Praise for Anne Perry
and her
CHARLOTTE AND THOMAS PITT NOVELS

PENTECOST ALLEY

"Stands as one of her most intricately constructed plots . . .
Perry packs a triple wallop into the final pages, one climax
following another."

—*Chicago Sun-Times*

LONG SPOON LANE

"Perry has once again delivered the tasty concoction her
readers have come to expect . . . and presents us with moral
and political puzzles that are all too close to our own."

—*Los Angeles Times Book Review*

ASHWORTH HALL

"Anne Perry pushes the English manor-house mystery into
dangerous new territory with *Ashworth Hall*. . . . [The] subtle play on sex roles, a constant in this rewarding series,
may well be the secret of its profound appeal."

—*The New York Times Book Review*

SEVEN DIALS

"Perry's as good as it gets. . . . The final courtroom scene
produces more victims and left me breathless."

—*The Providence Journal*

BY ANNE PERRY

FEATURING CHARLOTTE AND THOMAS PITT

FEATURING WILLIAM MONK

SILENCE IN HANOVER CLOSE

A CHARLOTTE AND THOMAS PITT NOVEL

ANNE PERRY

Ballantine Books Trade Paperbacks

New York

2011 Ballantine Books Trade Paperback Edition

Copyright © 1999 by Anne Perry
Excerpt from *Treason at Lisson Grove* copyright © 2011 by Anne Perry

Published in the United States by Ballantine Books, an imprint of
The Random House Publishing Group, a division of
Random House, Inc., New York.

BALLANTINE and colophon are registered trademarks of
Random House, Inc.

Originally published in the United States by St. Martin's Press in 1988.
Subsequently published in paperback by Fawcett Books,
an imprint of The Random House Publishing Group,
a division of Random House, Inc., in 1989.

ISBN 978-0-345-52373-0

Printed in the United States of America

www.ballantinebooks.com

6 8 9 7

Dedicated to
Aunt Ina

who was part of the inspiration
for Great-aunt Vespasia

1

"POLICE STATION, sir!" the cabbie said loudly, even before the horse's feet were still. His voice was thick with distaste; he did not like these places. The fact that this one was located in the aristocratic elegance of Mayfair was no compensation.

Pitt climbed out, paid him, and went up the stone steps and in through the doors.

"Yes sir?" the sergeant at the desk said without interest.

"I am Inspector Pitt from Bow Street," Pitt said crisply. "I'd like to see the senior officer in charge."

The sergeant took a deep breath, eyeing Pitt critically. He did not meet the sergeant's conception of a senior officer, not by a long way: he was quite casual. In fact he was downright scruffy, clothes all a mismatch, pockets full of rubbish. The man let the force down. Looked as if he'd never met with a barber's scissors—more like a pair of garden shears. Still, the sergeant had heard Pitt's name and spoke with some respect.

"Yes sir. That would be Inspector Mowbray. I'll let 'im know you're 'ere. Can I tell 'im what for, sir?"

1

Pitt smiled dryly. "No, I'm sorry. It's a confidential matter."

"Is that so, sir." The sergeant turned stolidly and went out, leaving Pitt standing until he returned several minutes later, still without haste. "If you go through that door, second on the left, sir, Inspector Mowbray will see you."

Mowbray was a very dark, balding man with an intelligent face; he looked decidedly curious when Pitt came in and closed the door.

"Pitt," he introduced himself, and held out his hand.

"Heard of you." Mowbray took Pitt's hand firmly. "What can I do?"

"I need to see the records of your investigation of a burglary in Hanover Close, about three years ago—October seventeenth, 1884, to be precise."

Mowbray's face showed rueful surprise. "Bad business, that. Don't often get murder in a household burglary, not in this area. Ugly, very ugly. Never found a thing." His eyebrows rose hopefully. "Have you got something? One of the stolen pieces turned up at last?"

"No, nothing at all. Sorry," Pitt apologized. He felt both guilty for taking the man's case from him and angry because this further poking around was evasive, not his real purpose, and probably futile anyway.

Pitt hated the way he had been brought into the case. Mowbray should have been the one doing this, but because the case involved the delicate question of a woman's reputation, a distinguished victim from a powerful family, and above all the almost inaudible whisper of the possibility of treason, the Foreign Office had used its influence to place the investigation through Ballarat, where they felt they could keep some control over it. Superintendent Ballarat was a man with excellent judgment of what his superiors required, and a rich ambition to rise high enough in his profession to become socially acceptable, perhaps even a self-made gentleman. He did not realize that those he most wished to impress were always able to distinguish a man's origins simply by the way he carried himself, by the turn of a vowel in his mouth.

Pitt was a gamekeeper's son who had grown up on a large country estate. He had been educated as a companion to the son of the house and had a manner acceptable to the gentry. He had also married considerably above himself, gaining an understanding of a social class closed to most ordinary policemen. Ballarat disliked Pitt and resented his manner, which he considered insolent. But Ballarat was obliged to admit that Pitt was unquestionably the best man for this investigation. He had done so with an ill grace.

Mowbray was staring at Pitt with only slight disappointment, and it quickly disappeared; apparently he had expected nothing. "Oh. Well, you'd better speak to Constable Lowther first; he found the body. And of course you can read the reports that were written at the time. There isn't much." He shook his head. "We tried hard, but there were no witnesses, and none of the stolen pieces ever turned up. We thought of the possibility of an inside job—we questioned the entire staff and came up with nothing."

"I daresay I'll do the same," Pitt said in an oblique apology.

"Have a cup of tea while I send for Lowther?" Mowbray offered. "It's a vile day. I wouldn't be surprised if it snows before Christmas."

"Thank you," Pitt accepted.

Ten minutes later Pitt was sitting in another small, chilly room with a gas lamp hissing on the wall above a scratched wooden table. A thin file of papers rested on it, and opposite Pitt a stiff, self-conscious constable stood at attention, buttons gleaming.

Pitt told him to sit down and be easy.

"Yes sir," Lowther said nervously. "I can remember that murder in 'anover Close pretty clear, sir. What is it as yer wants ter know?"

"Everything." Pitt took the teapot and filled a white

3

enamel mug without asking. He passed it to Lowther, who took it with round-eyed surprise. "Thank you, sir." He swallowed gratefully, composed himself, and began in a low voice, "It was five past three on the mornin' of October seventeenth, just over three year ago. I were on night duty then, an' I passed along 'anover Close—"

"How often?" Pitt interrupted.

"Every twenty minutes, sir. Reg'lar."

Pitt smiled very slightly. "I know that's what it's meant to be. Are you sure nothing held you up anywhere that night?" He deliberately gave Lowther the chance to escape blame if necessary without telling less than the truth. "No trouble anywhere?"

"No sir." Lowther faced him with totally guileless blue eyes. "Sometimes I do get 'eld up, but not that night. I were round exact, give or take no more'n a minute. That was why I noticed the broken winder at number two partic'lar, because I knew it weren't broke twenty minutes afore. An' it were a front winder, too, which is kind o' funny. Burglars usually goes ter the back, wiv a little nipper skinny enough to get through the bars and whip round an' let 'em in."

Pitt nodded.

"So I went to the door o' number two an' knocked," Lowther went on. "I 'ad ter raise an 'ell of a row—" He flushed. "Beg yer pardon, sir; a lot o' noise, before anyone came down. Arter about five minutes a footman opened up. 'Alf asleep, 'e were; 'ad a coat over 'is nightshirt. I told 'im abaht the winder as was broke, an' 'e was startled like, an' took me straight to the room at the front, which was the libr'y." The constable took a deep breath, but his eyes held Pitt's without wavering. "I saw immediate that there was trouble: two 'ard-back chairs was turned over, lyin' on their sides, there was 'alf a dozen books knocked on the floor, upset like, and a decanter spilled on a table near the winder as was broke and the glass lyin' on the floor, shinin' in the light."

4

"Light?" Pitt asked.

"Footman turned up the gas lamps," Lowther explained. " 'E were fair shook, I'd swear to that."

"Then what?" Pitt prompted.

"I went further into the room." Lowther's face puckered as the memory of the hard stab of human mortality came back to him. "I saw the body of a man on the floor, sir, 'alf on 'is face, sort o' legs bent a bit, like 'e'd bin took by surprise from be'ind. 'Is 'ead were matted wi' blood"—he touched his own right temple at the hairline—"an' there were a big bronze 'orse on a stand, 'bout ten inches 'igh, lyin' on the carpet 'bout eighteen inches away from 'im. 'E were wearing a dressin' robe over a silk nightshirt, an' 'ad slippers on 'is feet.

"I went over to 'im ter see if there were anythink I could do for 'im, though I thought 'e were dead even then." The look of an adult compassion for a child crossed his face. "The footman can't 'a bin more'n twenty, if 'e were that, an' 'e got took queer an' sat down rather sudden. 'E said, 'Oh Gawd—it's Mister Robert! Poor Mrs. York!' "

"And the man was dead?" Pitt said.

"Yes sir, quite dead. But 'e were still warm. An' o' course, I knew the winder 'adn't bin broke when I passed twenty minutes afore."

"What did you do then?"

"Well, it were plain 'e were murdered, an' it looked like someone'd broke in: the glass were all inside, and the catch were undone." His face clouded. "But a shockin' amacher job it were; no star-glazin' nor nuthin'—an' such a mess!"

Pitt did not need to ask what star-glazing was; many expert thieves used the trick of pasting paper over glass to hold all the shards while cutting a neat, silent circle which could be lifted out so a hand could be inserted to open the latch. A master cracksman could do the job in fifteen seconds.

"I asked the footman if they 'ad one o' them telephone instruments," Lowther continued. " 'E said as they 'ad, so

I went out o' the libr'y an' told 'im to stay at the door. I found the instrument and called the station an' reported the crime. Then the butler came down—'e must 'ave 'eard the noise and when the footman didn't go back upstairs, 'e come ter see what was goin' on. 'E formally identified the dead man as Mr. Robert York, the son o' the Honorable Piers York, the master o' the 'ouse. But 'e was away from 'ome on business, so there was nothin' for it but to tell the elder Mrs. York, the victim's mother. The butler sent for 'er lady's maid, in case she were overcome at the news. But when she came down and we 'ad ter tell 'er, she were very calm, very dignified.'' He sighed in admiration. "Makes yer realize what real Quality is. She were white as a ghost an' looked like she were dead 'erself, poor soul, but she never wept in front of us, just asked 'er maid to steady 'er a bit.''

Pitt knew of many great women who were bred to bear physical pain, loneliness, or bereavement by always showing the world a serene face, shedding all their tears in private. They were the sort of women who had sent their husbands and sons to battle on the fields of Waterloo and Balaklava, or to explore the Hindu Kush or find the source of the Blue Nile, and then to settle and administer the empire. Many had gone themselves into unknown lands, enduring appalling privation and the loss of every familiar sight and sound. In his mind Mrs. York was such a woman.

Lowther went on quietly, recalling the somber house and its grief. "I asked them if anything were missing as they knew. It were 'ard to 'ave ter ask a lady at such a time, but we 'ad ter know. She were quite calm and jus' walked round the room careful like, and she told us that as far as she could say, there was two silver framed minicher portraits dated 1773, a crystal paperweight engraved with a design o' scrolls and flowers, a small silver jug used fer fla'hers—and that weren't 'ard ter come at, because the fla'hers theirselves was on the floor and the water spilled on the carpet; don't know 'ow we missed seein' it before—an' a first edition of a book

6

by Jonathan Swift. She said as she couldn't see anythin' else."

"Where was the book kept?"

"On the shelves with the other books, Mr. Pitt—which means as 'e knew it were there! I asked, and she said as it didn't look nothin' special from the back of it you'd see ordinary."

"Ah." Pitt let out his breath slowly. He changed the subject.

"Was the dead man married?" he asked.

"Oh yes. But I didn't disturb 'is wife, poor creature. She 'adn't woke, an' I couldn't see no point in 'avin' ter tell 'er in the middle o' the night. Better to let 'er own family do that."

Pitt could hardly blame him. Having to tell the sad news to the loved ones of the victim was one of the hardest duties in a murder case; the only thing even more difficult was seeing the faces of those who loved the guilty when at last they understood.

"Material evidence?" he said aloud.

Lowther shook his head. "Nothin', sir; least nothin' as means much. There weren't nothin' in the 'ouse as didn't belong, nothin' to show the intruder went anywhere 'cept the libr'y. No footmarks, no 'airs nor bits o' cloth, nothin' ter see. Followin' day, we asked all the servants in the 'ouse, but they 'eard nothin'. No one 'eard the winder break. But then servants sleeps at the top o' the 'ouse, up in the attics like, so maybe they wouldn't."

"Anything outside?" Pitt pressed.

Lowther shook his head again. "Nothin' sir. No footmarks outside the winder, but it were 'ard frost, wicked that night, an' the ground were like iron. Didn't leave no marks meself, an' I weighs near fourteen stone."

"Dry enough so you left no footmarks on the carpet either?" Pitt questioned.

"Not a one sir; I thought o' that."

"Any witnesses?"

"No, Mr. Pitt. I saw no one meself, and never did find anyone else as 'ad. Y'see 'anover Close is a real close, no through road, so no one as didn't live there'd 'ave any reason to pass that way, specially in the middle of a winter night. An' it's not exac'ly an 'arlots' patch."

That was more or less what Pitt had expected to hear, but there was always the chance. He tried the last obvious avenue. "What about the stolen articles?"

Lowther made a face. "Nothin'. An' we tried 'ard, because of it bein' murder."

"Is there anything else?"

"No, Mr. Pitt. Mr. Mowbray took over talkin' to the family. 'E could tell you more, maybe."

"I'll ask him. Thank you."

Lowther looked puzzled and only slightly relieved. "Thank you, sir."

Pitt found Mowbray back in his office.

"Get what you wanted?" Mowbray asked, his dark face puckering into an expression of curiosity and resignation. "Lowther's a good man: if there'd been anything he'd 'ave found it."

Pitt sat down as near the fire as he could. Mowbray moved fractionally to make room for him and lifted the teapot, offering more tea by raising his eyebrows. Pitt nodded. It was dark brown, stewed, but it was hot.

"You went the following day?" Pitt pursued the subject.

Mowbray frowned. "Early as seemed decent. Hate having to do that, go and talk to people the moment they're bereaved, before they've even got over the first shock. Still, has to be done. Pity. York himself wasn't there, only the mother and the widow—"

"Tell me about them," Pitt interrupted. "Not just the facts; how did they impress you?"

Mowbray took a deep breath and sighed slowly. "The elder Mrs. York was a remarkable woman. Been something

8

of a beauty in 'er day, I should think, still fine-looking, very . . ."

Pitt did not prompt him; he wanted Mowbray's own words.

"Very womanly." Mowbray was not satisfied with this description. He frowned and blinked several times. "Soft, like—like one of them flowers in the botanical gardens. . . ." His face eased with the flash of memory. "Camellias. Pale colors and perfect shape. All ordered, not higgledy-piggledy like a wildflower, or one o' them late roses that falls open."

Pitt liked late roses: they were magnificent, exuberant; but it was a matter of taste. Perhaps Mowbray found them a little vulgar.

"What about the widow?" Pitt kept his voice level, trying not to betray any extra interest.

But Mowbray was too perceptive. A very slight smile curved his mouth and he kept his eyes on Pitt's face.

"She were 'it so 'ard wi' shock she were as white as a corpse 'erself, I'd swear to that. I've seen a lot o' women in times o' grief; it's one o' the rottenest parts o' the job. Them as are puttin' it on tend to weep an' faint and talk a lot about 'ow they feel. Mrs. York 'ardly spoke a word an' seemed sort o' numb. She didn't look at us, like liars do; in fact I don't think she cared what we thought."

Pitt smiled in spite of himself. "Not a camellia?"

A bleak humor flickered at the back of Mowbray's eyes. "Quite different sort o' woman altogether, much more . . ."

Again Pitt waited.

"More delicate, more easy to 'urt. I suppose partly because she were younger, o' course; but I got the feelin' she didn't 'ave the same strength inside 'er. But even shocked as she were, she were one o' the best-lookin' women I ever seen, tall and very slight, like a spring flower, 'ceptin dark. Fragile, you might say; one of those faces you don't forget, different from most. 'Igh cheeks, fine bones." He shook his head a little. "Face all full o' feelin'."

9

Pitt sat quietly for a moment, trying to picture the woman. What did the Foreign Office really fear—murder, treason, or merely scandal? What was the real reason they had asked Ballarat to open this case again now? Was it just to make sure there was nothing sordid that could come out later and ruin an ambassador? Even in this short interview Pitt had formed a respect for Mowbray. He was a good professional policeman. If Mowbray believed Veronica York was stunned by the shock, then Pitt probably would have thought so too.

"What did the family say?" he asked.

"The two ladies had been out to dinner with friends. They'd come home about eleven and gone straight up to bed," Mowbray replied. "Servants confirmed that. Robert York had been out on some business; he worked at the Foreign Office, and he quite often had business in the evenings. He came home after the ladies, they don't know when. Neither did the servants. They'd been told not to wait up, by York himself.

"It looks as if he was still awake when the burglar broke in. He must have come downstairs, interrupted the intruder in the library, and then got killed." Mowbray pulled a face. "Don't know why. I mean, why didn't the burglar simply hide, or better still, get out that window again? The latch was open. Unnecessary. Very unprofessional."

"What did you conclude, finally?"

Mowbray's eyebrows rose. "Case unsolved," he said, then hesitated for several seconds, as though weighing whether to commit himself further.

Pitt finished his tea and set the empty mug on the hearth. "Odd case," he said casually. "Man knows exactly when to break in without P.C. Lowther seeing him coming or going, even though Lowther passes every twenty minutes; yet instead of going round the back, away from the street, and using a snakesman to wriggle through the pantry bars, or a ratchet and pinion to loosen them, he breaks a front window—and doesn't even star-glaze it to stop the noise and hide

10

the hole. Yet he knows enough to find a first-edition Swift, which is not an obvious thing at all—Lowther said it was on the shelf with other books—but on the other hand he's so clumsy he makes enough noise to disturb Robert York, who comes down and catches him. And when York does come, instead of hiding or running away, the intruder attacks him so fiercely he kills him.''

"And doesn't sell any of his haul,'' Mowbray finished. "I know. Rum, very rum. Wondered if it were someone Mr. York knew personal like, some gentleman 'ard up turned to robbin' 'is friends. Started lookin' in that line, very discreet like. Even looked very casual at young Mrs. York's acquaintances—and got told very gracious and very cool by the powers that be as I should keep to me place and not add to the distress o' them as is already sufferin' 'orrible bereavement. Nobody actually said as I was to mark it unsolved; nothin' so blunt. Just an expression o' sympathy for the family, and a cold eye on me. But I don't need to 'ave it spelled out for me.''

It was what Pitt had expected; he had experienced the same unspoken but unmistakable sort of thing himself. It did not necessarily indicate any suspicion of guilt; just a deference for breeding, money, and the vast indefinable power that went with it.

"I suppose I had better pursue the next line.'' Pitt stood up reluctantly. It was raining outside; he could see the long wet streaks beating against the window, blurring the shadows of the roofs and gables outside. "Thank you for your help, and the tea.''

"Don't envy you,'' Mowbray said wryly.

Pitt smiled back. He liked Mowbray and resented having to retrace the man's steps as though he were in some way incompetent. Damn Ballarat and the Foreign Office!

Outside Pitt turned up his coat collar, tightened his muffler, and put his head down against the rain. He walked for a little while, feet sloshing up spurts of water, hair dripping down his forehead, thinking over what he had just learned. What was the Foreign Office after? A decent resolution of a case which involved one of their own, so it would cause no future embarrassment, as Ballarat had said? The widow of Robert York was informally betrothed to one Julian Danver. If Danver were headed for an ambassadorship, or higher, no shadow must touch the reputation of any of his family, especially his wife.

Or had some new discovery pertaining to the murder of Robert York pointed to treason, and were they using Pitt to unravel it for them? He would take the blame for the tragedy and the scandal which would inevitably follow, the careers and reputations ruined.

It was an ugly job, and everything Mowbray had told him only made it uglier. Who had been the other person in the library, and why?

Pitt turned from Piccadilly down St. James's, then across the Mall and down the Horse Guards' Parade past the bare trees and wind-whipped grass of the park, up Downing Street to Whitehall and the Foreign Office.

It took him a quarter of an hour to persuade the right officials and finally to reach the department where Robert York had worked until the time of his death.

He was met by a distinguished man in his late thirties with black hair, and eyes which at first appeared to be equally dark, but as he turned to the light proved to be a startling, luminous gray. He introduced himself as Felix Asherson and offered to be of any help within his power. Pitt took that for the limited offer it was.

"Thank you, sir. We have had occasion to look again into the tragic death three years ago of Mr. Robert York."

Asherson's face showed immediate concern, but then it would, in the Foreign Office where impeccable manners were part of his trade. "Have you caught someone?"

Pitt approached the subject obliquely. "No, I am afraid not, but there were several articles stolen at the time. It seems very possible the burglar was not a casual housebreaker but a person of education, perhaps after something in particular.''

Asherson waited patiently. ''Indeed? And you didn't know that at the time?''

''We did, sir. But I have been asked by certain persons in authority''—he hoped Asherson's Whitehall training in discretion was sufficient to keep him from asking who —''to pursue the matter again.''

''Oh.'' Asherson's face tightened almost imperceptibly, just a faint movement of muscles around the jaw, a thickening of the neck, so the stiff wing collar hugged the skin. ''How can we help you?''

Interesting how he used the plural, making himself a representative of the office, not personally involved.

Pitt selected his words carefully. ''Since the burglar chose the library and not one of the more obvious rooms, like the dining room, where the silver was, we have to consider that he may have been looking for documents, perhaps something Mr. York was working on at the time.''

Asherson was noncommittal. ''Indeed?''

Pitt waited.

Asherson took a deep breath. ''I suppose that's possible— I mean, he may have hoped to find something. Does it help now? After all, it was three years ago.''

''We never abandon a murder case,'' Pitt replied blandly. Yet they had buried this one after six fruitless months. Why had they opened it again now?

''No—no, of course,'' Asherson conceded. ''What can the Foreign Office do to assist you?''

Pitt decided to be blunt. He smiled very slightly, holding Asherson's eye. ''Has any information been missed from this office since Mr. York first came to work here? I appreciate that you may not be able to tell when it was taken, only when the discovery was made.''

Asherson hesitated. ''You make us sound remarkably inefficient, Inspector. We do not mislay information; it is far too important."

"So if information has reached unauthorized places, then it was deliberately given?" Pitt asked innocently.

Asherson breathed out slowly, grasping for time to think. Confusion was momentarily naked in his face. He did not know what Pitt was leading up to, nor why.

"There has been information . . ." Pitt said gently, testing, making it something between a question and a statement.

Asherson affected immediate ignorance. "Has there? Then perhaps that was why poor Robert was murdered. If he took papers home with him, and somehow people got to know of it, a thief may have . . ." He left the rest unsaid.

"Then he could have taken such papers home on several occasions?" Pitt pursued. "Or are you suggesting it might have been only once, and by some extraordinary chance the thief chose the precise night?"

It was preposterous, and they both knew it.

"No, of course not." Asherson smiled faintly. He was caught, but if he was resentful, he hid it superbly. "I really don't know what happened, but if he was indiscreet, or had friends who were unworthy of his trust, it hardly matters now. The poor man is dead, and the information cannot have reached our enemies or we should have suffered for it by now. And we haven't. That I can tell you with certainty. If there really were such an attempt, it was abortive. Can't you leave his memory in peace—not to mention his family?"

Pitt stood up. "Thank you, Mr. Asherson. You have been most frank. Good day, sir." And he left the uncertain-looking Asherson standing on the bright blue and vermillion Turkish carpet in the middle of the floor.

Back at Bow Street in the icy dusk, Pitt climbed the stairs to Ballarat's office and knocked on the door. At the command he went in.

Ballarat was standing in front of the fire, blocking it. His room was quite different from the functional quarters of the lesser police on the beat, downstairs. The broad desk was inlaid with green leather, the chair behind it was padded and moved comfortably on a swivel. There was the stub of a cigar in the stone ashtray. Ballarat was of average height, portly, a trifle short in the leg. But his rich side whiskers were immaculately barbered and he smelled of cologne. His clothes were perfectly pressed, from his bright oxblood boots to the matching brown tie round his stiff white collar. He was the antithesis of the disheveled Pitt, whose every garment was at odds with another, pockets weighted down by nameless objects. Even now, a piece of string trailed from one, and a hand-knitted muffler half obscured his soft collar.

"Well?" Ballarat demanded irritably. "Close the door, man! I don't want half the station listening. The matter is confidential, I told you that before. Well, what have you got?"

"Very little," Pitt replied. "They were pretty thorough at the time."

"I know that, damn it! I've read the papers on the case!" Ballarat pushed his short fingers further into his pockets, fists clenched. He rocked back and forth very slightly on the balls of his feet. "Was it a chance break-in? Some amateur who got caught in the act and panicked, killing young York instead of escaping like a professional? I'm sure any connection with the Foreign Office was coincidental. I have been told by the highest authority," and he repeated the words, rolling them on his tongue, "the highest authority, that our enemies have no knowledge of the work York was engaged in."

"More probably some friend of York's who ran up a debt and turned his hand to burglary to try to get out of it," Pitt answered frankly, and saw the look of displeasure on Ballarat's face. "He knew where the first-edition Swift was."

"Inside help," Ballarat said immediately. "Bribed a servant."

15

"Possibly. Assuming there was a servant who knew a first-edition Swift when she saw it. Not the sort of thing the Honorable Piers York would discuss with the tweeny."

Ballarat opened his mouth to tell Pitt not to be sarcastic with him, then thought better of it and changed course. "Well, if it was one of their social acquaintances, you'd better be damn careful in your questions, Pitt! This is a very delicate investigation we've been entrusted with. A careless word and you could ruin reputations—not to mention your own career." He looked increasingly uncomfortable, his face flushed to a dull purplish hue. "All the Foreign Office wants us to establish is that there was nothing—untoward, nothing unseemly in Mrs. York's conduct. It is no part of your business to blacken the name of a dead man, an honorable man who gave distinguished service to his queen and to his country."

"Well, there has been information disappearing from the Foreign Office," Pitt said, his voice rising in frustration, "and the burglary at the York house needs a great deal more explanation than it's had so far."

"Then get on with it, man!" Ballarat snapped. "Either find out which friend it was, or better still, prove it wasn't a friend at all! Clear Mrs. Veronica York of the slightest possible mark against her character, and we'll all be thanked."

Pitt opened his mouth to retort, but saw the pointlessness of it reflected in Ballarat's black eyes. He swallowed his temper. "Yes sir."

He went out with his mind seething. Then the cold air hit his face, stinging with rain, and he was jostled by passersby on the dark pavements. He heard carriages clattering by, saw shops with windows lit and gas lamps burning in the streets, smelled chestnuts roasting on a brazier. Pitt heard someone singing a carol, and he was overtaken by other things. He imagined his children's faces on Christmas morning. They were old enough now to be excited; already Daniel asked every night if it was Christmas tomorrow yet, and Jemima, with a six-year-old's elder-sister superiority, told him he must wait. Pitt smiled. He had made a wooden train for Daniel, with an engine and six carriages. He had bought a doll for Jemima, and Charlotte was sewing dresses, petticoats, and a fine bonnet for her. Lately he had noticed that when he came in unexpectedly she pushed her sewing in a bundle under a cushion, and looked up far too innocently at him.

His smile broadened. He knew she was making something for him. He was particularly pleased with what he had found for her, a pink alabaster vase about nine inches high, simple and perfect. It had taken him seven weeks to save up enough. The only problem was Emily, Charlotte's widowed sister. She had married for love, but her husband George had had both title and wealth. After the shock of her bereavement last summer it was only natural that she and her five-year-old son, Edward, should come on Christmas Eve to spend the holiday with her sister.

But what could Pitt possibly afford to give Emily that would please her?

He had still not solved the problem when he arrived at his front door. Pitt took off his wet coat and hung it on the hook, undid his sodden boots, and started towards the kitchen in his stocking feet.

Jemima met him halfway along the passage, cheeks flushed, eyes shining.

"Papa, isn't it Christmas yet? Isn't it even Christmas Eve?"

"Not yet." He swung her up into his arms and hugged her.

"Are you sure?"

"Yes, my sweetheart, I'm sure." He carried her into the kitchen and put her down. Gracie, the maid, was upstairs with Daniel. Charlotte was alone, surveying the final touches to her Christmas cake, a wisp of hair curling over her brow. She smiled at him. "Any interesting cases?"

"No. An old case that will go nowhere." He kissed her once; then kissed her again with growing warmth.

"Nothing?" she persisted.

"Nothing. It's only a formality."

2

At first Charlotte accepted Pitt's brief dismissal of his new case, because she was preoccupied with Christmas and all the arrangements. There was so much that had to be done in the kitchen: the hiding of carefully wrapped threepenny pieces in the plum pudding, the making of sweets, jam for tarts and chopped fruits for mince pies. And there were presents to finish and wrap in colored paper. On top of that, everything must be kept secret, to be a surprise on the day.

At any other time she would have been more inquisitive, and considerably more persistent. In the past Charlotte had involved herself in some of Thomas's most complex and personally tragic cases, drawn in by deliberate curiosity or outrage at some event. It was only last summer that her sister Emily's husband had been murdered, and that case had seemed endless. Emily herself had been the main suspect. George had had a short-lived but intense affair with Sybilla March, and Emily was the only one who knew it had ended the night before he died. Who could be expected to believe her when all the evidence was to the contrary? And Emily, in her efforts to win back George's attention, had been so indiscreet with Jack Radley that she had deliberately given everyone the impression that she herself was romantically involved.

Charlotte had never been so afraid as during that period, nor felt true tragedy as close. When their elder sister Sarah had died it had been a loss, sudden and stark, but imposed from outside, a chance event that might have stricken anyone. George's death was different. It had seemed a failure from within; all their assumptions about safety and love had been shattered in a simple, reverberating act, touching everything and marring it all with doubt. What lack in Emily, what emptiness in the trust she had thought so deep, had turned George to another woman with such passion? Their reconciliation after had been so brief, so delicate and so private it had not had time to blossom, and no one else had known of it. And the next morning George was dead.

There had been no pity, no attention of concerned friends as when Sarah died. Rather there had been suspicion, even hate, all sorts of old enmities and mistakes raked up and added to in the fear that blame would run over and scald everyone, leaving other people's secrets and weaknesses exposed—as indeed they had been.

It was six months ago now, and Emily had recovered from the shock. The social acceptance had returned; indeed, people fell over themselves to make up for their guilt at having been suspicious and their social cowardice at the time. But for all that, Society still required that widows be seen to mourn, especially those of men from old and titled families such as the Ashworths. The fact that Emily was not yet thirty would not in any way excuse her from remaining at home, receiving only relatives, and wearing unrelieved black. She must not attend any social functions that might appear frivolous or enjoyable, and she must maintain an attitude of gravity at all times.

She was finding it almost unendurable. To begin with, as

soon as George's murderer was found and the matter closed, she had gone into the country with Edward, to be alone and spend her time helping him to understand the death of his father and his own new position. With the autumn she had returned to the city, but all the usual parties, operas, balls, and soirees were closed to her. The friends who did call on her were sober to the point of stultification, and no one gossiped or discussed fashion or the latest play, or who was flirting with whom, considering those topics too trivial to disturb her grief. The time Emily spent sitting at home writing letters, playing the piano, or stitching endless needlework felt like a constant scraping of the skin, the source of a raging discontent.

Naturally Charlotte had invited Emily to come for Christmas with Edward, who would find the company of other children the best present of all.

But what about after Christmas? Emily would have to return to the Ashworth town house, alone and bored to tears!

And to tell the truth, as deeply as she loved her home and her children, six months of uninterrupted domesticity was beginning to hang a little heavily on Charlotte also. She had asked Pitt about his new case with more than wifely concern—there was as well a desire for adventure in the question.

The following evening, Charlotte prepared her ground a little more carefully. She waited until after dinner, when they were sitting in front of the parlor fire; the children were long in bed, and she was carefully stitching butterfly ornaments to put on the Christmas tree.

"Thomas," she began casually. "If the case is really nothing of importance—just a formality, as you said—do you think you will be able to leave it over Christmas?" She did not look up, keeping her eyes on her thread and the delicate gossamer she was sewing.

"I . . ." He hesitated. "I think there may be more to it than I supposed."

Charlotte kept her curiosity subdued with great difficulty. "Oh dear. How is that?"

"A burglary that is hard to understand."

"Oh." This time she did not need to pretend indifference. Burglaries were impersonal, the loss of possessions held no interest for her. "What was stolen?"

"Two miniatures, a vase, a paperweight, and a first-edition book," he replied.

"What is difficult to understand about that?" Then she looked up and found him smiling. "Thomas?" Instantly she knew there was more, an element of mystery or concealed emotion.

"The son of the house disturbed the burglar and was killed." His eyes were steady on hers, speculative. He was amused by her curiosity and her attempts to disguise it, yet he respected her perceptiveness. "And none of the stolen articles ever turned up," he finished.

"Yes?" Without realizing it she had let her sewing fall. "Thomas!"

He slid down into his chair, crossing his legs comfortably, and told her what he knew, adding Ballarat's warning about discretion and the reputations that could be ruined, and the information that the Foreign Office had mislaid.

"Mislaid?" she repeated the word skeptically. "Do you mean stolen?"

"I don't know. I don't suppose I ever will. If information was taken it would have been copied, not removed. If Robert York had papers in his house, that might have been what the burglar was after, and he merely took the other things to cover up the fact. More likely it had nothing to do with it."

She took up her sewing again, setting it on the side table so she should not lose the needle. "But what in goodness' name does the Foreign Office expect of you?" she pressed. "If there is a spy, isn't it desperately important he should be caught, quite apart from his having murdered poor Robert York?"

"I daresay he has been," he said ruefully. "And the Foreign Office wishes to keep quiet about it. What they really want is for us to test their skill, make sure the mislaid information is hidden beyond recall. It will do our reputation in the world little good to make such things public. Or perhaps there never was anything missing."

"Do you believe that?" she challenged.

"No. But it may have been carelessness more than deceit."

"What are you going to do about Robert York's murder? Someone killed him."

"Follow the burglary as far as I can," he said with a slight shrug.

"What is the widow like?" Charlotte was not willing to let it go yet. There must be something interesting that she could relay to Emily.

"I don't know. I have had no excuse yet to call on her without making her suspicious, and that is the last thing the Foreign Office wishes. It would immediately raise all sorts of ugly questions. You haven't mentioned Jack Radley lately. Is Emily still keeping his acquaintance?"

That was a matter much closer to Charlotte's heart, and she was prepared to abandon the unpromising mystery for it. Jack Radley had begun as a diversion, someone Emily had flirted with to prove to George that she could be every bit as charming, as poised, as witty as her rival. As the events of the case progressed he had become a prime suspect. But Jack had turned out to be a generous friend, far less superficial and self-seeking than his reputation had led Emily to believe. He had no money and fewer prospects. The obvious thought, unkind as it might be, was that he pursued Emily for the wealth she had inherited on George's death. His success with women was well known; his vanity might have led him to murder George, then court Emily and marry her.

He had proved to be quite innocent of any crime, but he was still far from the suitor Society would have wished for

Emily when the time was right. Certainly their mother would be appalled!

None of that bothered Charlotte greatly: whatever people thought, it could not possibly be worse than what they had thought of Charlotte herself for marrying a policeman! Jack Radley was impecunious, but he was very definitely a gentleman; policemen barely ranked above bailiffs and ratcatchers. But was Jack Radley capable of love? To imagine that everyone was, if only given the right companion, was a romantic mistake that was very easily made. But it was still a mistake. Many people desire no more than a convention—the sharing of a home, a social position, children, and the wider family; they do not wish to share their thoughts or their leisure, above all they do not wish to reveal their inner selves, where dreams are held, where they may be known, and thus wounded. They will not take risks. In the end there is no generosity of soul, only safety. There is no giving where there may be cost. Regardless of his charm or his wit, his warm and friendly manner, if Jack Radley was one of these, in the end he would bring Emily only pain. And Charlotte would do everything in her power to prevent that.

"Charlotte?" Pitt interrupted her thoughts, a little sharply. The answer mattered to him also. He was very fond of Emily, too, and he understood how it would hurt her if Charlotte's unspoken fear were justified.

"I think so," she said quickly. "We haven't spoken of him much lately, we have been so busy discussing Christmas. She is bringing a goose, and mince puddings."

He sank a little lower in the chair and stretched his feet towards the fire. "I think if you want to play detective"—he looked up at her through his lashes—"you would do more good exercising your judgment on Jack Radley than speculating about Mrs. York."

She gave him no argument. What he said was undoubtedly true, and although he phrased it gently, it was something in the nature of a command. Beneath his comfortable sprawl and his light manner, Pitt was worried.

However, Charlotte had every intention of combining the two. She could think of no more effective way of seeing enough of Emily to be able to exercise her judgment, as Thomas had said, than to encourage her to play detective in another case. At Christmas, any discussion or judgment would be next to impossible, but later, if Charlotte were to visit Emily at her home, where she might meet Jack Radley herself, she might be in a position to form a more valid opinion of him without being obvious about it.

She was ready, her plan prepared, when Emily called the following morning, a little after eleven. She came straight into the kitchen in a whirl of black barathea trimmed with black fox fur up to her chin, her fair hair coiled under a sweeping black hat. For a moment Charlotte was envious; the expensive coat looked so indescribably elegant. Then she remembered the reason her sister wore black and was instantly ashamed. Emily looked pale, apart from the spots of color stung into her cheeks by the ice on the wind, and there were gray smudges under her eyes where the skin looked bruised and papery. Charlotte did not need to be told her sister was restless and sleeping too little. Boredom is not by any means the worst of afflictions, but it carries its own kind of debilitation. Christmas would be all too brief, and what would Emily do after that?

"Have a cup of tea," Charlotte offered, turning to the big kitchen range without waiting for an answer. "Have you ever been to Hanover Close?"

Emily took off her coat and sat at the kitchen table, resting her elbows on its scrubbed wood. Her dress beneath the coat was equally elegant, although there were places where she did not fill it out as she used to.

"No, but I know where it is. Why?" The answering inquiry was merely polite.

25

Charlotte plunged in at the deepest point. "There has been a murder there."

"In Hanover Close?" This time she had Emily's full attention. "Good heavens. That's terribly exclusive. The best possible taste—and money. Who is dead?"

"Robert York. He used to work at the Foreign Office—until he died, I mean."

"How was he killed? I didn't read of it." Normally a lady of Emily's position would not have read a newspaper at all, apart from perhaps the society pages and the Court Circular. But unlike their papa, George had been very lenient where such things were concerned—as long as she did not offend people by discussing them. And, of course, since his death she did as she pleased.

Charlotte poured the water from the kettle into the teapot, then placed it on the table with a cream jug and two of her best cups. "It happened three years ago," she said as carelessly as she could. "Thomas has just been asked to reopen the case, because the widow is to marry again, to someone else in the Foreign Office."

Emily perked up. "Is she betrothed yet? I haven't seen news of that either, and I always read the society pages. That is about the only way I get to hear anything. No one tells me anything anymore; it's as if the whole subject of relationships between men and women were something I should not be reminded of." Unconsciously her fist clenched.

Charlotte noticed it. "That is the point!" she said quickly. "Thomas has been asked to investigate, to see if she is a suitable person to marry someone as important as Mr. Danver will become, when he is promoted."

"Might she not be?" Emily asked. "Please do pour the tea, I'm as dry as the Sahara, and it's had plenty of time to brew. Has she a reputation? I wish I could hear more. I'm so cut off it's as if I were a leper! Half the people I used to know are embarrassed to see me, and the other half spend their time sitting around solemnly and talking in whispers, as if I were dying myself.'' She sniffed fiercely, searching in her reticule for a handkerchief. It was not self-pity so much as the sudden warmth of the kitchen after the cold air in the carriage which provoked the necessity.

Charlotte shook her head. ''No, that's as much as I have learned, but the crime itself is very unexplained.'' She poured the tea and pushed Emily's cup across towards her, along with a piece of fresh ginger cake, which was taken readily. ''It is rather odd.'' And she told Emily all that Pitt had told her.

''Very odd,'' Emily agreed at last. ''I wonder if she had a lover, and there was a quarrel. I suppose that is really what the Foreign Office wants Thomas to discover, but they are afraid to say so, in case it should get back to Mr. Danver, who would be furious. And of course, it would prejudice him terribly; he would never have any peace of mind at such a slur.''

''Neither would she!'' Charlotte said hotly. ''If it is untrue, it could be the most appalling injustice. But I don't know how Thomas will be able to make any inquiries. It is hardly the thing a policeman can ask of her social acquaintances.''

Emily smiled. ''My dear Charlotte, you don't need to labor the point so hard. You are being singularly unsubtle, even for you! Of course we will find out. We have done nothing but bake cakes and stitch seams for six months, and I am ready to scream with it. We shall prove Veronica York's impeccable reputation, or ruin it entirely. Where shall we begin?''

Charlotte had already anticipated the difficulties. Emily could no longer move in Society as she had when George was alive; and Charlotte, as the wife of a policeman, had not the money to dress appropriately, nor the friends upon whom to call. There was only George's great-aunt Vespasia, who would understand and assist, but she was over eighty, and since George's death had taken a less active part in affairs than before. She was devoted to a number of causes, and believed that the battle against poverty and injustice could be tackled through reform of the law. She was currently engaged in a struggle to improve the working conditions in factories which employed children, especially those under the age of ten.

Charlotte poured more tea into her cup and sipped it. "Are you still in acquaintance with Jack Radley?" She asked, trying to sound casual, as if the question were entirely to do with the problem of Veronica York.

Emily reached for the ginger cake again. "He calls upon me from time to time. Do you think he might involve himself?" She cut a large slice of the cake and bit into it hungrily.

"Perhaps he might help us to—to arrange a meeting," Charlotte suggested.

"Not us." Emily made a face. "You." She poured herself more tea, spilling it. At this she swore, using a word she had heard George use in the stables. Charlotte knew her reaction had nothing to do with the mess in the saucer; she was frustrated by the imprisonment of mourning, and above all the loneliness.

"I know I shall have to do it this time," Charlotte agreed. "And you will have to instruct me. I shall gather what information I can, and together we will unravel what it means."

It was not like being there herself, catching the nuances of tone, the expression fleeting across the face, the glance from one to another, but Emily knew that Charlotte's idea was the best she could hope for, and she was grateful for it. It would have been ladylike to wait until Jack Radley called upon her. She did not imagine it would be long before he did; he had made his admiration plain enough six months ago and in the intervening time had visited her on many occasions. It was not the depth of his regard she doubted, but the quality. Did he court her for herself, or because she

28

was George's widow, with George's position and George's money? She enjoyed his company as much as she had ever enjoyed anyone's—and that was a rather startling admission, considering her suspicions. But how close is liking to loving?

When she had married George, he had been the catch of the season. Emily had been perfectly aware of his faults; she had considered them part of the bargain and accepted them graciously. He in turn had proved to be all that she had hoped, and had never criticized any of her imperfections. What had begun as a perfect understanding had grown into something much warmer. Her first perception of him had been as the handsome, reckless Lord George Ashworth, the ideal husband. Her feelings for George had matured into a gentle and loyal love, as she had begun to see the reality of a man who was worldly in sport and finance, charming in society, without the least duplicity in his nature, nor the least subtlety. She had always had enough wisdom to hide the fact that she was probably both more intelligent than he and more courageous. She had also been less tolerant and less generous in her judgments. He had had a quick temper, but it passed like a squall; he had overlooked the foibles of his own class and ignored the weaknesses of others. She did neither. Injustice infuriated her, more now than when she was younger. As time passed she was becoming more like Charlotte, who had always been opinionated, quick to anger, and a fighter against all she perceived to be wrong, even though that perception was sometimes hasty, and far too outspoken. Emily had been more sensible—at least until now.

Today she sat down and wrote a letter to Jack Radley, inviting him to call upon her at his earliest convenience, and dispatched the footman with it as soon as it was sealed.

His reply was satisfactorily rapid. He arrived in the early evening, the hour when in happier times she would have been dressing for an evening at dinner, or perhaps a ball or the theater. Now she sat by the fire reading Robert Louis Stevenson's *The Strange Case of Dr. Jekyll and Mr. Hyde,* published the previous year. She was glad to be interrupted; the story was darker and far more frightening than she had supposed, and she could see the elements of tragedy already. She had it in a brown paper cover, in case the servants should be scandalized.

Jack Radley entered the moment after the parlormaid announced him. He was casually dressed, but his tailor was clearly his chief creditor. The cut of his trousers was immaculate, the jacket fit perfectly. It was his smile she looked to, however, and those remarkable eyes, which were full of concern.

"Emily, are you all right?" he asked, searching her face. "Your message sounded urgent. Has something happened?"

She felt a trifle foolish. "I'm sorry. It is not an emergency, and I am perfectly well, thank you. But I am bored to distraction, and Charlotte has discovered a mystery." There was no point in lying to him; he was too like her to be deceived.

His face relaxed into a smile and he sat down on the chair opposite her. "A mystery?"

She tried to sound nonchalant, suddenly realizing that he might imagine she had dredged up an excuse to call him. "An old murder," she continued quickly, "that may have a scandal behind it, or may not, in which case an innocent woman might be ruined and unable to marry the man she loves."

He looked puzzled. "But what can you do? And how can I help?"

"There is a great deal the police can discover, of course, about facts," she explained. "But they can't make the sort of judgments we might, because it all has to be terribly discreet." She saw with a flicker of excitement that she had caught his interest. "And naturally no one would speak in front of the police as they might with us, nor would the police understand the shades of meaning if they did."

"But how can we find ourselves in a position to observe

these people?'' he said seriously. "You haven't told me who they are—but regardless of that, Emily, you cannot introduce yourself into Society again for some time.'' His face tightened, and for an unpleasant moment she feared she saw pity in his eyes. She might have accepted pity from someone else, but coming from Jack it grated surprisingly, like an abrasion of the skin.

"I know I can't!'' she said, and instantly regretted the tartness in her voice, and yet was unable to stop it. "But Charlotte can, and then we can discuss it together. At least, she can if you will be prepared to help her.''

He smiled a little ruefully. "I am very good at scraping an acquaintance. Who are they?''

She looked up at his face, trying to read his expression. His eyelashes still shadowed his cheek the way she remembered. How many other women had thought precisely the same thing? Really, this was the utmost foolishness. Charlotte was right; she needed some occupation for her mind, before it became completely addled!

"The man who was murdered was Robert York,'' she said briskly. "The widow is Mrs. Veronica York, of Hanover Close.'' She stopped. He was smiling broadly.

"Not difficult at all,'' he said confidently. "I used to know her. In fact . . .'' He hesitated, apparently uncertain how indiscreet to be.

Emily felt a stab of jealousy that was quite uncharacteristic. She knew it was extremely silly; she was thoroughly aware of his reputation. And anyway, she was a woman who had never cherished delusions. She knew perfectly well that men held themselves accountable to quite a different set of standards from those they expected of women. It was only necessary never to be so flagrant that others could not affect ignorance; what they suspected was irrelevant. All realistic people knew as much. Judicious blindness was the only way to preserve peace of mind. But it was a standard Emily was

31

becoming increasingly impatient with, even though she knew her feelings were foolish, and highly impractical.

"Did you part in a manner which would allow you to take up the acquaintance again?" she said crisply.

His face fell. "Certainly!"

She looked down, not wanting him to guess at any emotion in her, certainly nothing as unattractive as the truth.

"Then will you? With Charlotte? As you say, it would be impossible for me."

"Of course," he said slowly, and she knew he was looking at her. "But will Pitt approve? And I can hardly introduce her as a policeman's wife. We'll have to think of something better."

"Thomas won't have to know. She can come here first, borrow one of my dresses, and go as . . ." She searched her imagination. "As a cousin of yours up from the country. A close cousin, so it will not be in the least improper for you to accompany her without a chaperone."

"Will she agree to that?" There was already interest in his voice, and not the incredulity he might have felt towards someone else. Perhaps he was remembering Cardington Crescent.

"Oh yes," Emily said with intense determination. "Certainly she will."

Two days later, handsomely dressed in one of Emily's winter gowns adapted from last season—she had bought nothing but black this winter—Charlotte found herself in a smart carriage bowling along Park Lane towards Hanover Close, with Jack Radley beside her. He had called at the York house immediately upon parting from Emily. He left his card and asked if he might introduce to them his cousin, Miss Elisabeth Barnaby, who was newly come up from the country after nursing her aunt through a long and distressing illness, from which she was at last mercifully recovered. Now Miss Barnaby was in need of a little diversion, and for this reason

Jack had presumed on an old acquaintance, in the hope he might introduce her.

The reply had been brief, but perfectly civil, quite enough upon which to call.

Charlotte pulled the rug tighter round her knees. The carriage was bitterly cold and it was raining hard outside, daggers of water stabbing the gutters, hissing under the wheels and spraying high. The leather upholstery inside felt damp to the touch—even the wood of the window frames was clammy. Emily's dress was excellent, since her maid had let it out across the bosom and lengthened the cuffs an inch, all very suitable for a young woman recently come up from the country: while not obviously secondhand, neither was it of the latest fashion, such as might be worn by someone in no need of introduction. But Charlotte was still cold.

The carriage stopped. She glanced quickly at Jack Radley beside her and swallowed, feeling a tight flicker of apprehension. This was a very rash thing she was doing. Pitt would be furious if he knew, and the chance of being caught was very real. It would be easy enough to make a crucial mistake or slip of the tongue; she might have the misfortune to meet someone who had known her before her marriage, when she still moved in such circles.

The door was opened and Jack waited to hand her down. She stepped out, wincing against the cold needles of rain. She felt no better about the impending visit, but she could hardly remain in the carriage and say she had changed her mind. She weighed her sense of caution and the anticipation of Thomas's anger against the excitement she had felt when she and Emily discussed the plan.

She was still of two minds when the parlormaid opened the front door and Jack handed her his card, which was engraved with his name. *And Miss Elisabeth Barnaby* had been added by hand. Now it was too late; the die was cast. Charlotte put on her most charming smile and stepped inside.

The parlormaid had a creamy complexion and dark hair.

She was very pert, with wide eyes and a handspan waist; but then parlormaids were usually chosen for their looks. A handsome parlormaid was a mark of one's status and taste.

Charlotte barely had time to glance round the hall, except to notice that it was spacious. The stair was wide and remarkably fine, with beautifully carved bannisters, and the chandelier blazed with light on this dark winter afternoon.

They were shown into the withdrawing room. There was no time to look at the furnishings or the paintings; all Charlotte's attention was taken up by the two women who sat opposite each other on the overstuffed and buttoned red settees. The younger, who must be Veronica York, was tall, and perhaps a good deal too slender for the current fashion, but there was an intense femininity in the delicate lines of her shoulders and throat. Her soft black hair was swept up and off her face, showing a lovely brow and fine features, slightly hollow cheeks, and a startlingly sensuous mouth.

The older woman had thick, curly light brown hair; her curls were so rich no rags or irons could have created them, only nature. She looked to be considerably shorter than the other woman. Although she was of heavier build, she was still extremely comely in an embroidered gown of the latest fashion. Her features were regular and she had obviously been something of a beauty well into her prime. She was only just beyond it now, and the telltale lines on her pink and white skin were few, and round the mouth rather than the eyes. It was a face of arresting strength. This must be Loretta York, the dead man's mother, whom Thomas had said behaved with such dignity on the night of the tragedy.

As mistress of the house she welcomed them, inclining her head to Jack and offering her hand. "Good afternoon Mr. Radley, how agreeable of you to call, and to bring your cousin." She turned to Charlotte with a scrutinizing eye. "Miss Barnaby, I believe you said?"

Charlotte put on the most innocent air she could imagine and all but curtsied. She was supposed to be shy and grateful, seeking London Society and, as a single woman of desperate age, a husband.

"How do you do, Mrs. York. It is most kind of you to receive us."

"I hope we find you as well as you look, ma'am." Jack's flattery was automatic; it was the usual coin of exchange, and he had dined out most of his adult life on his charm. "You make me forget it is winter outside, and several years since we last met."

"I see your manners have not changed," she said a trifle tartly, but there was a flush of pleasure in her cheeks. She might protest, discard it as convention, but she liked it all the same. "Of course you know my daughter-in-law," she said, indicating the younger woman with no more than a glance in her direction.

Jack bowed again, very slightly, but enough for grace.

"Of course. I was most grieved to hear of your loss, and I hope that the future will hold some happiness for you."

"Thank you." A tiny smile touched the corners of Veronica York's lips. Watching closely, Charlotte could see there was an old understanding between them that had been picked up effortlessly. A thought of Emily flashed into her mind, and she pushed it aside. That was another problem, to be faced at another time.

Veronica was looking past Jack and assessing Charlotte, judging the cut of her gown, its newness, its cost, as was Loretta. Charlotte was satisfied that it communicated her new status precisely—it was the gown of a country woman somewhat retired from Society by duties of compassion, but of good family and more than adequate means.

"I do hope you will find London to your liking, Miss Barnaby," Veronica said graciously. "There will be much to divert you, but of course you must take care, because there is also company you would not wish, and it is easy enough to find yourself in distasteful places if you are not wise in your choices."

Charlotte seized the chance. She smiled shyly. "That is most kind of you, Mrs. York. I shall be sure to take your advice. A woman's reputation can be so quickly ruined."

"Quite," Loretta agreed. "Pray do be seated, Miss Barnaby."

Charlotte thanked her and sat carefully on a stiff-backed chair, arranging her skirt. For a moment she was reminded with unpleasant clarity of the time before her marriage when she had often been in situations something like this. She had been escorted by her mother to all the right functions, shown off to best advantage in the hope that some eligible man would be attracted and a suitable marriage arranged. Always she had ended by expressing too forceful an opinion upon something, or laughing inappropriately, or being altogether too willful and failing to charm—quite often on purpose. But then she had thought herself in love with her elder sister's husband, and the idea of marrying anyone else had been unspeakable. How long ago, how girlish, that seemed now! Nevertheless she remembered the relentless good manners, the pursuit of fashion, and all directed towards finding a husband.

"Have you been in London before, Miss Barnaby?" the elder Mrs. York was inquiring, her cool gray eyes summing up Charlotte's very handsome figure and noting the tiny needle holes where the bodice had been let out.

For once Charlotte did not mind. This was only a part she was playing. And she must remember to observe closely, so as to have something to report back to Emily.

"Oh yes, but not for some time, owing to my aunt's illness. Happily she is quite recovered, and I am free to take up my own life again. But I do feel I have missed so much. I imagine a great deal has happened in Society since."

"No doubt," Mrs. York said with a tiny smile. "Although there is a certain sameness in events from year to year, and only the people's names change."

"Oh, I think the people are quite different also," Veronica argued. "And certainly the theater is."

Mrs. York shot her a glance that Charlotte noted with interest: critical, then instantly muted; there was no gentleness in it. "You know very little of the theater," she pointed out. "You have scarcely been till this year." She turned to Charlotte. "My daughter-in-law is a recent widow. Naturally she has remained in mourning until quite lately."

Charlotte had already decided to pretend complete ignorance of the affair in Hanover Close and anything to do with it. She put on an instant expression of sympathy.

"I am so sorry. Please accept my deepest condolences. I should not have troubled you had I known." She turned to Jack, who studiously avoided her eye.

"It has been three years," Veronica said into the rather awkward silence. She looked not at her mother-in-law's face but downward to the rich wine-colored brocade of her own skirt, then back at Charlotte. "We too are taking up our lives again."

"*You* are." Mrs. York's tone made the distinction delicate, but perfectly plain. It was charged with emotion, but try as she might, Charlotte could not define it. Was she reminding the younger woman that her own loss of a son was irreplaceable, and somewhat deeper than the loss of a husband, since Veronica planned to remarry? There seemed more in her face than awareness of her daughter-in-law's pain, or even envy, or anything so vulnerable as self-pity. Her small, strong hands were white in her lap, and her eyes were glittering and sharp. Had not such an idea been so out of place, even ridiculous, Charlotte might have thought it a warning of some sort. But that was groundless, and an inaccurate observation.

Veronica's full lips curved upwards in a tiny smile. Clearly she understood the significance of the reply.

"Indeed, Mr. Radley, you may congratulate me," she said, looking up at him. "I am to be married again."

In that instant Charlotte made a mental note that Veronica

York and Jack Radley had certainly had a friendship that was more than merely amicable, at least on her part.

Jack smiled as if it were a happy surprise to him. "I hope you will have every blessing and good fortune."

"And so do I," Charlotte added. "I hope sadness will be completely in the past for you."

"You are something of a romantic, Miss Barnaby," Mrs. York remarked with her eyebrows raised. She was almost smiling, but there was a coldness in her that was palpable, something hard deep inside that was unresolved. Perhaps it was an old wound, and nothing to do with this. One never knew what pain or disillusion lay in other people's lives, what lost hopes. Charlotte must endeavor to meet the Honorable Piers York at some time; it might explain much that she could only guess at now.

She smiled as dazzlingly at Mrs. York as she could. "Oh, but of course. Even if the reality is not always as one would wish, I hope for the best." Was that the right sort of naiveté, or had she overdone it? She must not sit here for the brief half hour that was socially acceptable, and then leave again without having learned a thing. It would be some time before she could call again.

"So do I," Veronica reassured her. "And it is most kind of you. Mr. Danver is an excellent man, and I am sure I shall be very happy."

"Do you paint, Miss Barnaby?" Mrs. York asked, changing the subject abruptly, this time without looking at Veronica. "Perhaps Mr. Radley might take you to see the winter exhibition at the Royal Academy. I daresay it may interest you."

"I don't paint very well." Let them take that as modesty, or the truth, as they chose. Actually, like all well-bred young ladies, she had been taught to paint, but her brush was never equal to her imagination. Since she had married Pitt and had two children, her only hobby had been meddling in his cases and detecting a great deal. She had a gift for it—even Pitt admitted so—but she could hardly own to that now!

"I had not supposed you to enter a work, Miss Barnaby, merely to observe," Mrs. York replied with a small gesture of her hand, a wry dismissal of foolishness that stung Charlotte. But in her role as Miss Barnaby she was helpless to retaliate. "No skill would be required," Mrs. York continued, "except to look elegant and speak modestly. I am sure you could do both of those with the greatest of ease."

"You are very kind," Charlotte said between her teeth.

Veronica leaned forward. She really was a beautiful woman, her face combining both fragility of bone with strength of mouth and eye. Her manner was as friendly as if they had known each other for some time. Charlotte found herself hoping Pitt would find her blameless enough to satisfy the people at the Foreign Office. The thought of their judgments lit a spark of anger inside her.

"Perhaps you would care to come with me," Veronica offered. "I should be delighted to have your company. We could make all the remarks we wished and be utterly frank about what we like and dislike." She did not look at her mother-in-law, but raised one slender shoulder in the smallest gesture of exclusion.

"I should be delighted," Charlotte accepted sincerely. "It would be the greatest pleasure." She was aware of Jack coughing in the chair next to hers and reaching for a handkerchief to hide his smile.

"Then it is settled," Veronica said firmly. "It is not a favorite outing of Mama-in-law's. I am sure she will be grateful for being spared it this year."

"I have accompanied you to many places that were not especially to my liking!" Mrs. York said with cold eyes on Veronica. "And doubtless will do so again. Family responsibilities are something one never grows out of, nor is one able to escape them. I am sure you would agree with me, Miss Barnaby?" She spoke to Charlotte, but it was Veronica her glance fell on first, before turning with a change of expression so slight it was barely definable. Charlotte had the sudden, intense feeling that the two women disliked each other, perhaps even more than that.

Veronica stiffened, and a tightness crept into her neck, the long line of her throat, and her passionate mouth. She said nothing. Charlotte believed they were speaking of something quite different, and for all the tension between them and the underlying violence, they understood each other perfectly.

"Of course," Charlotte murmured. After all, she was supposed to have spent the last two years nursing a sickly relative. What sacrifice to duty could an unmarried woman have greater than that? "Families are bound by both love and obligation." It was almost time for them to leave. She must make one last effort at learning something deeper, beyond this sharp, unhappy impression. She discreetly glanced rapidly round the room, without turning her head. She noticed an ormolu clock. If she were going to lie, she might as well do it in the grand manner.

"Oh what a delightful clock," she said admiringly. "My cousin used to have one very like that, only a trifle smaller, I think, and one of the figures was clothed differently." She shivered to add verisimilitude. "Unfortunately it was taken in a robbery. Such a dreadful experience." She ignored Jack's horrified expression and plunged on. "Quite as painful as the loss of possessions was the awful feeling that someone had broken into your house and perhaps actually stood within yards of your bedroom as you lay asleep! It took us all ages before we could retire again with the slightest peace of mind." Through her lashes she was watching their faces. She was rewarded by a gasp from Veronica and a sudden rigidity in Mrs. York's body under its folds of sumptuous silk. "We called the police, of course," she went on relentlessly, "but no one was caught. And none of our precious things was ever recovered."

Veronica opened her mouth, sat perfectly still, then closed it without speaking.

"What a misfortune for you." Mrs. York's voice was quite low, but there was a curious edge to it, and her words were unusually distinct, as if her control over them were precarious. "I am afraid it is part of present-day life. One is seldom as safe as one imagines. Be thankful, Miss Barnaby, that it was only goods of which you were robbed."

Charlotte maintained her facade of innocence, although it stabbed her conscience. She gazed back at Mrs. York in bewilderment. Jack had already affected ignorance of the affair, so he could not now help. Charlotte saw the color drain from Veronica's face. Again she seemed about to speak but then to lose the words. She raised her eyes to her mother-in-law, then before their glances met she looked away again.

Finally it was the older woman who broke the hot silence.

"My son was killed by an intruder in the house, Miss Barnaby. It is something we still find too distressing to discuss. That is what made me say you were fortunate to have lost only material possessions."

"Oh, I am so sorry!" Charlotte said instantly. "Please forgive me for having brought you pain. How could I have been so clumsy." A real feeling of guilt was burning inside her already. Not everything can be justified by the need for solutions to mysteries, however intriguing, or needed for Emily's sake.

"You could not know," Veronica said huskily. "Please do not feel at fault. I promise you, we do not hold you so."

"I am sure your sensitivity will prevent you from raising the subject again," Mrs. York said levelly, and Charlotte felt the heat rise in her cheeks.

Veronica was quick to see her embarrassment and rushed to ease it. "That hardly needs to be said, Mama-in-law!" Her tone carried reproof, and the undertone of dislike was there again, bleak and painful in this opulent and comfortable room. It was not a flash of irritation but a long-lived and

41

bitter thing, surfacing suddenly. "I am sure Miss Barnaby needs to feel no blame for having mentioned her own misfortune; how could she have known of our—our tragedies? One cannot cease from all conversation in case it should waken a painful memory in someone else."

"I believe that was the substance of my remark." Mrs. York stared at her daughter-in-law, her brilliant eyes almost hypnotic in their concentration. "If Miss Barnaby is the person of sensibility I take her to be, having discovered our loss, she will not mention any subject close to it again while in our company. Surely that is plain enough?"

Veronica turned to Charlotte and put out her hand. "I hope you will call on us again, Miss Barnaby, and that you will come to the academy with me. I most sincerely meant my invitation; it was not merely a pleasantry."

"I shall be delighted," Charlotte said, taking the offered hand warmly. "It will be the greatest pleasure, and I look forward to it." She rose. It was now time to leave; after that conversation it was the only possible course. Jack rose also and together they expressed their thanks and good wishes, and five minutes later they were in the chilly carriage with the clatter of hooves and the hissing of wheels in the rain. Charlotte wrapped the rug round herself more tightly, but nothing could keep all the icy spears of the draft away. Next time she borrowed a gown from Emily she would take a fur muff to go with it!

"I assume you will be going to the academy with Veronica?" Jack said after a moment or two.

"Of course!" She turned in her seat to look at him. "Don't you think there is a great deal between Veronica and Mrs. York which the police could never discover? I think they both know something about the night of the burglary—although how we'll ever learn it I can't imagine."

3

PITT HAD NO IDEA that Charlotte had gone to Hanover Close. He both knew and understood her concern for Emily, and he expected her to use all her powers of judgment and deduction to find out just how Emily felt about Jack Radley and to measure his worthiness if Emily truly cared for him. And if it turned out he was not satisfactory, there would be the major challenge of either dissuading Emily from pursuing it any further or discouraging Radley himself. Pitt suspected that it might well take all Charlotte's skill to bring the affair to the conclusion that would cause Emily the least pain. Therefore he did not mention the York burglary or Robert York's death to Charlotte again, nor keep her up to date on his own pursuit of a solution.

Ballarat was evasive about the precise reason for opening the case again; it was unclear whether they hoped to discover who had murdered Robert York at this late date, or whether learning the motive was the real purpose of the investigation. Perhaps they wanted to establish beyond a doubt that it had been no more than a simple robbery that had erupted into unplanned violence, putting an end to the rumors of treason once and for all. Or were they really concerned that Veronica York was somehow involved, the unwitting catalyst of a crime of passion inexpertly covered to look like robbery? Or did they know the truth, and simply wish to make doubly sure it was successfully concealed forever by having the police test it, and if it did not break, then they could rest easy that it was buried beyond anyone's recall?

Pitt found this last possibility acutely distasteful, and possibly he wronged his superiors by letting it enter his mind, but he was determined to think it through until he could present Ballarat with an answer that was beyond denial or dispute.

He began with the stolen articles, and the curious fact that none of them had turned up in the places one might have expected despite the vigorous search the police had kept up throughout the following year. All the well-known fences, pawnbrokers, and less fastidious collectors of objects d'arts had been questioned at regular intervals as a matter of course, and on each occasion the York pieces had been on the list of goods mentioned.

But Pitt had been in the Metropolitan Police for nearly twenty years and he knew people Ballarat had never heard of, secretive, dangerous people who tolerated him for past and future favors. And it was to these he went while Charlotte was arranging her visit to the drawing rooms of Hanover Close.

He left Bow Street and walked sharply eastward towards the Thames, disappearing into one of the vast dockland slums. He passed crowded, warped buildings, dark under the lowering skies and filled with the sour reek of the fog that crept up from the slow, gray-black water of the river. There were no carriages with lamps and footmen here, only dim wagons laden with bales for the wharves and carts with a few limp vegetables for sale. A tinker with pans clattered as he jiggled over the uneven cobbles, an old-clothes seller shouted, "Ol' clo'! Ol' clo'!" in a mournful, penetrating voice. His horse's hooves had no echo in the drenching gloom.

Pitt walked quickly, his head down and his shoulders hunched. He wore old boots with loose soles and a grimy jacket, torn at the back, which he kept for such visits. He pulled the thin collar up round his ears now, but still the rain trickled down his neck to his back, a wandering, icy finger that made him shudder. No one paid him any attention apart from the occasional glance when a peddlar or coster half hoped he might buy something. But he did not look like a man who had the means to purchase, and with face averted and body tight with the knowledge of the warmth he had left behind, he hurried deeper into the alleys and passages of the warren.

Finally he found the door he sought, its wood black with age and dirt, metal studs worn smooth by countless hands. He knocked sharply twice, and then twice again.

After a moment or two it opened six inches on a chain, stopping with a clunk as it reached its limit. Even though it was midmorning the daylight scarcely penetrated these narrow alleys, their jettied stories almost meeting overhead, eaves forever dripping in incessant, uneven rhythm. A rat squeaked and scuttled away. Someone tripped over a pile of rubbish and swore. In the distant street the wail "Ol'! clo'!" came again, and down on the river the moan of a foghorn. The smell of rot filled Pitt's throat.

"Mr. Pinhorn," he said quietly. "A matter of business."

There was a moment's silence, then a candle flame appeared in the gloom. He could see little beyond it but the outline of a large, sharp nose and the black sockets of two eyes. But he knew Pinhorn always answered the door himself, afraid that his apprentices would keep the trade for themselves and do him out of a few pence.

"It's you," Pinhorn said sourly, recognizing him. "Wotcher want? I got nuffink for yer!"

"Information, Mr. Pinhorn, and a warning for you."

Pinhorn made a sound deep in his adenoids as if he were going to spit, then changed it into a bark. It expressed ineffable contempt.

"Robbery's one thing, and murder's another," Pitt said carefully, not at all disturbed. He had known Pinhorn for over a decade and this reception was exactly what he expected. "And treason is a third thing, nastier than both."

Again there was silence. Pitt knew better than to push his case. Pinhorn had fenced stolen goods for forty years; he understood his risks perfectly, or he would not still be alive, a prisoner only of poverty, ignorance and greed. He would be in one of Her Majesty's prisons, like Coldbath Fields, where labor such as the treadmill or passing the shot would have broken even his thick, hard body.

The chain rattled as he took it off and the door swung wide noiselessly on oiled hinges.

"Come in, Mr. Pitt."

He locked the door behind him and led the way down a passage piled with old furniture and smelling of mold, round a corner, and into a room that was surprisingly warm. A fire in an open grate shed a flickering light on the stained walls. A piece of heavy red carpet, no doubt garnered from some burglary, lay before the grate between two plush-covered armchairs. All the rest of the room apart from that cleared space was piled with dimly perceived objects: carved chairs, pictures, boxes, clocks, pitchers and ewers, piles of plates. Balanced at a crazy angle, a mirror caught the firelight and winked a red eye.

"Wotcher want, Mr. Pitt?" Pinhorn asked again, eyeing Pitt narrowly. He was a big man, barrel-chested, bullet-headed, his gray hair in a terrier crop such as prisoners wore, although he had never actually been caught or tried. In his youth he had enjoyed something of a reputation as a bare-knuckle fighter, and he was still capable of beating a man senseless if he lost his temper, which happened suddenly and violently from time to time.

"Have you seen a pair of miniature portraits?" Pitt asked. "Seventeenth-century, man and a woman? Or a silver vase, a crystal paperweight carved with a design of scrolls and flowers, and a first edition of *Gulliver's Travels* by Jonathan Swift?"

Pinhorn looked surprised. "That all? You come all the way 'ere ter ask me vat? Vat lot in't worf much."

"I don't want them; I just want to know if you've heard of them. About three years ago, probably."

Pinhorn's eyebrows shot up incredulously. "Free years ago! Yer bleedin' eejut! D'yer fink I'd 'member vat sort of 'aul fer free years?"

"You remember everything you've ever bought or sold, Pinhorn," Pitt said calmly. "Your trade depends on it. You're the best fence this side of the river, and you know the worth of everything to the farthing. You'd not forget an oddity like a Swift first edition."

"Well, I 'an't 'ad none."

"Who has? I don't want it, I just want to know."

Pinhorn screwed up his little black eyes and wrinkled his great nose suspiciously. He stared at Pitt for several seconds. "You wouldn't lie ter me, Mr. Pitt, nah would yer? It'd be very unwise, as then I wouldn't be able ter 'elp yer no more." He tilted his head to one side. "Might not even be able ter stop yer gettin 'urt on yer little hexpiditions inter places where rozzers in't nat'ral—like 'ere."

"Waste of time, Mr. Pinhorn," Pitt replied with a smile. "Same as you lying to me. Have you heard of the Swift?"

"Wot's it yer said abaht murder an' treason? They're strong words, Mr. Pitt."

"Hanging words, Mr. Pinhorn," Pitt elaborated distinctly. "There's murder for certain, treason only maybe. Have you heard anyone speak of the Swift, anyone at all? You hear most things this side of the river."

"No I 'an't!" Pinhorn's face remained in the same tortured expression of concentration. "If anybody's fenced anyfink like vat, vey done it outside o' the Smoke, or they done it private to someone as vey already know as wanted it. Although why anybody'd want it stole I dunno; it in't worf vat much. You said first edition, dincher, not 'andwrit ner nuffink?''

"No, just a first-edition printing.''

"Can't 'elp yer.''

Pitt believed him. He was not ingenuous enough to believe past gratitude for small favors would have any weight, but he knew Pinhorn wanted him on his side in the future. Pinhorn was too powerful to be afraid of his rivals and he had no conception of loyalty. If he knew anything that it was in his own interest to tell Pitt, he would undoubtedly have done so.

"If I 'ear anyfink I'll tell yer,'' Pinhorn added. "Y'owe me, Mr. Pitt.''

"I do, Mr. Pinhorn,'' Pitt said dryly. "But not much.'' And he turned round to make his way back to the great wooden door and the dripping alley outside.

Pitt knew many other dealers in stolen goods; there were the dollyshops, those poorest of pawnbrokers, who lent a few pence to people desperate enough to part with even their pots and pans or the tools of their trade in order to buy food. He hated such places, and the pity he felt was like being kicked in the stomach. Because he was helpless, he turned to anger as being better than weeping. He wanted to shout at the rich, at Parliament, at anyone who was comfortable, or who was ignorant of these tens of thousands who clung to life by such a frail and dangerous thread, who had not been bred to afford morality except of the crudest sort.

This time he was free to avoid them, along with the thieves' kitchens, where kidsmen kept schools of children trained to steal and return the profits to them. Similarly he did not need to scour the slop trade: those who dealt in old clothes, rags, and discarded shoes, taking them apart and making up new articles for the poor, who could afford no better. Often even the worst rags were laboriously unraveled and the fiber rewoven into shoddy—anything to cover those who might otherwise be naked.

The articles from the York house had been taken by a thief not only of taste but also of some literacy, and would have been fenced similarly. They were luxuries that could not be converted into anything useful to the patrons of dollyshops.

He made his way back through the tangle of passageways uphill away from the river towards Mayfair and Hanover Close. Thieves usually worked their own areas. Since he could not trace the goods, the best place to start was with those who knew the patch. If it was one of them, word of the theft would probably have reached the old hands. If it had been an outsider, that too would be known by someone. The police had investigated at the time, it had been no secret. The underworld would have its own information.

It took him half an hour after reaching Mayfair to track down the man he wanted, a skinny, lop-legged little man of indeterminate age called William Winsell and known, contrarily, as the Stoat. He found him in the darkest corner of a tavern of particularly ill repute, staring sourly at half a pint of ale in a dirty mug.

Pitt slid into the vacant seat beside him. The Stoat glared at him with outrage.

"Wot you doin' 'ere, bleedin' crusher! 'Oo d'ya fink'll trust me if vey see me wiv ve likes o' you?" He looked at Pitt's fearful clothes. "D'yer fink we don't granny yer, just 'cos yer aht o' twig in them togs? Still look like a crusher, wiv yer clean 'ands wot never worked, and crabshells"—he did not even bother to glance at Pitt's feet—"like ruddy barges! Ruin me, you will!"

"I'm not staying," Pitt said quietly. "I'm going to the Dog and Duck, a mile away, to have lunch. I thought you might like to join me in, say, half an hour? I'm going to have steak and kidney pudding, hot; Mrs. Billows does that a treat. And spotted dick, made with suet and lots of raisins, and cream.

And maybe a couple of glasses of cider, brought up from the West Country.''

The Stoat swallowed hard. "Yer a cruel man, Mr. Pitt. You must want some poor bastard cropped!'' He made a sharp gesture with his hand at the side of his throat, like a noose under the ear.

"Perhaps, in the end," Pitt agreed. "Right now it's only burglary information. Dog and Duck, half an hour. Be there, Stoat, or I shall have to come and see you somewhere less agreeable—and less private.'' He stood up, and without looking backwards, head down, he pushed his way through the drinkers and out into the street.

Thirty-five minutes later he was in the more salubrious parlor of the Dog and Duck, with a mug of cider, bright and clear as an Indian summer, in front of him, when the Stoat crept in nervously, ran his fingers round his grimy collar as if easing it from his neck, and wriggled onto the seat opposite him. He glanced round once or twice, but saw only dull, respectable minor traders and clerks; no one he knew.

"Steak and kidney pudding?'' Pitt offered unnecessarily.

"Wotcher want orf of me first?'' the Stoat said suspiciously, but his nostrils were wide, sucking in the delicious aroma of fresh, sweet food. It was almost as if the steam itself fed him. " 'Oo're yer after?''

"Someone who robbed a house in Hanover Close three years ago,'' Pitt replied, nodding over the Stoat's head to the landlord.

The Stoat swiveled round furiously, his face suddenly creasing with outrage. " 'Oo're yer signin' at?'' he snarled. " 'Oozat?''

"The landlord.'' Pitt raised his eyebrows. "Don't you want to eat?''

The Stoat subsided, vaguely pink under the gray of his skin.

"A robbery three years ago in Hanover Close,'' Pitt repeated.

The Stoat sneered. "Free years ago? Bit slow, incher? Runnin' be'ind vese days, are we? Wot was took?"

Pitt described the articles in some detail.

The Stoat's lip curled. "Yer in't after vem fings! Ye're after 'oo croaked ve geezer wot caught 'em at it!"

"I'd be interested," Pitt conceded. "But primarily I'm concerned to prove someone innocent."

"Vat's a turnup!" the Stoat said cynically. "Friend o' yours?"

"Hungry?" Pitt smiled. The landlord appeared with two steaming dishes piled high with meat, gravy, and feather-light suet crust. A few green vegetables decorated the side, and a maid stood by with an earthenware jug of cider sweet as ripe apples.

The Stoat's eyes glazed a little.

"Murder's not good for business," Pitt said very quietly. "Gives robbery a bad name."

"Bring on the scran!" the little man snapped, then licked his lips and smiled. "Yer right—it's clumsy and it in't nec-essary." He watched with rapture as his plate was set in front of him, inhaling the delicate steam and sucking his teeth as the cider was poured, eyeing it right to the brim of the tan-kard.

"What do you know about it, Stoat?" Pitt asked before he took the first mouthful.

The Stoat's eyes opened very wide. They were a clear gray; the redeeming feature of a cramped face, they must once have been handsome. He filled his mouth with food and chewed slowly, rolling it round his tongue.

"Nuffin'," he said at last. "And that in't nuffin', if yer sees wot I mean. Usual yer 'ears a word, if not straight orf, then in a munf er two. Or if 'e's in lavender 'cos it turned a bit nasty, then a year, mebbe. But vis 'un clean mizzled!"

"If he was in lavender in some nethersken, you'd know?" Pitt pressed. "In lavender" meant in a hiding place from the police, but the Stoat was indicating that this particular thief had vanished.

The Stoat filled his mouth again and spoke round the food with difficulty. " 'Course I'd know!" he said contemptuously. "Know every slapbang, lurk, nethersken, flash 'ouse, and paddyken fer miles."

Pitt understood him. He was referring to cheap eating houses, hiding places, low lodging houses, criminal pubs, and taprooms.

"An' I tell yer vis," the Stoat went on, sipping his cider appreciatively. " 'E weren't no professional. From wot I 'ear 'e got no crow, no snakesman, and 'oo but a fool'd go in the front like 'e did in a place like 'anover Close? Yer gotta know the crushers'd be rahnd every bleedin' twenty minutes!"

A snakesman was a thin or underdeveloped child who could creep through the bars of a window and, once inside, open the doors for the real thief. A crow was a lookout, frequently a woman, to warn of police or strangers approaching. Pitt already knew the thief was no professional from P.C. Lowther, but it was interesting that the Stoat knew this also. "So he was an amateur," he said. "Has he done anything else, anything since?"

The Stoat shook his head, his mouth full. He swallowed. "Told yer—mizzled. Never done nuffink afore ner since. 'E in't on our patch, Mr. Pitt. I never 'eard o' ven fings fenced, ner no one in lavender 'cos o' the feller topped—an' vey would be. It's no stretch in Coldbath, ner even takin' ve boat like it used ter be: murder's croppin' business, no cockchafers ner scroby, just Newgate, and a long drop early one mornin' wiv a rope collar. A long drop and only the devil ter catch yer."

"Cockchafer" was the graphic term for the treadmill used in prisons, a device to keep a man perpetually in motion; "scroby" meant the prison sentence of the lash.

The Stoat sat back and patted his belly. "Vat was a fair tightener, Mr. Pitt," he said, gazing at his empty plate. "I'd 'elp yer if I could. Ve best I can tell yer is ter look fer some toff wot fought as thievin' was simple and tried 'is 'and at it an' fahnd it weren't.'' He pulled over the plate of spotted dick pudding, thick with fruit, and dipped his spoon in it, then looked up with a sudden idea. ''Or mebbe the lady o' ve 'ouse 'ad a lover, an' 'e did away wiv 'er 'usband, an' it weren't nuffink ter do wiv thievin' at all. 'Ad yer fought o' vat, Mr. Pitt? It ain't one of ve family, vat I know.''

''Yes Stoat, I had thought of it,'' Pitt said, pushing the cream across to him.

The Stoat grinned, showing sharp, gappy teeth, and poured the cream generously. ''Y'in't daft, fer a crusher, is yer!'' he said with grudging respect.

Pitt believed the Stoat, but even so he felt compelled to pursue any other contacts he had right up until Christmas Eve. He found nothing but a blank ignorance and a total absence of fear, which was in itself a kind of evidence. He tramped miles through dingy alleys behind the grand facades of the great streets; he questioned pimps, fences, footpads, and keepers of bawdy houses, but no one told him anything of a thief who had broken into Hanover Close and tried to sell or dispose of the missing property, or who was hiding from a murder charge. The whole underworld turned a dirty, conniving, but quite innocent face to his inquiries.

It was a fine, sharp evening, dark by half past four after a pale green sunset. Gas lamps burned yellow, carriages rattled back and forth over a shining film of ice on the cobbles. People called out greetings, drivers shouted abuse, and street sellers cried their wares: hot chestnuts, matches, bootlaces, old lavender, fresh pies, penny whistles, toy soldiers. Here and there little knots of youths sang carols, their voices thin and a little sharp in the frosty air.

Pitt felt a slow, blessed cleanliness wash over him as the smell of despair receded and the grayness was infused with the beginnings of color. The excitement around him drove out memory and buoyed him up, even expunging the pity and guilt he usually felt when leaving the rookeries and returning to his comfortable home. Today he cast off those feelings like a soiled coat and was left with only gratitude. He flung open the front door and shouted out, "Hello!"

There was an instant's silence, then he heard Jemima jump from her stool and the clatter of shoes on linoleum as she ran up the hall to meet him.

"Papa! Papa, is it Christmas Eve yet? It is, isn't it!"

He threw his arms round her and lifted her high into the air. "Yes, my sweetheart, it is! It is Christmas Eve, right now!" He kissed her and held her on his arm, striding into the kitchen. All the lights were blazing. Charlotte and Emily sat at the table, putting the finishing touches on the icing of a great cake, and Gracie was stuffing the goose. Emily had arrived an hour earlier with a footman in tow, laden with colored paper, boxes, and ribbons. Edward, Daniel, and Jemima had clustered round him, speechless with excitement, Edward hopping up and down from one foot to the other, his blond hair flopping on his head like a silver-gold lid. Daniel was doing a little dance on the floor, round and round in circles until he fell over.

Pitt put Jemima down, kissed Charlotte, welcomed Emily, and acknowledged Gracie's presence. He took his boots off and stretched out in front of the stove, warming his feet and legs, and watched contentedly as Gracie moved the kettle over onto the hot surface and got down the teapot and his large breakfast cup.

After the meal he could hardly wait for the children to go to bed so he could bring out his carefully hidden gifts and begin to wrap them up. He and Emily and Charlotte sat round the scrubbed kitchen table, now piled with scissors, bright paper, and pieces of ribbon and string. Every so often someone would disappear into the parlor, demanding not to be disturbed, and returning with a satisfied smile and gleaming eyes.

They went to bed a little before midnight, and Pitt only heard Charlotte get up once in the pitch darkness when a small voice on the landing asked plaintively, "Isn't it morning yet?"

He woke properly at seven to find Daniel at the door in his nightgown and Charlotte fully dressed at the window.

"I think it's snowing," she said softly. "It's too dark to see, but there's a sort of gleam in the air." She turned round and saw Daniel. "Happy Christmas, darling," she said, bending over to kiss him. He stood still; he was nearly five and not sure about being kissed anymore, at least not in front of other people.

"Is it Christmas?" he whispered into the soft hair around her cheek.

"Yes—yes it is! Get up Thomas, it's Christmas." She held out her hand to Daniel. "Do you want to come and see what is under the tree in the parlor before you get dressed?"

He nodded, his wide eyes never leaving her face.

"Then come on!" And she whisked him out, leaving the door wide open behind her and calling for Edward and Jemima to follow.

Pitt scrambled out of bed, pulled on his clothes in even worse disarray than usual, and, after splashing his face from the pitcher on the dresser, ran downstairs. Charlotte, Emily, and the children stood in the parlor staring at the tree and the pile of bright parcels under it. No one spoke.

"Breakfast first, then church; then we'll see what's in there," Pitt said, breaking the spell. He did not want Emily to turn and see his face, and think of George.

Jemima opened her mouth to protest, then thought better of it.

"Where's Gracie?" he asked.

"I sent her home last night," Charlotte replied. "With two of us we can do everything quite easily."

"Wouldn't she rather have been here, with us?" Pitt thought of the difference between Gracie's home and this

55

house with its warmth, its happiness, and the goose in the oven.

"Maybe," Charlotte agreed, leading the way to the kitchen. "But her mother wouldn't. Emily gave her a chicken," she added under her breath, then went on briskly. "Breakfast in thirty minutes. Everyone go and get dressed—come on!" She clapped her hands and Emily took the children back upstairs while she went to prepare porridge, bacon, eggs, toast, marmalade, honey, and tea. Pitt went back up to shave.

Outside there was a fine dusting of snow and banners of pearl-gray cloud across the winter blue of the sky between the rooftops. They walked together to the church half a mile away. Everywhere bells were ringing; the cold air was full of the sound.

The service was short, and they sat packed together in the narrow pews while the vicar told the familiar story, the organ pealing out all the familiar hymns. "Oh Come All Ye Faithful" and "God Rest Ye Merry Gentlemen," and everyone sang till the sound seemed to roll round them like an ocean.

They walked back in a shower of snow, making footprints in its newness, taking another look at the pile of parcels under the tree. Then, after a short stage of flurry in the kitchen, they all sat down to roast goose with savory stuffing and all the trimmings, crisp brown roast potatoes and parsnips, and a good French wine, and plum pudding fired with brandy, to the delight of the children, and covered with cream. Charlotte had made it and cut it with great care so everyone got a silver threepence.

Finally the presents could be kept no longer. Bursting with excitement, they all trooped into the parlor to portion them out and watch as three children tore off paper, scattered it in mounds, and were lost in a daze of boundless wonder. For Daniel there were the engine and wagons Pitt had made him and a jack-in-the-box Emily had brought; for Edward a box of bricks of every color, shape and size which Pitt had carved and painted, and a set of tin soldiers from Emily; and for Jemima a doll for whom Charlotte had sewn three different outfits of clothing, and from Emily a kaleidoscope which when she shook it and held it to her eye presented an ever-changing magic world of glittering designs.

From Charlotte's mother they each had books: Lewis Carroll's *Alice's Adventures in Wonderland* for Jemima; Charles Kingsley's *The Water Babies* for Daniel; and Robert Louis Stevenson's *Treasure Island* for Edward.

Charlotte was thrilled with her pink alabaster vase, and the garnet brooch Emily gave her; and Emily was equally delighted with the lace collar from Pitt and Charlotte. Pitt was totally happy with the shirts Charlotte had sewn for him, and the gleaming leather Wellington boots Emily had brought. He thanked her for them sincerely, not only for the gift, but for the tact she had shown in not giving too much. She knew quite well that as a constable, Pitt had earned about the same as a chimney sweep, and even now as an inspector his entire month's salary was less than her month's dress allowance.

Emily in turn was grateful for the emotional warmth and the sense of belonging, and she let them see her pleasure as the most delicate way of thanking them. When the flurry of gifts and thank-yous subsided at last, they sat in front of the fire, sparing no expense in letting it roar red and yellow up the chimney. Emily and Charlotte talked and Pitt dozed with his feet on the fender.

In the evening, when the children had gone up to bed, exhausted, clutching their presents, Charlotte, Pitt, and Emily took out a giant jigsaw puzzle of the coronation of Queen Victoria. They sat up till midnight, when Emily finally put in the last piece with a crow of triumph.

Two days later, in a crisp north wind that froze the slush on the pavements into slippery, crackling ridges and scattered ice from the gutter like broken glass, Pitt went back to work. After leaving various instructions regarding the other burglaries in his charge, he left Bow Street for Hanover Close. He was increasingly curious to meet the Yorks, and he had an idea.

A somewhat surprised cabbie set him down in the calm, elegant Close with its Georgian facades and the complicated filigree of bare, black trees against a heavy white sky. He opened his mouth to ask Pitt if he was sure this was where he meant to be, then saw the look on his face and changed his mind. The cabbie took the money and slapped the reins on the horse's faintly steaming rump.

Pitt walked up to the front door, prepared for the scorn of the footman, who would tell him a policeman's place—if he must come at all—was at the tradesmen's entrance in back. He was used to this sort of treatment, but he still felt his shoulders tighten.

The door opened almost immediately and a footman in his late twenties failed to keep the slight surprise out of his face.

"My name is Thomas Pitt." Pitt did not mention rank yet. "It is possible I may have some information about a matter of interest to Mr. York. I would be obliged if you would ask if I may see him."

The footman did not dare turn down such a request without reference to his master, a fact which Pitt had counted on.

"If you will wait in the morning room, sir, I will inquire." The footman stepped back and opened the door invitingly. He had a tray in his hand, but Pitt did not have a card to place on it. Perhaps that was something he should consider: just a plain one, with his name and nothing else.

The morning room was spacious and comfortable, a man's room, with cool green furnishings and sporting prints on the walls. There were leather-bound books in two glass-fronted cases and a rather fine sphere on a table by the window, with all the nations of the empire marked in red, and encircled by vast reaches of Canada, Australasia, India, most of Africa all the way up to Egypt, and islands in every ocean. An engraved brass meridian encircled it.

The footman hovered. "May I tell Mr. York what the matter is in connection with?" he said earnestly.

"With the death of Mr. Robert York," Pitt answered, stretching the truth only slightly.

The footman found no reply to that, bowed very minutely, and left, closing the door behind him.

Pitt knew he would not have long to wait, and there would be little point in studying the books to learn the personalities of those in the house. Handsome books were all too often purchased for their appearance rather than their content. Instead he rehearsed again what he intended to say, preparing himself to lie to a man for whom he felt profound pity, and might well develop a liking.

The Honorable Piers York appeared within five minutes. He was tall, with the build of a man who had been slender in his prime. Approaching seventy, he held himself erect, except for a slight rounding of the shoulders, and his lean face was full of a wry, private humor, which was deeply ingrained beneath the present patina of grief and the years of self-restraint.

"Mr. Pitt?" he inquired curiously, closing the door and indicating one of the armchairs in a tacit invitation. "John said you have something to say about my son's death. Is that correct?"

Pitt felt more ashamed than he had expected, but it was too late to withdraw now without explaining his lie. "Yes sir." He swallowed. "It is possible that some of the articles stolen may have been discovered. If you would give me a closer description of the vase and the paperweight . . . ?"

York's eyes were puzzled. The shadow of loss was there, also a gleam of something which might have been humor or irony as he took in Pitt's shining and perfectly fitted boots.

"Are you from the police?" he asked.

Pitt felt the heat in his face. "Yes sir."

York sat down with an elegant movement despite a faint stiffness in his back. "What have you found?"

Pitt had his story prepared. He sat down opposite and avoided York's eyes as he replied. "We have found a great deal more stolen property lately, and among it are several pieces of silver and crystal."

"I see." York smiled bleakly. "I can't see that it matters much now. They were not of great value. It was just a small vase; can't really remember the thing myself. The paperweight had engraving on it, I think, flowers or something. I wouldn't go to too much trouble, Mr. Pitt. Surely you must have more important work."

There was no alternative but to say it. "It may be through the articles that we can trace the thief, and thus the man who killed your son," he explained gravely.

York smiled, polite but weary. He had already divorced the matter from his emotions. "After three years, Mr. Pitt? Surely it will have changed hands many times since then." It was an observation, not a question.

"I don't think so, sir. We have many contacts with the dealers in stolen goods."

"I suppose it is necessary?" York said with a sigh. "I really don't give a damn about the vase, and I'm sure my wife doesn't either. Robert was our only son; can't we . . ." His words died away.

Was it necessary? Would the whole charade he had planned really lead to any information about Robert York's murderer? Would it even shed any light on the possible involvement of his widow? Was it not merely a further exercise in pain inflicted upon a family that was already deeply hurt?

But there was something different about this crime. It was not a common housebreaking. He believed Pinhorn, the Stoat, and all the others who said it had not sprung from the underworld. Perhaps an acquaintance of the York household had turned to sudden crime, and when Robert had recognized him, the burglar had killed Robert in his panic, rather than be betrayed. Or else it was a murder first and a burglary second: Robert York had surprised his wife with a lover, and the perpetrator had taken the articles to mask the real crime. Or worse still, perhaps it had been premeditated.

There was, of course, the possibility feared by the Foreign Office: that the real theft involved papers Robert York had taken home, and not only was this murder, but also treason.

"Yes, I'm afraid it is necessary," Pitt said firmly. "I'm sorry, sir, but I am sure even in her grief Mrs. York would not wish a murderer to go free when there is a possibility we may catch him."

York stared at him levelly for several seconds, then stood up slowly. "I suppose you know what you're doing, Mr. Pitt." There was no slight in his voice; he spoke as one gentleman to another. He pulled the bell rope near the door, and when the footman answered he sent him for Mrs. York.

She was several minutes in coming, but neither of them spoke again until she appeared. Pitt stood up immediately and regarded her with interest. This was the woman whose composure had so impressed Lowther on the night of her son's death, and Mowbray the day after. She was of barely average height, her slender build a little thickened at the waist, with well-covered shoulders and a white neck draped in lace, not an old lady's lace, but expensive, heavy French lace such as Great-aunt Vespasia might have chosen. Even from a distance of several feet Pitt could smell the faintest aroma of an elusive sweet perfume like gardenia. She had smooth, rounded features, an almost Greek nose, and lips that were still well defined. Her skin was flawless, and her hair, though faded in color, still rich-textured and full, with natural wave. She had been a beauty, in her own fashion. She regarded Pitt with cold surprise.

"Mr. Pitt is from the police," York said in explanation. "He may have found some of our belongings that were stolen. Can you describe the silver vase? I'm afraid I wouldn't know it if I saw it."

Her eyes widened. "After three years you may be able to return me one silver vase? I am unimpressed, Mr. Pitt."

The criticism was just and he knew it. Pitt's voice sounded sharper than he intended. "Justice is frequently slow, ma'am, and sometimes the innocent suffer as well. I'm sorry."

She forced herself to smile, and he respected her for that.

"It was about nine inches high, on a round base but squared up the body, with a fluted lip. It was solid silver, and took about five or six stems. I usually put roses in it."

That was very precise; there was nothing vague or distorted about her description. He looked at her closely. She was intelligent, in complete command of herself, but there was no lack of emotion in her face. In fact Pitt could easily imagine great passion there. He glanced down at the small, strong hands at her sides and saw that they were stiff, but not clenched.

"Thank you, ma'am. And the crystal paperweight?"

"Spherical, with two Tudor roses engraved on it, and something else, a ribbon or scroll. It was about three or four inches high, and heavy, of course." Her brow puckered. "Have you found the thief?" There was a slight tremor in her voice now and a tiny muscle flickered under the pale skin of her temple.

"No ma'am"—at least that was the absolute truth—"only property, through a dealer in stolen goods. But he may lead us to the thief."

York was standing several feet away from her. For a moment Pitt thought he was going to reach out to her in a gesture of comfort, or merely of companionship, but he changed his mind, or else Pitt had misunderstood the slight movement. What lay behind his wry patrician face, her regular, carefully preserved beauty? Did they suspect that their daughter-in-law had had a lover? Or that their son had been murdered for his country's secrets? Or that some associate, even a family friend, had fallen deeply into debt and had turned in desperation to robbery rather than face the disgrace and perhaps even imprisonment brought by financial ruin?

He would learn nothing from staring at them. All their nurturing in the cool, obedient childhood of the aristocracy had bred into them self-mastery, the knowledge of duty to dignity and to class. Whatever fear or grief lay inside, no policeman, no gamekeeper's son was going to see it naked in a wavering voice or a shaking hand. Pitt almost wished Charlotte could see them; she might be able to read far more into their manner.

He could not prolong it anymore, and he could think of no appropriate excuse to meet the widow. He thanked them and allowed the footman to show him to the door and the gray, ice-whipped street.

It took him three days to find a vase that fit Mrs. York's description, and even then it was an inch and a half short and had five sides rather than four, but it was near enough. The paperweight was impossible; the stolen goods hauls presented nothing remotely like it, and he would betray his deceit if he brought one that differed vastly from the description he had been given.

It was New Year's Eve and snowing hard. He rode through muffled streets, the wheels of the hansom almost silent in the pall, and stepped out at number 2 Hanover Close a little after three. He had asked the constable on the beat and knew that this was the best opportunity to catch the younger Mrs. York at home, while the elder Mrs. York was out visiting.

This time the door was answered by a pretty young snip of a parlormaid with a crisp lace apron and a cap on her dark head. She eyed Pitt up and down suspiciously, from the tousled hair poking out under his tall hat and his well-cut but ill-used coat, its pockets stuffed with all manner of objects he had thought he might find useful, to Emily's beautiful boots.

"Yes sir?"

He smiled at her. "I have called to see Mrs. York. She is expecting me within these few days."

She considered his smile more than the information, which she found hard to believe. "Mrs. York has company at the present, sir, but if you come into the morning room I'll inform her you are here."

"Thank you." He stepped in and handed her one of the cards he had acquired since his last visit. Perhaps it was a trifle presumptuous for a policeman to have a card, but he liked it, and it might justify its expense one day. He had not told Charlotte about it, in case she secretly thought him foolish.

The morning room was unchanged, a banked-up slow fire glowing in the grate. This time Pitt deliberately opened the door to the hall after the maid had gone and stood a little out of the way of it, so that he could overhear any conversation unseen. The visitors were probably irrelevant, but he was curious. There had been no carriages outside, so they must intend staying long enough to be worth sending them round to the mews at the back; that meant more than the half hour or so of a normal afternoon call.

The misunderstanding he hoped for materialized. It was the younger Mrs. York the parlormaid informed, and after nearly ten minutes it was she who came, accompanied by a fair-haired man of about forty with a face not handsome, but of intelligent and compelling cast. They were both civil but extremely guarded.

Veronica York was indeed a beautiful woman, very slender, with delicate shoulders and bosom, and she moved with an unusual grace. Her face was more sensitive than her mother-in-law's, more finely boned. It appealed to Pitt instinctively. There was a haunting quality in it, and he had the impression that beneath the calm lay an intense passion, poised to break through.

"Mr. Pitt?" she said with obvious doubt. "I hope you do

64

not mind, Mr. Danver has accompanied me. I regret I do not recollect our acquaintance.''

Danver put one arm half round her, as if he would protect her from any attack of discourtesy. But there was no hostility in his face, only caution, and an awareness of her vulnerability.

"I'm sorry," Pitt apologized immediately. "It was Mrs. Piers York who was expecting me. I should have made myself plainer. But I expect, if you would not mind, you could assist equally well." He took the silver vase out of his coat pocket and held it up. "It is possible that this is the vase stolen from you some three years ago. If it is, would you be kind enough to assure yourself, and then confirm it to me?"

The blood fled from her face and her eyes widened as if he had held up something appalling and incomprehensible.

Danver tightened his arm round her as though he feared she might faint. Then he turned on Pitt furiously.

"For heaven's sake, man, have you no pity at all? You walk in here without the least warning and hold up a vase that was stolen the very night Mrs. York's husband was violently murdered!" He looked at Veronica York, and his voice rose as he saw her anguish deepen. "I shall complain to your superiors about your gross insensitivity! You might at least have asked for Mr. York!"

Pitt did feel compassion for her, but he had felt it for the guilty as well as the innocent many times before. For Julian Danver it was different: either he was a superb actor, or it had not occurred to him that the truth was anything other than what had already been presumed.

"I'm sorry," Pitt apologized honestly. "Mr. York told me on a previous visit that he would not know the vase again. It was Mrs. Piers York who described it to me. I can ask a servant, if you prefer: with your permission?"

Veronica was struggling to master herself. "You are being unfair, Julian," she said with some difficulty. She swallowed dryly and caught her breath. She was still bloodlessly pale.

65

"Mr. Pitt is only doing his duty. It would not be any less distressing to Mother-in-law." She raised her eyes to meet Pitt's, and he was struck again by the power of emotion in her; she was no mere society beauty but a woman who would be unique and compelling anywhere. "I am afraid I am not sure whether it is our vase or not," she said, struggling to keep her voice in control, "I never took much notice of it. It was in the library, which is a room I did not frequent a great deal. Perhaps if you would ask one of the servants, rather than distress my mother-in-law with seeing it?"

"Of course." Pitt had hoped to find an excuse to speak to the servants, and this was ideal. "If you will instruct your butler or housekeeper that you have given your permission, I shall go through to the servants quarters and perhaps find the housemaid who dusted the library at that time."

"Yes," she agreed, unable to hide her relief. "Yes, that would be an excellent idea."

"I'll attend to it," Danver offered. "Would you prefer to go to your room for a while, my dear? I'll make your apologies to Harriet and Papa."

She swung round quickly, "Please don't tell them."

"Of course not," he assured her. "I'll merely say you felt a little faint and went to lie down for half an hour and will rejoin them later. Would you like me to call for your maid, or your mother-in-law?"

"No!" This time there was a fierceness in her voice, and her hand on his arm was clawlike in its grip. "No—please don't! I shall be perfectly all right. Don't disturb anyone else. I shall go up for a little eau de cologne and then return to the withdrawing room. If you will be kind enough to call Redditch and explain to him about Mr. Pitt and the vase?"

He acquiesced with some reluctance, uncertainty still plain in his face.

"Good afternoon, Mr. Pitt," she said courteously, turning away. Danver opened the door for her, and she disappeared into the hall.

66

Danver rang for the butler, a mild, slightly anxious-looking man of middle age who still retained some of the bewildered innocence of extreme youth. It was an odd combination in the dignity and responsibility of his position. Pitt's errand was explained to him, Danver excused himself, and Pitt was conducted across the hall, through the green baize door, and into the housekeeper's sitting room, which was unoccupied at present.

"I'm not sure who was downstairs maid at the time, sir," the butler said dubiously. "Most of the staff have changed since Mr. Robert was killed. I'm new myself; so is the house-keeper. But the scullery maid was here then. She might remember."

"If you would?" Pitt agreed.

He was left for some twenty minutes to sit and wait, turning over his thoughts on Veronica York, until at last a pleasant-looking girl in her early twenties came in. She was wearing a blue stuff gown and a small white apron and cap. Obviously she was not the scullery maid; her looks were trim and soft and her hands were not reddened by constant water. It had been a long time since she had scrubbed a floor. The butler came with her, presumably to make sure she was discreet in her answers.

"I'm Dulcie, sir," she said with a tiny bob. Policemen did not rank a full curtsy; they were something like servants themselves. "I was the tweeny 'ere when Mr. Robert was killed. There's only me and Mary, the scullery maid, left. Mr. Redditch said as I could 'elp you, sir?"

It was a pity the butler remained, but Pitt should have expected that: any senior servant in his position would have.

"Yes, if you please." Pitt took out the silver vase again and held it up for her. "Look at this carefully, Dulcie, and tell me if it is the vase that used to be in the library, up to the time of Mr. Robert York's death."

"Oh!" She looked startled. Apparently Redditch had been very fair and told her only that she was wanted because she had been a housemaid three years ago. Her eyes widened and fixed on the vase in Pitt's hand. She did not touch it.

"Well, Dulcie?" Redditch prompted. "Is that the vase, girl? You must have dusted it often enough."

"It's very like it, sir, but I don't think that's it. Like I remember it, it had four sides to it. But I could be wrong."

It was the best answer she could have given. It allowed him to pursue the subject.

"Never mind," he said easily, smiling at her. "Just think back to what you used to do three years ago. Do you remember that week?"

"Oh yes," she said, her voice hushed.

"Tell me something about it. Were there many visitors to the house?"

"Oh yes." Memory brought a momentary smile to her face. "There was lots of people then." The light vanished. "Of course, after Mr. Robert's death all that stopped, only people coming to give their condolences."

"Ladies calling in the afternoons?" Pitt suggested.

"Yes, most days, either on Mrs. Piers or Mrs. Robert. There was usually one of them in, and one out paying visits 'erself."

"Dinner parties?"

"Not very often. More often they dined out, or went to the theater."

"But some came here?"

"Of course!"

"Mr. Danver?"

"Mr. Julian Danver, and 'is father Mr. Garrard, and Miss 'arriet," she replied quickly. "And Mr. and Mrs. Asherson." She mentioned half a dozen more names which Pitt wrote down under the disapproving eye of the butler.

"Now see if you can recall a particular day," he went on, "and go through your duties one by one."

"Yes, sir." She looked at her folded hands and recited slowly, "I got up at 'alf past five and came downstairs to clean out all the grates, taking out the cinders to the back. Mary'd give me a cup o' tea, then I'd make sure all the 'arths was clean and things blacked as should be, and the brasses, firedogs, and the like polished, and I'd lay the fires and light them so when the family came down in the rooms'd be warm. I'd make sure the footman brought in the coals and the scuttles was full—sometimes you 'ave to be be'ind them all the time. Then after breakfast I'd start dusting and cleaning—"

"Did you clean the library?" He had to press for an identification to justify his position.

"Yes sir—sir! I remember now: that's very like the vase we 'ad, but it in't it!"

"You're sure?" the butler put in sharply.

"Yes, Mr. Redditch. That in't our vase; I'd swear to it."

"Thank you." Pitt could think of nothing else to ask. At least he had some names and could begin looking for a possible amateur thief. He stood up and thanked them.

Redditch relented.

"Would you like a cup of tea in the kitchen, Mr. Pitt?"

Pitt accepted immediately. He was thirsty, and he would very much like a hot cup of tea. He would also like an opportunity to observe as many of the servants as he could.

Half an hour later, after three cups of tea and two slices of Madeira cake, he went back to the main hallway and opened the library door. It was a gracious room, lined with bookshelves on two sides, the third taken up with windows from floor to ceiling curtained in rust red velvet. On the fourth side was a huge marble fireplace flanked by semicircular tables inlaid with exotic wood. There was a massive desk in oak and green leather, its back to the windows, and three large leather-covered armchairs.

Pitt stood in the middle of the floor, imagining the scene on the night Robert York was killed. He heard a slight sound behind him and turned to find the maid, Dulcie, in the doorway. As soon as he saw her she came in. Her brow was puckered and her eyes bright.

"There was something else?" he asked quickly, sure he was right.

"Yes sir. You asked about guests, people callin' 'ere . . ."

"Yes?"

"Well, that week was the last time I saw 'er, or anything belonging to 'er." She stopped, biting her lip, suddenly uncertain whether she should be so indiscreet.

"Saw who, Dulcie?" He must be gentle, not attach too much importance to it and frighten her. "Saw who?"

"I don't know 'er name. The woman what wore the cerise-colored gowns, always something o' that shade. She weren't a guest—at least, she never came in the front door with other people, and I never saw 'er face except that one time in the light from the gas lamp on the landing; there she was one moment, and gone a second later. But she wore cerise always, either a gown or gloves or a flower or something. I know Miss Veronica's things, and she 'adn't nothing that color. But I found a glove one day in the library, 'alf under one of them cushions." She pointed to the furthest chair. "And once there was a piece o' ribbon."

"Are you sure they weren't the elder Mrs. York's?"

"Oh yes, sir. I knew the lady's maids then, and we talked about the mistresses' clothes. It's a hard color, that; I know as neither of them wore it. It was the woman in cerise, sir, but 'oo she was I swear I don't know. 'Cept she came and went like a shadow, like no one should see 'er, and I 'aven't seen 'er since that week, sir. I'm sorry as it weren't the right vase, sir. I wish as you could catch 'ooever done it. It in't the silver: Mr. Piers says as you can always get money from the insurance, like 'e did when Mrs. Loretta lost 'er pearls with the sapphire clip." She bit her lip and suddenly stopped.

"Thank you, Dulcie." Pitt looked at her worried face. "You did the right thing to tell me. I shan't repeat it to Mr. Redditch unless I have to. Now show me to the door, and no one will notice your being here."

"Yes sir. Thank you sir. I . . ." She hesitated a moment,

as if she would say more, then changed her mind and bobbed a brief curtsy before leading him out across the large hall and opening the front door.

A moment later he was outside in the silent close, ice crackling under his boots. Who was this woman in cerise, who apparently had never called again after Robert York's murder, and why had no one else spoken of her?

Perhaps she did not matter; she might be a friend of Veronica's, a relative with eccentric or unacceptable behavior. Or she might be just what the Foreign Office was concealing and hoping he could not trace—a spy. He would have to speak to Dulcie again, when he knew a little more.

4

E*MILY RETURNED HOME* the day after Boxing Day.
The Ashworth town house was large and extremely gracious.
George had had much of it redecorated to please Emily's
taste the first year after they were married, and he had been
characteristically generous. Nothing that added charm or
personality had been denied, and yet the overall effect was
not ostentatious in the least. There were no ornate French
pieces, no gilt or curlicues; the furniture was Regency and
Georgian, in keeping with the architecture of the house itself.
Emily had argued with George at the time about his parents'
love of tassels and fringes and had banished most of the
indifferent family portraits to unused guest rooms. The result
had both surprised and pleased George, who had compared
it with satisfaction to the crowded houses of their friends.

Now, as Emily stood in the hallway while the servants
obeyed her instructions, carrying in cases, preparing luncheon for Edward and herself, she felt a void of loneliness
close round her as if the house were alien. She drew in her
breath, wanting to tell them to stop, that she would be returning to Charlotte's much smaller house. It was positively

cramped by comparison, with secondhand furnishings, and located in a narrow, unfashionable street. But Emily had been happy there; for a few days she had entirely forgotten about her new state of widowhood. Physical differences had been irrelevant, they had all been together, and if she woke once or twice in the night in her bed alone and thought of Charlotte lying in a warm bed with Thomas just beyond the wall, those were short moments, quickly banished by returning sleep.

Now the contrast was like a newly whetted blade, making the spacious air of this house, of which she was sole mistress, feel chilly, as if cold water were touching her skin.

It was ridiculous! The servants had fires burning in every grate, and there were the sounds of quick, busy feet in the passage, the clink of silver in the dining room and the chatter of maids on the landing, and the green baize door swung with a faint bump as a footman came through.

She walked quickly up the stairs, undoing her coat as she went. Her lady's maid appeared and took it from her, along with her hat; she would unpack the cases, sort out what needed laundering, and hang up the gowns. The nursery-maid would do the same for Edward.

Downstairs again, the cook knocked on the boudoir door and inquired for instructions about dinner, and whatever Emily might care for on the menu over the next few days. There was nothing Emily had to do herself but make decisions about things that hardly mattered. That was the trouble. Day after day stretched before her, empty of any necessary or interesting occupation: all the bleak January days she might fill with needlework, writing letters, playing the piano to an empty room, or messing around with brushes and paints and failing to create what she envisioned.

Whatever she did, she did not want to do it alone.

But most of the people she knew were merely acquaintances; to consider them friends would be to devalue the word. Their company would disturb the silence without giving her a sense of companionship, and she was not yet so desperate that she craved any presence at all, regardless of its quality.

In the sensible part of her mind was the realization that company of any value meant relationships, and Emily was not sure what relationship she was prepared for, outside of her family. Although her mother was also fairly recently widowed, Emily felt she had little in common with her. Caroline Ellison had been married a long time, and had been comfortable enough by everyday standards. But she had discovered an aloneness in widowhood that was not at all unmixed with exhilaration. For the first time in her life she answered to no one, neither her autocratic father, her ambitious mother, nor her agreeable but essentially opinionated husband. Even her mother-in-law was not the dictatorial old matriarch she had been while her son was alive. At last Caroline was free to express her own ideas. On more than one occasion she had startled the old lady into a paroxysm of rage by telling her to mind her own business, something she would never have dared do when Emily's father was alive. It would simply not have been worth the ensuing unpleasantness, nor the impossibility of explanation.

But then Emily's father had died peacefully after a short illness, and he had been sixty-five. George had been murdered while scarcely in his prime, and Emily had never really lacked the freedom to do things as she wished anyway. The restrictions placed upon her were those of Society, and she was more tightly bound by them now George was dead than she had been while he was alive. Her hollow feeling of loneliness frightened her; it would probably only get worse, and she might be driven to fill her life with pointless activities and silly conversation with people who cared nothing for her.

The alternative seemed remarkably attractive: to pursue her friendship with Jack Radley. At the moment she did not feel it would be too hard to force out of her mind the sort of questions her more rational self would ask: Was there more to him than charm, humor, the ability to make even quite ordinary pastimes seem fun and to understand her so well that explanations were seldom necessary, and justification never?

Liking was fine, for friends. But Emily knew that in a man one was to marry there must also be trust, the knowledge that the important values were shared, that if she were ill or in distress, if she were maligned by others he would support her. And if he were unfaithful—the thought hurt with almost physical sharpness, as the wounds George had dealt were not completely healed—if he were unfaithful it would be meaningless, and he would be discreet enough that she would never know about it, and above all neither would her friends.

And there must be respect. What could she possibly share with someone who did not possess the courage to fight for what he believed, or the largeness of heart to be moved to pity? She would quickly grow to despise a man whose imagination never went beyond his own concerns.

She caught herself with a start of horror and embarrassment. What on earth was she thinking? Marriage? She must be mad! Jack needed to marry into money; she knew that from his presence at Cardington Crescent. That was why Uncle Eustace had originally invited him: as a suitable husband for Tassie, he was to provide the family connections, and she the money. But of course Emily herself was many times wealthier than Tassie March, now she had inherited George's estate. And that ugly thought must be forgotten. She was a wealthy widow. The fortune hunters would begin to come, circling like vultures round the dying, waiting their turn: not too soon, or they would appear unseemly and spoil their chances, not too late, or they would be beaten to the prize.

The thought was so repellent it was sickening. Her first time in the marriage market, Emily had enjoyed the game. She had everything to win, and she had won. She had deserved to; she had played the game superbly. She had all the innocence and arrogance of inexperience.

Now she felt so much less sure of herself. She had tasted failure, very recently, and she had everything to lose.

Was Veronica York in the same position? Had she turned over these same thoughts in her mind? Her husband had been murdered, and presumably she was heir through him to whatever fortune the Yorks possessed. Did she now regard admirers with suspicion, in her imagination devising tests for them, to see if their love was truly for her or merely for her means?

What monumental arrogance! Jack Radley had never mentioned marriage, nor given Emily the slightest indication that it was what he intended or wished. She must control her thoughts, or she would end up saying something idiotic in front of him and betraying herself completely, which would make this entire situation impossible!

If only there were an urgent crime that she and Charlotte could come to grips with, something real and undeniably important, that would drive all this ridiculous speculation and dreaming out of her mind! How could any woman of the least intelligence occupy all her thoughts with giving orders to servants who knew perfectly well what to do anyway? The parlormaid could have easily organized the running of a household for one woman and a small boy!

So it was with very mixed and somewhat turbulent emotions that Emily greeted the butler the following morning when he came into the withdrawing room to announce that Mr. Jack Radley presented his compliments. He was in the morning room and wished to know if Lady Ashworth would receive him.

She swallowed and sat still for a moment, composing her features; it would not do for the butler to see her confusion.

"What an odd time to call," she said casually. "There is

76

a matter he was looking into for me; perhaps he has some news. Yes, Wainwright, ask him to come in."

"Yes m'lady." If Wainwright noticed anything at all it was absent from his smooth face. He turned slowly and went out of the room, as though he were part of a procession. He had been with the Ashworths since he was a boy, and his father before him, as head gardener. Emily still felt uncomfortable around Wainwright.

Jack came in a moment later, unhurriedly, as decorum required, but there was a lightness to his step and his face was eager. As always he was fashionably dressed, but he wore his clothes with such ease his elegance seemed a happy accident rather than something contrived. It was a look men paid fortunes to achieve.

He hesitated on the edge of telling her she looked well, discarding that lie in favor of a fleeting smile, and the truth.

"You look as bored as I am, Emily. I hate January, and it's almost here. We must do something terribly interesting, to make it pass quickly, while we are too occupied to notice.

In spite of herself she was moved to smile. "Indeed? And what do you suggest? Pray do sit down."

He obeyed with elegance and looked at her candidly. "We must pursue our detecting," he replied. "Surely Charlotte will go back to the Yorks, won't she? I got the distinct impression she was as keen as we were. In fact, was it not her idea?"

It was the ideal excuse, and Emily seized it without thinking.

"Yes it was! I'm sure she would welcome a chance to call again." She did not need to add that it would require Jack's assistance; they both knew that. No single woman in the position Charlotte had pretended to would press such an acquaintance herself. And anyway, Charlotte had not the financial means even to come in a carriage, let alone suitably dressed. Emily could provide those things, but not an escort.

Charlotte must be prompted, in case she had forgotten about the Yorks in the excitement of Christmas.

"I will send her a note," she added aloud. "And it is always possible Pitt will learn something further, so we should keep abreast of that too."

Jack looked thoughtful, gazing at the floor. "I have tried, extremely discreetly, to sound out one or two acquaintances about the Danvers, but I discovered very little. The father, Garrard Danver, is fairly senior in the Foreign Office, which may be how they came to know the Yorks so closely. Although Society is surprisingly small. Everyone knows everyone else, at least by sight or repute, if not to speak to—but of course that is a different thing from calling upon them. There were two sons: one was killed in the Indian Army some time ago, the other is Julian Danver, who may or may not marry Veronica York, depending upon Pitt's inquiries."

Emily gave a little snort of irritation. She was developing an empathy with Veronica York which made the concern about her reputation all the more infuriating.

"I wonder if anyone has bothered to consider whether he is good enough for her!" she said tartly. Instantly Emily regretted the words; she would have bitten her tongue rather than say something so betraying of her own loathsome suspicions. Please God he would not make the connection! She opened her mouth to rush into speech and smother it, then was afraid he would realize that was what she was doing. Instead she brazened it out.

Jack looked a little startled. "You mean his reputation?"

Now she had no answer. To expect a man's reputation to have the same purity as a woman's was absurd; she would mark herself as eccentric to the point of idiocy if she suggested such a thing.

But the alternative was the truth, and that was worse. But how could she back out of this discussion without being caught in a lie? She could feel the hot blood in her cheeks. She must say something! The silence positively prickled.

"Well, they might be concerned that he was a man of honor as much as he seems," she said, scrambling for something that sounded better, more specific. "Some men have most disreputable habits. Perhaps you don't know, but having assisted in the investigation of one or two crimes, I have learned of some terrible things, which were quite unknown to their families." She forced herself to look at Jack. She was talking too much.

"Would it have anything to do with Robert York's murder?" he asked. His eyes revealed nothing.

"No," she said slowly. "Unless, of course, he killed him."

"Julian Danver?"

"Why not?"

"Because he was already Veronica's lover?" He took her point. "Yes, that's possible." He said it with assurance. Apparently the idea did not seem farfetched to him. Divorce would not have been open to Veronica, even with grounds such as proven adultery, let alone with no grounds at all! Emily knew that. Only men could divorce for unfaithfulness, and even then the woman was ruined. Women were expected either to prevent such a misfortune or else to put up with it with grace. And if Veronica herself were cast aside as an adulteress, then Julian Danver would lose all prospect of a career if he were to marry her; in fact, they would not even be received in Society. To all intents and purposes, they would cease to exist.

"Do you suppose he was so infatuated with her that he lost his head, his morality, enough to do that?" she asked, not because she thought Jack could possibly know but because she wanted to test his opinion of Veronica. Did he see her as a woman who could inspire such a reckless passion?

The answer was the one she had feared.

"I don't know Danver," he answered seriously. "But if he was capable of it, then Veronica would be just the woman to waken such a feeling."

"Oh." Emily's voice was tight, a little high. "Then we had better pursue the matter forthwith, for justice's sake if nothing else." She sounded businesslike, very crisp. "I shall write to Charlotte to follow up on the invitation to visit the winter exhibition, and you must do what you can to obtain an invitation for her to meet the rest of the people who might be involved." Her frustration boiled up suddenly and erupted despite her intentions. "I *wish* I were not shut up here like a hermit! It's damnable! I could do so much if only I were free to socialize—oh *hellfire!*"

He looked startled for a moment, but there was laughter in his eyes. "I don't think you're ready for the Honorable Mrs. Piers York's withdrawing room yet, Emily," he said wryly.

"On the contrary," she snapped, her face hot. "I'm over-ready!"

But there was nothing she could do, and her choice lay between accepting it with a good grace or an ill one. After another few minutes of general chatter Jack took his leave with a commission to contrive the necessary invitation. Emily was left alone again to go over and over in her mind all that she had said, changing a word or two, an inflection here and there to make it more gracious, less revealing. She wished she could go back and conduct the whole meeting again, and this time be more casual, perhaps occasionally say something witty. Men liked women who amused them, as long as they were not too clever or too spiteful.

Could she possibly be in love with Jack? That would be indecent so soon after George's death. Or was it just that she liked him, and she was bored, and so crushingly lonely?

It was six days later, past New Year's and into January with all its bleak and desperate cold, snow lining the streets and freezing fog creeping up like a white presage of death, clogging the throat, devouring light, distorting sound, and isolating each person who ventured out into it, when Emily's carriage called for Charlotte in the late afternoon. It took her to Emily's house, where she changed into a royal blue silk dinner gown while Emily and her maid fussed over her. Then, wrapped in wool and fur, she rode in Jack's carriage to the house of Garrard Danver and his family in Mayfair, at the farther end of Hanover Close.

The carriage moved slowly through the swirling fog, and Charlotte could barely see the faint luminescence of gas lamps above, one moment clear yellow and the next swathed and blinded with dirty white rags of vapor.

She was glad when they pulled up and it was time to begin being Elisabeth Barnaby again. It was easier to take the plunge into activity than to sit hunched up in the dark turning it over in her mind and worrying about all the things that might go wrong. If they were to catch her out, how could she possibly explain herself? It would be ghastly: she would be stuck there wriggling like a moth on a pin while everyone stared at her and thought how absurd and tasteless she was. She would have to say she had lost her wits—it was the only possible excuse.

And even if she were entirely successful in duping them, would she discover anything at all that could shed any light on Robert York's death? Perhaps this whole attempt was nothing to do with Robert or Veronica York, but was merely a silly farce to take Emily's mind off her boredom, and an opportunity for Charlotte to make some judgment on Jack Radley, and only a temporarily successful attempt at that!

The carriage door was open and the footman was waiting to hand her down. She stepped out, glad of his grip for a moment or two as the cold, acrid air hit her like wet muslin. Then she went quickly up the steps and into the wide, warm hallway.

There was no time to look at the furnishings or the pictures beside the flight of stairs that swept upwards to the landing. The butler took her coat and muff and a maid held open the door into the withdrawing room. Charlotte took Jack's arm and tried to sweep in with confidence, holding her chin high, her silk skirt swishing—or to be accurate, Emily's silk skirt.

Jack nudged her sharply and she realized she was over-doing it. She was supposed to be modest, and obliged for their help. She lowered her gaze with a sense of irritation. She was tired of being obliged.

They were the last to arrive, which was very suitable, since they were the only ones not known closely to the others already. The six people in the room turned to look at them with varying degrees of interest. The first to speak was a young woman in her late twenties with a most individual face which only just missed being pretty; her nose was tip-tilted too far from the classic, and there was a frankness in her dark eyes that seemed out of place in an unmarried woman. Her figure was not nearly rounded enough for fashion, but her dark hair was shining and thick enough to have pleased any-one. She came forward to greet Charlotte with a good-mannered smile.

"How do you do, Miss Barnaby. I am Harriet Danver. I am so pleased you were able to come. Are you finding Lon-don agreeable, apart from this wretched weather?"

"How do you do, Miss Danver," Charlotte replied cour-teously. "Oh yes, thank you for asking. Even in this fog it is such a nice change from the country, and people are so kind."

A tall, lean man with an aquiline, highly ascetic-looking face came forward from where he had been half sitting on the back of a huge armchair. Charlotte judged him to be in his mid-forties, until he passed directly under the chandelier and she saw that the graying at the temples touched the rest of his head as well; the lines on his face were finer and more numerous than the shadows had betrayed.

"I am Garrard Danver." His voice had a fine timbre to it. "I am delighted to meet you, Miss Barnaby." He did not take her hand but instead smiled at Jack, bidding him wel-come also, and introduced them to the remaining people in the room. Of these the most interesting by far was Julian

Danver; indeed he was the principle reason Charlotte had been so keen to come. He was about the same height as his father, with a more athletic build, but it was his face that held her attention. He must have gotten his features from his mother, because Charlotte could see no family resemblance to Garrard at all, whereas in Harriet it was quite recognizable, especially about the eyes. Julian was fair, his eyes were gray or blue—she could not tell in the light of the chandelier—and his hair was brown with a fair streak across the front. His features were strong, and there was intelligence and restraint in his bearing. She could well imagine that Veronica York found him most attractive.

The last member of the Danver family was Garrard's maiden sister, Miss Adeline Danver. She was rakishly thin, her deep green dress failing to mask the sharp bones of her shoulders. Her features exaggerated the flaws in Harriet's face—her chin was smaller, her nose more prominent—but she had the same dark eyes and fine head of hair, more faded but still thick.

"Aunt Adeline is hard of hearing," Harriet whispered softly to Charlotte. "If she says something odd, please smile and disregard it. She frequently gets quite the wrong sense of what is said."

"Of course," Charlotte murmured politely.

The only other guests were Felix Asherson and his wife. A striking man with black hair and unexpectedly vivid gray eyes, he worked in the Foreign Office with Julian Danver. But it was his mouth Charlotte noticed. She could not make up her mind about it; was it sensuous and strong, or was that wide lip a sign of self-indulgence? His wife Sonia was a handsome woman with bland, regular features, empty of expression, the sort of face fashion advertisers like because it sets off a hat without drawing the eye from it in the least. Her figure was well-proportioned, and on this occasion she wore a gown in a most becoming shade of coral pink, revealing plump, milk-white shoulders.

After the formal greetings had been exchanged, the usual small talk began. Since all the others were known to each other, it centered upon Charlotte and Jack Radley, and Charlotte concentrated on giving answers that made sense factually and were also in keeping with the character she had created for herself. She was supposed to be a young woman of modest means and good breeding, and, naturally, in search of a husband. Maintaining this role required all her attention, and it was not until they were at dinner round a table gleaming with silver and crystal, partaking of a rather too salty soup, that she was able to take time to observe the rest of the company.

The conversation was still very general: comments upon the unpleasantness of the weather, then minor points of news—nothing political or even remotely contentious—and then remarks about a play that most of them had seen. Charlotte replied only when good manners demanded, which gave her time to think. She might not get this opportunity again, so she must take full advantage of it.

The things she hoped to discover were few, but they would add to the little she had learned from Pitt. How long had Julian Danver and Veronica been acquainted? Did their love predate Robert York's death, and thus cause it? Was Julian Danver an ambitious man, either in his profession or socially? Was there a noticeable difference in their financial status, so that money might have been a motive, either for Veronica or for him?

Charlotte had grown up in a home where quality was intensely admired, even on those occasions when it could not be afforded. It was one of a well-bred young lady's attributes that she should be able to distinguish the excellent from the merely good, and naturally also its cost. She had been in the hall and withdrawing room of the York house, and she judged that they had had money long enough to be comfortable with it. There was none of the tendency to show off which so often accompanied recent acquisition. They felt no necessity to parade new furnishings or decorations, or put objets d'art in prominent positions.

Of course, she was quite aware that people's circumstances can change; she had seen many houses with fine rooms where guests were received, while the rest of the building lacked even a carpet and grates did not know a fire from one Christmas to another. And some prefer to keep a full complement of servants while they themselves eat barely enough to keep alive, rather than be seen to have a poor establishment. But Charlotte had noticed the women's clothes. They were of the latest cut and there were no worn places on cuffs or elbows; nothing had been altered to fit another season, or turned to hide patches. And she had done enough of that kind of thing herself to know precisely where to look for the telltale needle holes, the slightly different shading of fabric.

Now as she pretended to listen to the conversation across the table, she glanced as discreetly as she could at the dining room and its furnishings. The whole effect was silver and blue, pale on the immaculate wallpaper, dark royal blue in the curtains, which seemed to be without the usual faded marks that the sun so quickly made in blues, which meant they were not above a season old. Perhaps that indicated a tendency to extravagance? There was a painting of a Venetian scene on the wall opposite her, but Charlotte could not tell whether it was excellent or merely agreeable. The table itself was mahogany, or at least the legs were; the top was completely covered by crisp damask of heavy quality. The chairs and two sideboards were of the Adam style, and might well be genuine.

After checking that no one was watching her, she took a quick glance to see the hallmark on the reverse of her silver spoon. Perhaps the salty soup was a mere mischance; even the best people could have an accident with a cook. Perhaps they even liked it like this.

She considered the women's clothes again with an eye to

cost as well as to the indications to character they might show. Presumably both Harriet and Aunt Adeline, as unmarried women, were dependent upon Garrard for their support. Adeline's gown did not have the panache of high fashion, but then nothing she wore ever would; she was not that kind of person, and Charlotte guessed she never had been. Nonetheless, the dress was well cut and of excellent fabric. Much the same could be said of Harriet's gown.

No, unless there was some hidden factor, some inheritance or the like, it did not seem as if money entered into the match.

"Don't you, Miss Barnaby?"

She realized with a start that Felix Asherson was talking to her—but what on earth had he said?

"I find Mr. Wagner's operas a little long-winded and I am tired some time before the end," he repeated, looking at her with a slight smile. "I prefer something rather closer to life, don't you? I don't care for all this magic."

"I'm not surprised," Aunt Adeline put in suddenly, before Charlotte had time to find an answer. "There's enough of it we can't avoid as it is."

Everyone stared at her, and Charlotte was totally confused. The remark seemed to make no sense.

"He said 'magic,' Aunt Addie," Harriet said quietly. "Not 'tragic.' "

She did not seem in the least put out. "Oh, really? I don't care for the magic element very much. Do you, Miss Barnaby?"

Charlotte swallowed. "I don't think so, Miss Danver. I am not sure that I ever met with it."

Jack coughed discreetly into his napkin, and Charlotte knew he was laughing.

Julian smiled and offered her more wine. A footman and two maids served the fish course.

"Unrequited love seems to be the theme of a great many

86

operas and plays," Charlotte said to break the silence. "In fact, it is almost a necessity."

"I suppose it is something most of us can imagine, even if we have been fortunate enough not to feel it," Julian answered.

"Do you think such tales are true to life?" Charlotte asked gently, watching his face for sympathy or contempt.

He gave her the courtesy of a thoughtful answer. "Not in detail. Drama has to be condensed, or as Felix says, it becomes too boring; our attention is short. But the emotions are real, at least for some of us—" Suddenly he stopped and looked down at the table, then quickly up again at her. In that moment she found herself liking him. He had said something he had not meant to, but she was certain his embarrassment was not for himself—there was no anger or resentment in it at all—but for someone else at the table.

"My dear Julian," Garrard said irritably. "You are far too literal. I don't suppose Miss Barnaby intended anything so grave."

"No, of course not," Julian agreed quickly. "I apologize."

Charlotte was intensely aware that they were talking about something real and known to both of them. It had to be either Adeline or Harriet. Harriet was past the age when one might have expected a personable and well-bred woman of sound financial prospects to marry. Why had they not arranged a suitable match for her?

Charlotte smiled charmingly; her warmth was quite truly felt. "Indeed, I was only thinking, as you were, that too much magic or coincidence spoils one's belief in the story, and therefore one's emotional rapport with the characters. It was quite a trivial remark." She plunged on. "Mrs. York has been kind enough to invite me to go and view the winter exhibition at the Royal Academy with her. Have any of you been yet?"

"I went," Sonia Asherson said mildly. "But I can't say that I recall anything in particular."

"Any portraits?" Aunt Adeline inquired. "I love faces."

"So do I," Charlotte agreed. "As long as they are not idealized so that all the flaws are removed. I often think the true character lies in those lines and proportions that depart from the classic—where the individuality is revealed, and the marks of experience."

"How perceptive of you," Aunt Adeline said with sudden pleasure, and for the first time she looked with interest directly at Charlotte. Charlotte realized at once what a vivid creature lived inside the thin, rather quaint exterior. How shallow to judge from smooth, conventional looks, like Sonia Asherson's. Instinctively her eyes went to Felix. How trivial of him to have preferred a bland creature like Sonia rather than someone unconventional but full of feeling, like Harriet.

But perhaps he didn't. She had no right to assume he was happy; anything might lie behind Felix's polished manners and elusive face. This was another line of thought altogether, Charlotte reminded herself, and nothing to do with Veronica York, or Robert's death.

"It was so kind of Mrs. York to invite me to accompany her," Charlotte repeated a little abruptly. She must keep the conversation to the point. "Do you know, does she paint? I like portraits, but I love those delicate watercolor pictures some travelers make so clearly and with such sensitivity that you can imagine yourself there. I recall some wonderful pictures of Africa; I could almost feel the heat on the stones, so well was it drawn." They were all looking at her now; right round the table their faces were turned towards her. Sonia Asherson was clearly surprised at her sudden garrulity, while Felix seemed amused; Harriet was looking but not listening, her thoughts elsewhere; Garrard gazed at Charlotte politely. Only Aunt Adeline had a brightness in her eyes that followed

88

her sentiment. Jack was uncharacteristically silent. Apparently he was going to leave the field to her.

It was Julian who answered.

"I don't think she does paint. We've never spoken of it."

"Have you known her long?" Charlotte asked, trying to be artless, and wondered immediately if she had been too blunt. "I imagine in the diplomatic service you must have traveled?"

"Not to Africa," he said with a smile. "But it is something I should like to do."

"Far too hot!" Felix said with a grimace.

"I can understand you'd rather not," Aunt Adeline said with a sharp glance at him, "but it might be an excellent thing all the same!"

Harriet caught her breath. Her fingers round the stem of her wineglass were so tight the knuckles paled. In that instant a dozen memories flooded back to Charlotte of how she had felt before she had met Thomas, when she was still in love with Dominic, her eldest sister's husband. She remembered the agonizing fear, the hopelessness of being left out, the wild moments of imagined intimacy, a glance, an accidental touch, the singing heart when he seemed to take extra care speaking to her, the tenderness she thought she saw, and underneath it all the cold, sane despair. But she would not have dreamed of marrying anyone else, no matter what efforts her mother made. Was this not what she was seeing now in Harriet's lowered eyes, pale lips, and hot cheeks?

"He did not say he would rather not, Aunt Addie," Julian corrected. "He said it was far too hot. I presume he meant for Veronica to accompany me."

Aunt Adeline dismissed the idea with scorn. "Nonsense! Some Englishwoman, I forget her name, went up the Congo all by herself. I'd love to do that!"

"What an excellent idea," Garrard said waspishly. "Shall you go in the summer or the winter?"

She looked at him with bright eyes of disgust. "It is on

89

the Equator, my dear, so it hardly matters. Don't they teach you anything in the Foreign Office?''

"Not how to row up the Congo in a canoe,'' he retorted. "It doesn't seem to serve any purpose. We leave it to spinster ladies, who, according to you, have a taste for it.''

"Good!'' she snapped. "You had better leave us something!''

Jack came to the rescue. He turned to Julian. "I knew Mrs. York several years ago, before her marriage to Robert, but I can't remember whether she was interested in travel, and of course one may change. I daresay marrying into the Foreign Office will have broadened her knowledge, and perhaps her ambitions.''

Charlotte silently blessed him, and composed her face into an expression of great interest. "Was Mr. York a traveler?''

There was a moment's silence. A knife clinked on someone's plate. Out in the hall a servant's footsteps sounded quite clearly.

"No,'' Julian replied. "No, I don't believe he was, although I did not know him well. I came to the department in the Foreign Office only a couple of months before his death. Felix knew him better.''

"He liked Paris,'' Sonia Asherson said suddenly. "I remember him saying so. I wasn't at all surprised; he was such a charming man, elegant and witty. Paris would be bound to please him.'' She looked at her husband. "I wish we could go abroad sometimes, to somewhere sophisticated like that. Africa would be terrible, and India only marginally better.''

Charlotte looked at Harriet, and this time she was almost sure her guess was right. The dark, hollow look in her eyes, the aura of loss surrounding her was exactly what Charlotte herself had once felt when Sarah and Dominic had talked quite lightly of moving away. Yes, Harriet was in love with Felix Asherson. Did he know it? Dominic had never had the faintest idea of the turmoil he had caused in his sister-in-law, the agony, the embarrassment or the idiotic dreams.

She looked at Felix Asherson, but he was staring at the white damask cloth in front of him.

"I shouldn't anticipate anything," he answered her irritably. "I can't imagine any circumstance in which I should be sent to any part of Europe, except perhaps Germany. All the interest in my department is with the empire, particularly Africa and who colonizes where. And if I went there it would be on business. I should be there and back in weeks, and most of the time would be spent on the voyage."

Harriet was still too absorbed in trying to hide her feelings from the company to say anything. Garrard was leaning backwards in his chair, admiring the sparkle of the wine in his glass as the light from the chandelier caught it. A little self-consciously elegant, Charlotte decided, although she felt there was more emotion behind that highly individual face than she had first imagined—deeper lines round the mouth, a sharper curve to the lips, gestures that told of control mastering an inner restlessness. He was not as unlike Adeline as he had seemed at first.

"I must ask Mrs. York about Paris," she said, smiling dazzlingly at no one in particular. "I have never traveled, and I daresay I will not have the opportunity, but I love to hear about other people's experiences."

"Mostly experiences of barbarous food and plumbing that doesn't work." Garrard looked at her with irony. "A much overrated occupation, I assure you, Miss Barnaby. You will usually be too hot or too cold, someone will mislay your baggage, the Channel crossing on the steamer will make you ill, and once you reach Calais you will not understand a word anyone says."

Charlotte was about to retort with asperity that she spoke French, when she realized she was being teased, and for his amusement, not hers. "Indeed?" She raised her eyebrows. "All experiences I am quite used to in England, except for the Channel crossing. Perhaps you have not lately left London, Mr. Danver?"

91

"Bravo!" Aunt Adeline said with satisfaction. "She has your measure, my dear."

His smile touched only his mouth. "Indeed," he said, but he left it more a question than a concession.

"You shouldn't spoil people's dreams, Papa." Julian began eating again slowly. "Anyway, Miss Barnaby may find things quite different if she comes to travel. I remember Robert's mother used to enjoy it. She mentioned Brussels in particular."

"Was that recently?" Charlotte asked eagerly. "Perhaps things have improved since you were there, Mr. Danver."

His face hardened. The light shone on the smooth, tight skin of his cheeks, and Charlotte sensed a powerful anger inside him. Why on earth should he be abraded by something so trivial? No one had proved him mistaken, merely expressed a different opinion. Was his temper so unstable?

"Perhaps my dreams will never be realized," she said quietly, "but it is pleasant to have them."

"God preserve us from dreaming women!" Garrard raised his eyes to the ceiling, and there was an edge to his voice that Charlotte would ordinarily have called him to account for.

"It is frequently the only way we can get anything," Aunt Adeline said, picking up her glass and sniffing at her Chablis. "But of course, you wouldn't realize that."

Everyone looked nonplussed. Felix glanced at Julian. Sonia's face, with its regular features and flawless skin, registered what Charlotte was convinced was stupidity, although it was totally unfair to judge her so harshly. She was being too partisan towards Harriet and she knew it.

"I beg your pardon, Miss Danver?" Jack said with a frown.

"Not at all your fault," she said graciously. "I daresay you are in a similar position."

Jack turned to Charlotte, totally confused.

"What are you talking about, Aunt Addie?" Harriet asked gently.

"Scheming women." Aunt Adeline's eyebrows rose above her bright eyes, too round for beauty. "Aren't you listening, my dear?"

"Henderson!" Garrard called loudly. "For heaven's sake, bring on the pudding, whatever it is!"

" 'Dreaming women,' Aunt Addie," Julian said patiently. "Papa said 'dreaming women,' not 'scheming.' "

"Oh, really?" She smiled quite suddenly at Jack. "I apologize, Mr. Radley, do forgive me."

"Nothing to forgive," he assured her. "One can very easily lead to the other, don't you think? One begins by dreaming, and without the restraint of morality, isn't it often too easy to end in working out ways to bring about whatever it is one wants?"

Charlotte glanced from one face to another, not daring to look at Julian too long. Had they any idea why she was here? Was she perhaps far more transparent than she supposed, and they were merely playing with her?

"You are overrating people's morality." Garrard's smile still curved his lips upward, but there was derision in it rather than pleasure. "It is more often a perception of what is practical and what is not—although, God help us, there are some hideous exceptions. Thank you, Henderson; put it down, man!" He accepted the steaming treacle pudding and syrup and brandy sauce. "Miss Barnaby, let us talk of something less sordid. Have you any plans to go to the theater? There are plenty of amusing plays on; one is not restricted to Mr. Wagner by any means."

The subject had been changed, and she realized that without the most extraordinary ill manners she could not pursue the topic further. Even if she did, it would be profitless now; she would betray herself and ruin all future plans.

"Oh, I certainly hope to," she said eagerly. "Is there

93

anything you recommend? It would be lovely to go to the theater, wouldn't it, Jack?''

And so the meal concluded and nothing more was said that seemed to have any bearing upon Robert York's life or death, or the Danver family's relationship with the Yorks.

The ladies left the table before the port was brought in, and returned to the withdrawing room. Charlotte had expected the conversation to be stilted, as she sensed what Harriet's feelings for Felix were. Whether Sonia was aware of them or not, they could not possibly feel at ease with each other. As for Felix himself, Charlotte had not yet decided whether he knew of Harriet's love, or whether he returned it, and if so, with what sincerity or honor. Aunt Adeline's sharp tongue and dull hearing were unlikely to help matters.

Charlotte was ready to do her best to smooth the awkwardness with small talk, but she found her assessment mistaken. Apparently they had all known each other long enough to have found their own accommodation. Either by trial or by instinct, they knew what harmless comments to make on fashion, what gossip of mutual acquaintances to exchange, and which short stories in the *London Illustrated News* they all had read.

Charlotte did not have the time, or the money, to take the *Illustrated News*, nor had she ever heard of their friends. She sat with a smile of polite interest which became more fixed and less natural as the minutes dragged by. Once or twice she caught Aunt Adeline's eye, saw a flash of amusement there, and looked away.

Finally Aunt Adeline stood up.

"Miss Barnaby, you expressed an interest in art. Perhaps you would care to see one of the landscapes in the boudoir? It was my sister-in-law's favorite room, and she was quite fond of travel. She hoped to visit so many places.''

"And did she?'' Charlotte asked, rising also.

Adeline led the way. "No. She died young. She was twenty-six. Harriet was barely walking; Julian was seven or eight.''

Charlotte was touched with a sudden sharp sense of loss

for the woman whose life had ended when she was on the brink of so much—a husband and children, one a mere baby. How would she feel, if she had to leave Daniel and Jemima, and Thomas, to manage alone?

"I'm so sorry," she said aloud.

"It was a long time ago," Aunt Adeline replied half over her shoulder as she crossed the hall, going down a wide passage and opening the door into a lady's sitting room, known as a boudoir. It was decorated in cream and a muted tone the color of dry sand, with touches of cool liquid green, and one splash of pale coral provided by a single chair. It was most unusual, and rather out of character with the rest of the house. It led Charlotte to a sudden thought that perhaps the young Mrs. Danver had not felt at home here; perhaps she had made this room into an island for herself, contrasting it with the other rooms as strongly as she dared?

On the wall opposite the fireplace was a painting of the Bosphorus, looking down from the Topkapi Palace on the Golden Horn. Fleets of little boats plied the blue-green waters, and in the distance, blurred by the haze of heat and the dazzle of the sun, loomed the shore of Asia. A strong man might easily swim as far, as Leander had done for Hero. Had young Mrs. Danver thought of that when she chose it?

"You say nothing," Aunt Adeline remarked.

Charlotte was very weary of triteness. She wanted to discard the convention-imprisoned Miss Barnaby and be herself, especially with this woman, whom she liked more and more.

"What could I possibly say that could meet the loveliness of this, or all the ideas and the dreams one might find in it?" she demanded. "I refuse to add any more platitudes to the evening."

"Oh my dear child, you are doomed to disaster!" Adeline said candidly. "You will take wings like Icarus, and like Icarus, fall into the sea. Society does not permit women to fly, as you will doubtless discover. For heaven's sake, do not

95

marry suitably; it may well be like walking into cold water, inch by inch, until it covers your head.''

Charlotte had a tremendous impulse to tell Adeline she had already married, highly unsuitably, and was extremely happy. Remembering Emily, she held her tongue at the last moment.

''Shall I marry unsuitably, if I can?'' she asked with only half a smile; it was wry, and she knew it, a little painful.

''I don't suppose your parents will allow it,'' Aunt Adeline demurred. ''Mine wouldn't.''

Charlotte drew breath to say again that she was sorry, then knew it would sound too condescending. Adeline was not the sort of person for whom one should feel ever the most glancing touch of that pity which has no fellow feeling. She did not believe that Adeline Danver had shrunk from any decision out of cowardice; but even if she had, passing judgment on it now was none of Charlotte's right, nor desire.

Instead, she drew a little on truth, remembering what had actually happened to her. ''My grandmother is the one who would make the worst fuss,'' she said.

Adeline smiled bleakly, but her eyes held no self-pity. She sat sideways on the arm of one of the big sand-colored chairs. ''My mother enjoyed poor health. She played it for every second of obedience and attention she could extract from it. But when I was young we all believed she might die from one of her 'turns.' Eventually it was Garrard who called her bluff, for which I shall always respect him. But then it was too late for me.'' She took a deep breath. ''Of course, had I been a beauty, I should have lived a life of glamorous sin. But having never been asked, I am obliged to pretend that I would not have accepted.'' Her brown eyes were brilliant. ''Have you noticed how one condemns most self-righteously that which one has never had the opportunity to do?''

''Yes,'' Charlotte agreed with a candid smile. ''Indeed I have. It casts a new meaning upon 'making a virtue of necessity.' It is one of the hypocrisies that irritates me the most.''

"You'll see a great deal of it. You'd do well to hide your feelings and learn to hold conversation with yourself."

"I fear you are right."

"I am most certainly right." Adeline stood up. She really was very gaunt, but there was a strength of vitality in her which made her the most interesting person in the house. She looked at the picture again. "Do you know that a courtesan named Theodora rose to be empress of Byzantium?" she said quite casually. "I wonder if she wore outrageous colors. I love royal blues and peacock greens and scarlets and saffron yellow—even the names of them sound good— but I dare not wear them. Garrard wouldn't give me a moment's peace. He would certainly stop my dress allowance." She stared fixedly at the picture as if she could see beyond it. "You know, there was a woman who used to visit this house, once or twice, in the middle of the night, very beautiful, like a black swan. She wore gowns of blazing cerise, not fiery, not a yellow red like flames, but shot with blues. Fearful color on anyone else. I should look like a nightmare in it." She turned round with a look of faint surprise. "But she looked marvelous. Can't imagine what she was doing here, except to see Julian, perhaps; but he really should have been more discreet. Garrard would have been furious. Still, since he began courting Veronica York, as far as I know, he has been above reproach, and that is all one can reasonably expect of a man. A man's past is his own affair. I wish it were so for a woman, but I am not ingenuous enough to believe it ever will be."

Charlotte's mind was whirling. Adeline had said so much, she needed time to disentangle it.

"I have an aunt whom you would like," she said, realizing even as she spoke how daring she had become. "Lady Cumming-Gould. She is nearly eighty, but she is marvelous. She believes in women having the vote for Parliament, and she is prepared to fight to help bring it about."

"How unselfish of her." Adeline's eyes were bright, although there was self-mockery as well as enthusiasm in them. "She will not live to see it."

"Don't you think so? If we all pressed as hard as we could, would not men eventually see the justice of it, and . . ." The expression on Adeline's face made Charlotte feel naive, and her voice died away.

"My dear," Adeline said, shaking her head slightly. "Of course if we all spoke together we could persuade men, or even force them—but we never do speak together. How often have you seen half a dozen women agree and band together for a cause, let alone half a million?" Her thin fingers smoothed over the velvet back of the chair. "We all live our separate lives, in our own kitchens if we are poor, our withdrawing rooms if we are well-to-do; and we do not cooperate for anything, but see ourselves as rivals for the few eligible and well-financed men that are available. Men, on the other hand, work fairly well together, imagining themselves the protectors and providers of the nation, obliged to do everything they can to preserve the situation precisely as it is—in their control—on the assumption that they know best what is right for us and must see that we get it, come hell or high water." Her head jerked up. "And there are only too many women who are happy to assist them, since the status quo suits them very well also, and they are invariably the people with power."

"Miss Danver! I think you are a revolutionary!" Charlotte said with delight. "You *must* meet Great-aunt Vespasia; you'd love each other."

Before Adeline could respond there were footsteps in the passageway and Harriet appeared at the door, her face pale and her eyes heavy, as if she lacked sleep.

"The gentlemen have rejoined us. Won't you come back, Aunt Addie?" Then she remembered her manners. "Miss Barnaby?"

A look of pity passed over Adeline's face and vanished so rapidly that Charlotte was almost doubtful she had seen it; perhaps she had only imagined an echo of her own quick understanding. "Of course." Adeline moved towards the door. "We were admiring your mother's painting of the Bosphorus. Come, Miss Barnaby, asylum is over for this evening. We must leave Theodora and Byzantium and return to the world and the pressing matters of the present, such as whether Miss Weatherly will become engaged to Captain Marriott this month, or next, or whether perhaps he will evade her entirely"—she shrugged her thin shoulders—"and go to sea in a sieve."

Harriet looked puzzled, glancing uncertainly at Charlotte.

"Edward Lear," Charlotte hazarded an explanation. " 'Their heads were blue and their hands were green,' or the other way round, and they went to sea in a sieve—I think. But he was also an excellent artist. His paintings of Greece are beautiful."

"Oh." Harriet looked relieved, but no wiser.

"Well?" Jack asked her as soon as they were alone in the carriage, huddled together in biting cold, breath white as steam. Outside the wind moaned and rattled and the gutters were filled with freezing slush, dark with mud and frozen manure, for once odorless. The horses' hooves thudded heavily on the ice.

"All sorts of things," she replied with chattering teeth. She decided not tell him that Harriet was in love with Felix Asherson; it was young Miss Danver's own private heartache, and if he had not noticed it, then it should remain so. "They seem to have quite as much money as the Yorks, so that is not a motive. And apparently the two families have known each other for some time, so Julian and Veronica might have fallen in love before Robert died. On the other hand, and this really is most interesting, Aunt Addie—"

"Whom you like enormously," he interrupted.

"Whom I like enormously," she agreed. "But that doesn't blind my wits."

"Of course not."

"It doesn't! Aunt Adeline said that twice at least she had

99

seen a strange and beautiful woman in the house, at night, up until three years ago, but not since! She wore an outrageous shade of cerise, always.''

"You mean both times?"

"All right, both times. But who was she? Maybe she was the spy, after Julian's secrets from the Foreign Office. Perhaps she inveigled him.''

"Then why hasn't she been seen since?"

"Perhaps after Robert York's death she went away, or into hiding. Or maybe he was the one with the secrets, and since he is dead, there is nothing for her anymore. Maybe Julian Danver wouldn't fall for her—he loved Veronica. I don't know!"

"Are you going to tell Thomas?"

She took a deep breath and let it out slowly. Her hands deep in Emily's muff were numb with cold. It was so late that she was going to have to stay the night with Emily and go home tomorrow, which would not please Pitt. She could tell him Emily was upset, so she had remained, which was true after a fashion, but she hated lying to him, and it was a lie at heart.

The alternative was to tell him the truth, and the reasons for pursuing the York murder. "Yes," she said slowly. "I think so.''

"Are you sure that's wise?" he said doubtfully.

"I'm an awfully bad liar, Jack.''

"You amaze me!" he said, his voice rising mockingly. "I would never have guessed it!''

"Pardon?" she asked sharply.

"I should say I'd witnessed a bravura performance this evening.''

"Oh—that's quite different. It doesn't count.''

He started to laugh, and although she was furious, she liked him for it. Perhaps Emily would be all right.

Charlotte got up before dawn the following morning, and by seven o'clock she was at home in her own kitchen frying prime bacon and fresh eggs, a peace offering from Emily.

"Is Emily ill?" Pitt looked worried, but she knew he was on the edge of losing his temper if her answer was not satisfactory. She knew perfectly well that she looked too excited, too pleased with herself, to have been up all night by a sickbed.

"Thomas . . ." She had thought about this a long time, at least an hour of the short night.

"Yes?" His voice was guarded.

"Emily isn't ill, but she is very lonely, and being in mourning is pretty wretched."

"I know that, my dear." Now there was compassion in his voice, and it made her feel guilty.

"So I thought we should get involved in something," she hurried on. She poked the bacon and it hissed gently, sending out an exquisite aroma.

"Something?" he pressed with heavy skepticism. He knew her far too well for this to succeed.

"Yes, something totally absorbing—like a mystery. So we started to look into Robert York's death, which you told me about." She reached for an egg and cracked it into the pan, then another. "Jack Radley—and that's another reason: I really do want to get to know him rather better, just in case," she hurried on, taking a deep breath, "Emily considers marrying him. Someone has to look after her interests—"

"Charlotte!"

"Well, I did have two reasons," she insisted, then went on hastily. "Anyway, I went to tea with Veronica York and her mother-in-law. Emily arranged it so that Jack Radley took me—that way I was able to observe him while making some discoveries about the Yorks." She could feel Pitt's presence behind her as she turned the eggs gently, then took them out and put them on his plate next to the bacon. "There you are," she said, smiling sweetly. "Last night I dined with the Danvers. I met them all, and they are most interesting. By the way, the Yorks and the Danvers appear to have about the same financial status, so neither Veronica nor Julian Danver would marry the other for money." As she spoke she

101

made the tea and set it on the table, all without meeting his eyes. "And Aunt Adeline told me the oddest thing: she saw a beautiful, glamorous woman wearing an outrageous shade of cerise in the house. Do you suppose she was a spy?" At last she looked at her husband, and was immensely relieved to see amazement in his face. His eyes were wide and his hand had stopped halfway to his mouth.

"A woman in cerise?" he said after a moment's silence. "Did she say in cerise?"

"Yes. Yes, why? Have you heard of her? Is she a spy? Thomas!"

"I don't know. But the maid at the Yorks' saw her too."

Charlotte slipped into the seat opposite him and leaned forward, forgetting her own bacon. "What did she say? When did she see her? Do you know who she is?"

"No. But I shall go back and speak to the maid again, I think, and ask her for a closer description, and exactly when she saw this woman. I must find out who she is, if I can."

But before he went to Hanover Close again, he called by at the Bow Street station to attend to a few other inquiries, particularly a burglary in the Strand. He was halfway through reading the reports when a constable came in, a mug of tea in one hand. He put it down on Pitt's desk.

"Thank you," Pitt said absently.

"Thought you'd like to know, Mr. Pitt," the constable said with a sniff as he reached for a large cotton handkerchief, sneezing into it and blowing his nose, "been a haccident yesterday, sir, at 'anover Close. Very sad. One of the upstairs maids fell out o' the window, poor soul. Musta leaned out too far for suffink or other, maybe to call to someone. Any'ow the poor girl is dead, sir."

"Dead?" Pitt looked up, startled and chilled. "Who?"

The constable looked down at the paper in his hand. "Dulcie Mabbutt, sir. Lady's maid."

5

WHEN CHARLOTTE LEFT to go back home, Emily was wide awake, an endless day stretching ahead and nothing planned. She tried to go back to sleep again—quarter to six was far too early—but her mind was restless.

At first she contemplated Charlotte's evening with the Danvers. Who was the mysterious woman in the cerise gown? Probably just an old love of Julian's he had been indiscreet enough to entertain under his father's roof.

No, that would not do. No man with half an ounce of intelligence would do such a thing, and by Charlotte's account Julian Danver was quite a presence. She had spoken of him with some admiration and said she completely understood why Veronica York should wish to marry him. And Charlotte could never abide a fool, even though she imagined she was tolerant.

There was another answer: either Julian, or Garrard, was a traitor, and the woman in cerise was the spy who had turned the man's loyalty. It was simply coincidence that she had not been seen since Robert York's death—she had been more careful, that was all.

103

No, that was silly too. If the woman in cerise had had nothing to do with Robert York's death, why bother to think about her at all? She was just what she seemed, a paramour being indiscreet. Perhaps Julian had tired of her—or Garrard, at a stretch of the imagination—and she had become desperate and foolish enough to pursue him to his house.

Or again, maybe Harriet was leading a double life— possibly even keeping an assignation with Felix. And in such flamboyant clothes, so different from her usual attire that Aunt Adeline had failed to recognize her. In the middle of the night, when Aunt Adeline had presumably woken from sleep, that seemed more than likely. She sounded like a quaint old lady, at the best.

Would Emily herself grow into a quaint, lonely old lady, visiting relatives too often and so bored she lived other people's lives vicariously, misunderstanding everyone and seeing things that were not there?

With this wretched thought Emily decided to get up, even though it was still only five minutes to seven. If the servants were startled, let them be. It would do them good.

She rang for her maid and had to wait several minutes for her to come. Then she had a bath and dressed carefully, as if she were to entertain someone of great importance—it was good for her morale—and went downstairs. Of course, her lady's maid had warned the rest of the house, so she took no one by surprise. Whatever they felt, there was nothing in their faces but bland good-mornings. Carrying in the poached eggs, Wainwright looked like a church warden with a collection plate, and he put it down in front of her with the same reverence. She would have loved to startle him enough to make him drop it!

When she had finished breakfast and had taken three cups of tea she went to the kitchen. She thoroughly irritated the cook by interfering with the week's menus, and then tried the patience of her own maid by checking on the mending and ironing of her gowns. When she finally realized how unfair she was being, she went into her boudoir, closed the door, and began to write a letter to Great-aunt Vespasia, simply because she would have liked to talk to her. She was on the fourth page of her letter when the footman knocked and came in to tell her that her mother, Mrs. Ellison, was in the morning room.

"Oh, ask her in here," she answered. "It's much brighter." She covered the letter and with mixed feelings prepared to welcome her mother.

Caroline came in a moment later, dressed in a fashionable wine-colored barathea trimmed with black fur and a rakish hat which made her look more elegant than Emily could remember. There was a flush in her cheeks, doubtless the bitter weather, and she was full of good spirits.

"How are you, my dear?" She kissed Emily delicately and sat in one of the most comfortable chairs. "You look peaked," she observed with maternal candor. "I hope you are eating well. You must look after your health, for Edward's sake and your own. Of course, this first year is terribly difficult, I know, but another six months and it will be past. You must prepare for the future. By midsummer it will be acceptable for you to start mixing in a few suitable gatherings."

Emily's heart sank. The word *suitable* was like a damnation. She could imagine those gatherings: coteries of black-clad widows sitting round like crows on a fence, making pious-sounding, meaningless remarks, or else tutting over the latest giddiness of Society, picking it over endlessly because it was the only way they could participate in its life.

"I think I'll take up good works," she said aloud.

"Very commendable," Caroline agreed with a little nod. "As long as you do it in moderation. You might speak to your vicar about it, or if you prefer, I will speak to mine. I am sure there are committees of ladies who would welcome your contributions in time, when it is appropriate for you to begin going out of your home to such meetings."

Sitting on committees of women was the last thing Emily had in mind. She was thinking of the sort of work Great-aunt Vespasia did—visiting workhouses and campaigning for better conditions and agitating for changes in the employment laws for children, trying to increase the number and scope of "ragged schools" for pauper children, perhaps even fighting for the political franchise for women. Now that she had the money, there might be quite a lot she could do, Emily decided. "You don't look dressed for good works," she said critically. "In fact, I've never seen you look so well."

Caroline was startled. "There is no need to dress like a dowd or to look wretched in order to do good works, Emily. I know this has been tragic for you, but you must not allow yourself to become eccentric, my dear."

Emily could feel her temper boil up inside her, mixed with frustration and despair. Imprisoning walls seemed to be closing in around her. It was as if someone were padlocking a gate and she could hear her mother's calm, reasonable voice like the swish of closing curtains shutting out everything that was spontaneous, bright, and exhilarating.

"Why not?" she demanded. "Why shouldn't I become eccentric?"

"Don't be foolish, Emily." Caroline's tone was still gentle, but overly patient, as if she were speaking to a sickly child who would not eat her rice pudding. "In due course you will want to marry again. You are far too young to remain a widow, and you are extremely eligible. If you behave circumspectly during the next two or three years you may quite easily marry at least as well as you did before and be most comfortable and happy. But this next short time is crucial. It could make or mar everything."

Emily raised her eyebrows high. "You mean if I do something immodest or unseemly, no duke will have me, and if I am seen to be eccentric I may not even manage a baronet!"

"You are in a very trying mood this morning," Caroline said, struggling to remain patient. "You know the rules of

Society quite as well as I do. Really, Emily, you used to be the most sensible of the three of you, but you seem to be getting more like Charlotte every time I see you. Perhaps I should have counseled you against spending Christmas with her, but I thought it would be nice for Edward to have some other children to play with. And to be quite frank, I know Charlotte must have been grateful for all the financial assistance you were able to give her—discreetly.''

"Charlotte is perfectly happy!" Emily said far more waspishly than she had wished to. She was being unfair, and she knew it even as she was unable to prevent herself from going on. "And I enjoyed Christmas with her and Thomas—in fact, I loved it.''

Caroline's face eased into a smile and she quickly put her hand over Emily's. "I'm sure you did, my dear. Your affection for each other is one of the nicest things in my life.''

Emily felt a ridiculous prickle of tears and was furious with herself. She did not wish to distress her mother, and yet with the best will in the world Caroline was devising a future for her which so utterly misunderstood what she wanted, it was unbearable.

"Mama, I refuse to sit on parish committees, so on no account speak either to your vicar or mine; you will only embarrass yourself, because I shall not turn up. If I do any good work it will be something real, perhaps with Great-aunt Vespasia. But I won't sit around pontificating on other people's morals, handing out saving tracts and homemade broth from a great height!''

Caroline sighed, gritting her teeth. "Emily, at times you are most childish. You really cannot behave like Lady Cumming-Gould. She has quite a name in Society. People tolerate her because she is very old, and because they still retain a certain respect for her late husband. And at her age it doesn't matter a great deal what she does; it can always be discounted as senility.''

"I never met anyone in my life less senile than Great-aunt

Vespasia!'' Emily defended her furiously, not only in her affection for Vespasia but for the wit and pity she represented. ''She has more good judgment about what really matters in her little finger than most of the rest of Society in all its fatuous heads put together!''

''But no one would marry her, my dear!'' Caroline said, exasperated.

''She's nearly eighty, for goodness' sake!'' Emily shouted.

Caroline would not be diverted by reason. ''Exactly the point I am trying to make. You are barely thirty. Consider your position with some sense. You are a pretty woman, but you are not a great beauty, as Vespasia was; nor are you born of a great family. You have no alliances to offer, no connections with power.'' She looked at Emily seriously. ''But you do have a considerable amount of money. If you marry beneath yourself you will lay yourself open to fortune hunters and men of the most dubious sort, who may well court you out of greed and the desire to gain entry to Society on the strength of your past connections with the Ashworths. It is a sad thing to have to say, but you are not a child; you know that as well as I do.''

''Of course I know!'' Emily turned away. Jack Radley's face came vividly to mind. He was charming and seemed so frank, with those marvelous eyes fringed with long lashes. Was he a superb liar, capable of skilled and sustained deceit? All his future might depend on it: if he wooed and won her he could stop worrying about money for the rest of his life. For the first time since his childhood he would be secure; he could dress as he liked, buy horses and carriages, gamble, go to the races, invite people to dinner instead of incessantly seeking invitations in order to dine well. He would no longer have to curry favor, he could afford at last to like and dislike as he chose. The thought was intensely ugly, and it hurt more deeply than she would have believed even a few weeks ago. Emily took a deep, rather shaky breath. ''Of course I know!''

she said again loudly. "But I have no intention of marrying a bore simply to be sure his motives are not financial."

"Now you are being ridiculous." Caroline's patience was wearing positively threadbare. "You will make a reasonable accommodation, as we all do."

"Charlotte didn't!"

"I think the less said about Charlotte the better!" Caroline said in exasperation. "And if you imagine for one instant that you could marry someone like a policeman, or any other sort of tradesman or artisan, and be happy, then you really have taken leave of your wits! Charlotte is extremely fortunate that it hasn't turned out to be worse than it has. Oh, certainly Thomas is a pleasant enough man, and he has treated her as well as he is able, but she has no security. If something should happen to him tomorrow she will be left with nothing at all, and two small children to raise by herself." She sighed. "No, my dear, do not delude yourself into thinking that Charlotte has everything her own way. It would not suit you to be cutting down last year's dresses to do this year, and cooking in your own kitchen, with Sunday's meat having to last you through till Thursday. And don't forget you would have no wealthy sister to help you as she has! Have your daydreams, by all means, but remember that is all they are. And when you have woken up from them, behave yourself like a widow of charm and dignity, with a considerable fortune and a social position that is very much worth your while to maintain undamaged by eccentric behavior. Give tongues no cause to whisper."

Emily was too crushed to argue.

"Yes, Mama," she said wearily. The whole realm of answers and explanations was too tangled in her mind, too alien to Caroline, and too little understood even by herself for her to begin to unravel and present them.

"Good." Caroline smiled at her. "Now perhaps you will offer me a dish of tea—it is extremely cold outside. And in a few months I shall speak to the vicar. There are committees

109

for various things that would do very nicely as suitable places for you to begin to associate again.''

''Yes, Mama,'' Emily said again hollowly, and reached for the bell rope.

The rest of the day was thoroughly miserable. Outside, the wind blew showers of sleet against the windows, and it was so dark all the gas lamps were burning even at midday. Emily finished her letter to Great-aunt Vespasia, and then tore it up. It was too full of self-pity, and she did not want Aunt Vespasia to see that side of her. It was understandable, perhaps, but it was not attractive, and she cared very much what Vespasia thought of her.

When Edward finished his lessons they had afternoon tea together, and then the long evening stretched to an early bed.

The following day was utterly different. It began with the morning mail, which contained a letter from Charlotte posted late the previous evening and marked ''Most Urgent.'' She tore it open and read:

Dear Emily,

Something very sad has happened, and if we are right, then it is also evil and dangerous. I think the woman in cerise is the key to it all. Thomas knew of her too, from the lady's maid at the Yorks'. Of course he didn't tell me about her at the time, because then he did not know we had any interest. She saw Cerise—I shall call her that—at the <u>York</u> house in the middle of the night. When I told him what Aunt Addie said you can imagine his reaction!

But the dreadful thing is that when he went into the station at Bow Street before going back to question the maid at Hanover Close again, he heard that she had been <u>killed</u> the day before! Apparently she fell out of an upstairs window. Thomas is very upset. Of course, it could have been an accident and nothing to do with his inquiries or the fact that she told him about Cerise, but on the other hand someone may have overheard her. And this is the

110

interesting thing: all the Danvers were in the house when Thomas was there, so anyone might have been in the hall at the time she and Thomas were in the library talking.

What we need to do is find out who was there when she fell. Thomas can't do it because there is no reason to suspect it wasn't an ordinary domestic accident. People do sometimes fall out of windows, and one cannot start casting suspicions on a family like the Yorks. And if the whole investigation of Veronica should come out, then there would be the most dreadful scandal and goodness knows who would be hurt. Julian Danver would probably be ruined, and Veronica most certainly would.

You must tell Jack when next he calls.

If there is anything else, I shall tell you as soon as I hear it.

Your loving sister,
Charlotte

Emily held the paper with tingling fingers. Her hands were numb and already her mind was racing. The woman in cerise! And the lady's maid who had seen her in the York house in the middle of the night was now dead.

But they would never get beneath the smooth, supremely disciplined surface of the Yorks' facade by going for the odd afternoon tea, or walking round the Winter Exhibition and exchanging a few slight confidences on fashion or gossip. Pitt had disturbed something much deeper than an old burglary, or the question of Veronica's suitability to become the wife of Julian Danver. This was something of such passion and horror that even three years later it could erupt without warning into violence—and now, it seemed quite possible, murder.

They must get closer, much closer—in fact, they must get inside the Yorks' home.

But how?

An idea occurred to her, but it was preposterous! It would

111

never work. To start with, she would not be able to carry it off; she was sure to be found out immediately. They would know.

How would they know? It would be difficult—of course, it would—she would have to behave entirely differently, alter her appearance, her face, her hair, even her hands and her voice. An Englishwoman's background could be identified by her voice the moment she spoke; no servant had those rounded vowels, the precise consonants, even if the grammar had been meticulously copied. But Veronica York would be needing a new lady's maid, someone who would be there all the time, in the unguarded moments, someone who would see everything, as only those who are invisible can. And domestic servants are invisible.

Knowing it was absurd, Emily went on planning how it might be done. She had had a lady's maid all her life—first her mother's, then her own—and she knew the duties by heart. Some she would certainly not be very good at; she had never really tried to iron, but surely she could learn? She was rather good at doing hair; she and Charlotte had played at doing each other's before they had been allowed to wear their hair up. She was adequate with a needle; there could not be all that much difference between embroidering and mending.

The difficulty—and the danger—would be in altering her manner so that she passed for a servant. What was the worst that could happen if she were discovered?

She would be dismissed, of course, but that hardly mattered. They would think she was a well-bred girl who had fallen into some sort of disgrace that necessitated taking a menial position. They would almost certainly assume she had had an illegitimate child, that was the kind of disgrace women fell into. It would be a humiliation, but a brief one. If they ever met her again as Lady Ashworth they would be unlikely to recognize her, because it would never occur to them that it was she; if it did, she could brazen it out. She would look daggers at them and suggest they had lost their wits to make such an offensive and tasteless suggestion.

As a lady's maid she would not meet any guests to the house; she would never be asked to wait at table, or answer the door. Perhaps the idea was not so absurd after all. They would never discover who had murdered Robert York if they continued as they were. They were playing at it, touching the fringes, knowing there was a terrible passion under the conventional surface, but only throwing around guesses as to what it was, and whom it had pushed into murder. Inside the York house she could learn infinitely more.

She shivered suddenly, thinking of the danger. Being dismissed as a fallen woman would be nothing, a brief embarrassment. But if by some horrendous mischance they did recognize her as Emily Ashworth, they would assume she had taken leave of her senses, that George's death had robbed her of her sanity. The scandal would be appalling! But there was no reason why that should happen.

No, the real danger was from the person who had already killed Robert York, and possibly Dulcie, killed her simply because she had seen or heard something. Emily would have to be exquisitely careful! She must pretend to be stupid, and innocent, and she must always, always guard her tongue.

The alternative was to give up—to go on sitting here in black, either alone or talking polite rubbish to the few people who called on her, until Caroline arranged some wretched committees for her to be righteous on. She would get nothing but secondhand reports from Charlotte. She would not contribute anything at all herself. Even Jack would be bored with her soon.

By the time Jack called at midmorning she had made the decision. Thank goodness she had not sent that wretched letter to Aunt Vespasia. She was going to need her help. She would call on her that afternoon.

"I'm going to the Yorks'," she announced as soon as Jack came in.

"I don't think you can do that, Emily," he said with a slight frown.

"Oh, not socially!" She waved her hand, dismissing the notion. "Their lady's maid saw Aunt Addie's woman in cerise at the Yorks' house as well, in the middle of the night. She told Thomas—and now she's dead!"

"The maid?"

"Yes, of course the maid!" Emily said impatiently. "The woman in cerise has vanished, and she must have something to do with treason, and almost certainly Robert York's murder. We must find out all we can, and we shan't do that by calling for tea now and then."

"What else? We can hardly walk in and start interrogating them," Jack pointed out.

"Even if we could, that wouldn't do any good." Emily was excited now. Whatever Jack said it was not going to put her off. For the first time since George's death she was going to do something totally outrageous, which he would certainly have forbidden, and she was glad there was no one who could command her obedience. "We must be subtle," she continued. "We must observe them when they have no idea, and little by little they may betray themselves."

He was at a loss to understand, and with delight she dropped her bombshell.

"I am going to take the position of lady's maid! I shall write one reference myself, and get another from Great-aunt Vespasia."

He was stunned. "Good God! You can't! Emily, you can't go as a servant!"

"Why not?"

The first minute spark of humor lit in his eyes. "You wouldn't know how, for a start," he said.

"I would!" Her chin came up, and she knew she must look and sound ridiculous. "For goodness' sake, Jack, I've had a very good lady's maid for years. I know perfectly well

114

what she does, and I can do it myself in a pinch. I certainly had to learn how when I was a girl.''

He started to laugh, and at any other time she would have thought it a delightful sound, full of joy and vitality. Now she heard derision in his laughter, and it was extremely provoking.

"I'm not saying it will be easy!" she said sharply. "I am not used to having people tell me what to do, and I shan't like being at someone else's beck and call, but I can do it! It will be something of a change from sitting here all day doing nothing at all!''

"Emily, they'll find you out!" His laughter vanished as it dawned on him that she might be serious.

"Oh no they won't! I shall be a model of good behavior.''

Disbelief was written all over his face.

"Charlotte has got away with being Miss Barnaby," she carried on determinedly. "And I'm a far better liar than she is. I shall go this afternoon, otherwise I may be too late. I have written myself a glowing reference, and I shall obtain another from Aunt Vespasia. I have already telephoned her—did I tell you I have acquired a telephone? It's a wonderful thing; I don't know why I didn't get one before—and she is expecting me this afternoon. She will write an introductory letter for me if I ask her.'' She was not at all sure that Aunt Vespasia would do anything of the sort, but she would do all she could to persuade her.

Now he looked really concerned. "But Emily, think of the danger! If what you are supposing is true, then someone murdered the maid. If they have even a suspicion of you, you could end up the same way! Leave it to Thomas.''

She swung round on him immediately. "And what do you suggest he do? Go as a footman? He wouldn't have the slightest idea how to get on, apart from the fact that they know him already and that he is with the police. From what Charlotte says, his superiors aren't interested in Robert York's death. All they want to do is make sure Veronica is suitable to marry Julian Danver!"

"Oh come on!" Jack turned sideways in the chair opposite her. "That's what they said, but it's obviously an excuse. They don't care in the least what Veronica does, if she's discreet about it. And if she weren't they'd know without anyone's finding out for them. They're suspicious about York's death and whether Veronica had a lover or not, and if he or even Veronica herself murdered Robert. They are just too devious to have said so outright."

She stared at him. "Are they? What about treason? What about the woman in cerise?"

He thought for a moment. "Well, that could have been Veronica herself after an assignation with Julian Danver, if they were lovers then."

"Then it was Julian who killed Robert York?"

"Possibly. The fact that he's an agreeable fellow is irrelevant. Some of the worst cads I've known have been charming, as long as you didn't stand in their way. Or it could have been Harriet leading a double life, with Felix Asherson. She's obviously in love with him."

"Charlotte didn't tell you that!"

"My dear girl, she didn't need to! Do you think I'm a complete fool? I've seen too many flirtations not to know when a woman's in love. She was polite, she pretended he was a friend and of no romantic interest. She avoided his eyes, and looked at him when he was turned away. She was so careful it must matter to her very much."

She had had no idea he was so perceptive. It came as a sobering surprise, puncturing her confidence.

"Indeed," she said coldly. "And of course you are never mistaken—you can read women just like that!" She tried to snap her fingers and failed to make the sharp sound she wished, producing instead only a faint thump. "Hellfire!" she said under her breath. "Well anyway, I am going to the

116

Yorks. There is something hideously wrong in that house, and I shall discover what it is."

"Emily, please." His voice changed completely, the lightness vanished. "If they catch you out in the least thing they may well realize why you are really there! If they pushed one maid out of the window they won't hesitate to get rid of you, too!"

"They can't push two maids out of the window," she said with chill reason. "Eyebrows would be raised, even at the Honorable Piers York!"

"It doesn't have to be a window," he said, getting angry himself. "It could be the stairs, or a ladder. They could push you under a carriage wheel, or it might be something you ate. Or you could simply disappear, along with a couple of good pieces of the family silver. Emily, for God's sake, use a little sense!"

"I am bored to screaming with using sense!" She turned round fiercely and glared at him. "I have worn black, seen no one, and been sensible for six months, and I am beginning to feel as if it was me they buried! I am going to the Yorks' to be a maid and discover who murdered Robert York, and why. Now, if you wish to come to Great-aunt Vespasia's with me, you are welcome. Otherwise, will you please excuse me, because I have work to do. I am telling my own staff that I am going to stay with my sister for a while. Of course I shall tell Charlotte the truth. If you want to help, that will be very nice; if not, if you prefer to disassociate yourself, I shall understand completely. Playing detective is not for everyone," she finished with immense condescension.

"If I don't help, Charlotte will be left high and dry," he pointed out with a slight smile.

She had forgotten that. She was obliged to climb down, but it was hard to do it gracefully.

"Then I hope you will feel able to continue." She did not look at him. "We must keep in touch with the Danvers; they are certainly part of it."

"Does Charlotte know about this—plan of yours?"

"Not yet."

He drew in breath to comment, then let it out again in a sigh. Seeing men behave like fools was one thing, but he was not accustomed to this behavior in women. He had to readjust his thinking, but Jack was adaptable and had remarkably few prejudices. "I'll work out a way to keep in touch with you," he said after a moment's consideration. "Don't forget, most houses don't allow maids to have 'followers.' And they'll comment on letters, maybe even read them if they suspect it's an admirer."

She stopped. She had not thought of that. But it was too late to withdraw now. "I'll be careful," she conceded. "I'll say it is my mother or something."

"And how will you account for the fact that your mother lives in Bloomsbury?" he asked.

"I . . ." At last she faced him.

"You haven't thought," he said candidly.

For a moment she blessed him for not being patronizing. If he had been gentle it would have been the last straw. She remembered her own early days of social aspiration, the constant struggle to keep up, to say the right thing, to please the right people. Those born to acceptance can never understand the feeling. That was one of the things she and Jack shared, a sense of being outside, accepted as long as they charmed and amused, but not by right. He had felt the sting of unconscious superiority too often to practice it himself.

He was waiting for her to flare up; instead Emily was reminded of how much she liked him. He had said nothing of the risk to her social position.

"No," she agreed with a small smile, quite calmly. "I would be obliged if you would help me sort out such details. I shall have to say my sister is in service, if they ask me. There are plenty of residential servants in Bloomsbury."

"Then she must have the same surname. What are you going to call yourself?"

118

"Er, Amelia."

"Amelia what?"

"Anything. I can't use Pitt, they might remember it from Thomas. I once had a maid called Gibson; I'll use her name."

"Then you'll have to remember to write to Charlotte as Miss Gibson too. I'll tell her."

"Thank you, Jack. I really am very obliged."

He grinned suddenly. "I should think so!"

"You are going to do what?" Great-aunt Vespasia's silver eyebrows arched high above her hooded eyes. She was seated in her spare, elegant withdrawing room, dressed in mulberry silk with a pink fichu at the neck that was fastened with a seed pearl star. She looked frailer than before, thinner, since George's death. But some of the fire had come back into her glance, and her back was as straight as ever.

"I'm going to go to the Yorks' as a lady's maid," Emily repeated. She swallowed hard and met Aunt Vespasia's eyes.

And Vespasia stared unflinchingly back at her. "Are you? You won't like it, my dear. Your duties will be the least part of your burden; even obedience will be less irksome to you than assuming an air of meekness and respect towards the sort of people you normally treat as equals, whatever your private thoughts may be. And do remember, that goes for the housekeeper and the butler as well, not just the mistress."

Emily could not dare to think of it or her nerve would desert her. A small timorous voice inside her wished Aunt Vespasia would come up with some unanswerable reason why she could not possibly go. She knew she had been unfair to Jack; he had been concerned for her, that was all. She would have been hurt if he had not objected to the plan.

"I know," she admitted. "I expect it to be difficult. I may not even last very long, but this way, I can learn things about the Yorks that years of visiting couldn't achieve. People forget servants; they think of them as furniture. I know. I do it myself."

"Yes," Aunt Vespasia agreed dryly. "I daresay your own maid's opinion of you might be a salutary thing for you to learn, if you ever get above yourself. No one knows your vanity, nor your frailties, quite like a maid. But remember, my dear, for precisely that reason one trusts a maid. If you break that trust, do not expect to be forgiven. I do not imagine Loretta York is a forgiving woman."

"You know her?"

"Only in the way everyone in Society knows everyone else. She is not my generation. Now, you will need some plain stuff dresses and some caps and aprons, some petticoats without lace, a night shift, and some ordinary black boots. I am sure one of my maids will be near enough to your size. And a plain box to carry them in. If you do this highly bizarre thing, you had at least better do it properly."

"Yes, Aunt Vespasia," Emily said with a sinking heart. "Thank you."

Late that afternoon, without perfume or the merest rouge to heighten her pale color and clad in a dowdy brown dress and a brown hat, Emily alit from the public omnibus carrying a borrowed and much used box. She walked to number two Hanover Close to present herself at the servants' entrance. She had in her reticule, also borrowed, two letters of recommendation, one from herself and the other from Great-aunt Vespasia. She had been preceded by a call on the new telephone, which Aunt Vespasia delighted in, to announce her coming. After all, there was no point in applying for this position if it were already filled. Aunt Vespasia had learned that it had not been filled, although there were applicants in mind. The elder Mrs. York was very particular, even though the maid was actually to serve her daughter-in-law. Still, she was mistress of the house, and would say who worked in it and who did not.

Aunt Vespasia had asked after Mrs. York's health, then

proceeded to commiserate with her about the distress and in-convenience of losing a maid in such circumstances. She had remarked that her own lady's maid, Amelia Gibson, who had served her most satisfactorily, was now, in Aunt Vespasia's declining years and semiretirement from Society, really more than she required, and was consequently looking for a new position. She was a girl of reliable family, long known to Vespasia, who had also been in the service of her great-niece, Lady Ashworth, whose accompanying testimonial would bear witness. Vespasia hoped that Mrs. York might find Amelia of satisfactory skill and disposition. Vespasia would vouch for her character.

Mrs. York thanked her for her courtesy and agreed to see Amelia if she presented herself forthwith.

Emily clutched her reticule with the letters and three pounds, fifteen shillings in silver and copper (maids would not have gold sovereigns or guineas) and lugged the unaccustomed weight of a box containing a change of dress, aprons, caps and her underwear, a Bible and some writing paper, pen and ink, as she descended the area steps, her heart knocking in her ribs, her mouth dry. She tried to rehearse what she was going to say. There was still time to change her mind. She could turn round and simply go away and write a letter making some excuse: she had been taken ill, her mother had died—anything!

But her feet kept going, and just as she was about to weigh up this lunatic decision in the last moment left, the back door opened. A scullery maid who looked to be about fourteen came out with a bowl full of peelings to throw in the waste bin.

"You be come fer poor Dulcie's position?" she said cheerfully, eyeing Emily's shabby coat and the box in her hand. "Come on in then, you'll freeze out 'ere in the yard. Give yer a cup o' tea afore yer see the mistress, make yer feel better. Yer look 'alf starved in the cold, yer do. 'Ere, give that there box ter Albert, 'e'll carry it for yer, if yer staying."

Emily was grateful, and terrified now that the decision to come had been made. She wanted to thank the girl, but her voice simply refused to obey. Mutely she followed the scullery maid up the steps into the back kitchen, past the vegetables, the hanging corpses of two chickens and a brace of game birds complete with feathers, and into the main kitchen. Her hands were numb in her cotton gloves and the sudden warmth engulfed her, bringing tears to her eyes and making her sniff after the stinging cold on the walk from the omnibus stop.

"Mrs. Melrose, this is someone applyin' ter be the new lady's maid, and she's fair perished, poor thing."

The cook, a narrow-shouldered, broad-hipped woman with a face like a cottage loaf, looked up from the pastry she was rolling and regarded Emily with businesslike sympathy.

"Well, come in, girl, put that box down in the corner. Out of the way! Don't want folk falling over it. If you stay, we can 'ave it taken upstairs for you. What's your name? Don't stand there, girl! Cat got your tongue?" She dusted the flour off her bare arms, flipped the pastry the other way on the board, and began again with the rolling pin, still looking at Emily.

"Amelia Gibson, ma'am," Emily said falteringly, realizing she did not know exactly how deferential a lady's maid should be to a cook. It was something she had forgotten to ask.

"Some folk call lady's maids by their surnames," the cook remarked. "But we don't in this 'ouse. Anyway, you're too young for that. I'm Mrs. Melrose, the cook. That's Prim, the scullery maid, as let you in, and Mary, the kitchen maid there." She pointed with a floury finger at a girl in a stuff dress and mob cap who was whisking eggs in a bowl. "You'll find out the rest of the 'ousehold if you need to know. Sit down at the table there and Mary'll get you a cup o' tea while we tell the mistress you're 'ere. Get on with your work, Prim, you got no time to stand around, girl! Albert!'' she called shrilly. "Where is that boy? Albert!''

A moment later a round-eyed youth of about fifteen appeared, his hair standing on end where it grew away from his forehead in a cowlick, a double crown at the back giving him a quiff like a cockatoo.

"Yes, Mrs. Melrose?'' he said, swallowing quickly. He had obviously been eating on the sly.

The cook snorted. "Go up and tell Mr. Redditch as the new girl's 'ere after Dulcie's place. Go on wi' you! And if I catch you in them cakes again I'll take a broom to yer!''

"Yes, Mrs. Melrose,'' he said, and disappeared with alacrity.

Emily accepted her cup of tea and sipped it, giving herself hiccups and then feeling ridiculous when Mary laughed at her and the cook scowled. She tried holding her breath and had only just conquered them when the trim, pretty parlormaid came to say that Mrs. York would see her in the boudoir. She led the way and Emily followed. All along the passage, past the butler's pantry, through the green baize door and into the main house she kept rehearsing in her mind what she must say, how she must behave. Eyes candid but modest, speak only when spoken to, never interrupt, never contradict, never express an opinion. No one cared or wanted to know what maids thought, it was impertinence. Never ask anyone to do anything for you, do it yourself. Call the butler sir, or by his name. Address the housekeeper and the cook by name. And remember to speak with the right accent! Always be available, night or day. Never have headaches or stomachaches—you were there to do a job, and short of serious illness there were no excuses. The vapors were for ladies, not for servants.

Nora, the parlormaid, knocked on the door, opened it, and announced, "The girl to see you, ma'am, about being Miss Veronica's maid.''

The boudoir was ivory and pink with touches of deeper

123

rose, very feminine indeed. There was no time to look for character or quality now.

Mrs. Loretta York sat in an armchair. She was a small woman, a little plump around the shoulders, an inch or two thicker at the waist than she probably wished, but otherwise the beauty she had been in her youth was excellently preserved. Emily knew instantly that there was steel under the woman's soft, white skin, and for all the lace handkerchiefs, the waft of perfume, and her thick, soft hair, there was nothing remotely vague in her wide eyes.

"Ma'am." Emily bobbled a very small curtsy.

"Where do you come from, Amelia?" Loretta inquired.

Emily had already decided the safest thing would be to copy her own maid's background—that way she would be certain not to contradict herself. "King's Langley, ma'am, in Hertfordshire."

"I see. What does your father do?"

"He's a cooper, ma'am. Makes barrels and the like. My mam used to be a dairymaid for Lord Ashworth, as was the old gentleman, before he passed on." She knew not to say *died*; it was too blunt a word for a servant to use on such a delicate subject. One did not speak of death.

"And you have worked for Lady Ashworth and Lady Cumming-Gould. Do you have your references?"

"Yes ma'am." She took them out of her reticule, fingers stiff with nervousness, and passed them over. She looked at the floor while Loretta first read them and then refolded them and passed them back. Both letters were written on crested paper, she had taken care to see to that.

"Well, these seem to be satisfactory," Loretta observed. "Why did you leave Lady Ashworth's service?"

She had thought of that. "My mam passed on," she said, catching her breath and swallowing hard. Please heaven the hiccups did not return! It would be disastrous if Loretta thought she had been tippling at the cooking sherry. "I had to go back home to care for my younger sisters, until we could find places for them. And of course Lady Ashworth, being a lady of Society, had to find someone to take me place: but she said she'd speak well for me. And then Lady Cumming-Gould took me on."

"I see." The chill eyes regarded her unemotionally. It was odd to be looked at as if one were a property to be purchased or passed by, without regard to manners or feelings. It was not peculiar to Loretta York; anyone else would have been similar. And yet she would be employed to care for her on the most intimate terms, brush her hair, launder, iron and mend her clothes, even her underwear, wake her in the morning, dress her for dinners and balls, wait on her if she were ill. No one else knew a woman as intimately as her maid. Her husband certainly did not.

"Well Amelia, I presume you can sew and iron and care for a wardrobe properly, or Lady Ashworth would not recommend you. She has a reputation for being in the height of fashion, without vulgarity, although I cannot recall meeting her myself."

Emily felt a rush of blood into her face, then an immediate chill as fear washed through her. The chance of recognition had brushed close sooner than she had anticipated. The peril had come and gone in one awful moment, and when it had passed she opened her mouth to thank Loretta for the compliment, realizing with a start that a reply would have betrayed her into the very pitfall she had just avoided. In her new station no comment was expected of her.

"You may begin immediately," Loretta continued, "and if you prove satisfactory after a month, we shall make you permanent. You will attend my daughter-in-law. You will be paid eighteen pounds a year, and have one afternoon off every second week, if it is convenient, but you will be home again before nine. We have no girls out late. You may have a day off to go home and see your family every three months."

Emily stared at her. "Thank you, ma'am," she said in a

rush. She had been given the position. It was decided. She felt at once frightened and victorious.

"Thank you, Amelia, that will be all. You may go." Loretta's voice brought her back to reality.

"Thank you, ma'am," she said again, letting the relief show in her face. After all, she really did want the place! She bobbed very briefly and turned to leave, feeling an overwhelming sense of freedom just at being out of the room and past the first obstacle.

"Well?" The cook looked up from the apple pie she was finishing off with carefully cut pastry leaves.

Emily smiled at her more broadly than she should have. "I got it!"

"Then be about your unpacking," the cook said pleasantly. "Don't stand around 'ere, girl. You're no use to me! 'Ousekeeper's sitting room is second on the left. Mrs. Crawford should be in there this time o' day. Go and see 'er and she'll tell you where you'll sleep—Dulcie's room, I daresay—and she'll have Joan, the laundry maid, show you where your iron is, and the like. I daresay someone'll find Edith for you—that's Mrs. Piers York's maid. You'll be for Miss Veronica."

"Yes, Mrs. Melrose." Emily went to the corner to pick up her box.

"Don't you bother wi' that! Albert'll take it up. Liftin' and carryin's not your job, 'less you're asked. On wi' you!"

"Yes, Mrs. Melrose."

She went to the housekeeper's sitting room and knocked on the door. She was told sharply to come in.

It was small, crowded with dark furniture, the smell of polish mixing with the thick, greenhouse odor of a potted lily on a jardiniere in one corner. There were embroidered antimacassars on the backs of the chairs and along the sideboard, which was littered with photographs. Two hand-stitched samplers framed in wood hung on the walls. Emily felt overpowered even before she stepped inside.

The housekeeper, Mrs. Crawford, was short and thin, with the face of an irritable sparrow. Gray hair escaped a screwed-back hairstyle that was considerably out of date and crowned with white lace like froth.

"Yes?" she said sharply. "Who are you?"

Emily stood up straight. "The new lady's maid, Mrs. Crawford. Mrs. Melrose said as you would tell me where I should sleep."

"Sleep! At four o'clock in the afternoon, girl? I'll tell you where you can put your box! And I'll show you to the laundry and Joan can give you your iron and table. I daresay Edith is sitting down; she's not so well these days. You'll have met Nora, the parlormaid, and there's Libby the upstairs maid and Bertha the downstairs maid, and Fanny the tweeny, but a useless little article she is! And of course Mr. Redditch, the butler, but you'll not have much to do with him, nor John the footman, who valets for Mr. York, and Albert the boot-boy."

"Yes, Mrs. Crawford."

"And you'll have met Mary the kitchen maid and Prim the scullery maid. Well, that's all. Outside staff, grooms and the like, don't need to concern you. And you'll not have anything to do with anyone outside the house unless Mrs. York sends you on an errand. You'll have Sunday mornings off to go to church. You'll eat in the servants hall with the rest of us. I expect that dress'll do you." She looked at it without favor. "You've got caps and aprons, of course? I should think so. If Miss Veronica wants them changed she'll tell you. I hope I don't need to remind you, you'll have no followers, no gentlemen callers of any sort, unless you've a father or brother, in which case if you ask permission, I daresay they'll be allowed to see you, at convenient times."

"Thank you, ma'am." Emily could feel the walls tightening round her as if she were a prisoner. No callers, no admirers, one half day off a fortnight! How was she going to keep in touch with Charlotte, and Jack?

"Well, don't stand there, girl!" Mrs. Crawford rose and smoothed her apron briskly, her keys jangling at her waist. She led the way out, moving like a little rodent, with busy, jerky steps. In the laundry she patted and touched things, showing Emily coppers for boiling linen, bins of soap, starch, ironing tables, flatirons, and airing rails, all the time clicking her tongue over the absence of Joan.

Upstairs Emily was shown Veronica York's bedroom. It was cool green and white with touches of yellow, like a spring field, and her dressing room had cupboards full of clothes, all fashionable and of high quality—but nothing in pink, let alone cerise.

Upstairs on the servants' floor, she was led to a small room about one fifth the size of her own at home, bare but for an iron bedstead with a ticking-covered mattress, gray blankets, and a pillow; one small cupboard; and a table with a basin on it, no pitcher. Under the bed was a plain white china chamber pot. The ceiling sloped so that in only half of the room could she stand upright, and the dormered window had thin, unlined brown curtains. The linoleum on the floor was like ice to the touch; there was one small rag mat by the bedside. Her heart sank. It was clean and cold and infinitely grim compared with home. How many girls had stood in doorways like this with tears welling up inside them, knowing there was no possible escape, and this was the best they could hope for, not the worst?

"Thank you, Mrs. Crawford," she said huskily.

"Albert's put your box there; you unpack it, and when Miss Veronica rings"—she pointed to the bell Emily had not noticed before—"you'll go down and attend to her dressing for dinner. She's out now, or I'd have taken you to her."

"Yes, Mrs. Crawford."

And the next minute she was alone. It was ghastly. All she had was a box of clothes, a narrow bed as hard as a bench, three blankets to keep warm, no fire, no water except what she fetched for herself to put in that basin, and no light but for one candle in a chipped enamel holder; and she was at the beck and call of a woman she had never met. Jack was right: she must have lost her wits! If only he had forbidden her, if only Aunt Vespasia had begged her not to do it!

But Jack was not worried about her loneliness, the bare floor, the cold bed, the chamber pot, the strip wash in one basin of water, or the obedience to a bell. He was afraid because someone had committed murder in this house—twice—and Emily was an intruder who had come to try and catch the murderer.

She sat down on the bed, her legs shaking. The springs creaked. She was cold and her throat ached with the effort not to weep. "I am here to find a murderer," she said to herself quietly. "Robert York was murdered—Dulcie was pushed out of a window because she saw the woman in cerise and told Thomas. There is something terrible in this house, and I am going to find out what it is. Thousands of girls, tens of thousands all over the country live like this. If they can do it, so can I. I am not a coward. I do not run away just because things are frightening, and certainly not because they are unpleasant. They are not going to beat me before I've even begun!"

At half past five the bell rang, and after straightening her cap in front of the piece of mirror on the mantel shelf and retying her apron, Emily went down to meet Veronica York, carrying the candle.

On the landing she knocked on the bedroom door and was told to go in. She did not glance at the room; she had seen it before, and curiosity would not do. And indeed, her real interest was in Veronica herself.

"Yes ma'am?"

Veronica was sitting on the dressing stool in a white robe tied at the waist, her black hair falling loose like satin ribbons down her back. Her face was pale but the bones were beautiful, her eyes large and dark as peat water. At the moment her fragile skin was a little blue around the slender nose and across her high cheeks, and she was definitely too thin for current fashion. She would need a bustle to plump out those narrow hips, and swathes to make her bosom look fuller. But Emily had to admit she was a beautiful woman, with the qualities of delicacy and character that haunt the mind far longer than mere regularity of feature. There was passion in her face, and intelligence.

"I'm Amelia, ma'am. Mrs. York employed me this afternoon."

Suddenly Veronica smiled and all her color returned; it was like illumination in a gray room.

"Yes, I know. I hope you'll like it here, Amelia. Are you comfortable?"

"Yes thank you, ma'am," Emily lied bravely. What she had been given was all a maid could expect. "Will you be dressing for dinner, ma'am?"

"Yes please. The blue gown; I think Edith put it in the first cupboard."

"Yes ma'am." Emily went through to the dressing room and brought back a royal blue velvet and taffeta gown, cut low, with balloon sleeves. It took her a few moments to find the right petticoats and lay them out.

"Yes, that's right, thank you," Veronica agreed.

"Would you like your hair done before your gown, ma'am?" It was the way Emily herself dressed—it was so easy to drop a hair or a pin, a smudge of powder or a perfume stain.

"Yes." Veronica sat still while Emily took the brush, then polished the long shining hair with a silk scarf. It was lovely, thick and dark as a moonless sea. Had Jack looked at it with such admiration? She forced that idea away. This was no time to tease herself with jealousies.

"You will find we are a little behind," Veronica said, interrupting her thoughts. Emily saw her shoulders stiffen and the muscles pull across the back of her neck. "I am afraid my previous maid had—a terrible accident."

Emily's hand with the comb stopped in the air. "Oh." She had decided to affect ignorance. None of the servants had told her, and the sort of person she was pretending to be would never have read about the "accident." "I'm sorry, ma'am. That must have been distressing for you. Was she hurt badly?"

The answer was very quiet. "I'm afraid she was killed. She fell out of the window. Don't worry, it wasn't the room you are in."

Emily saw Veronica's eyes on her in the mirror. Deliberately she put on an expression of surprise and sympathy, knowing she must be careful not to overact.

"Oh, that's terrible, ma'am! The poor creature. Well, I'll be very careful. I don't like heights anyway, never did." She began coiling Veronica's hair and pinning it, sweeping it away from her temples. At any other time she would have enjoyed the task, but now she was nervous. She must look skilled, they had to believe this was her profession. "How did it happen, ma'am?" It would be only natural to ask.

Veronica shivered. "I don't know. No one does. Nobody saw it happen."

"Did it happen at night then?"

"No, it was in the evening. We were all at dinner."

"How awful for you," Emily said with what she hoped sounded more like compassion than curiosity. "I hope you didn't have guests, ma'am."

"Yes we did, but fortunately they left before we discovered what had happened."

Emily did not probe any further. She would be able to find out from one of the other servants who the guests had been, although she was prepared to wager one had been Julian Danver.

"What a terrible time you've had." She curled the last strand of hair and put in the pins. "Is that comfortable, ma'am?"

Veronica turned her head one way and then the other in

front of the glass. "You've done that very well, Amelia. It's not how I usually wear it, but I think it's an improvement."

Emily was greatly relieved. "Oh thank you, ma'am."

Veronica stood up and Emily helped her into the petticoats and then the gown, fastening it carefully. Veronica looked very striking indeed, but Emily was uncertain whether a compliment might be considered too familiar. She decided against it. After all, a maid's opinion hardly mattered.

There was a sharp rap on the door, and almost before Veronica had said "Come in" it opened and Loretta York, elegant in lavender silk embroidered in black and silver, swished in, regarding Veronica up and down critically. She appeared not even to see Emily.

"You look pale. For goodness' sake, pull yourself together, my dear. We have a duty to do. The family deserves our best courtesy, as well as the guests. Your father-in-law will be expecting us. We do not wish him to think we crumble to pieces because of some domestic tragedy. He has enough to concern himself with. What happens at home is our affair, and we must protect him from any disturbances. A man has a right to a calm and well-ordered home." She looked at Veronica's hair carefully. "People do die. Death is the inevitable end of life, and you are not some tuppenny bourgeoise to fall into the vapors at the first affliction. Now pinch a little color into your face and come downstairs."

Veronica's body stiffened, the blue silk tightening as the line of her jaw hardened into a sharp angle.

"I have quite as much color as usual, Mother-in-law. I do not wish to look as if I have a fever."

Loretta's face froze. "I am thinking of your welfare, Veronica," she said icily. "I always have your good in mind, which you will realize if you think back." The words were reasonable, even kind, but her voice cut like a knife.

Veronica grew paler, and she spoke with difficulty. "I am aware of that, Mother-in-law."

Emily was transfixed. The emotion was so strong she could feel it prickling her skin. And yet the issue was so slight!

"Sometimes I wonder if it slips your mind." Loretta did not alter her fixed gaze. "I want your future happiness and security, my dear. Don't ever forget that."

Veronica swiveled, her throat jerking with the effort. "I never, never forget what you do for me," she whispered.

"I will always be here, my dear," Loretta promised—or, in the hot motionlessness of this room, was this a veiled threat? "Always." Then, as Emily's paralyzed figure caught the corner of her vision, "What are you staring at, girl?" she asked. Her voice stung like a sudden slap. "Be about your business!"

Emily leapt to attention and the dressing robe slid from her hands to the floor. She bent and picked it up clumsily, fingers stiff. "Yes ma'am!" She almost ran from the room, her face burning with frustration and embarrassment for having been caught eavesdropping. The words had been so ordinary, any mother and daughter-in-law might have exchanged them, but there had been no lightness or ease in the air; it was charged with multiple layers of meaning. And Emily felt with a crawling electricity under her skin that beneath it all was an immense hatred.

Emily took her first meal in Hanover Close in the servants' hall, at a large table presided over by Redditch, the butler. He was in his mid-forties and just a trifle pompous, but his face had such an inoffensive air of slight surprise about it that she could not dislike him.

It was late by the time the meal had been served in the dining room, found satisfactory, and cleared away. The scullery was filled with dirty dishes. At the foot of the table sat the cook, who was still solicitous, since Emily was a newcomer, but there was no doubt that motherly concern would be quickly replaced by motherly discipline should Emily speak out of turn or fall short in her duty. Mrs. Crawford, the housekeeper, was dressed in black bombazine with an immaculate lace-trimmed cap, more elaborate than the one she had worn previously. She was very much on her dignity. She obviously considered herself the mistress in any other part of the house and only tolerated the cook's supremacy here because Mrs. Melrose was so immediately concerned with preparing the meal. Throughout the conversation Mrs. Crawford made sharp little remarks, reminders of rank.

Edith, the other lady's maid, apparently felt recovered enough to come to the table. She was in her mid-thirties, plump and sullen, her black hair still shiny but her country complexion dulled with two decades of London fog and soot and too little air. Whatever her indisposition, and although she seemed ill pleased with the food, she managed to eat all of it and came back for second helpings of the bread, cheese, and pickles, which was all there was offered, the main meal having been eaten at luncheon. Emily had the strong suspicion that Edith was more lazy than unwell, and she determined to find out why the disciplinarian Mrs. York tolerated her.

She spent what was left of the evening in the servants hall, listening to scraps of conversation and learning all she could, which was little enough, because they spoke mainly of their own affairs, domestic matters, the tradesmen and their shortcomings, and the general decline of the national character as exhibited by other people's servants and the standards of households in general.

Edith sat next to the fire and sewed a chemise, and the mystery of her employment was solved—she was an exquisite needlewoman. Idle and ungracious she might be, but there was genius in her fingers. Her needle flashed in and out, drawing the gleaming silk behind it, and flowers took shape under her hand, delicate as gossamer and perfectly proportioned. Emily glanced at her work and saw the reverse was almost indistinguishable from the top. She realized that she might well be expected to pull Edith's weight in fetching and carrying, and she would have to do it without complaint, or she would be replaced. Girls who would run errands were two a penny since the coming of machinery and the consequent disappearance of hundreds of home crafts; the traditional occupations for women no longer existed. Tens of thousands of them poured in from the country to take domestic service, most of them with nothing to offer but willingness and the need to survive. Girls who could stitch like Edith were worth their weight in gold. It was a lesson to be remembered.

Fanny, the tweeny, who was only twelve, was sent to bed at half past nine so she could be up at five to clean out the grates and polish the brasses. She went with a halfhearted complaint, made more from habit than any hope she would be reprieved, and Prim, the scullery maid, followed fifteen minutes later, for similar reasons, and with a similar complaint.

"On with you!" the housekeeper said sharply. "Quick sticks! Up them stairs, girl, or you'll be late in the morning."

"Yes, Mrs. Crawford. G'night. G'night, Mr. Redditch."

"Good night," came the automatic reply.

"I know there is a big dinner party tomorrow—will there be many guests?" Emily asked as casually as she could.

"Twenty," Nora replied. "We don't do very big parties here, but we have some important people." She sounded a little defensive. She looked at Emily coldly, prepared to counter any slight, should it be offered.

"We used to 'ave more," Mary said, looking up from the mending she was doing. "Afore Mr. Robert was killed."

"That'll do, Mary!" the cook said quickly. "We don't want to talk o' things like that. You'll be givin' them girls bad dreams again!"

Emily deliberately misunderstood. "I love parties. I love to see the ladies all dressed up."

"Not parties!" the housekeeper said crossly. "Talking about death. You can't be expected to know, Amelia, but

Mr. Robert died terrible. I'll caution you to hold your tongue about it. You go tattling all over the place and upsetting people and you'll have no position in this house, and no character to take with you! Now you go upstairs and put out Miss Veronica's things for the night an' make sure you got your tray set for the morning. You can come down here again for cocoa at half past nine."

Emily sat motionless, her temper rising. Her eyes met the housekeeper's and she saw the start of surprise in them. Maids do not question their orders, least of all new maids. It was her first mistake.

"Yes, Mrs. Crawford," she said demurely, her voice thick with anger, both at herself and at being subjected to discipline.

"Uppity, that girl," Mrs. Crawford said as Emily was almost out of the door. "You mark my words, Mrs. Melrose: uppity! Can see it in her eyes and the way she walks. Got airs, that one. She'll come to no good—I can always tell."

Emily's first night in Hanover Close was wretched. The bed was hard and the blankets thin. She was used to a fire, and a feather quilt, and thick velvet curtains over the windows. These curtains were plain cloth and she could hear the sleet lashing against the glass until sometime in the shivering darkness when it froze and turned to snow. Then there was silence, thick, strange, and penetratingly cold. She hunched up her knees but she could not get warm enough to sleep. Finally she got up, the air so bitter that the touch of her gown against her skin made her wince. She swung her arms sharply but was too tense to succeed in warming herself. Instead she put her towel on top of the bed, and then the mat from the floor over that, and climbed back in.

This time she slept, but it seemed only moments before there was a sharp rap on the door and the tweeny's pale little face came round it.

"Time to get up, Miss Amelia."

For a moment Emily could not think where on earth she was. It was cold and the room was stark. She saw iron bed-posts and a heap of gray blankets and the floor mat over her. The curtains were still closed. Then with a rush of misery it all came back to her, the whole absurd situation she had got herself into.

Fanny was staring at her. "You cold, miss?"

"I'm freezing," Emily admitted.

"I'll tell Joan; she'll find you another blanket. You'd better get up. It's near seven o'clock, and you'll 'ave ter get yerself ready, then make Miss Veronica's tea and fetch it up, and draw 'er bath. She usually likes to be up by eight. An' if nobody told yer, Edith'll prob'ly sleep in an' you'll 'ave ter make Mrs. York's tea, too, and draw 'er bath maybe."

Emily threw the bedclothes off and plunged out, her body shaking. The floor without the mat was like dry ice. "Does Edith often skive off?" she asked with chattering teeth. She pulled open the curtains to let in the light.

"Oh yes," Fanny answered matter-of-factly. "Dulcie always did 'alf 'er work, as I 'spec' you will too, if you stay. It's worf it. Anyway, if Miss Veronica likes you she'll prob'ly take you wif'er when she marries Mr. Danver, an' then you'll be all right." She smiled and her eyes moved up to look at the gray sky through the window. "Maybe you'll get ter meet someone real nice—'andsome, an' kind—what 'as 'is own shop, maybe, and fall in love. . . ." She let the thought hang in the air, beautiful and bright as a bubble, too precious to touch.

Emily felt tears prickling her eyes. She turned away, but she was too cold to stop dressing, nor was there time.

"Is Miss Veronica going to get married? How exciting. What's he like, Mr. Danver? I expect he's well-to-do?"

Fanny let the dream go and came back to reality. "Lor' miss, I dunno! Nora says 'e is, but then she would! Got eyes for the gentlemen, she 'as. My ma used ter say all parlor-maids 'as. Fancies theirselves rotten."

"What was Mr. Robert like?" Emily put on her apron and reached for a brush to untangle her hair and pin it up.

"I dunno, miss. 'E died afore I come 'ere."

Of course—she was only twelve, she would have been nine when Robert York was murdered. Stupid question.

Fanny was not to be deterred. "Mary says 'e was ever so good-looking, and a real gentleman. Never tried it on, like some gentlemen do, and lovely spoken. 'E liked nice fings, dressed a treat, but not showy like. In fac' she says 'e was the best gentleman she ever saw. She thought the world of 'im. O' course I fink she 'eard it all from the front servants like, 'er being scullery maid then. Devoted to Miss Veronica, 'e was; an' she to 'im." She sighed and looked down at her plain gray stuff dress. "Terrible sad, 'im bein' killed like that. Fair broke 'er 'eart. She wept suffink wicked, poor soul. I reckon as 'ooever done it should be topped, but nobody never caught 'im." She sniffed fiercely. "I'd like to find someone as'd love me like that," she said, then sniffed again. She was a realist and half of her knew it would always be a fantasy, but it was precious. In the long day of practicalities, she needed to let go for a moment and permit the mind to take wing. Even the remotest chance was infinitely cherished.

Emily thought of George with a vividness she had learned to avoid for months now. A year ago her life had seemed so safe, and here she was, shaking with cold in an attic at seven in the morning, dressed in plain blue stuff and listening to a twelve-year-old tweeny pour out her dreams.

"Yes," she said honestly, "it would be the best thing imaginable. But don't run off with thinking that it only happens to ladies. Some of them cry themselves to sleep too; you don't see all that happens. And some people you'd never think of can find happiness. Don't give up, Fanny. You mustn't give up."

Fanny wiped her nose on a rag from her apron pocket. "You're a caution, miss. Don't let Mrs. Crawford 'ear you

138

say that. She don't approve o' girls wif ideas. Says it's bad for 'em: unsettles 'em, like. She says 'appiness comes from knowing yer place an' keepin' to it."

"I'm sure she does," Emily said. She dashed the cold water from the bowl onto her face and snatched the towel from the bed to rub it dry. It hurt her skin, but at least the roughness made her blood sing.

"I gotta be goin'," Fanny said, turning to the door. "I only done 'alf me grates, and Bertha'll be arter me to 'elp 'er wi' ve tea leaves."

"Tea leaves?" Emily did not know what she meant.

"On the carpet!" Fanny stared at her. "The tea leaves on the carpet to clean it afore the master and mistress comes down! Mrs. Crawford'll 'ave me if I don't get on!" And with a note of real fear in her voice she scuttled away. Emily heard her rapid feet along the uncarpeted passage and down the stairs.

The day was an endless whirl of one task after another. Emily began by cutting fine bread and butter and taking a tea tray to Veronica, pulling back the curtains, inquiring for instructions for bathing and dressing; then she did the same for Loretta and suddenly felt idiotically nervous. Her fingers fumbled and she nearly spilled the tea; the cup rattled and for a moment she was afraid she was going to knock it over. The curtains stuck and she had to yank them and her heart stopped as she had visions of the whole rail coming down on top of her. She felt Loretta's eyes boring two holes in her back.

But when she turned round Loretta was busy with her bread and butter and had no interest in her whatsoever.

"Would you like me to draw your bath, ma'am?" she asked.

"Certainly." Loretta did not look up. "Edith has already put out my morning dress. You can come back in twenty minutes."

139

"Yes, ma'am," she said, and excused herself as hastily as she could.

When both the ladies were bathed and dressed Edith deigned to put in an appearance, so Emily had only Veronica's hair to do, after which she was permitted to hurry down to the kitchen and take her own snatched breakfast. Then she was required to go back upstairs and help Libby the upstairs maid with turning out the bedrooms. Each room had to be aired thoroughly, and before this could be done the cheval glasses must be laid down so the draft could not knock them over and break them. Then in the freezing wind from the open sashes they turned the bottom mattresses, plumped up the middle ones, and thoroughly kneaded and pummeled the top feather ones till they were as light as soufflés. Finally they remade the beds. The carpets were rolled and taken downstairs to be beaten only once a fortnight, and thank heavens it was not today. This time they only swept the carpets, dusted every surface, emptied and washed all the basins and chamber pots, cleaned the baths thoroughly and laid out fresh towels.

By the time they were finished Emily was tired and dirty. Her hair had fallen out of its pins, and Mrs. Crawford caught her on the stairs and told her that she looked a disgrace, she had better smarten herself up if she wished to remain. Emily was on the point of retaliating that if Mrs. Crawford had done a hand's turn herself she would also look a little untidy when she caught sight of Veronica. Pale and tight-faced, she was walking quickly away from Loretta, and the butler with the morning newspapers freshly ironed, going across the hall towards the dining room.

"Yes, Mrs. Crawford," Emily said obediently, remembering why she was there. She was so thirsty she could taste feathers in her mouth and her back was stiff from bending and lifting. But she would not be defeated by a housekeeper! This was the only place to discover who had killed Robert

York and why—and who had pushed poor Dulcie out of the window to her death.

Already she had learned more about the characters of the two women than she could have in a month of social visiting. It was Loretta, not Veronica, who slept in shell pink satin sheets with pillowcases embroidered in self-colored silks. Either Veronica was happy with linen, or she had not been offered anything else. It was Loretta who had the expensive oil of musk perfumes in crystal and Lalique bottles with silver filigree stoppers. Veronica was more beautiful by nature's gift, with her slender height and grace and those haunting eyes; but it was Loretta who was the more elegantly feminine. She bothered with the details of care, the perfume in the handkerchief and in the petticoats to waft to the nostrils as she moved, or passed, the taffeta to rustle and whisper as she walked, the many pairs of boots and slippers to match every gown and be shown in a glimpse under her skirts. Had Veronica not thought of these things, or did their subtlety elude her? Was there some reason for this difference that Emily did not yet understand?

There was obviously a strong emotional bond between the two women, although its exact nature still eluded Emily. Loretta seemed protective, guarding the younger and seemingly weaker woman after the grief of her widowhood, yet at the same time her patience was thin and she was highly critical. And Veronica resented her mother-in-law while appearing to depend upon her a great deal.

When they changed for luncheon after the morning's outing, Emily was busy taking care of wet coats and soiled skirts, humping them back and forth to be dried out, brushed off, sponged and pressed—and she had both to do since Edith was missing again. She overheard a sharp exchange as Veronica's voice rose and Loretta's remained calm and cold in what was seemingly a warning. Emily tried to overhear, but just as she was about to bend to the keyhole the upstairs maid came by and she was obliged to continue with her duties.

Luncheon in the servants hall was called dinner, and Emily was caught out in misnaming it and received a curious look from the cook.

"Think you're upstairs, do you, my fine lady?" the housekeeper said tartly. "Well, there'll be no giving yourself airs down here, and you'd best remember it! You're just the same as the rest of the girls; in fact, you're not as good until you prove yourself!"

"Oh, maybe some gentleman acquaintance of Miss Veronica'll take a fancy to 'er an' she'll become a duchess!" Nora pulled a face. " 'Ceptin' you need to be a parlormaid to meet dukes, and you 'aven't got the looks for it. You aren't tall enough, for a start. An' you 'aven't got the colorin' either. Peaked, you are!"

"I don't suppose there are enough dukes to go around anyway," Emily snapped back. "Since even parlormaids have to wait till all the ladies are suited!"

"Well, I've a sight more chance than you 'ave!" Nora retorted. "At least I know my job; I don't 'ave to 'ave a tweeny show me 'ow to do it!"

"Duchess!" Edith giggled. "That's a fine name for 'er. Walks with 'er 'ead in the air like she already got a tiara on an' was afraid it might slip over 'er nose." She made a mock curtsy. "Don't wobble yer 'ead, Yer Grace!"

"That's enough!" the butler said with a frown of disapproval. "She's done most of your work this morning. You should be obliged to her! Maybe that's what's wrong with you."

"Edith was busy with mending, and she's not strong." Mrs. Crawford gave Redditch a look of irritation which would have quelled anyone less than a butler. "You've no call to pick on her."

"Edith is bone idle and wouldn't be kept if she wasn't the best seamstress in the city," Redditch replied quickly, but his reproach was robbed of some of its bite by the slightly wary air with which he immediately followed it.

142

"I'll thank you to attend to your own responsibilities, Mr. Redditch. The maidservants are mine and I'll look after them my own way, which suits Mrs. York well enough."

"Well, it doesn't suit me, Mrs. Crawford, to see girls lowering themselves to make mock of each other, and if I hear it again someone'll have their notice."

"We'll see who has their notice, Mr. Redditch," Mrs. Crawford said darkly. "You mark my words, it'll be them as can best be replaced."

That seemed to be the end of the matter for the time being, but Emily, glancing at their faces, knew that battle lines had been drawn and the exchange would not be forgotten. She had made enemies of both Edith and Nora, and the housekeeper would be happy to catch her in any shortcoming from now on. If she wanted to survive, she would have to cultivate the butler's regard till her position became a matter of his pride as well.

The afternoon was dreadful. Emily had superintended her own maid often enough and had imagined she knew her duties, but watching someone use a flatiron on lace ruffling was a very different thing from doing it oneself, and it was much more difficult than she had thought. The only good thing about it was that she did not scorch anything, so it was possible for Joan to rescue her, and the outcome was a debt to Joan. Emily had no break all afternoon, not even for a cup of tea, and finally rushed upstairs at half past five, exhausted, her head throbbing, back aching and feet pinched in the unfamiliar boots, barely in time to help Veronica change for the dinner party.

After receiving several callers for tea Veronica seemed tired also, and more nervous than Emily could understand. She was not the hostess; the responsibility for the dinner's success rested with her mother-in-law, so all she had to do was be charming. Nevertheless she changed her mind three times about which gown to wear, was dissatisfied with her hair, and when Emily had taken it all down and put it back up again she still did not feel confident. She stood in front of the cheval glass and frowned at her reflection.

Emily was exhausted, her mind crowded with thoughts of how selfish this woman was. She had done nothing whatsoever all day except visit, eat, and chatter, while Emily had worked like a Trojan, missed afternoon tea, and been picked on and jeered at, and all Veronica could think of was to tell Emily to take her hair down yet again and do it a third time.

"It becomes you very well the first way, ma'am." Emily only barely controlled the tone of her voice.

Veronica picked up the perfume bottle and it slipped through her fingers, splashing perfume down the front of her skirt.

Emily could have wept. Now the whole thing had to be changed—there was no possible alternative. And on top of that she did not know how to get rid of the stain and would have to ask Edith, who would crow over her ignorance, almost certainly letting Mrs. Crawford know about it, and probably the rest of the staff. She did not trust herself to speak. It was only when she was in the dressing room fetching a fourth gown that she realized that she herself often gave no more thought to her own maid's feelings than Veronica was doing now.

Back in the bedroom with the fresh gown she saw Veronica sitting on the bed in her petticoats and chemise, her head low, her hair fallen forward. She looked very slight, her shoulders almost childlike, and painfully vulnerable. This was an acutely private moment. Did anyone else ever see her like this, without the glamor and the confidence? Emily wanted to put her arms round her, she looked so bitterly alone; she, too, understood widowhood in the shadow of murder. But she knew that would be impossible. There was a gulf between them, at least from Veronica's side.

"Don't you feel very well, ma'am?" she said gently. "I can get you a tisane, if you like? As lovely as you are, no one will mind if you are a minute or two late. Come down after the other ladies and cause a bit of a flutter!''

Veronica looked up, and Emily was surprised to see the gratitude in her face. She smiled faintly. "Thank you, Amelia. Yes, I would like a tisane. I can drink it while you're doing my hair."

It took five minutes for Emily to sort through the ingredients available and select a soothing camomile, and another three for the kettle to boil, after which she had to carry the herb tea back upstairs. She met Mrs. Crawford in the hall.

"What are you doing down here, Amelia?"

"An errand for Mrs. York," Emily replied tartly, and whisking her skirts around the corner of the stairpost she went up without looking back. She heard Mrs. Crawford snort and the muttered words, "We'll see about you, miss!" but she could not take time to worry over it now.

Veronica greeted her with pleasure, and sipped the tisane as if it were indeed a life restorer. She made no demur when Emily put her hair up as she had the first time and helped her on with the fourth gown, black taffeta stitched with beads. It was very dramatic, and on a less beautiful woman it would have been overwhelming.

"You look marvelous, ma'am," Emily said sincerely. "There won't be a man in the room has eyes for anyone else."

Veronica blushed, the first color in her cheeks Emily had seen all day.

"Thank you, Amelia. Don't flatter me or you'll make me immodest."

"A little confidence doesn't do any harm." Emily picked up the stained gown to take it away. She would have to attend to the stain immediately. Perhaps Joan would help her.

She had just got through the dressing room door and was turning to close it when she heard the bedroom door open and saw Loretta come in. She was wearing dove gray and silver and looked very feminine.

145

"Good gracious!" Her eyebrows rose when she saw Veronica. "Do you really think that's suitable? It is most important you impress the French ambassador favorably, my dear, especially in front of the Danvers."

Veronica drew a deep breath and let it out slowly. Emily could see her hand clench in the folds of her skirt.

"Yes, I think it's perfectly suitable," she said unsteadily. "Mr. Garrard Danver is an admirer of elegant clothes; he does not care for the ordinary."

Loretta's face colored deeply, then the blood drained away. "As you wish." Her voice was tight. "But I don't know why you are so late. You came up in plenty of time. Is your new maid no good?"

"She's perfectly good—in fact she's excellent. I changed my mind about what I was wearing. It wasn't Amelia's fault."

"A pity. You were probably better advised the first time. Still, it's too late now. Is that a tisane cup?"

"Yes."

There was a moment's silence. Then Loretta's voice came quietly, with an edge to it but remaining perfectly controlled. She had moved slightly, so Emily could no longer see her face.

"Veronica, you must not start giving in to nerves. It is a self-indulgence you cannot afford. If you are ill we will call the doctor; otherwise you must exercise a little discipline, put a smile on your face, and come downstairs. You are already close to being late. It won't do!"

There was silence. Emily pulled the door open an inch wider, but dared do no more in case the movement caught Loretta's eye.

"I'm perfectly ready," Veronica said at last.

"No you are not! Being ready is more than having your gown on and your hair done, Veronica." Her voice sank lower and there was an urgency in it. "You must have your mind prepared as well. You are going to marry Julian Danver; don't give anyone cause to doubt your happiness, least

146

of all Julian himself, or his family. Smile; no one likes a sulky or nervous woman—women are expected to add to a man's comfort and pleasure, to be easy company, not a strain! And no one willingly marries a woman whose health is not robust. We hide our petty complaints. Courage and dignity are expected of us—in fact, they are required.''

''Sometimes I hate you,'' Veronica said so softly Emily only just heard her, but with a passion that made her skin crawl.

''And that too,'' Loretta answered with stonelike calm, ''is a self-indulgence you cannot afford, my dear, any more than I can.''

''Perhaps it would be worth it!'' Veronica said between her teeth.

''Oh think again, my dear, think again,'' Loretta answered her softly. Then quite suddenly her voice changed and became rasping, choked with fury. ''Pull yourself together and stop your weak, stupid whining! I can only carry you so far, then you must look after yourself! I have done everything for you that I can, and it has not been as easy for me as you sometimes seem to think.''

There was a rustle of skirts, then the outer door opened and Emily heard an entirely new voice, a man's, intelligent and individual.

''Are you ready, my dear? It's time we went to greet our guests.''

That must be Piers York, the only person in the house Emily had not met. ''Veronica, you look quite ravishing.''

''Thank you, Papa-in-law.'' Veronica's voice shook even with those few words.

''I am quite aware of the time, Piers,'' Loretta said briskly, no trace of her previous emotion remaining; she had transformed it into a slight irritation at being checked up on. ''I was reminding Veronica. She has a new maid, and new maids always take a little longer.''

"Oh, has she?" he said mildly. "Don't think I've seen her."

"No reason why you should," Loretta answered. "You have enough to do without organizing the servants."

Veronica was disposed to argue. "It wasn't Amelia's fault, it was mine. I changed my mind."

"A costly thing to do." There was warning under Loretta's polite comment, and Veronica must know that as much as Emily. Only Piers was seemingly unaware of it.

"Nonsense, my dear. Lady's privilege."

This time Loretta did not argue. Again she changed, her tone becoming courteous and familiar. "Oh, Veronica and I know each other very well. We have shared much grief, so I assure you, my dear, we have no misunderstandings. She knows exactly what I mean. Come, it is past time we were downstairs. Our guests are due, and the Hollingsworths at least are never late. Most tedious."

"I think they're all rather tedious," he said frankly. "I don't know why we keep on having them here. Can't see that it's necessary."

The rest of the evening was miserable. The kitchen was chaotic as the cook superintended the finishing and serving of a dozen different dishes. Mary was frantic with pastries, gravies, sauces and puddings. Redditch was busy in the cellars and the dining room, where John was, and Albert kept rushing back and forth. Nora was primped up and sweeping around with her skirts swishing, her apron so white and full of lace it looked like a breaking sea as she ordered the housemaids around imperiously. Prim was up to her elbows in the sink trying to get a start on the washing up, at least the saucepans, but as soon as she finished one pile another descended on her. Everyone's temper was short, and any supper was to be snatched as the opportunity arose, only cold game pie being available—about the last thing Emily felt like eating.

148

It was not part of her duty, but Emily helped with the clearing up, washing and polishing glasses and putting away extra silver and plates. She could not comfortably go to bed leaving Mary, Prim, and Albert with that monstrous pile, and she needed as many allies as she could earn. Mrs. Crawford was now unalterably an enemy, since the butler had made his regard unfortunately plain. Nora was jealous and kept referring to Emily as "the Duchess," and Edith made no secret of her contempt.

It was quarter to one, the wind whining outside and seeking every crack in the windows and every open door to send daggerlike drafts. Sleet battered against the glass when Emily climbed the last bare flight of the attic stairs and crept into her small, icy room. There was only a candle to light it and the bed was so cold it felt wet to the touch.

She took off her outer clothes and pulled on her nightgown over all her underwear, then turned back the blankets and slid into bed. She was so cold she was shaking and the tears came to her eyes in spite of all her determination. She rolled over, burying her face in the frozen pillow, and cried herself to sleep.

149

6

For once Charlotte managed to contain both her astonishment and her anxiety when she heard from Jack Radley about Emily's extraordinary decision to disguise herself and go to the Yorks in service. Fortunately Jack had called early in the afternoon, so she had had plenty of time to recover her composure by the time Pitt returned home a little after six. Consequently he knew nothing about it and assumed in contented ignorance that Emily was sitting at home, where all Society and Pitt himself expected her to be.

He was deeply distressed over the death of the maid, Dulcie, not only because he had liked her but because he felt guilty. It was unreasonable, and he told himself so. She might very well have fallen out of her window accidentally and the whole matter was merely one of the numerous domestic tragedies that happen every year; but he could not seem to shake the fear that had she not told him about the strange woman in the house and the missing jewels, and had he not been careless enough to listen to her with the library door open, then she would still be alive.

At first he did not mention her death to Ballarat, sure that he would dismiss it as the Yorks' misfortune and no business of Pitt's. And he did not want to run the risk that Ballarat would actually forbid him to look into it.

But as he thought more and more about the woman in cerise, Pitt became convinced he must pursue her identity before he could give any answer to the Foreign Office regarding Veronica York's reputation, and her suitability to marry a rising diplomat, his determination to keep quiet weakened.

When Ballarat sent for him two days later he was caught mentally on the wrong foot.

"Well, Pitt, you don't seem to have accomplished much in the York case," Ballarat began critically. He was standing by the fire, warming the backs of his legs. A malodorous cigar burned in the stone ashtray on his desk. There was a small bronze lion beside it, rampant, one paw in the air.

Pretentious ass! Pitt thought angrily. "I was doing quite well until my principal witness was killed!" he said aloud, and instantly knew he had been unwise.

Ballarat's face darkened, the blood ruddying his cheeks. He rocked backwards and forwards on his feet very slightly, his hands behind his back. He blocked most of the heat from the rest of the room; with wet boots and trouser legs, Pitt would have welcomed the warmth.

"Witness to what, for heaven's sake?" Ballarat demanded irritably. "Are you trying to tell me you've uncovered some scandal about the Yorks after all, and the man who might have betrayed them has died?"

"No I'm not!" Pitt retorted. "I'm talking about murder. It's none of the police's business if they all had lovers; that's their own affair. But Robert York's death was murder, and that was our responsibility to clear up, and we haven't yet."

"For heaven's sake, man!" Ballarat interrupted him. "That was three years ago, and we did our best. Some thief broke in and poor York caught him in the act. The wretch will have disappeared into the slums he came from. He might even be dead himself by now. Your trouble is you're not man enough to admit failure even when it's obvious to everyone else." He glared at Pitt, daring him to argue.

Pitt rose to the bait. "And if it was an inside job?" he said rashly. "A friend turned amateur thief, or someone in the house who was in debt and stealing. It wouldn't be the first time. Or what if Veronica York had a lover, and it was he who murdered her husband? Do you want to know about that, or, assuming it was Julian Danver, would the Foreign Office rather we covered it up?"

A series of expressions chased over Ballarat's face, first sheer horror, then anger and confusion, then fear, as he understood the full implications of the last possibility. He would be caught between two masters; the Foreign Office, who had ordered the inquiry, and the Home Office, who were in charge of the police and justice. Either one could easily ruin his career. He was furious with Pitt as the instigator of such a dilemma.

Pitt saw this as quickly as Ballarat and took a distinct and deep satisfaction from it, even as he realized that Ballarat would make him the butt of his otherwise impotent anger.

"Damn you, Pitt! You incompetent, interfering . . ." He searched for an adequate word, and failing to find it, began again. "You idiot! That's a—a totally irresponsible suggestion, and the Yorks, not to mention the Danvers, will sue you for slander if you whisper one word of it to anyone!"

"Shall we decline the case?" Pitt asked sarcastically.

"Don't be insolent!" Ballarat shouted. Then his duty towards the Home Office, who were, after all, his employers, reasserted itself. Ballarat controlled his temper with an effort. "What conceivable grounds have you for making such an appalling suggestion?"

This time Pitt was less prepared, and Ballarat saw the second of hesitation with victory in his eyes. His body relaxed slightly, becoming more jaunty, and he resumed rocking on the soles of his feet. Still he blocked the fire, glancing down at Pitt's wet legs with satisfaction.

Pitt tried to organize his thoughts. His reply must be unassailable. "No fence in London has handled or seen any of the goods," he began. "No thief in the area has heard of them or knows of any strangers working the patch, no one has seen anyone hiding up or running from a murder." He saw Ballarat's face hover between belief and disbelief. He was a climber, a currier of favor, and it was a long time since he had been personally involved in the investigation of a crime. But he was neither ignorant nor stupid, and although he profoundly disliked Pitt, deploring his manners and his social judgments, he respected his professional skill.

"The thief knew where to find a first edition among the other books in the library and yet has apparently not disposed of it, and he left all the silver in the dining room," Pitt went on. "I've started looking in their social circle for anyone with debts." He noticed Ballarat's alarm with satisfaction. "Discreetly. And I've got someone inquiring into York's own affairs," he added spitefully. "But the curious circumstance I was investigating was the appearance in the small hours of the morning of a glamorous and furtive woman in a cerise gown—twice at least in the York house, prior to Robert York's death, and also in the Danver house, again in the small hours of the morning, and again wearing a startling shade of cerise and apparently not wishing to be seen. The maid who described her at the Yorks fell out of a window to her death the day after she spoke to me."

Ballarat stopped rocking and remained motionless, his round little eyes on Pitt's face. "Veronica York?" he said slowly. "Wouldn't this maid have recognized her?"

"I would have thought so," Pitt agreed. "She was the lady's maid. But people see what they expect to see, and it was only for a moment in the gaslight, and the woman was dressed entirely differently. From the slight description it

153

could have easily been Veronica; same height and build, same coloring."

"Damnation!" Ballarat swore furiously. "I suppose it couldn't have been Robert York's mistress, and Mrs. York knew nothing about her?"

"Possibly. But what was she doing in the Danver house?"

"Obvious—Danver's sister!"

"She's a loose woman?" Pitt raised his eyebrows. "Who goes in for married diplomats, first Robert York, now Felix Asherson?"

Ballarat scowled. "What about Felix Asherson? What has he to do with it?"

Pitt sighed. "Harriet Danver is in love with him. Don't ask me how I know; I do. And I think it's pretty unlikely she was the woman in cerise, but if she was, then the Foreign Office should know."

"Damn it, Pitt! It could be this woman in cerise is just some daft relative who likes to dress up and creep about. Lots of families have their embarrassments; a damn nuisance, but no actual harm."

"Of course," Pitt agreed. "She may be just gently mad. Or she may be an expensive harlot who entertained Robert York, or conceivably his father"—he saw Ballarat's face darken but he did not stop—"or Julian Danver, or Garrard Danver. And maybe Dulcie Mabbutt fell out of the window in a curiously timed domestic accident." He held Ballarat's eyes. "Or maybe the woman in cerise was a procurer or carrier of treason, a blackmailer or a lover, and she was working on Robert York before she either murdered him herself, or some of her colleagues did."

"Good God—are you saying young Danver was her master?" Ballarat exploded.

"No." For once Pitt could deny it honestly. "I don't see why he should need to be. Isn't he in the Foreign Office as well?"

"Another traitor?" Ballarat's jaw set. His cigar was crumbling away to little rings of ash unnoticed.

"Maybe?"

"All right! All right!" Ballarat's voice rose. "Find out who she was! The security of the empire may be involved. But if you want to keep your job, Pitt, be discreet. If you're clumsy I can't and won't protect you. Do you understand me clearly?"

"Yes, thank you, sir," Pitt said with open sarcasm. It was the first time he had called Ballarat sir in years; he had always managed to evade it without being downright rude.

"My pleasure, Pitt," Ballarat replied, showing his teeth. "My pleasure!"

Pitt left the Bow Street station and stepped out into a pea soup fog feeling savage and determined. There was always Charlotte, and he would certainly rely upon her judgment as much as possible. He had to admit now that he was glad she had been able to connive an invitation to the Yorks' and the Danvers'. At least she might give him an informed opinion of Veronica York's character, and whether she had been devastated by her husband's death or freed by it to marry Julian Danver. If the latter were true, then the woman had remarkable control to have waited a full three years and behaved throughout with such apparent decorum. Or had Julian insisted upon that, in order to keep his career? All the same, it was remarkable if there had been no indiscretion, no self-indulgence in all that time. Especially if Veronica had been the woman who dressed dramatically in cerise for her assignations.

Or perhaps she still did, and that had made waiting bearable for her.

The fog in the Strand was so thick he could not see across to the opposite pavement. It hung, thick and yellow-gray, full of the fumes from thousands of smoking chimneys, as the filth suspended in the dampness rose up from the wide coils of the river that laced through the suburbs, past Chelsea, the Houses of Parliament, the Embankment, Wapping, and Limehouse, down to the Pool of London, Greenwich, and the Arsenal, and finally the estuary.

If Cerise, whoever she was, had dressed as glamorously as Dulcie said, then she had not done it merely to flit around landings in the middle of the night. She had gone out somewhere in public. It was a disguise, an alter ego for some woman who would be known in Society; or else she was a courtesan with whom neither the Yorks nor the Danvers would be seen by their own friends. So where would she have been able to meet her lovers?

He stood on the curb as carriages, hansoms, and carts clopped by him slowly in the yellow mist, looming suddenly and disappearing, swallowed up, the horses only dark shapes and muffled sounds. The road was slimy and more spattered with dung than usual. This was the sort of weather when crossing sweepers got knocked over, sometimes even killed. There was a one-legged sweeper in Piccadilly who had lost his limb that way.

Pitt knew there were hotels, restaurants, and theaters where such assignations could be kept, places where if a gentleman saw an acquaintance both men would have enough tact to overlook the meeting, neither wishing it referred to. These places were dotted round the borders of fashionable London, in the Haymarket, Leicester Square, Piccadilly. He knew where to find them and the touts and doormen to ask.

"Cabbie!" he shouted into the street, catching his breath as the fog threatened to choke him, making him cough. "Cabbie!"

A hansom slowed up and stopped, harness dripping, horse's head down, driver's voice disembodied in the gloom.

"Haymarket," Pitt requested, and climbed in.

It was the following day, the fog still clamped heavily over the city, acrid in the throat, sharp to the nose, before he found his first success. He was in a private hotel a little off Jermyn Street near Piccadilly. The doorman was a richly mustached ex-soldier, with liberal ideas on morality and an injury from the Second Ashanti War which prevented him from doing any physical labor. He was also illiterate, which precluded any clerical work. He was quite amenable to answering Pitt's questions, for a consideration. Ballarat had been very little help with information or influence, but he had given Pitt as much financial license as he could.

"You're goin' back a bit, guv," the doorman said cheerfully. "But sure I remember 'er. Right 'andsome she was, an' always wore them sort o' colors. Looks wicked on most people, but suited 'er summink marvelous. Black 'air and dark eyes she 'ad, an' graceful as a swan. Tall woman, not a lot o' shape to 'er, but she 'ad summink special all the same."

"What sort of something?" Pitt said curiously. He wanted to know what this man thought, his judgment; even with his limited vocabulary, his opinion would be worth a great deal. He knew street women, he watched them every night, and he saw their clients too. He would see them working and yet not be part of it. Few of them would fool him.

The man pulled a slight face as he considered. "Quality," he said at last. "She 'ad a quality about 'er; never acted like she was 'ustling people, anxious like; it was always them as was after 'er; she didn't give a cuss." He shook his head. "It were more'n that, though. It were—it were like she were doin' it fer fun. Yeah, that's it—she 'ad fun! She never laughed, not out loud, she 'ad too much class for that. But she were laughing inside, like."

"Did you ever talk to her?" Pitt pursued.

"Me?" He looked a little surprised. "No, I never did. She didn't say a lot, and always spoke quiet like. Only saw 'er, oh, maybe 'alf a dozen times."

"Can you remember who she was with?"

"Different blokes. Elegant—she liked 'em real elegant,

didn't like any scruff. And money o' course, but then so do they all. No one without a bit o' real money comes 'ere.'' He gave a short laugh.

"Can you describe any of them?''

"Not so's you'd know 'em again, no.'' He smiled.

"Try a little,'' Pitt pressed him.

"You couldn't pay me that much, guv. You goin' ter give me another job when they throw me out of 'ere an' black me name?''

Pitt sighed. He had known before he started that describing the woman was very different from being indiscreet about her clients. Clients had money, position, they expected privacy and no doubt bought it for a generous price. Selling the secrets of one would lose the trust of all. "All right,'' he conceded. "Be general. Old or young, dark, fair or gray, what sort of height and build?''

"Yer goin' ter search all London, guv?''

"I can eliminate a few.''

The doorman shrugged. "If yer like. Well, those as I can recall was older, above forty. Don't think she took 'em fer the money; dunno why, but I 'ad the feelin' she could afford ter pick and choose.''

"Gray?''

"None I recalls. An' none 'efty—all on the slim side.'' He moved closer to Pitt. "Look, guv, for all I know it could 'ave bin the same gent. It don't pay me ter peer into their faces! They comes 'ere discreet—that's what they pays for! Like I said, she could afford ter pick. I always 'ad the feelin' she was doin' it fer fun.''

"Did she always wear that color?''

"Shades of it, yeah; it was like—'er trademark. Why you so keen ter know about 'er anyway? She ain't bin 'ere in, oh, two or three years.''

"Which? Two, or three?''

"Well if yer want it that precise, guv, three, I reckon.''

"And you've not seen or heard of her since then?''

"Come ter think of it, no I 'aven't." His faced relaxed into a grin. "Maybe she married well. Sometimes they do. Maybe she's a duchess sitting in some grand 'ouse by now, ordering around the likes o' you an' me."

Pitt pulled a face. The chance was slight at best, and they both knew it; it was far more likely she had lost her looks by disease, or assault, in a fight with another prostitute or a pimp who felt he had been cheated, a lover whose demands had become too perverted or possessive; or that she had simply moved downmarket from a hotel such as this to a simple brothel. He did not mention the possibility of treason or murder; that would complicate the question unnecessarily.

The doorman looked at him closely. "Why you after 'er, guv? She puttin' the black on someone?"

"It's a possibility," Pitt conceded. "It's a definite possibility." He took out one of his new cards and gave it to the man. "If you see her again, tell me. Bow Street Police Station. Just say you've seen Cerise again."

"That 'er name? What's it worth?"

"It'll do. And it's worth my goodwill—which, believe me, is a lot better than my ill will."

"You wouldn't pick on me, just 'cause I ain't seen someone! I can't see 'er if she in't 'ere! An' you wouldn't want lies, now, would yer?"

Pitt did not bother to answer. "What theaters and music halls do your clients patronize?"

"Geez!"

Pitt waited.

The man bit his lip. "Well, if ye're after 'er yer call Cerise, I 'eard she bin ter the Lyceum, an' I suppose she tried the 'alls, although don't ask me which ones 'cause I dunno."

Pitt's eyebrows rose. "The Lyceum? A lady of courage to ply her trade there."

"I told yer, she 'ad class."

"Yes you did. Thank you."

The man tipped his hat a little sarcastically. "Thank you, guv!"

Pitt left him and went out into the street again. The fog wrapped round him again like a cold muslin, damp and clinging to the skin.

So Cerise had both courage and style. She was certainly not Veronica York on a mere affair with Julian Danver! If it was Veronica, then she led a secret life of the sort to scandalize the Foreign Office to the core of its collective soul. For a diplomat to have a wife who was a practicing prostitute, of whatever price or degree of discrimination, was impossible. He would be dismissed instantly, and ruined.

Neither was she Harriet Danver pursuing her affair with Felix Asherson, although he had never actually thought that. Charlotte had said Harriet was in love; as yet he had no knowledge of whether Asherson returned her feelings. But either way, that answer offered no explanation as to why Cerise should be in the York house.

No, it seemed she was what he had first thought, a woman who used her beauty and unusual quality of allure to trap and then blackmail her Foreign Office lovers for the secrets of their work. Robert York had refused, either immediately or after some time, and as a result either she herself or perhaps her accomplices had had to murder him to avoid betrayal.

It was getting dark and the fog was beginning to freeze, the air filling with tiny pellets of ice, which sent shivers through him as they crept into the folds of his muffler and touched his skin. He began to walk briskly north into Regent Street, then turned left towards Oxford Circus. There were other people he could ask: upmarket prostitutes who would know the competition and be able to tell him more about Cerise, where she plied her trade, what clients she chose, whether she only picked men who were of use to her, and whether she was a real threat to the others by taking general business.

An hour later, after some persuasive argument and the

exchange of more money, he sat in an overheated, overfurnished little room off New Bond Street. The woman in the pink chair opposite him was well past her prime, her bosom overflowing from the strict corsets and loose flesh visible under her chin had lost its elasticity, but she was still handsomer than most women ever are. There was an ease about her, from years of being desired, but the bright bitterness in her eyes reflected the underlying knowledge that she had not been loved. She picked at some candied fruit in a pink tissue-lined box. "Well?" she said guardedly. "What do you want, luv? It isn't my style to tell tales."

"I don't want tales." Pitt did not waste his time or insult her with flattery they both knew he did not mean. "I want a woman who almost certainly tried putting on the black. That's bad for your trade; you don't need that sort."

She pulled a face and ate another piece of fruit, nibbling all round the edges before putting the center whole into her mouth. Had her walk of life been different, led to different dress, less paint on her skin, the hardness of survival out of her eyes and the small lines now clearly formed round the corners of her lips, she might have been one of her generation's great beauties. The thought passed through Pitt's mind with irony and sadness as he watched her eat.

"Go on," she prompted. "I don't need telling my business. If I wasn't the best you wouldn't be 'ere asking me favors. I don't need your money. I earn more in a day than you do in a month."

Pitt did not bother to remark that her risks were higher and her time short. She knew it.

"A woman who always wore a shade of cerise, dark or light, anything from plum to magenta, always something that color. She was tall and slender, not much flesh on her, but loads of style, dark eyes and black hair. Have you ever seen her, or heard your girls mention her?"

"Doesn't sound like she'd 'ave much to offer. Thin, black 'air?"

"Oh, she had something," Pitt said with certainty, and in spite of himself Veronica York's face with its high cheekbones and haunting eyes came back to his mind. Could she have been Cerise, and have killed Robert when he discovered that? He looked at the lush, feminine woman in the pink chair opposite him, with her glowing, almost Titian hair and her apple-blossom skin. "She had fire, and style," he finished.

The woman's eyes opened wide. "Know 'er well, did yer?"

Pitt smiled. "I never met her. I'm going on the impression she made on others."

She gave a little laugh, part derision and part genuine humor. "Well, if she put the black on people she was a fool! That's a sure way ter kill business. In the long run it's suicide. I don't know anything about 'er. Sorry luv."

Pitt did not know if he was pleased or disappointed. He had to find Cerise, and yet he did not want her to be Veronica York.

"Are you sure?" he said automatically. "It may be three years back."

"Three years! Well, why didn't yer say so?" She reached for another piece of fruit and bit into it. She had beautiful teeth, white and even. "I thought yer meant now! There was one like that about three or four years ago. Terrible color she wore, but she could carry it. Black 'air an' eyes, thin as a washboard, need pounds of 'orse 'air to pad 'er out. But she 'ad fire, the sort that comes from inside; yer can't get it out of a pot or in a glass. All the champagne in London wouldn't give it yer. Lit up like she enjoyed 'erself every minute, like she was 'avin' the time of 'er life, on the edge o' danger and loved it. Mind, she were a real beauty, none o' yer powder an' paint jobs. Bones to break yer 'eart, she 'ad."

Pitt felt suddenly suffocated in this overstuffed room, and at the same time there was a coldness inside him. "Tell me more about her," he said quietly. "How often did you see or hear of her; where, who with, and have you any idea what happened to her?''

The woman hesitated, her eyes wary.

"I'll be very unpleasant if I have to," Pitt said levelly. "It's murder. I'll turn over this entire place and make such a fuss none of your clients will dare come back."

"All right!" she snapped angrily. But there was no outrage in her; that required the element of surprise, and she had known the dangers too long and felt them too often for that. "All right! I an't seen or 'eard of 'er in three years, an' only a few times before that. She weren't reg'lar. In fact, for what it's worth it's my opinion she weren't professional anyway; that's why I never took no trouble to find out more about 'er. She weren't no rival. She didn't take gen'ral trade; just paraded around, showed off, and picked up one or two. All in all she were good fer us, 'cause she drew attention, stirred up appetites, and then left. More for us."

"Did you see her with anyone you can remember? It's important."

She considered for several minutes and Pitt did not hurry her.

"Seen 'er once with a real elegant gent, good-looker. One of the other girls said she'd seen 'er with 'im before, because she'd tried to pick 'im up 'erself, but 'e 'ad eyes for Cerise and no one else."

"Did you ever learn her name?"

"No."

"Anything about her?"

"No, 'cept what I told yer."

"All right, you know the world, and the business. What's your best guess? What sort of woman was she, and what happened to her?"

The woman laughed abruptly, then the bitterness softened into pity, for herself and all those who shared her lot, even peripherally. "I dunno," she said. "Could be dead, for all I know, or more like come down in the world. Life in this

163

business can be short. 'Ow the hell do I know what 'appened to 'er, poor bitch?''

"She was different, you said that; so did the others who saw her. What's your best guess as to where she came from? Come on, Alice, I need to know, and you've the best chance of being right.''

She sighed. "My guess is she was Quality out slumming it, God knows why. Maybe she was just bent that way. Some is. Although why any woman that's got a roof over 'er 'ead and food for the rest of 'er life should want ter risk it is beyond me. Still, I reckon insanity can 'it the Quality like the rest of us. Now that's all, I in't got nothing else to add to it. You 'ad your time; I got things to do. I bin more'n fair—an I 'ope you'll remember that.''

Pitt stood up. "I will,'' he promised. "As far as I know, you keep a lodging house. Good day.''

He spent two more days going from one place to another in the haunts of the demimonde, the theaters and restaurants where such women plied their trade, and he heard occasional mention of Cerise or someone who might have been her or might not, but he learned nothing that added to what he already knew. No one remembered who she had been with, whether it was several men or only a few, although it was certainly more than one in every account. No one knew her name nor where she came from. She was tolerated because she came very seldom and robbed them of little business. It was a hard world and they expected competition. If a man preferred one woman to another there was nothing to be done about it except in extreme cases; usually it was better to take defeat gracefully. Scenes embarrassed the clientele.

Whether any of the men with her had been Robert York it was impossible to say. She frequented places where he was likely to have been, but then so had half London Society, at least among the men. The descriptions of her companions were general enough to have fit him, or Julian Danver, or

164

Garrard Danver, or even Felix Asherson—or just about anyone else with elegance and money.

In the early evening of the second day, a little after six, as the fog cleared at last, leaving only a few dark pockets, Pitt took a cab to Hanover Close, this time not to the York house but further along, to where Felix Asherson lived. Pitt had chosen to see him at home in order to form a more complete impression of the man, to make some judgment as to his circumstances and possibly his character. Away from the formal and rather intimidating atmosphere of the Foreign Office he might be more inclined to relax his caution. In his own home he would feel safer and could be certain none of his colleagues would interrupt, perhaps suspecting him of indiscreet disclosures to the police. Also, inside the house Pitt might form a more precise picture of his financial situation. There was still the possibility that Robert York had surprised a friend burgling his house and his recognition had sparked a murder. Pitt had not forgotten that possibility.

He knocked on the front door and waited till a footman came.

"Yes, sir?" There was no expression in the polite inquiry.

Pitt produced one of his cards.

"Thomas Pitt. I have a matter of some importance to discuss with Mr. Asherson, if he is free. It concerns one of his colleagues at the Foreign Office." That was literally true, if not true in its implication.

"Yes, sir. Will you come in, sir, and I will inform Mr. Asherson you are here." He looked at Pitt dubiously. His boots were not Emily's new ones; those were too good for all the walking he had been doing lately, and he did not want to wear them out. His jacket was serviceable but no more; only his hat was of quality. He was not library material; the morning room was good enough for him. "If you will come this way, sir?"

The fire had died to a few embers but the room was still warm, at least compared with the cab Pitt had just taken. He found the room pleasant enough, modest compared with the Yorks', but agreeably furnished, and with at least one good picture on the wall. If Asherson were short of money he could have sold it for enough to keep a housemaid for several years. So much for debt.

The door opened and Asherson came in, his dark brows drawn together in a frown. It was a handsome face, but too volatile. There was something uncertain about it. Pitt would not want to rely on this man in a crisis.

"Good evening, Mr. Asherson," he said pleasantly. "Sorry to disturb you at home, but the matter is delicate, so I thought it would be more private here than at the Foreign Office."

"Oh damn!" Asherson pushed the door closed behind him. "Are you still ferreting around after poor old York's killer? I told you before I didn't know anything remotely useful. I still don't."

"I'm sure you aren't aware of knowing anything," Pitt agreed.

"And what do you mean by that?" Asherson was plainly annoyed. "I wasn't there that night, and nobody's told me anything."

"I know a great deal more than when I first spoke to you, sir," Pitt said, watching Asherson's face. The gas lamps threw shadows in the room, exaggerating his expression as a yellow gleam highlighted the planes of his cheeks and nose and created darkness where sunlight would have eliminated it. "There was a woman who seems to have had a role in it."

Asherson's eyes widened. "In York's death? You don't mean it was a woman burglar? I didn't know there were such things." There was nothing but surprise in his face.

"The burglary may be incidental, Mr. Asherson. Possibly even the murder was too. Perhaps the only thing that really mattered was the treason."

Asherson stood absolutely motionless; not a muscle moved

166

in his face or his body. It was an unnatural stillness, a silence that hung too long. Pitt could hear the hiss of the gas in the lamps on the wall and a slight sound as the coals settled in the hearth.

"Treason?" Asherson said at last.

Pitt did not know how far he dared stretch the truth. He decided to evade an answer. "What was Robert York working on before he was killed?" he asked.

Again Asherson hesitated. If he said he did not know, Pitt would have to believe him.

"Africa," he answered finally. "The, er . . ." He bit his lower lip gently. "The partition of Africa between Germany and Britain. Or perhaps it would be more fortunate to phrase it as the division of spheres of influence."

Pitt smiled. "I take the point. Is it confidential? Secret?"

"Very!" There was a shadow of humor in his alarm, perhaps at Pitt's ignorance. "Good God, if all the terms of a treaty we'd accept were known to the Germans in advance, it would ruin our bargaining position, but far, far worse than that would be the impression it would make on the rest of the world, particularly France. If the French were to make our deliberations public, the rest of Europe would prevent us from making the agreement at all."

"Three years ago," Pitt reaffirmed, watching his face.

"Oh yes, it's not a hasty negotiation; it's not all over in a few months, you know."

There had been hesitation in his face, a shadow of doubt— or cunning? There was a lie in it somewhere, a deceit by implication if not in actual words.

Pitt took a guess, but he made it a statement rather than a question, as if he already knew. "And some of this information has leaked through. Your negotiations have not been without difficulty."

"Yes," Asherson said slowly. "Only odd pieces—they could even be educated guesses. They're not fools."

Pitt knew what Asherson was doing: he was building escape routes—but for whom? Robert York was dead. Was Asherson using him as a decoy for someone who was still alive? Himself? Cerise? Veronica? One of the Danvers?

"When was the last instance in which this information might have been stolen and passed to the Germans?" Pitt asked. "I presume we can be certain it was not given to the French?"

"Oh . . ." Asherson was confused. "Yes, it certainly wasn't given to the French, but the Germans, I don't know. It isn't possible to say. Information like that may not be used for some time after it is received."

That was true, but Pitt believed it was also an evasion. Was Asherson just naturally reluctant to trust anyone outside his own office, or was he still protecting someone?

Pitt tried approaching it from another direction. "It hasn't seriously impeded your negotiations?"

"No," Asherson agreed quickly. "As I said, it could even be the natural ability of the Germans. It isn't the French, that is certain."

"Then it's hardly worth murdering over."

"What?"

"Not worth murdering to hide," Pitt repeated carefully.

Asherson said nothing. His lips tightened and he stared back across the lamplit room. Pitt waited.

"No," Asherson said at last. "I think you must be mistaken. It was a burglary that went wrong."

Pitt shook his head. "No, Mr. Asherson, that is one thing it was not. If it wasn't treason then it was murder, personal and intentional, by someone who knew Robert York."

Again Asherson waited, then his face eased. Pitt could spot the exact moment the idea came to him. "You mean York was robbed by someone he knew, some acquaintance who had been to the house and knew where to look for valuables?"

"No. All they took amounted to barely a hundred pounds

168

at best, less by the time it would have been fenced—which it wasn't.''

"Fenced?"

"Resold to a receiver of stolen goods."

"Wasn't it?" he said carefully. "Can you know that?"

"Yes, Mr. Asherson."

"Oh." Asherson looked down at the floor, his face heavy with concentration. The gaslight caught the curious gray of his eyes and the black lashes.

Again Pitt stood motionless, allowing the silence to settle. Somewhere out in the hall a servant's feet made a brisk sound on the parquet floor; the sound died away again along the passage as a door thudded.

At last Asherson reached his decision. He faced Pitt.

"Other information has gone missing," he said very quietly. "More important information. But none of it has ever been acted on by our enemies, as far as we can tell. God knows why not."

Pitt was not surprised, but it gave him no satisfaction. He had still hoped he was wrong, that some other explanation would present itself. Was this the whole truth yet, or only part of it? He looked at Asherson's grim, unhappy expression and believed at least this much was honest, as far as it went.

"And would you know?" he asked.

"Yes." This time Asherson did not hesitate. "Yes. Papers that have been temporarily missing, a copy replaced instead of the original. Don't ask me for anything more; I can't tell you."

"No doubt they'll use it when they're ready," Pitt said, flatly. "Perhaps if they used it now you'd know their source, and they're protecting him as long as he's useful."

Asherson sank down onto the arm of one of the chairs, sitting awkwardly. "This is awful. I had hoped it was simply Robert's carelessness, but if he really was murdered over it, then that doesn't seem reasonable. God, what a tragedy!"

"And none of it has gone since his death?"

169

Asherson shook his head.

"Have you seen a beautiful woman, tall and slim with dark hair, wearing an unusual shade of cerise?"

Asherson looked at him incredulously. "What?"

"A sort of hot bluish pink, like magenta or cyclamen."

"I know what color cerise is, you fool!" He shut his eyes suddenly. "Damn it! I'm sorry. No, I haven't seen her. What the hell does that have to do with it?"

"It seems likely it was this woman who lured York into betrayal of his country," Pitt replied. "He may have been having an affair with her."

Asherson looked surprised. "Robert? I never saw him take the slightest notice of any woman but Veronica. He—he just wasn't a womanizer. He was very discriminating, a quiet sort of man with excellent taste. And Veronica adored him."

"It seems he was two men," Pitt said sadly. He would not tell Asherson that it could have been Veronica herself in cerise. If Asherson had not thought of it, it would not help. And just in case Asherson himself were the traitor, no need to warn him of Pitt's closeness.

"Well, he's dead now." Asherson stood up. "Let the poor devil rest in peace. You won't find your mysterious woman in Hanover Close. I'm sorry I can't help."

"You have helped, Mr. Asherson." Pitt said smiling bleakly. "Thank you for your frankness, sir. Good evening."

Asherson did not reply, but stepped back so Pitt could pass him and go out of the door. In the hall a footman appeared from the shadows and showed him to the step and the dark street beyond.

Outside in the Close the last fog had blown away in the north wind, bitter as the Pole, and the stars were glittering in a sky barely marred by an occasional smear of smoke. Ice crackled underfoot in the frozen puddles and gutters. Pitt stepped out briskly; in a tidier man it could almost have been called a march.

He climbed the immaculate porch steps of number two and pulled the brass bell. When the footman opened the door he knew precisely what he was going to say, and to whom.

"Good evening. May I see Mr. York please? I require his permission to speak to his staff about one of them who may have had knowledge of a crime. It is most urgent."

"Er, yes sir. I 'spect you may." The youth looked taken aback. "You'd better come in. Library fire's lit, sir; you can wait in there."

It was a few minutes until Piers York came in, his benign, slightly quizzical face marked with an unusual frown. "What is it this time, Pitt? Not the damn silver again, surely?"

"No sir." He stopped, hoping York would not press the point. But he stood staring at Pitt, his eyebrows raised, his eyes small and gray and intelligent. There was no avoiding an answer.

"Treason and murder, sir."

"Balderdash!" York said smartly. "I doubt the servants even know what treason is, and they never leave this house except on their half days off, which are only twice a month." His eyebrows rose even higher. "Or are you suggesting this treason took place here?"

Pitt knew he was on very dangerous ground. All Ballarat's warnings jangled in his ears.

"No sir, I think an agent of treason may have visited your house, unknown to you. Your maid Dulcie Mabbutt saw her; others may have."

"Saw *her*?" York's eyebrows shot up. "Good God! You mean a woman? Well, Dulcie can't help you, poor child. She fell out of one of the upstairs windows and died. I'm sorry." His face was pinched and sad. Pitt found it impossible to believe he was not genuinely grieved. Probably he knew nothing about any of it—Cerise, or Robert's or Dulcie's death. He was a banker; he alone of the men in the case had nothing to do with the Foreign Office, and Pitt could not imagine a spy wasting her energies on this wry, rather charming man

171

well into his sixties. And he had too much innate humor to harbor the vanity necessary to be so ridiculous.

"I know Dulcie is dead," Pitt agreed. "But she may have confided to the other maids. Women do talk to each other."

"Where and when did Dulcie see this woman of yours?"

"Upstairs on the landing," Pitt replied. "In the middle of the night."

"Good heavens! What on earth was Dulcie doing out of her own room in the middle of the night? Are you sure she wasn't dreaming?"

"This woman's been seen elsewhere, sir, and Dulcie's description was very good."

"Well, go on, man!"

"Tall and slender, with dark hair, very beautiful, and wearing a gown of a startling shade of fuchsia or cerise."

"Well, I certainly haven't seen her."

"May I speak to some of your girls who might have been friendly with Dulcie, and then perhaps to the younger Mrs. York? I believe Dulcie was her maid."

"I suppose so—if it's necessary."

"Thank you, sir."

He spoke to the upstairs maid, the downstairs maid, the laundry maid, the other lady's maid, the kitchen maid, the scullery maid, and finally the tweeny, but it seemed Dulcie had been remarkably discreet and had kept total confidence on all that she saw of her mistress's household. He wished she had been less honorable, and yet there was a kind of bitter satisfaction in it. Virtue of any sort kept its sweetness whatever surrounded it. He saved the questions about Dulcie's death for Veronica. If she was innocent it was cruel, but he could not afford kindness now.

Her mother-in-law was out, the first stroke of good fortune Pitt had had in some time, and Veronica received him in the boudoir.

"I don't know how I can help you, Mr. Pitt," she said

172

gravely. She was dressed in deep forest green, which heightened her slightly ethereal quality. She was pale, her eyes shadowed as if she had slept badly, and she remained standing some distance from him, not facing him but staring at a gold-framed seascape on the wall. "I see no purpose in going over and over the tragedies of the past. Nothing will bring my husband back, and we don't care about the silver or the book. We would much prefer not to be constantly reminded of it."

He hated what he was doing, but he knew of no other way. If he had pressed harder and been cleverer, if he had solved it the first time, Dulcie would still be alive.

"I'm here about Dulcie Mabbutt, Mrs. York."

She turned quickly. "Dulcie?"

"Yes. While she was in this house she saw something of great importance. How did she die, Mrs. York?"

Her gaze did not waver, and she was so pale anyway he could detect no change in her aside from the distress he would have seen in almost anyone. "She leaned too far out of a window and lost her balance," she replied.

"Did you see it happen?"

"No—it was in the evening, after dark. Perhaps in the daylight—perhaps she would have seen what she was doing and it would not have happened."

"Why should she lean so far out of a window?"

"I don't know! Maybe she saw something, someone."

"In the dark?"

She bit her lip. "Perhaps she dropped something."

Pitt did not pursue it; the unlikeliness was obvious enough. "Who was in the house that evening, Mrs. York?"

"All the servants, of course; my parents-in-law, and dinner guests—perhaps Dulcie was talking to one of the footmen or coachmen of the guests."

"Then they would have raised the alarm when she fell."

"Oh." She turned away, blushing at her foolishness. "Of course."

173

"Who were your guests?" He knew the answer before she spoke.

"Mr. and Mrs. Asherson, Mr. Garrard Danver and Mr. Julian Danver and the Misses Danver, Sir Reginald and Lady Arbuthnott, and Mr. and Mrs. Gerald Adair."

"Did any of the other ladies or you yourself wear a gown of a brilliant cerise or magenta color, ma'am?"

"What?" Her voice was barely a whisper, and this time her face was so ashen the skin looked like wax.

"A brilliant cerise or magenta," he repeated. "It is a bluish pink, the sort of color cinerarias grow."

She gulped and her lips formed the word *no*, but no sound came from her throat.

"Dulcie saw a woman in such a dress, Mrs. York, upstairs in this house—" Before he could finish she gasped and pitched forward onto the floor, hands out to save herself, knocking into the chair as she went.

He dived forward too late to catch her, and half falling over the chair himself, knelt down beside her. She was completely unconscious, her face ivory in the gaslight. He uncrumpled her limbs and picked her up. It was awkward, because she was a deadweight, but she was so slender there was hardly any substance to her. He laid her on the sofa, arranged her skirts to cover all but her feet, then rang the bell, almost yanking the cord from the wall.

As soon as the footman appeared Pitt ordered him to get the lady's maid with some smelling salts. His voice sounded rough, even frightened. He must steady himself. There was a violence of emotion inside him; he feared he had been too clumsy and had provoked the very scandal Ballarat would pay any price to avoid, anger at the loss of life, pity for it, a sense of betrayal because he had not wanted it to be Veronica. But surely the gay and daring Cerise would not have crumpled into a faint at the first suspicion of the law.

The door opened and the lady's maid came in, a pretty, slight creature with fair hair and—

"God Almighty!" The breath hissed out between his teeth and Pitt felt the room lurch a little round him also. "Emily!"

"Oh!" Her hand flew to her mouth and she dropped the bottle of salts. "Thomas."

"All right!" For a moment there was a silence of utter incredulity. Then his fury broke. "Explain yourself!" he ground out between his teeth.

"Don't be foolish!" she whispered. "Keep your voice down! What happened to Veronica?" She knelt down, picked up the salts, and unstoppered them, waving them gently under Veronica's nose.

"She fainted, of course!" Pitt snapped back. "I asked her about Cerise. Emily, you've got to get out of here. You must be mad! Dulcie was murdered, and you could be next!"

"I know she was—and I'm not leaving." Her face was determined as she stared at him defiantly.

"You are!" He grasped her arm.

She snatched it away. "No, I'm not! Veronica isn't Cerise. I know her far better than you do!"

"Emily—" But it was too late; Veronica was beginning to stir. Her eyes opened, dark with horror. Then, as memory came back and she recognized Pitt and Emily, the mask returned.

"I beg your pardon, Mr. Pitt," she said very slowly. "I'm afraid I am not very well. I—I haven't seen the person you spoke of. I cannot help."

"Then I'll not disturb you any further. I'll leave you with your—maid." Pitt forced himself to be civil, even gentle. "I apologize for having disturbed you."

Emily rang the bell for the footman, and when he came she gave him his instructions. "John, please show Mr. Pitt to the front door, and then ask Mary to bring Mrs. York a tisane."

Pitt glared at her and she looked back with her chin high.

"Thank you," he said, and followed the footman out.

He took a hansom home and strode up his own hallway to the kitchen.

"Charlotte! Charlotte!"

She turned round with innocent surprise at the rage in his voice, then saw his face.

"You knew!" he said furiously. "You knew Emily was in that house as a maid! God Almighty, have you no wits at all, woman?"

It was the wrong approach and he knew it even as he shouted at her, but he was too angry to control himself.

For a moment she glared back at him, then she changed her mind and lowered her eyes meekly. "I'm sorry, Thomas. I didn't know until it was too late, I swear, and then there was no point in telling you. You couldn't have done anything about it." She looked up with a very small smile. "And she will learn things there that we can't."

He gave up, swearing long and savagely under his breath before he ran out of vocabulary he could use in front of Charlotte and accepted the cup of tea she was pouring.

"I don't give a damn what she learns!" he said fiercely. "Have you thought for one moment in all your idiotic plans about the danger she's in? For God's sake, Charlotte, two people have been murdered in that house already! If she were found out, what could you do to help her? Nothing! Nothing at all!" He flung his arm out. "She's there completely on her own; I can't get in there. How could you be so bloody stupid?"

"I am not stupid!" she said hotly, indignation bright in her cheeks and eyes. "I didn't know anything about it—I told you that! I only heard about it afterwards."

"Don't equivocate!" he snapped back. "You drew Emily into this; she would never have heard about it if you hadn't started meddling. Get her out! Sit down now and write to her telling her to go home where she belongs—now!"

Charlotte's face was set. "There's no point; she won't come."

"Do it!" he roared. "Don't argue with me, just do it!"

There were tears in her eyes, but no obedience or submissiveness. "She won't listen to me!" she said furiously. "I know the danger! Do you think I can't see it? And I know you're in danger too! I sit at home and wait for you when you're late, wondering where you are, if you are safe—or lying bleeding in the street somewhere."

"That's unfair! And it has nothing to do with Emily," he answered more levelly. "Get her out, Charlotte."

"I can't. She won't come."

He said nothing. He was too angry—and too frightened.

7

E*MILY WAS APPALLED* when she came into the library in answer to Albert's summons and saw Pitt standing there. Thank heaven the circumstances had given him little time to express his outrage or to press his demand that she leave. When Veronica returned to consciousness, Pitt had been obliged to remain silent, except for the few remarks to excuse himself, leaving Emily alone with her mistress propped up against the cushions, looking like death warmed over.

Emily felt so intense a pity for her it was like a new wound, but she also knew that she would probably never have a better chance than now, when Veronica was shocked and off balance, to draw some unguarded word from her as to what had frightened her so profoundly.

She bent down beside her and touched her hand. "Ma'am, you do look ill," she said gently. "Whatever did he say to you? He ought not have been allowed!" She stared so intently at Veronica's ashen face that some sort of answer was unavoidable.

"I—I think I fainted," Veronica whispered at last.

Mentally Emily apologized to Pitt for the injustice she was about to do him; then with all the skill she could muster, she let genuine compassion fill her eyes. "Did he threaten you, ma'am? What did he say? He has no right! You should report him: What was it?"

"No," Veronica said quickly, then bit her lip, struggling with the lie. "No—he—he was really quite civil. I . . ." For a moment her eyes met Emily's and she hesitated on the brink of speech, the temptation to trust so vivid that Emily could trace every thread of it, the wavering, the rival fears.

Emily held her breath.

But the moment passed. Veronica turned away and the tears spilled and ran down her cheeks. She lay back and closed her eyes.

Emily longed to put her arms round her and tell her she understood, she knew what it was like to lose your husband suddenly, violently, in the horror of murder, with the knowledge that someone must hate so much that only death could satisfy them. And she also knew the fear that grew day by day, fear of confusion, of a whole world become incomprehensible and full of secrets, some of them hideous; and the fear that the truth might be worse than you could bear. And there was the fear that with knowledge you, too, might become a victim—and at the back of every other fear, the one that you might be guilty of some stupidity, or some neglect that had contributed to it all, a permanent rising, whispering guilt!

And for Emily, too, there had been the fear that the police would suspect her. Her motive had looked to be so obvious!

Was that what Veronica was afraid of now? Did she feel Pitt treading closer? Was it terror for herself that had made her faint?

Or was she afraid for someone she was protecting— someone like Julian Danver? It was more like Pitt to be oblique, to go for the weakest link in the chain of events:

not the murderer himself but the person most likely to yield to pressure.

Or was Veronica afraid, as Emily had been, of the people in her husband's family who believed she was guilty, or who wanted her to be—not only of errors of judgment, of the occasional selfishness, but literally physically guilty of murder? Was that the passion between Loretta and Veronica—that Loretta believed her daughter-in-law had killed her son? Was taking her revenge in her own way, slowly, day by day, turning the knife, collecting one word after another until she had proof? It was a far more delicate torture than the simple hangman's noose, and Loretta could administer it herself—and watch.

Or was it Cerise she was afraid of?

Or in spite of the fear now, was she Cerise herself? And was it her paymasters of whom she was terrified, now that the net was closing in?

Whatever the truth, there was no point in pursuing it at present. The moment when she might have spoken was gone, and Emily knew it would be foolish to betray her curiosity. She felt a little sick. She did not want it to be Veronica. She could not help liking her, even feeling a kind of identity. But Emily was angry also, because of her own inability to judge. Her emotions were strong, she wanted to protect the victims and attack the offenders, of all sorts, whether guilty of murder, or only of hatred and meanness of soul; but she could not discern who they were.

"Would you like to go upstairs, ma'am?" she said, perhaps less tactfully than she might have. "Before anyone comes and—" She realized how far she was committing herself and stopped.

But Veronica understood. She swung her legs down from the sofa and sat up very slowly, still dizzy.

"Yes—yes, I would rather." There was no need to add Loretta's name; all the implications hung in the air between

180

them, perfectly understood, but it would not do to speak them aloud.

Slowly, side by side, they left the library, crossed the hall to the stairs, and went up.

That evening Edith had another one of her "spells," and Emily was asked to lay out the dinner gowns for both Veronica and Loretta.

"Poor Edith. She should see a doctor," she said with cloying sweetness. "Shall I ask Mrs. York to call one for her? I'm sure she would; she thinks so highly of Edith."

Fanny tittered and then stopped abruptly when the housekeeper glared at her.

"There's no need for you to tell us what to do and what not to, miss!" Mrs. Crawford snapped at Emily. "We'll call a doctor if it's necessary! You're a sight too ready with your advice!"

Emily affected innocence and a slight air of having been hurt.

"I'm sure I was only trying to help, Mrs. Crawford, being that I shall see Mrs. York in the line of duty. To save you going out of your way."

"I'll go where I please, miss, and none of your business!"

"The girl was only trying to help," the butler said reasonably. "And maybe we should get a doctor to Edith. She has more turns than a hurdy-gurdy!"

Libby burst into a fit of giggles and half slid under the table.

"Oh, you are so witty, Mr. Redditch," Bertha said admiringly.

Nora snorted. She had observed Bertha's eye for Redditch and, having tried her own hand there and failed, regarded it with scorn. Anyway, she had every intention of doing better than a butler—Bertha could have him and welcome! She wasn't going to spend the rest of her life living in someone

181

else's house! She was going to have one of her own, with nice linen and crockery, and a maid of all work.

Redditch smirked slightly; admiration was very pleasant.

"Control yourself, Libby," he said sententiously. "No call for all that. Yes, Mrs. Crawford, I think Amelia might mention it to Mrs. York."

"Yes, Amelia," Nora agreed with a little sniff. "Why don't you do that?"

Joan opened her mouth to say something, then changed her mind. But she stared at Emily and shook her head so slightly it might have been an illusion of the gaslight, except for the expression of warning in her eyes.

"Scorch any slips today?" Nora asked sarcastically.

Emily smiled back. "No, thank you. Did you spill any soup?"

"I never spill soup! I know my job!"

"You used to," Albert said with satisfaction. In his opinion Nora was a step above herself. He had tried to be friendly with her, and she thought herself too good for a junior footman. And she had ticked him off in front of the tweeny. "I remember when you dropped a potato in the French ambassador's lap."

"And I remember a few of your mistakes, too!" Nora said fiercely. "Do you want me to begin?"

"Do as you please, I'm sure," Albert said airily, but his face was bright pink.

"I will! How about the day you stood on Lady Wortley's train? I can still hear the taffeta rip!"

Redditch decided to take control. "That'll do!" The butler straightened himself in his chair and fixed them with a stern eye. "I won't have name-calling and interfering with other people's jobs. Nora, what you said was uncalled for!"

Nora made a face behind his back.

Emily stood up. "The wind'll change and you'll get stuck like that!" she said simply, betraying to everyone what Nora had done. "Anyway, it's time I went upstairs."

"It's more than time!" the housekeeper added. "Seeing as you have both ladies to care for. Should have gone quarter of an hour since."

"I didn't know Edith would be taken with one of her spells again," Emily answered back. "Although I suppose I might have guessed, seeing how often they happen."

"I'll have none of your impertinence!" the housekeeper snapped. "Watch your tongue, miss, or you'll be out on the street without a character!"

"And there's only one way to make your living then," Nora added spitefully. "We all know what 'appened to Daisy. Not that you'd be much good at that either. You're too thin, and you've no color at all."

"And I should imagine you'd be perfect!" Emily returned instantly. "You've just the face for it. You're wasted here— at least, I suppose you are."

"Oh!" Nora flushed scarlet. "I've never been so insulted!" She stood up and flounced out of the room, slamming the door behind her.

Albert started to giggle and Libby slid down under the table again, burying her face in her apron. Only Fanny stared in horror; she understood the power of jealousy instinctively, and she had seen enough to be frightened of it.

Emily left the room on the crest of her victory, but she had only got as far as the doorway when she heard the whispers start behind her.

"She's a bad lot, that one!" the housekeeper said sharply. "She'll have to go! Mark my words. Airs above herself— trying to talk with a fancy voice!"

"Nonsense!" The butler was very quick. "She's got a bit of spirit, that's all. Nora's been queening around here too long; time someone matched up to her. She's just not used to having another girl as handsome as Amelia is."

"Handsome! Amelia?" Mrs. Crawford snorted. "Thin as a tuppenny rabbit, she is, and all that pale hair, and skin like a dish of whey. If you ask me, she's not healthy!"

"She's a sight healthier than Edith!" Redditch said with evident satisfaction.

Emily closed the door on Mrs. Crawford's gasp of temper, and went along to the green baize door and up the main stairs.

By the time Emily had laid out Veronica's clothes and gone to Loretta's room, Loretta was already waiting for her. For several minutes she merely gave instructions, almost absent-mindedly, then at last she seemed to make up her mind to speak.

"Amelia?"

"Yes, ma'am?" Emily heard the difference in her tone, something peremptory in it. Or perhaps she was anxious?

"Is Miss Veronica unwell this evening?"

Emily considered her answer for a moment. If only she knew more about Loretta and her relationship with her son. Had the marriage been arranged? Had Loretta selected Veronica? Or had she and Robert fallen in love, against Loretta's wishes? Perhaps she had been one of those possessive mothers for whom no woman could have been good enough to marry her son.

"Yes ma'am, I think she was." She must be careful. If Veronica herself said otherwise she would create trouble by betraying her to her mother-in-law and at the same time destroy the trust she needed in order to learn anything. "I didn't like to ask her, in case I intruded."

Loretta was sitting on the stool in front of the dressing table. Her face was grave, her blue eyes wide. Cascades of deep, wavy hair framed her perfect pink and white skin.

"Amelia, I must confide in you." Her eyes met Emily's in the glass. "Veronica is not very strong, and her health needs care, at times perhaps more than she realizes. I hope you will help me to protect her. Her happiness is very important to me, you understand. Not only was she my son's wife, but in the time she has lived here we have grown very close."

Emily was startled into attention. She had been mesmerized for a moment by the steady, almost unblinking gaze in the glass.

"Yes, ma'am," she agreed hesitantly. Surely it was a lie—wasn't it? Or could the violent emotion between them be a form of love, of dependence and resentment? How should she answer this? She must behave like a maid and yet not lose the chance to learn. Did Loretta already know about Pitt's visit? Emily must not be caught in a lie, or she'd be thrown out and would fail completely. "Of course I will do whatever I can," she said, smiling back nervously. "The poor lady does seem . . ." What word should she use? Frightened—terrified was the truth—but of what? Loretta was watching her, waiting. "Delicate," Emily finished desperately.

"Do you think so?" Loretta's perfect eyebrows rose. "What makes you say that, Amelia?"

Emily felt ridiculous. She could not possibly respond with the truth; she was left with fatuous answers. Was she being tested for loyalty, to see if she would recount Veronica's fainting that afternoon, which Albert had seen and might have reported? There was no time for judgment. She answered instinctively.

"She was overcome with a faint this afternoon, ma'am. It passed quickly, and she seemed quite well again afterwards." That would not be so remarkable. Ladies did faint; tight stays, waists pulled into a handspan often made one ill.

Loretta stopped fiddling with the pins in the silver tray on her dressing table. "Indeed? I didn't know. Thank you for telling me, Amelia. You have done the right thing. In the future you will tell me anything else concerning Miss Veronica's health and inform me if she is distressed or seems nervous, so I may give her all the assistance I can. This is a most important time in her life. She is shortly to become engaged to marry a very fine man. I am deeply concerned

185

that nothing whatsoever should jeopardize her happiness. You understand me, Amelia?''

"Oh yes, ma'am," Emily said with a sickly smile. "I'll do everything I can to help."

"Good. Now you may dress my hair, and you had better hurry because you have Miss Veronica's to do as well."

"Yes ma'am. It seems Edith is poorly again."

Emily met Loretta's eyes in the glass, and there was a dry humor in them, startling and unexpected; it indicated a sharpness of perception that was unnerving.

"She'll be completely better tomorrow," Loretta said with conviction. "I promise you."

Edith was indeed up with the lark the next morning, but she was in a vile temper. Whatever had been said to her, she blamed Emily for it and held a bitter grudge. She followed Emily around, overseeing her work—especially the ironing, which she knew was her weakest point—criticizing the slightest error, until Emily lost her temper and told her she was a fat, idle, mischief-making slut, and if she put half as much effort into doing her own job as she did into meddling in other people's, then no one else would need to cover for her.

Edith threw a bucket of cold water at her. Emily's first thought was to retaliate by hitting Edith as hard as she could across her stupid face. But that would undoubtedly get her dismissed, and then she would discover nothing. She took the opposite course and stood in the middle of the laundry room floor, shivering and dripping. Joan, who had heard Edith shriek in fury, appeared in the doorway and saw Edith with the empty bucket in her hand and Emily's pathetic state.

Emily thought for a moment what she must look like, how furious her mother would be and how absurd the whole situation was, and was terrified she would burst into giggles. To smother the slight hysteria she felt rising inside her she pulled her apron up to cover her face and stifled her laughter in its ample folds.

Joan disappeared, and two minutes later the butler came in, his face pink, his sideburns bristling.

"Edith! Whatever's come over you, girl? You can stay here till Mrs. York wants you, and iron all the rest of the sheets."

"That's not my job!" Edith protested with outrage.

"Hold your tongue, and do as you're told! And there'll be no dinner for you today, or tomorrow either, if you give me any impertinence!" He turned to Emily gently and put his arm round her, holding her far more firmly than necessary. "Come now, get out of those wet things and then Mary'll get you a hot cup of tea. You haven't been hurt. You'll be all right soon. Come, come. Stop crying, you'll make yourself ill."

Emily did not know if she could; her laughter was too close to tears to stop easily. After the loneliness, the cold, the tension and the strangeness it was a relief to let go and pour her feelings out. She felt Redditch's arm around her, warm, surprisingly strong. It was really quite pleasant and she relaxed into it—then the appalling thought struck her that he might well misread her compliance. She had already noticed he seemed to like her a great deal, and had championed her more than once. That would be all she needed to lose control of this altogether!

She sniffed fiercely, commanded herself to behave, dropped her apron from her eyes and straightened up.

"Thank you, Mr. Redditch. You are quite right; it is nothing but shock because the water was cold." She must not forget she was supposed to be a maid. She could hardly afford arrogance, or the kind of distance a lady might affect. "Thank you. You're very kind."

His arm fell away reluctantly. "Are you sure?"

"Oh, yes—yes, thank you!" She moved away slowly, keeping her eyes averted. This was preposterous! She was thinking of him as a man, not a butler! Or on second thought, he was a man! All men were men! Perhaps it was Society that was preposterous?

"Thank you, Mr. Redditch," she said again. "Yes, I'll go and get changed. I'm frozen, and a hot cup of tea would be lovely." She turned and all but ran out of the room and along the corridor to the stairs.

By the time she came down into the kitchen again everyone had heard of the affair, and she was met with wide-eyed stares, whispers, and a snigger or two.

"Ignore them!" Mary said softly, bringing her a steaming cup and sitting down beside her. Her voice dropped till it was barely audible. "Did you really call her names? What did you say?"

Emily took the tea carefully, her hands still shaking. "I told her she was a fat, lazy slut," she whispered back. "But don't repeat that: Mrs. Crawford would have me out! I expect Edith's been here for years and Mrs. Crawford's always known her."

"No, she hasn't." Mary moved a little closer. "She's only bin 'ere two year, and Mrs. Crawford fer three."

"Everyone seems new," Emily said artlessly. "Why? It's a good place; lovely house, fair wages, and Miss Veronica's not hard."

"Dunno. I suppose it must be the murder. I didn't 'ear no one say as they would leave; all the same, everyone did."

"That's silly." Emily kept her voice down, but she was excited. Perhaps she was on the verge of some real detecting. "Did they think the murderer would kill someone else— oh!" She affected amazement and horror, swinging round on her wooden seat to look at Mary directly. "You don't think Dulcie was murdered, do you?"

Mary's eyes, blue as the rings on the kitchen china, stared at her in disbelief. Then gradually the possibility took hold, and Emily was afraid she had gone too far. A second maid in hysterics in one day would certainly get her thrown out without any excuses. Even Redditch could not save her. She could have bitten her tongue for being so hasty.

"You mean pushed 'er outa the window?" Mary's voice was almost inaudible. But she was made of sterner stuff than Edith; she did not hold with hysterics. They usually made people cross, and men hated them. And her mind was quite sharp; she could read, and had a pile of penny dreadfuls under her pillow upstairs. She knew all about crime. "Well, Dulcie was 'ere when poor Mr. Robert was killed," she said with a tiny nod. "Mebbe she saw summink."

"So were you, weren't you?" Emily sipped her tea gratefully. "Well, you'd better be careful. Don't speak to anyone about anything that happened then! Did you see anything?"

Mary was apparently unaware of the contradiction in Emily's instructions. "No, I never did," she said regretfully. "Important people never come into the kitchen, and I 'ardly never got out of it. I was only scullery maid then."

"You didn't see any strange people upstairs ever? People who shouldn't have been?"

"No, I never."

"What was Mr. Robert like? The others must have talked."

Mary's brow puckered in thought. "Well, Dulcie said 'e was very partic'lar, never untidy like, an' always polite—least, as polite as Quality ever is. But then old Mr. York is always polite, too, although 'e's terrible untidy. Leaves 'is things all over the place, and forgets summink awful! I know 'e was out a lot. James as was footman then, 'e was always sayin' Mr. Robert was out again, but that was Mr. Robert's job. 'E was summink very important in the Foreign Service."

"What happened to James?"

"Mrs. York got rid of 'im. Said as since Mr. Robert was dead there wasn't no need. Sent 'im off the very next day, she did, on account of Lord somebody-or-other was lookin' for a valet, and she spoke for 'im."

"Mrs. Loretta?"

"Oh yes o' course. Poor Miss Veronica weren't in no state to do anything. Terrible grieved, she were; in an awful state, poor soul. Mr. Robert were 'er 'ole world. Adored 'im, she did. Not that Mrs. Loretta weren't terrible upset, too, o' course. White as a ghost, Dulcie said." Mary leaned so close her hair tickled Emily's cheek. "Dulcie told me she 'eard 'er crying summink wicked in the night, but she didn't dare go in, 'cause she couldn't do nuffink! People 'as to cry; it's natural."

"Of course it is." Suddenly Emily felt like an intruder. What on earth was she doing here in some unfortunate woman's house, deceiving everyone, pretending to be a maid? No wonder Pitt was furious! He probably despised her as well.

"Come on," Mrs. Melrose interrupted briskly, breaking her train of thought. "Drink up your tea, Amelia. Mary's got work to do, even if you 'aven't! An' I'd watch your tongue, if I were you, my girl. Don't do to be too smart! Edith's a lazy baggage, an' you got away with it this time—but you made enemies! Now drink that up an' get along with you!"

It was excellent advice and Emily thanked her for it meekly and obeyed with an alacrity that surprised them both.

The next two days were uncomfortable. Edith was nursing a resentment which she did not dare exercise, but it was the bitterer for that, and Emily knew she was only biding her time. Mrs. Crawford felt she had somehow been bested, and constantly found tiny faults with Emily, which provoked Redditch into criticizing the housekeeper until everyone was on edge. The laundry room became her only sanctuary, since once again Edith had contrived to get out of the ironing. She had bruised her wrist and the flatiron was too heavy for her. Mrs. Crawford let her get away with that, but she could not overrule Redditch on the matter of dinner, and two delicious midday meals went by without Edith's presence. Mrs. Melrose seemed to have made a special effort. As was customary, the servants shared the fine wine in the family cellars. In the evening, after supper, they drank hot cocoa and played games in which Edith did not join.

Emily's only immediate problem was how to fend off Redditch's friendship without hurting his feelings and thus forfeiting his protection. She had never had to be so diplomatic in her life, and it was a considerable strain. She sought refuge in unnaturally diligent attendance upon Veronica. That was how she came to be in the boudoir in the middle of the afternoon when Nora announced that a Mr. Radley had called, and would Miss Veronica see him?

Emily suddenly felt flushed; the book she had been reading aloud slid off her lap onto the floor. All this had begun as an adventure, but she was not sure she wanted Jack to actually see her as a maid. Her hair was back in a style far less flattering than usual, and there was no color in her face—as a servant it was not allowed unless it was natural, of course—and because she was inside all the time, sleeping in that cold bed, up too early, there were shadows under her eyes, and she was sure she was thinner. Perhaps she did look like a tuppenny rabbit! Veronica was thin, but in her gorgeous clothes she merely looked delicate, not bloodless.

"Oh, yes please," Veronica said with a smile. "How nice of him to call. Is Miss Barnaby with him, too?"

"No ma'am. Shall I bring him in here?" Nora glanced quickly at Emily, implying that she should leave.

"Yes, do. And have Mrs. Melrose prepare some tea and sandwiches, and cakes."

"Yes ma'am," Nora turned on her heel and went out, her skirts swishing round the door before she closed it. In her opinion lady's maids had no business being where they could meet gentlemen callers. That was a parlormaid's privilege.

Jack came in a moment later, smiling easily, graceful and full of life. He did not even glance at Emily, but his face lit with pleasure when he saw Veronica, and she held out her hand to him. Emily felt a shock of rejection, almost as if she had been slapped. It was idiotic. Had he spoken to her it would have spoilt everything, and she would have been angry with him. And yet she felt crushed inside because he had carried out his part perfectly. He had treated her like a servant, not a woman at all.

"How kind of you to see me," he said warmly, as if it was more than just a social ritual. "I should have sent my card, but it was a spur-of-the-moment call. How are you? I heard you had a misfortune in the house. I do hope you are beginning to recover?"

Veronica clung to his hand. "Oh Jack, it really was dreadful. Poor Dulcie fell out of the window, and she was crushed on the stone beneath. I can't think how it happened. No one saw anything!"

Jack! She had called him by his Christian name so naturally that it must be how she thought of him, even after all this time. Why had she not married him when they knew each other before? Money? Her parents? They might well have refused someone like Jack, who had no prospects. They had picked Robert York instead, an only son who had both money and ambition. But would she have preferred Jack? And infinitely more important, would he have preferred her?

They were talking as if Emily were not there; she could have been another cushion on the chair. Veronica was looking up at Jack, her cheeks flushed, looking happier than Emily had ever seen her. The light shone on that hair like black silk, and her eyes were wide. She was more than beautiful—there was individuality and passion in her face. Emily was caught in a turmoil of feelings that tightened her throat so she thought she might choke. As Amelia she liked Veronica, and pitied her because she realized she was desperately unhappy over something. It came to Emily with clarity, as she sat there like a fool watching Jack, that Veronica was wound up like an old-fashioned thumbscrew inside, hurting a little more each day. Was it still grief over Robert? Or was it fear?

Was it because she knew something—or because she did not know, and her sense of uncertainty warped everything?

And at the same time, Emily was burningly jealous. And jealousy brought back the agony of watching George become infatuated with Sybilla, of knowing the man she loved preferred, in fact adored someone else. It was a pain like no other, and the fact that George had woken up from his affair before he died did not wash away her knowledge of what it was like to be rejected. There had been no time for the wound to heal fully.

Emily could not help seeing Veronica as a rival. Jack had started as an amusement, a graceful and charming toy to be played with; then he had become a friend, far more comfortable to be with than almost anyone except Charlotte. But now he was a part of her life she could not lose without profound loneliness. Now he was laughing and talking with Veronica, and Emily was powerless even to speak, let alone to fight for his attention. It was a kind of pain she had never experienced before. Some other time she would give thought to what it must be like always to be a maid, condemned only to watch. Now she was full of her own anger and hurt and had no time for anyone else.

And she should slip away. Maids had no business remaining in the room as if they were guests. She did not excuse herself; that too was unnecessary, an interruption. She simply stood up and tiptoed out. Jack did not even turn his head. At the door she looked over her shoulder at him, but he was smiling at Veronica, and Emily might not have existed.

Charlotte was frightened when Pitt described Emily's danger with such clarity, but she was helpless to save her sister. Even if Charlotte went to the Yorks' as often as she could, she could hardly rescue Emily over the teacups and cucumber sandwiches. The only comfort was that she did not actually believe Veronica was Cerise; from what Pitt had said, she had not the nerve to be a spy.

She raised the subject again the next day, hoping to ease the rift between them. "If she is a spy, don't we have to discover her, for the nation's sake?"

"No, we do not," he said pointedly. "I do."

"But we can help! Nobody in Hanover Close is going to talk to you because you are police, whereas they take no notice of us. They don't think we have enough brains for them to have to lie!"

Pitt grunted and raised his eyebrows. He looked at her pointedly, and she decided to ignore him. It might be wiser to let the subject drop, in case he forbade her going to the Yorks': she really did not want to have to disobey him. She wanted very much to avoid another quarrel. She could not possibly allow Emily to face whatever danger there was alone, but there was nothing she could say that Pitt would believe. If she were too docile he would become suspicious, so she merely resumed eating her supper and presently spoke of something else.

The following morning, as soon as Pitt was out of the house, she wrote a letter to Jack Radley and had Gracie put it in the ten o'clock post. While she was ironing Pitt's shirts, Charlotte laid her plans.

It was Saturday, two days later, when they came to fruition, by which time she had been visited by Jack with an account of his call upon Veronica York. Emily had been in the room on his arrival, but had left shortly afterwards. He had been concerned that she looked very pale and rather unhappy, although he had not dared to do more than glance at her. The news of Emily was not good, but Charlotte was quite elated that he seemed so anxious for her. Looking at his face, which usually revealed nothing but charm and the superficial pleasure Society expected, she saw something of the man beneath, and found she liked it. Perhaps for Emily to be in danger was precisely what he needed, to show her that he had in him the depth she wanted for Emily.

Consequently it was with a high heart and some exhilaration that she set out alone from Emily's house in the early afternoon, dressed in one of her sister's older gowns, let out judiciously here and there because she was a couple of inches taller, and handsomer of bust than Emily, even before the tragedy of George's death. It was golden brown, the color of old sherry, and extremely becoming to her warm-toned complexion and her hair with its auburn lights. She chose a hat trimmed with black fur, and a muff to match. Altogether she had never looked so well in a winter outfit in her life.

She had sent a letter and received one in return from Veronica, so she was expected. She drew up in Emily's carriage, hoping no one would notice. If asked, she was going to explain that it had been lent for convenience, since Lady Ashworth was out of town.

Veronica was awaiting her in the withdrawing room and her face lit with pleasure as Charlotte was shown in. She rose immediately.

"How nice to see you. I'm so glad you came. Do sit down. I wish it were not so terribly cold, but all the same I thought we might go for a ride, just to be away from the same surroundings all the time. Unless you would like to see the winter exhibition again?"

Charlotte saw the urgency in her eyes as she waited for an answer.

"Not at all—a carriage ride is an excellent idea," Charlotte responded with a smile. It was not what she had planned, but it might serve, and she must court Veronica's friendship. If they were alone together in a carriage, secure from interruption, she might elicit some confidence. "I should enjoy that very much," she added for good measure.

Veronica relaxed, some of the tension easing out of her slender body. She smiled. "I'm so glad. I wish you would call me Veronica, and may I call you Elisabeth?"

For a moment Charlotte was startled; she had almost forgotten her alias. "Of course!" she said after a moment's hesitation, then in case Veronica thought she disapproved, "That is most kind of you. Where do you care to drive?"

"I . . ." Veronica's pale cheeks colored very slightly, and instantly Charlotte understood; she was not yet ready to commit herself to such trust.

"Why not let us see where the wish takes us?" Charlotte suggested tactfully. "No doubt something agreeable will occur to us once we are started."

Veronica was visibly relieved. "How sympathetic you are." The moment had passed without the need for explanation, and she was grateful. "Have you had a pleasant time since we visited the exhibition?" she asked.

Charlotte had to invent a reply on the spot. "If you wish for a frank answer, I am afraid nothing worthy of repeating."

Veronica's smile expressed her comprehension completely. She had endured years of being a model widow, a decorous wife, and before that a demure young lady seeking a suitable marriage. She had an intimate acquaintance with boredom.

Charlotte was about to introduce another topic when Loretta came in, her face registering good-mannered surprise.

"Good afternoon, Miss Barnaby," she said. "How pleasant of you to call. I hope you are well, and enjoying your stay in London?"

Before she could fumble for an appropriate response Veronica helped her by announcing their plans. "We are going to take a drive."

Loretta's eyes opened wide. "In this weather? My dear, it is bitterly cold and looks as if it might well snow again."

"Very bracing," Veronica said immediately. "And I am longing to get a little air."

The corners of Loretta's full-lipped mouth curved upward minutely. "Are you going to call upon anyone?"

This time Veronica was slower, and her eyes slid away from her mother-in-law's. "I . . . er—"

"We have not decided," Charlotte interrupted for her,

196

smiling at Loretta. "We thought we could go wherever the whim took us."

"I beg your pardon?" Loretta was put off her stride by such an unexpected answer.

"We have not decided," Veronica repeated, seizing on the escape. "We shall drive for pleasure. I have been inside too much lately. I am sure fresh air would do me good. I feel peaked."

"And what about Miss Barnaby?" Loretta inquired. "She is not in the least peaked. In fact she appears in the most robust good health."

Charlotte knew she had anything but the pale and languid look of fashion, but she did not care. "I am perfectly happy to take a ride," she insisted. "Perhaps we should see some sights."

"You are too amiable," Loretta said coolly. "I thought perhaps you might have considered visiting Harriet Danver."

They all knew she meant Julian, but they kept up the fiction.

With Charlotte's moral support Veronica had gathered courage. This time she met Loretta's eyes. "No," she said blandly. "We had merely said it would be nice to take a ride. I thought I might show Elisabeth some of the fashionable places in London that she has not seen."

"In this weather?" Loretta said again. "There is no sun whatever and it will be dark by four. Really, my dear, you are being a trifle impractical."

"Then we had better hurry." Veronica was not to be dissuaded. Her will was growing stronger; Charlotte could see it in the angle of her head and the increasing quickness of her answers.

Loretta smiled sweetly, taking them both by surprise. "In that case I shall come with you. Then if you do decide to call upon the Danvers you will not be unchaperoned, which would be most unsuitable. After all, it is Saturday, and Mr. Danver may well be at home. We must not be ill thought of."

Suddenly Veronica seemed seized by panic, as if she were enmeshed in a net and every new twist to free herself only bound her more tightly. Charlotte could see the rise and fall of her bosom as she fought for breath, and her hands clenched at her sides as if she would tear at her skirt.

"I shall have Elisabeth with me!" Her voice rose sharply, almost out of control. "I know the rules! I—"

Loretta stared at her, eyes careful, steady, almost warning, a tight smile on her lips. "My dear girl—"

"How generous of you." Charlotte immediately wished she had not stepped in: it might have been more productive to let the scene play itself out. She should have thought more of detection and less of friendship. But it was too late now. "I am sure we should enjoy your company, especially if we take a walk in the park." She thought of the raw wind slicing in off the open grass and whining through the wet, leafless trees.

But Loretta was not to be deterred so easily. "I think, Miss Barnaby, that when you step outside you will change your mind, but if that is what you wish then I shall wait in the carriage for you."

"You'll freeze!" Veronica said desperately.

"I am much stronger than you think, my dear," Loretta replied levelly, and as Veronica turned away Charlotte was startled to see tears in her eyes. What was this emotion between these two women? Veronica was afraid; Charlotte had seen fear often enough to know. And yet Veronica was not naturally submissive, and now that Robert was dead she ought to have no need to cater to his feelings for his mother. Financially she was secure, and she was all but engaged to marry again. Why was she so afraid? Everything Loretta had done, at least on the surface, had been in her interest.

If only Charlotte could learn what sort of a marriage it had been, how it had begun. Had Loretta adored her only son, and had she been too demanding of her daughter-in-law? Had she interfered, criticized, been open in her disappointment because there had been no grandchildren? There could be a dozen passions or griefs behind the driving emotion that bound these two women.

The tense silence in the room was broken when the door opened and Piers York came in. Charlotte had not met him before, but she knew him immediately from Pitt's description: elegant, a trifle stooping, face wry with self-deprecatory good humor.

"Ah!" he said with slight surprise on seeing Charlotte.

Veronica forced a smile; it was ghastly, a travesty of pleasure.

"Papa-in-law, this is Miss Barnaby, a new friend of mine who has been good enough to call. We were going to take a short drive."

"What an excellent idea," he agreed. "Rather cold, but better than sitting inside all day. How do you do, Miss Barnaby."

"How do you do, Mr. York," Charlotte replied warmly. He was the sort of man she liked without needing to think about it. "I'm so glad you approve. Mrs. York"—she glanced at Loretta—"was afraid we should not enjoy it because it is so chill outside, but I feel exactly as you do, that whatever the weather it is better to go out for a little while, even if only to better appreciate the fire when we return."

"What a sensible young woman." He smiled. "I have no idea why fashion so admires the drooping young creatures who lie about being bored with everything. They have no idea how tedious they are. I pity the man who is naive enough to marry one of them. Still, I suppose they are all taking a pig in a poke anyway!"

"Piers!" Loretta said tartly. "Please keep that sort of unfortunate language for your club! It has no place here. You will offend Miss Barnaby."

He looked surprised. "Oh, I'm sorry, Miss Barnaby, did I offend you? I assure you I only meant that one can get very little idea of a person's true nature from the sort of social twitterings that are all one is allowed before marriage."

Charlotte smiled broadly. "I am not in the least offended. I know precisely what you mean. And then when you do discover, of course it is too late. Mrs. York was just saying that if we come to call upon the Danvers it would be necessary for Veronica to be chaperoned. But I would be quite happy to make sure nothing is done that could be remarked upon, I give you my word."

"I am sure you mean well, Miss Barnaby, but that is not sufficient for Society," Loretta said firmly.

"Nonsense," Piers contradicted her. "Perfectly all right. Anyway, who would know about it? Harriet certainly isn't going to say anything."

"It would be as well if I were to go with you," she insisted, taking a step towards the door. "This is a most delicate time."

"For heaven's sake stop fussing, Loretta!" he said with unusual sharpness. "You worry over Veronica far too much. Danver's a decent enough fellow, and no stick-in-the-mud. Miss Barnaby is perfectly adequate as a chaperone, and it's good of her to oblige."

"Piers, you don't understand." Loretta's voice grated with the power of her emotion. "I wish you would accept my judgment. There is far more to this than you realize."

"About a carriage ride?" His disbelief was tinged with annoyance.

Her face was white. "There are delicacies, things that . . ."

"Indeed? What, for example?"

She was angry, but she had no answer that she was prepared to give him.

Charlotte looked at Veronica, wondering whether the brief escape would be worth the unpleasantness which would undoubtedly follow.

"Come, Elisabeth," Veronica said without looking at

Loretta. "We shall not be long, but it will be good for us to go out."

Charlotte excused herself and followed Veronica out into the hallway. She waited a few moments while the footman was dispatched to fetch Veronica's cloak and muff, and Veronica herself went to change her boots.

The withdrawing room door was ajar.

"You know nothing whatever about that young woman!" Loretta's voice rose angrily. "Most unsuitable. Brash. Totally unsophisticated!"

"She seemed very pleasant to me," Piers answered. "In fact, altogether attractive."

"For heaven's sake, Piers! Just because she has a handsome face. Really, you are so naive sometimes."

"And you, my dear, see complications where there are none."

"I anticipate, which is not the same thing."

"It is very often exactly the same thing."

Charlotte was prevented from overhearing any more by Veronica's return. Emily came downstairs, too, with a cloak over her arm. At first Charlotte hardly recognized her; she looked so different with her hair under a cap, wearing a blue stuff dress with no bustle and a plain apron over it. She looked thinner than before, although it was probably the clothes, and terribly pale. Their eyes met only for a moment, Emily's wide and very blue, then Veronica put on the cloak. Emily smoothed it over her shoulders, and Charlotte and Veronica went out of the front door as Albert held it open for them.

The drive was chilly, even with rugs over their knees, but it was exhilarating to be bowling along at a good pace with fashionable streets, wide avenues, and squares passing their windows. For a moment Veronica turned, her eyes almost black in the carriage interior, her lips parted, but Charlotte knew where Veronica wanted to go before she could ask.

"Of course," she said quickly.

Veronica clasped her hand inside the muff. "Thank you."

* * *

They were received without surprise at the Danver house
and shown into the withdrawing room. Since Charlotte had
written to Veronica two days ago, it was possible Veronica had
written to Julian, and they were expected. Julian Danver himself was there and greeted them, taking Veronica's hands and
holding them warmly for a moment before turning to Charlotte.

"How charming to see you again, Miss Barnaby." He
smiled at her. His gaze was very direct, and Charlotte remembered how much she had liked him. "I am sure you
remember my aunt, Miss Danver? And my sister Harriet?"

"Of course," she said quickly, looking first at Aunt Adeline, whose thin, intelligent face regarded her with interest,
and then at Harriet. This afternoon she seemed paler than
before; there was a deep shadow of unhappiness behind her
answering look. "I hope you are well."

"Very well, thank you, and you?"

All the usual greetings were exchanged and the polite,
meaningless topics of conversation touched upon. It was the
sort of formal ritual Charlotte had been used to as a girl but
had been able to cast aside after her marriage. Indeed with
the dramatic fall in her social standing, the opportunity had
been removed from her, a loss she had been grateful for. She
had never been skilled at it, her own opinions far too ready
on her tongue. No one wanted them: it was unseemly for a
woman to be opinionated, and a great deal of feminine charm
lay in listening and admiring, and making perhaps an occasional remark of optimism and good nature. Of course, it
was almost always acceptable to laugh, if one's laughter was
musical and not too loud; it should never be the rich mirth
of one who understood the absurd or the farcical. Charlotte
had lost the polish she had cultivated when her mother had
tried so hard to marry her successfully. Now she sat primly
on the edge of her chair with her hands folded in her lap and
watched, speaking only when civility demanded.

Veronica had practiced the feminine graces so long it was

second nature to her to find the words to courteously say nothing. But watching her face, which on the surface seemed so fragile until one looked at the balance of the bones and the strength of passion in the mouth, Charlotte could see her mind was occupied with other, more distressing thoughts. Her smile was brittle, and although she appeared to be listening to whomever was speaking at the moment, her eyes frequently flickered to Julian Danver's face. More than once Charlotte had the feeling Veronica was uncertain of his attention to her. It seemed foolish to wonder whether such a lovely woman, already experienced in marriage and the object of sympathy for her bereavement, but never of the kind of pity reserved for the unmarried like Harriet or Aunt Adeline, could be unsure of herself. Julian Danver's intentions were plain; all his actions, the way he conducted himself in front of others, made it obvious. No man would behave in such a manner unless he had promised marriage. To withdraw without the most drastic of reasons would open him to ruin. Such a promise once given was unforgivable to break.

So why did Veronica twine her fingers in her lap and keep glancing first at Julian, then at Charlotte? Why did she talk just a little too much, and with a fine, almost indiscernible edge to her voice, cutting Charlotte off in the middle of a remark and then smiling at her so frankly it was an apology? Charlotte thought she understood Harriet's pain perfectly. It was very simple to explain: if she really loved Felix Asherson, whether he returned it or not, there was nothing she could do about it, nor would there ever be, unless Sonia Asherson died. And why should she die? Sonia was an almost offensively healthy young woman, buxom and serene as a good country cow. She would probably live to be ninety. She was far too well versed in the arts of survival, not to mention contented with her lot, to abandon all sense and give Felix cause to divorce her, and it was quite impossible she should divorce him, even if she discovered he loved Harriet. Yes, Harriet's colorless face and quiet voice took no leap of the imagination to understand, and Charlotte grieved for her without being able to do anything at all; even compassion would only have been like vinegar to the wound, robbing her of the sole comfort of supposing her pain to be private.

Finally Charlotte could bear the tension no longer. She remembered seeing a doorway to the conservatory when they were shown in, and she turned to Julian.

"I believe I noticed your conservatory as we passed through the hall. I love conservatories so much. Perhaps you would be kind enough to show me? It would be like stepping in a moment from London's winter into a foreign land full of flowers."

Veronica drew in her breath with a sharp sound.

"How well you describe it. You have added instantly to my pleasure," Julian said quickly. "I should be delighted to take you. We have some very fine lilies—at least, that is what I believe they are. I'm not good at names, but I can find you the most beautiful, and those with the richest perfume." He stood up as he spoke.

Charlotte rose also. Veronica's back was to Julian, so he could not see her face; Charlotte smiled directly at her, meeting her hot gaze steadily. It was full of anger and dark, wounded bitterness. Charlotte extended her hand, palm upward in invitation.

At last, and quite suddenly, Veronica grasped her meaning; she came quickly to her feet, her face first pale, then a deep pink. "Oh—oh yes," she said awkwardly. "Yes."

"If you will be kind enough to excuse us?" Charlotte asked Aunt Adeline and Harriet.

"Of course," they murmured. "Yes, of course."

It was successful immediately. The conservatory was quite large, and there were elegant ferns and vines hiding one walk from another, and a small green pool with flawless lotuses, which Charlotte stopped to admire without needing to feign delight. Julian then pointed out the fragrant lilies he had mentioned. After making all the right comments Charlotte

204

at last caught Veronica's eye, and with the tiniest smile, she turned and walked back to the lotus pool. After enough time had passed, she tiptoed back out into the hall again.

She could not return to the withdrawing room or she would betray the whole fabric of the excuse—not that anyone was deceived, but forcing the others to acknowledge it was another thing entirely. She felt foolish standing there in the hall, doing nothing. She walked over to a large painting of a landscape with cows and stopped in front of it as if she were regarding it closely. Actually it was very agreeable, of the Dutch school, but her mind was busy with all she knew of Veronica and the Danvers.

She stood for some time with her eyes on the peaceful scene. She could hear in her mind the chewing of the cud, and almost see the jaws' gentle rhythm. They were beautiful creatures, oddly angular and yet graceful, the curve of their horns ancient as civilized man.

She turned away from the painting suddenly. She was not there to indulge her taste for art, nor even her friendship for Veronica. Veronica might be Cerise; she and Julian Danver might have murdered Robert York. Duty demanded that Charlotte creep back and attempt to overhear their conversation, distasteful as that was.

Just inside the conservatory door she stopped and solemnly regarded a red canna lily as if it held her interest. Then she sidled further in, glancing from the lilies on the ground up to the vines overhead and back again. She was several yards along the path and had nearly collided with a potted palm when she saw Veronica and Julian Danver in an embrace of such passion she blushed for having seen them. It was an intrusion which at any other time would have been inexcusable, and she could not possibly explain without betraying herself completely, and everything she hoped to achieve, even perhaps putting Emily in a position of the greatest embarrassment, culminating in social ruin.

Quickly she stepped back into the arms of a vine—and

almost fainted with horror at the first instinctive thought that the clinging touch was human. She swallowed a shriek, realizing the truth, and with an effort pulled herself together and stepped out smartly, only to come face to face with Aunt Adeline. She swore under her breath, feeling idiotic and knowing her hair was disheveled, her cheeks scarlet.

"Are you all right, Miss Barnaby?" Adeline raised her eyebrows. "You look a little distressed."

Charlotte took a deep breath. Only a really good lie would serve.

"I feel such a fool," she began with what she hoped was a disarming smile. "I was trying to see a flower overhead, and I overbalanced. I do beg your pardon." She put her hand to the trailing strands of her hair. "And then I got caught in a vine and I couldn't get loose. But I haven't hurt the plant."

"My dear, of course you haven't." Adeline smiled bleakly, her eyes like brown velvet boot buttons. Charlotte had no idea whether the woman believed a word of what she had said. "I think perhaps it is time we had some tea. Shall I call Julian and Veronica, or will you?"

"I, er . . ." Without thinking Charlotte moved to block the path. "I'm sure they'll come in a few moments."

Adeline's gaze was steady and skeptical.

"I wondered if it was bougainvillea," Charlotte said abruptly. "Such a wonderful shade of cerise. Is that not the color you said you saw Veronica wearing one night?"

Adeline looked startled. "That was not Veronica." For once she dropped her usually clear, fine voice, perhaps her most attractive feature. "I'm perfectly sure of that."

"Oh, I must have misunderstood you. I assumed . . ." Her words trailed away; she did not know how to finish. She had been trying to surprise something out of Adeline, while preventing her from going into the conservatory and seeing that wildly immodest embrace. And it was not only for Veronica she wished it, but for Adeline herself. Perhaps no one had ever held her so, or would do now.

"Oh no," Adeline said with a tiny shake of her head. "Her walk was quite unlike Veronica's. You can tell a great deal about a woman by the way she walks, and her walk was unique. There was a grace in it, a daring. She was a woman who had power and knew it—and yet, I think, she had much to be afraid of. If she were to allow herself to be afraid."

"Oh," Charlotte faltered. "Then—who?"

Adeline's face reflected wisdom, pain, and the merest shadow of humor. "I do not know, Miss Barnaby, and I do not ask. There are many old loves, and old hates, that are better left unspoken."

"You surprise me!" Charlotte's words were suddenly sharp, almost accusatory. "I had thought you were more candid than that."

Adeline's plain, sensitive mouth tightened. "The time for candor is past. You have no idea what pain may lie behind these things. A little blindness can allow them to ease, where to speak may make answer inevitable." She inclined her head towards the interior of the conservatory. "Now you have done your good turn for the day, Miss Barnaby. Either you will call Veronica, or I shall."

"I will," Charlotte said obediently, her mind in a whirl. Had Cerise been a lover of Julian's? Did Veronica know, or guess; was that the ghost she was fighting—an old mistress? Was that why she allowed herself such abandon before an engagement was even announced, let alone a marriage?

If so, then who had killed Robert York, and why?

They were back to treason. Could it possibly be that Veronica herself was hunting her husband's murderer? Could it be Julian who had killed Robert, and did she know it? Was that the terror consuming her—and what lay between her and Loretta?

"Veronica!" Charlotte said aloud. "Miss Danver says that tea will be served in a few minutes. Veronica!"

8

P*ITT CHOSE TO WALK* to Mayfair. It was not a pleasant day; a flat, gray sky closed over the city like a heavy lid and the wind scythed across the park, stinging his skin above his muffler. It crept into the space round his ears and its coldness hurt, making his body tighten against it. Carriages rattled along Park Lane but he saw no one on foot. It was too cold for pleasure; the street vendors knew there would be no business for them here where residents could afford to ride.

He walked because he was going to the Danvers', and he was putting off arriving there as long as he could. Dulcie was dead, so there was no one left to ask about Cerise except Adeline Danver. Part of the chill inside him was guilt— Dulcie's bright, frank face came back to his mind far too easily. If only he had taken the precaution of closing the library door before allowing her to speak! He still did not know which of her two remarks had caused her death—the mention of Cerise, or of the missing necklace. But Pitt's investigation of Piers York's affairs had proved him to be more than financially secure, and in spite of his remark to Dulcie, he did not seem to have claimed for the gems.

All inquiries into other friends of Robert York who might have acquired debt and turned to amateur burglary had also proved fruitless so far. Nor had Pitt succeeded in tracing many of the servants who had been employed in Hanover Close at the time, and dismissed soon after. The butler had taken a position in the country, the valet had gone abroad, the maids had disappeared into the vast mass of female labor in London and its environs.

He stopped; he was outside the Danvers' house already. The air was damp, raw in the throat, with the sour smell of too many fires jetting smoke out into the leaden sky. He could not stand around like a vagrant. Someone held a thread that eventually wound back to murder. If he picked at it, teased it, he thought he might find an end lying with Adeline Danver.

She received him civilly, but with undisguised surprise. He had formed a very clear picture of her in his mind from Charlotte's description; nevertheless he was taken aback by the sharp intelligence in her rather round eyes under their wispy brows. She was a plainer woman than Charlotte had implied: her nose was tip-tilted and narrow, her chin very receding. It was only when she spoke in a voice of remarkable timbre and diction that he saw her beauty.

"Good afternoon, Inspector. I have no idea how I might be of assistance, but of course I shall try. Please do be seated. I don't believe I have ever met a policeman before." She regarded him with open curiosity, as if he were some exotic species of creature imported for her entertainment.

For the first time in years Pitt felt self-conscious; he seemed all hands and feet and coattails. He sat down gingerly, trying to arrange himself with some neatness, and failing.

"Thank you, ma'am."

"Not at all." Her eyes never wavered from his face. "I

209

assume it is about poor Robert York's death? That is the only crime with which I have even the remotest connection—and believe me, it is remote. But I knew him, of course, although there are many others who knew him far better." She smiled very slightly. "I suppose I have the advantage of being an observer of life, rather than a player, so perhaps I have seen something that others may have missed."

He felt transparent, guilty of great insensitivity. "Not at all, Miss Danver." He smiled very faintly. He was not at all sure he should try to be charming—he might end up making a complete fool of himself. "I approach you because I have a very specific question in mind, and you are the person in the house least likely to have any involvement with this event, and therefore to be embarrassed by it, or distressed."

"You take trouble to be tactful," she said with a slight nod of approval. "Thank you for not insulting my intelligence with an idle courtesy. What event do you imagine I may know of? I confess I cannot think what it might be."

"Have you ever seen in this house, alone and not as an ordinary guest, a woman of striking appearance, tall, slender and very dark, wearing a gown of a vivid and unusual shade of magenta or cerise?"

Adeline sat motionless. She might not have been breathing but for the faintest stir of the fichu over her thin, almost bosomless chest.

Pitt waited, staring back at her bright brown eyes. Now there was no possibility of evasion between them. Either she would lie outright, brazenly, or she would tell him the truth.

Outside in the hall a clock struck eleven. The chimes seemed endless, until eventually the last one died away.

"Yes, Mr. Pitt," she said. "I have seen such a woman. But there is no point whatsoever in your asking me who she is, because I do not know. I have seen her twice in this house, and to the best of my knowledge, I have never seen her anywhere else, either before or since."

"Thank you," he said gravely. "Was she wearing the same clothes on both occasions?"

"No, but it was a very similar shade, one darker than the other, as I recollect. But it was at night, and gaslight can be misleading."

"Can you describe her for me, all that you do remember?"

"Who is she, Inspector?"

The use of his title set a distance between them again, warning him not to take her for granted.

"I don't know, Miss Danver. But she is the only clue I have as to who murdered Robert York."

"A woman?" Her eyes widened. "I assume you are suggesting something sordid." It was a statement.

He smiled broadly. "Not necessarily, Miss Danver. I think there may ʰave been a theft, unreported because only Mr. York himself knew of it, and that this woman may have been the thief, or may have witnessed the murder."

"You are full of surprises," Adeline Danver conceded with an answering softness touching the corners of her mouth. "And you cannot find this woman?"

"Not so far. I have been singularly unsuccessful. Can you describe her for me?"

"I am fascinated." She bent her head very slightly to one side. "How do you know she exists?"

"Someone else saw her, in the York house, also by gaslight."

"And their description is not adequate? Or do you fear they are misleading you deliberately?"

Should he frighten her? Dulcie's trusting face came back as sharply as if she had gone out of the library door only yesterday.

"Her description was very brief," he said without moderating the blow at all. "But I can't go back and ask her again because the day after she spoke to me she fell out of an upstairs window to her death."

211

Adeline's thin cheeks were white. She was well acquainted with tragedy. She was over fifty and had known many deaths, but none of them had left her untouched. Much of her life lay in the triumphs and the sorrows of others; it had had to.

"I'm sorry," she said quietly. "You are referring to Veronica York's maid, I assume?"

"Yes." He did not want to seem melodramatic, foolish. "Miss Danver—" He stopped.

"Yes, Inspector?"

"Please do not speak of our conversation to anyone else, even in your own family. They may inadvertently repeat it, without intending harm."

Her eyebrows rose and her thin hands gripped the arms of her chair. "Do I understand you correctly?" Her voice was little more than a breath, but still perfectly controlled, beautifully modulated.

"I believe she is still here, somewhere—at times very close," he replied. "Someone among your family, or your acquaintances knows where she is, who she is—and possibly what really happened on that night three years ago in Hanover Close."

"It is not I, Mr. Pitt."

He smiled bleakly. "If I thought it were, Miss Danver, I should not waste my time asking you."

"But you think one of us, someone I daresay I am fond of, does know this terrible thing?"

"People keep secrets for many reasons," he replied. "Most often out of fear for themselves, or to protect someone they love. Scandal can blow up out of sins that are very slight—if they catch the imagination. And scandal can be a worse punishment for some than imprisonment or financial loss. The admiration of our peers is a far greater prize than some realize—more blood has been shed for it than is seen, and more pain. Women marry men they do not love rather than be imagined to be unloved. People pretend all the time so that others will imagine they are happy. We need our

212

masks, our small illusions; few of us can bear to go naked into the world's gaze. And people will kill to keep their clothes."

She stared at him. "What an odd person you are. Why on earth do you choose to be a policeman?"

He looked down at the carpet. It did not occur to him to evade, still less to lie. "Originally because my father was convicted for something he did not do. The truth has its uses, Miss Danver, and although it can be painful, lies are worse in the end. Though there are times when I hate it, when I learn things I would rather not have to know. But that's cowardice, because we are afraid of the pain of pitying."

"And do you expect it to hurt this time, Mr. Pitt?" she asked, her eyes on his face, her thin fingers picking very slightly at the lace in her skirt.

"No," he said honestly. "No more than the murder already has done. What did she look like, Miss Danver? Could you describe this woman for me?"

She hesitated for a moment, searching her memory. "She was tall," she said slowly. "I think quite definitely taller than average; she had a kind of grace short women cannot possess. And she was slender, not . . ." She blinked, grasping for the word which eluded her. "Not voluptuous, and yet she—no. Her voluptuousness was not in her shape but it was there! Quite definitely it was there; it was in the way she moved. She had passion, style, a kind of daring, as if she were dancing a great ballet along a razor's edge. I'm sorry— do I sound ridiculous?"

"No." He shook his head without taking his eyes from hers. "No, if what I guess about her is right, then that is a fitting analogy. Go on."

"She had dark hair, black it seemed in the gaslight. I only caught the briefest glimpse of her face, and I remember she was very beautiful."

"What sort of face?" Pitt pressed. "There are many kinds of beauty."

"Unusual," she said slowly, and he knew she was trying to picture the moment again, the gaslight on the landing, the vivid dress, the turn of the head till she saw the features. "There was a perfect balance between the brow and the nose, the cheek and the curve of the throat; it was all a matter of bones and a sweeping hairline. It was nothing ordinary, like arched eyebrows or a pouting mouth, or dimples. She reminded me vaguely of someone, and yet I am perfectly sure I had never seen her before."

"Are you?"

"Yes. And you may choose to believe me or not, but it is the truth. It was not Veronica, which I assume you are imagining, and it was most certainly not my niece Harriet."

"Who did she remind you of? Please try to recall."

"I have tried, Mr. Pitt. I can only think it may be someone whose picture I have seen. Artists' impressions can be most misleading. They change so much with the fashion of the times, have you noticed? They paint you as they think you wish to look. But photographs give a remarkable likeness. I am sorry, I have no idea who it is, so there is no purpose in your pressing me. If at any time it comes to me, I shall certainly tell you. That I promise."

"Then promise me also, Miss Danver, that you will not discuss this with anyone else, nor entrust a message to anyone—anyone at all. I really do mean what I say." He leaned forward a little. If he frightened her it was a small price to pay for saving her life. "Robert York is dead, and so is Dulcie, both in their own homes, where they thought they were safe. Give me your word, Miss Danver."

"Very well, Mr. Pitt," she agreed. "If you really believe it is so serious. I shall discuss it with no one. You may cease to worry about it." She looked at him levelly, her round, clever eyes very grave. "Good gracious, Mr. Pitt—your concern is a trifle unnerving!"

* * *

214

Outside again in the gray street he turned and walked south. He must find the woman in cerise. He had already exhausted the easier avenues, the hotels and theaters where she would have been most likely to meet her clients. He had questioned the doorkeepers, the prostitutes who might have been her rivals, as well as the pimps and madams. They either did not know her or would not say. It all confirmed what he imagined from the beginning, that she was a spy, not a woman earning her living from prostitution. She was not interested in general trade, only certain men in particular. And she had taken great care not to be traced.

Finding Cerise would be a matter of laborious, detailed police work. He knew at least one place which she had patronized several times, and now he had a close and unusual description. No one in the business of sexual favors for hire was likely to help him further; all the middlemen reaped their profits from silence. But there were always people in a London street who were almost invisible, people who might remember, who made their livelihood from passersby, their hungry eyes watching each one for even the tiniest signs of willingness to buy.

He stepped over to the curb and raised his arm, shouting to a hansom as it plodded along Park Lane through the thickening mist. There was snow in the wind. He climbed in and gave the address of the hotel where he had found the doorman who remembered Cerise, sitting back to wait out the slow, cold journey. This was not the best time to begin—the vendors he wanted would be the ones who worked at night—but he had nothing else to pursue, and there was an urgency inside him.

He stopped short of the hotel itself and left the cab on the corner, opposite a stall where a man wearing a white apron and a black hat with a ribbon round it was selling hot eels. Beside him, a girl ladled out thick pea soup at a halfpenny a cup.

The aroma drifted on the wet air and Pitt automatically reached in his pocket. He had never acquired the native Londoners' taste for eels, but he was partial to pea soup. A red-faced woman was before him in the queue, but after she was served he produced his halfpenny and took the hot cup gratefully. The liquid was thick and a little lumpy, but the flavor was rich and its warmth rippled through him, creating a tiny heart of strength inside.

"You here in the evenings?" he asked casually.

"Sometimes, in the summer wiv ve eels," the man answered. "Vis time o' year anyone wiv an 'ome ter go to is in it! Vem as 'asn't usual don't 'ave money neither."

"Who'd be here in the evening?"

The man went on ladling eels. "Wot time yer talkin' abaht? Early on, till eight or nine, 'er." He gestured to a small girl about fifty yards up the pavement, who stood shivering in the cold, a box of sweet violets by her bare feet. She might have been ten or eleven years old.

"I'll take another cup of soup." Pitt gave the man a second halfpenny and took the cup from the girl. "Thank you." He turned to walk away.

"Hey! I want me cup back!" the man shouted behind him.

"You'll get it," Pitt said over his shoulder, "when it's empty." He approached the flower girl. She was only a few years older than Jemima, with a pinched face and few underclothes beneath her plain dark dress and faded shawl. Her feet were mottled red and blue with extreme cold.

He put the cup of soup down on the pavement and fished in his pocket for two more pennies.

"I'll have two bunches of violets for my wife," he said, holding out the coins.

"Thank you, sir." She took the pennies, glancing at him out of clear blue eyes, then stole a glance at the steaming soup.

He picked it up and took a sip, then set it down again.

"I've bought more than I can eat," he said. "You can finish it if you like."

She hesitated; nothing came into her life without a price.

216

"I don't want it," he repeated.

Very carefully she reached out her hand and picked it up, still watching him.

"Have you been on this street long?" he asked, knowing as he said it that she was probably too young to be any help to him. But he had bought the soup without thinking of Cerise.

"Two year," she replied, sipping soup with a slurp and sucking it round her mouth.

"Is it busy in the evenings?"

"Fair."

"Are there other traders here?"

"Some. 'Bout two or free."

"Who? What do they sell?"

"There's a woman wot sells combs, but she goes early. Girl wot sells matches sometimes. An' o' course there's 'im wot sells 'ot plum duff; 'e's 'ere of an evenin'. An' sometimes there's patterers. They moves abaht, mostly from Seven Dials way, 'cause vat's w'ere the printers is."

He did not need to question her, he knew what running patterers were: men of prodigious memory and usually a nice turn of humor, who sold red-hot news, generally of crime and seduction. And if there was nothing sufficiently grisly in truth, then they were not above inventing something, replete with detail, and frequently showing pictures.

"Thank you," he said civilly, picking up the empty cup. "I'll come back this evening."

He went home for dinner and gave Charlotte, to her surprise and delight, both bunches of violets. Then at about ten o'clock he forced himself to go out again into the freezing fog.

It was a vile night, and there was no one in the street outside the hotel except a fat, pasty-faced youth selling hot plum duff, a cooked dough filled with sultanas and kept at a good temperature with layers of steaming cloth. The youth was well patronized by the men leaving the hotel, but after half an hour of standing and stamping his feet to keep the circulation going and a couple of brisk turns round the block, Pitt had seen none of the women who used the hotel rooms for their trade.

He questioned the plum duff boy and learned nothing at all. The boy had been there five years, he thought, but he had never noticed a woman in cerise.

The following night he came again, but he was no more successful, and the night after that he went instead to the Lyceum Theatre. He spoke to a seller of peppermint water who had seen someone in brilliant pink but could not recall her height, and rather thought she had had red hair.

Then after midnight, angry with the futility of it all, his feet numb in the settling snow and with his collar up round his ears, he moved forward amid the din of shouting, laughter, and occasional jeers as the theater turned out. He saw a youth selling ham sandwiches and decided to buy one. He was not hungry, but he liked ham. He pushed his way through the throng, jostled by elbows and plump bustles, assaulted by the smell of perfume, sweat, and beery breath till he reached the sandwich man in the street beyond. There was a threepence in his pocket but his fingers were too cold to grasp it.

The youth looked at him expectantly. He was thin and there were hectic spots of color in his cheeks. It was a wretched living and Pitt knew it, standing outside in all weather, often half the night, and to make enough to survive they had to buy the meat on the bone and cook it themselves, then cut the sandwiches. He made less than a halfpenny profit on each sandwich sold, and Pitt knew that anything spoiled or lost could wipe out the day's takings.

"I'll have two, please." He gripped the threepenny bit at last and produced it. The youth gave him two sandwiches and a penny change.

"Thank you." Pitt bit into the first sandwich and found it surprisingly good. "Have you been here long?"

"Abaht eight hour," the boy replied. "But they're fresh, guv, I made 'em meself!" He looked anxious.

"They're excellent," Pitt agreed with more enthusiasm than he felt for anything except the idea of going home. "I meant, have you had this patch for long? For example, were you here three or four years ago?"

"Oh. Yeah, I bin 'ere since I were fourteen."

"Do you ever remember seeing a very beautiful woman in a dark, very bright plum pink dress, about three years ago? Very striking woman, tall, with dark hair. Please think carefully, it's very important."

"What sort o' woman, guv? Yer mean one o' them?" He inclined his head very slightly towards a lush-looking woman with a pile of loose fair hair and rouge on her plump cheeks.

"Yes, but more expensive, more class."

"One as I saw like that, wearing that sort o' color, looked more like a lady ter me—though she were with a gent as was never 'er 'usband."

Pitt deliberately quelled his feeling of excitement.

"How do you know?"

"Garn!" The boy pulled a face of disbelief. " 'E were all over 'er. Eyes like limpets, 'e 'ad. An' she were leading 'im on proper; all very tasteful like, but I seen too many not ter know. Some folks 'as class, and some 'asn't, but it's all the same in the end. Proper beauty, she were, though."

"Was she buxom?" Pitt made an hourglass in the air with his hands, almost losing his sandwich in the process.

"No." The youth's eyebrows rose in surprise. "No, she weren't. It were summer an' she 'ad a real low gown an' she were right scrawny! But ever so elegant!"

"Tall or short?" Pitt could not keep his voice from rising.

"Tall. Tall as me, I reckon, at least. Why? She someone you know? I an't seen 'er since then. I can't 'elp yer. She must 'ave moved uptown, or got married—which in't likely, ter be honest wiv yer. More like she come to a bad end. Got

219

some sickness, or someone carved 'er up. Mebbe she got the pox, or the cholera.''

"Maybe. Can you describe the man she was with? How did she leave? Which direction did she go?''

"You are keen! I didn't take no notice o' the gent she was wiv, 'cept 'e were dead elegant as well. Looked better-class than most yer get rahnd 'ere. 'E weren't no clerk or trades-man out for an evenin'. 'E were definitely a toff come slum-min'. But yer gets a few o' them, if they wants a bit o' relaxation wivout the missus, ner anyone as they know as'd tell on 'em.''

"Where did they go? Did they go together?''

The youth looked at Pitt scornfully. " 'Course they went together! No toff treats no tart to an evenin' at the theayter, 'owever classy she is, just ter wish 'er good night on the steps arterwards!''

"In a cab, or a carriage?''

"A cab, o' course! Don't take their own carriages if'n they're out on the sly! Use a bit o' common, guv!''

"Good. Where is the nearest rank of cabs from here?''

"Rahnd the corner an 'baht 'undred yards down the street.''

"Thank you.'' And before the youth could express his doubts, Pitt had disappeared into the swirl of falling snow beyond the canopy of the theater.

"Crazy,'' the boy said cheerfully and curled his fingers round the pennies in his pocket. " 'Am sammiches! Fresh 'am sammiches! Only a penny each!''

Over the next two days Pitt plowed through the snow, feet freezing, legs wet from the slush in the gutters, as he coughed in the smoke and fog clamped over the city roofs by an icy sky. He found every cabdriver from the rank and questioned them all. He also found two crossing sweepers who had worked the area at the relevant time. One had come up in the world and had an interest in a hot coffee stall, the other had found a better crossing. None of them could do more than describe Cerise and say that she had arrived at the hotel and the theater in a cab and left in one.

Only one cabbie could remember where he had taken her, and that was to Hanover Close.

Pitt returned home so cold he was sick inside. His hands and feet hurt, and failure seemed to close round him as completely as the thick sourness of the night.

It was long after midnight and the house was silent. Only the light just inside the hall was on. He put his key in the lock, finding it carefully with the tips of his frozen fingers. It took him several moments.

Inside it was warm. Charlotte had banked up the fire and there was note pinned on the parlor door where he could not miss it.

> Dear Thomas,
> The kitchen fire is still warm, the kettle is full, and there is hot soup in the pan if you want it. The oddest man came just before dark and left a letter for you. He said he knew about the woman in pink—I suppose he means Cerise. He was a "running patterer," whatever that is. I left the letter on the parlor mantelpiece.
> Wake me up if I can help.
>
> > Love,
> > Charlotte

He pushed open the parlor door and felt for the knob of the gas lamp and turned it up. He saw the letter and tore it open, ripping out the paper and straightening it.

> Dear Mr. Pitt,
> I heard as you been asking around after the woman who wears a strange color of pink, and you are very desirous of finding her. I know where she is, and if you are willing to make it worth my trouble I will take you to her.

If you are interested come to the Triple Plea public house in Seven Dials tomorrow evening about six o'clock.

S. Smith

Pitt smiled and folded the letter carefully, putting it in his pocket. He tiptoed through to the kitchen.

The following evening he walked slowly through the fine ice-cold drizzle, woolen muffler high round his ears, along a gray alley in the district of Seven Dials. He knew why the man had chosen this part of the city; it was, as the flower girl had said, where the news sheets were printed and the natural headquarters of the running patterers. They made their living selling news or song sheets by the yard, constantly on the move crying the thrills and dramas within their pages. Most were based on the latest crime—the more gruesome, the better. Occasionally it was love letters of the utmost indiscretion. They might be of a famous person, an international beauty, or more tantalizingly an unnamed "lady of this neighborhood—to a gentleman not a hundred miles away!" If the truth were currently a little flavorless, then they had wit and imagination enough to retell some of the old favorites: wronged women who murdered either their faithless lovers, or the poor infants of the union, which well told, would bring tears to many a reader's eye. Running patterers were usually men of some enterprise and a keen observation of human nature; it did not surprise Pitt that it should be one of these who had noticed and remembered Cerise. The man's occupation was the retelling of tales of passion, murder, and beautiful women.

It was bitterly cold, and the narrow alleys made funnels for the wind. The dim figures Pitt passed were hunched forward, heads sunk into their shoulders, faces averted. In doorways sleepers piled together like sacks for the heat of each other's bodies. The splinters of a broken gin bottle caught a gleam of light from a gas lamp.

Pitt found the Triple Plea after only one false turn. Pushing his way through the raucous drinkers in the public bar, he reached the counter. The landlord, in a beer-stained calico apron, shirt sleeves at half mast, looked at his unfamiliar face warily.

"Yeah?"

"Anyone asking for me?" Pitt asked quietly. "Name's Pitt."

"An' why should I know that? I in't a public service!"

"Oh, but you are." Pitt forced a civil expression to his face. He fished in his pocket and brought out a sixpence. "And services should be paid for, when they're worth it. When someone does ask, you tell me. Meantime I'll have a cider."

The man eyed the money ungraciously, pulled a draft cider into a tankard, and pushed it across. "There y'are. 'Is name's Black Sam, an' 'e's over in the corner wiv a blue shirt and a brown coat—an' the cider'll be extra."

"Naturally," Pitt agreed, and added another tuppence. He took the glass and sipped from it gingerly. Actually it was rough and sweet, and surprisingly good. Taking a long drink, he made his way quite slowly over to the corner indicated, his eyes roaming to find the patterer. Several of the men here were probably of that occupation; they were not far from the printing houses, and they had the mobile faces, the quick eyes and lean figures of men who were constantly on the move.

He saw a man with an unusually dark complexion and a bright blue shirt sitting over a jar of ale. Almost immediately their eyes met, and Pitt knew it was S. Smith; there was an air of waiting in him, a restless scanning of faces. Pitt forced his way through and stopped in front of the cramped table.

"Mr. Smith?"

"That's right."

"Pitt. You said that for a consideration you could help me."

"So I can. Drink yer cider; then when I leave, foller me

223

out a minute or two be'ind. Don't want ter give folks reason ter think, thinkin' in't good fer 'em. I'll be outside on the street opposite. I 'ope yer've brought summink gen'rous wiv yer? I don't give no credit. Noos is noos, an' I makes me livin' by it.''

"Sometimes it is," Pitt said coolly. "Sometimes it's lies. I've heard plenty of good cocks before.'' A "cock" was a colorful melodrama invented when real news was slow; there were several famous ones making the rounds.

Black Sam smiled, showing crooked teeth that were surprisingly clean. "Sure. But they're fer entertainin' ladies as like a good cry an' no 'arm done if the story is a bit— decorated like. That's art.''

"Quite. Well, I'd like nature, or nothing.''

"Oh, you'll get it, don't fret.'' And he stood up, tipped his mug back and drained it to the last drop, set it back on the bench, and pushed past Pitt without looking at him again. A moment later he had disappeared.

Pitt finished his cider without hurrying, then edged his way out into the night. The fine drizzle had stopped and it was beginning to freeze over. There were no stars because of the pall of smoke that hung over the city from the tens of thousands of chimneys. He could see the dim outline of Black Sam on the far curb. He crossed over and approached him.

"How much?" Sam said pleasantly without moving.

"If I find the woman in the pink dress and she's the right one, half a crown.''

"An' wot's ter stop yer sayin' it in't the right one?''

Pitt had already thought of that. "My reputation. If I fiddle you out of what's rightly yours for services rendered, no one'll give me information in the future, and then I can't do my job.''

Sam thought it over for a moment, but he was not long in his decision. Word spread fast among people who lived on the edge between survival and despair, and he made his own way by judging people. "Yer on," he agreed. "Follow me.''

And at last he straightened up and began to walk with a gait that was a deceptively rapid kind of lope. Pitt was hard pressed to keep up with him; although he was used to being on his feet all day it was with a measured tread, even back when he had been a constable. Now he was accustomed to riding, and the patterer's speed left him breathless.

Fifteen minutes later they were almost at the far side of Seven Dials and in a more salubrious neighborhood, but still the streets were narrow and a practiced eye could recognize cheap lodging houses, and several that were almost certainly used as brothels. If Cerise were here then she had indeed fallen on hard times since the days of the Lyceum and the hotel where the doorkeeper had remembered her.

The patterer stopped and stood still on the grimy pavement.

"Up them stairs," Black Sam said smoothly. He might have been on an evening's stroll for any difference the run had made to him. "Knock on the door at the top an' ask ter see Fred. 'E'll tell yer where yer party is. I'll wait 'ere, and if 'e does, I'll trust yer ter come back down an' give me me 'alf crown. Can't say fairer than that. If 'e don't, then we've 'ad a nice walk fer nuffin.''

Pitt hesitated, but it was hardly worth the haggling. Wordlessly he went across to the steps indicated and climbed them slowly, making as little noise as possible. The door at the top was heavy and closed. He knocked hard, hurting his knuckles. After a moment it opened and a thin youth with a knife scar across his cheek looked at him without interest.

"I want to see Fred," Pitt said, standing well back.

"Wot fer? I in't seen you afore!"

"Business," Pitt replied. "Get him."

"Fred! Geezer 'ere for yer—says it's business!" the youth shouted.

Pitt waited for several minutes in silence before Fred appeared. He was rotund, red-faced and surprisingly agreeable. He smiled toothlessly. "Yeah?"

225

"I'm looking for a woman in a pink dress, very vivid dark pink. Black Sam said you know where I can find her."

"Yeah, that's right. She rents a room orf me."

"Now?"

"Yeah o' course now! Wot's the matter wiv yer? Think I'm daft?"

"Is she there now, in this room of yours?"

"Yeah. But I don't let just anybody in. Mebbe she'll see yer, an' mebbe she won't. She might already 'ave company, like."

"Naturally. I don't expect something for nothing. What does she look like, this woman in pink of yours?"

"Wot does she look like?" His pale eyebrows rose up to his nonexistent hairline. "Geez! Wot do you care? You must 'ave a lot more money than yer look like if yer can afford ter care!"

"I care," Pitt said between his teeth. "That's what matters to me." A good lie came to his mind. "I'm an artist. Now, tell me!"

"All right, all right." He shrugged genially. "If you say so. But I don't know why yer want ter paint 'er; she's as thin as a washboard, don't 'ave no bosom and no 'ips. But she 'as got a face, I'll give 'er that. She 'as a curious fine face, an' black 'air. Now make up yer mind an' don't stand 'ere on the doorstep like a fool. I 'an't got the time, even if you 'ave!"

"I'll see her," Pitt said instantly. "I owe Black Sam. Let me go and pay him, then I'll be back to pay you for your trouble."

"Then get on wiv it!" Fred urged. "I got work ter do."

Ten minutes later Pitt, debts discharged, stood in a red-carpeted passageway with faded, dirty footmarks along the center and a gas lamp hissing gently on the wall. He knocked on the door at the end of the passage. Nothing happened. He knocked again, more loudly. Fred had assured him she was there, and he had described her too closely not to know who

226

she was. He had spoken of characteristics Pitt had not even mentioned.

A door opened behind him and a large woman with a cascade of blond hair came out, a shawl wrapped round her more than ample figure, her bare shoulders smooth, rippling with fat.

"Leave off that racket, mister!" she said curtly. "Yer want in, then go in! Door's not locked. Don't stand there disturbin' everyone! I got customers. You sound like a raid, put people off!"

"Yes ma'am," he said with a lift of excitement. So Cerise was actually in there. In a moment he would see her, and perhaps know the secret of Robert York's death. He turned away from the blonde, already returning to her customer, and twisted the handle of the door. She was right, it was not locked. It opened easily under his hand and he went in.

The room was more or less what he had expected: comfortable but messy, overfurnished, smelling of perfume, fine dust, and stale sheets. There were too many cushions and too much red. The bed was large and rumpled, two quilts thrown carelessly so he could not see at a glance whether there was anyone lying under them or not. He closed the door behind him.

When he was standing beside the bed he recognized the human outline of the form, and saw a flash of magenta satin, a strand of black hair like a loose band of silk. The woman's face was turned away.

He was about to address her, then realized he had no idea what her name was. He had thought of her as Cerise. When he knew of her, she had been on the crest of the wave. In three years she had fallen to this. She was hardly the same person. His excitement on the point of discovery was suddenly shot through with pity. The more dashing, the more reckless she had been, the deeper this reduction cut with its tawdry intimacy. She might have been an instrument of treason, a murderess or accessory to murder; still he felt intrusive now.

"Madam," he said inadequately.

She did not move. She must be very heavily asleep, perhaps even drunk. He leaned forward and touched her shoulder under the quilt, then shook her very slightly.

Still she did not move. He pulled her more strongly, turning her over, revealing the vivid magenta silk bodice with its low neck and slash of fuchsia. She had drunk herself insensible. He leant forward, taking both his hands to her shoulders, and shook her. Her hair fell back off her face and the quilt slipped.

At first he could not believe it. The head lolled a little sideways, unnaturally, not with the unresponsiveness of sleep but the limp finality of death. Her neck was broken. It must have been a single blow of great force. She was thin; he could see now the fragility of her bones. It was hard to tell if she had been beautiful. Without vitality there was only a certain grace of proportion left.

"Oh Gawd!"

For a moment he thought he had spoken himself, then he realized there was someone in the room.

"You bloody fool! Wot yer go an' do that fer? Poor little bleeder, she never done you no 'arm!"

Pitt straightened up slowly and turned to look at Fred; white-faced, he blocked the door.

"I didn't kill her," Pitt said impatiently. "She was dead when I got here. You'd better go out and find a constable. Who came in here before I did?"

"Oh, I'll send for a rozzer—yer can be sure o' that!" Fred said savagely. "But I can't leave you 'ere. Gawd knows 'oo else I might find dead if I did!"

"I didn't kill her!" Pitt said between his teeth, holding his temper with difficulty. "I found her dead. Go and get the police!"

Fred remained motionless. "And o' course you'll wait

'ere for me to come back wiv 'em. You must take me fer a fool!''

Pitt stood up and moved towards him. Instantly Fred stiffened and his fists came up. For the first time Pitt realized that for all his apparent civility, Fred had every intention of stopping him with violence if necessary, and he was built to succeed with it.

"I am the police," he said abruptly. "We've been looking for this woman in connection with a murder, maybe treason."

"Yeah? An' I'm the Duke o' Wellington!" Fred was wedged massively in the doorway, his arms hanging, loosely, in case Pitt should attempt any sudden attack. "Rosie!" he shouted without taking his eyes off Pitt. "Rosie! Come 'ere! Quick!"

Pitt began again, "I am—"

"Shut up, you!" Fred snapped. "Rosie! Get yerself 'ere afore I comes and gets yer!"

The huge blonde appeared, wrapped in a voluminous pink sheet and flushed with irritation. "Look, Fred, I pays good rent 'cos I do me business 'ere! I don't look to get yelled at an' disturbed every—" She stopped, sensing something serious. "Wot's the matter? Wot 'appened?"

"This 'ere geezer done fer the girl wot wears that 'orrible pink color. Strangled 'er, by the looks."

"Poor little cow." Rosie shook her head. "In't no call fer that."

"Well, go an' get the rozzers, yer fat bitch!" Fred said angrily. "Don't just stand there! There's bin murder!"

"Don't you go callin' me names, Fred Bunn!" she said tartly. "An' I in't goin' lookin' fer no rozzers. I'll send Jacko downstairs." And wrapping her sheet round her in a more dignified manner she turned her back and went towards the stairs.

Pitt sat down on the edge of the bed. There was no point

in arguing with Fred, who was set in his belief. When the police came it would all be sorted out.

Fred leaned against the doorpost. "Wot yer want ter go and do that fer?" he said sadly. "Yer didn't 'ave to kill 'er."

"I didn't," Pitt repeated. "I wanted her alive! I needed to ask her some very important questions."

"Oh, yeah. Treason!" Fred snorted. "Well, ye're original, I'll say that for yer. Poor little cow!"

"How long has she been here?" Pitt asked. He might as well make use of the time.

"I dunno. Couple o' days."

"Only a couple of days?" Pitt was surprised. "Where was she before that?"

" 'Ow the 'ell do I know? She paid 'er rent, that's all I care about."

Pitt felt inexpressibly weary. It was all so pathetic. Cerise, whatever her name really was, had had a childhood somewhere, then a brief career as a courtesan, glittering by night, perhaps dangerous even then; hidden by day. Then fortune had changed, her looks had faded and she had fallen out of fashion, reduced to the status of an ordinary prostitute. Finally she had had her neck broken in some senseless quarrel in this shabby rented room.

He turned back to look at her. This was the woman who had held such power, briefly, over Robert York and either Julian Danver or Garrard, such power that she had entered their houses, flouting every convention, running desperate risks. What if Veronica had seen her, or Loretta, or even Piers York? Loretta would not have turned the other way as Adeline had; she was of far more ruthless mettle. She would have tackled Robert and told him precisely where he should conduct his amours.

He looked down at the thin form on the bed. Her skin was dark, almost olive, and smooth as an old sepia print over her shoulders. But above the brilliant magenta ribbon round her neck it was already coarse-textured, and there were fine lines in her face, purplish shadows under her eyes. The bones were delicate, the mouth full-lipped, but it was hard to tell now if she had once been beautiful. But life could have wrought magic. She might have had wit, that rare smile that lights a face, the gift for listening with the kind of attention that makes the speaker feel for a moment that he is the center of all laughter and wisdom. Pretty faces were a shilling a dozen, charm was something else altogether.

Poor Cerise.

Pitt was jerked out of his thoughts by the heavy tramp of feet in the passage beyond Fred's motionless figure. He heard Rosie's voice, shrill and indignant, and somewhere a man wailed.

The constable appeared, his blue cape wet with the fine rain and his bull's-eye lantern at his belt, truncheon ready in his hand.

"Well?" he demanded. "Where's this 'ere woman you said as was dead, then?"

" 'Ere," Fred answered sullenly. He did not like policemen, and it was grudgingly he conceded the necessity now. "And this is the geezer wot killed 'er—Gawd knows why. But I let 'im in 'ere quarter hour ago, 'cause 'e was askin' for 'er most partic'lar. Then I 'as ter come up 'ere fer suffink else, and she's as dead as mutton, poor beggar. So I sends Rosie to tell Jacko ter fetch yer. She'll tell yer the same."

The constable pushed past Fred and stared into the room, his round face puckering with a mixture of sadness and distaste. He looked at Pitt and sighed.

"Now wot yer go an' do a fing like that fer? In't yer wife, or anyfink like vat, is she?"

"No, or course not!" Pitt said angrily. Suddenly all the pretense seemed ludicrous. "I'm a police officer, Inspector Pitt from the Bow Street station, and we've been looking for this woman for weeks. I tracked her down here, but I was too late to stop her being murdered. She was an important witness."

The constable looked up and down at Pitt's knitted muffler, his old coat, rather shapeless trousers, and worn boots. Disbelief was patent in his face.

"Check with Bow Street!" Pitt snapped. "Superintendent Ballarat!"

"I'll take yer ter Seven Dials; they can send ter Bow Street," the constable said stolidly. "Yer make no fuss and yer won't get 'urt. Get nasty an' I'll 'ave ter get rough wiv yer." He turned to Fred. " 'Oo else 'as bin up 'ere since you seen 'er"—he gestured to the dead woman on the bed—"alive?"

"Geez! A little skinny geezer wiv Newgate knockers," he said, putting his fingers up in a spiral to describe the cheek curls, "fer Clarrie. But she came down an' fetched 'em. An' a bald-'eaded feller, 'baht fortyish, fer Rosie, an' I brought 'im up 'ere and saw 'im inter Rosie's room. But 'e's a reg'lar."

"So no one else 'as bin up 'ere but 'im?"

"An' the girls," Fred finished. "Ask 'em."

"Oh, I will, you can be sure o' vat. An' yer better all be 'ere when we wants yer, or yer'll be 'unted down an' arrested fer 'idin' hevidence in a murder—an' end up in Coldbath Fields, or Newgate." He looked at Pitt. "Nah, you comin' quiet, or do I 'ave ter be unpleasant wiv yer? Gimme yer 'ands."

"What?" Pitt was startled.

"Yer 'ands, mister! You take me for a fool? I in't a walkin' yer back through the streets in the dark wivout the bracelets on yer."

Pitt opened his mouth to protest, then realized the pointlessness of it, and thrust out his hands obediently.

Two hours later, sitting in the Seven Dials police station, still manacled, he was beginning to feel panic rising hot inside him. A message had been sent to Bow Street, and a neatly written answer had been returned. Yes, they knew

232

Thomas Pitt, who answered the description precisely, but they could not agree that he had been sent to arrest anyone. They knew of no prostitute in a pink dress, and as far as they were concerned there was nothing of the sort connected with the case upon which Pitt was working. He had been assigned to look more carefully into the robbery at the home of Piers York in Hanover Close some three years ago, and the murder by an intruder of his son, Robert York. As far as Superintendent Ballarat knew, Pitt had failed to discover anything of material interest. The officer in charge of this unfortunate murder must handle it with all the justice and dispatch of which he was capable. Of course, Superintendent Ballarat wished, as a professional courtesy, to be kept informed of events as they should transpire, with the profound hope that Thomas Pitt was not guilty of anything except foolishness, and perhaps the kind of immorality that men fell prey to from time to time. Nevertheless, justice must be done. There could be no exceptions.

When Fred had first found him Pitt had only been able to think of Cerise, the futility of finding her when it was too late, the shabby reality of death. That they had mistaken him for the murderer had seemed farcical at the time. But now it was becoming appallingly clear that they did not believe him, and all his protestations, instead of making the truth obvious, were falling uselessly on their ears, like the excuses of any other criminal caught red-handed. And Ballarat had no intention of risking Society's indignation and his superiors' displeasure by stepping forward to defend Pitt or his actions. He did not want there to have been treason, he did not want to have to investigate the Yorks or the Danvers, or Felix Asherson, and he was only too happy to be rid of the one man who was pressing him to do it. If Pitt were convicted of murder he would be even more effectively silenced than if he were dead.

The sweat broke out on Pitt's skin, then chilled instantly, leaving him shivering and a little sick. What would happen to Charlotte? Emily would see to her financially, thank God! But what about the disgrace, the public shame? Policemen had few friends; a policeman hanged for murdering a prostitute had none at all. Charlotte would find every hand turned against her: neighbors and erstwhile friends would abhor her; the underworld that normally had some care for its own, who might have given something to an ordinary hanged man's widow, would have no pity for a policeman's family. And Daniel and Jemima would grow up with the shadow of the gibbet across their hearts, always hiding who they were, trying to defend him, never really knowing—Pitt stopped; these thoughts were unbearable.

"Come on!" The voice yanked him from his inner misery back to the urgency of the present. "Coldbath Fields fer you; yer can't sit 'ere all night. Let's be 'avin' yer!"

He looked up to see the chill boiled-blue eyes of a constable regarding him with the kind of loathing that police reserve for their own kind who have betrayed everything they have given their lives to preserve.

"On yer feet! Gotter learn ter do as ye're told, you 'ave!"

9

CHARLOTTE HAD expected Pitt to be late getting home, so she went to bed a little before eleven, unhappy that things between them were still unresolved. She woke with a start in the morning, aware even before she opened her eyes that something was wrong. There was a coldness, a silence. She sat up. Pitt's side of the bed was as neat and untouched as it had been when she put the sheets on clean the day before. She scrambled out and reached for her robe without any clear idea of what she was going to do. Perhaps there was a note downstairs. Could he have come in and had to go out again without time to sleep at all? For the moment she dared not think beyond that. She did not even bother with slippers and she winced as her bare feet touched the cold floor in the passageway.

She looked first in the kitchen, but there was nothing; the kettle was where she had left it and the cups were unused. She went to the parlor, but there was nothing there either. She tried to fill her mind with good reasons for Pitt's absence, so her fears could not intrude: he was on the trail of something, and so close to victory he could not leave it; he had actually made an arrest and was still at the police station; there had been another murder, and he was so busy with it he could not come home, and he had not sent a messenger during the night because he did not want to waken her, and no stranger could get in without his key—but her common sense stopped her there. There was always the letter box; it would have been simple to slip a note in to tell her.

Well, any minute now someone would come, perhaps even Pitt himself. She should get dressed. She was shuddering with the chill and her bare feet were numb. There was no point in standing here. Gracie would be up soon and the children must have breakfast. She turned and went upstairs quickly, into the oddly empty bedroom. She took off her robe and nightgown, still shivering, and put on her camisole, petticoats, stockings, and an old, dark blue dress. Her fingers were clumsy this morning and she could not be bothered to do anything with her hair except wind it in a loose coil and pin it up. She would wash her face in the kitchen downstairs where the water was hot. Surely by then there would be a message.

She had just reached for a rough, dry towel and felt its clean abrasiveness on her skin when the doorbell rang. She dropped the towel onto the bench accidentally dragging it with her elbow and pulling it onto the floor. She ignored it, running along the passage to the front door, which she flung open. A red-faced constable stood on the doorstep, misery so heavy in his features that she was instantly afraid. Her breath stopped.

"Mrs. Pitt?" he asked.

She stared at him speechlessly.

"I'm terribly sorry, ma'am," he said wretchedly. "But I 'as ter tell yer that Inspector Pitt 'as bin arrested fer killin' a woman in Seven Dials. 'E said as 'er neck was already broke when 'e found her—no doubtin' it was. 'E'd never do such a fing. But fer ve time bein' 'e's bin took to the 'Ouse o' Correction at Coldbath Fields. 'E's all right, ma'am! There's no

236

need ter—ter take on!'' He stood helpless, unable to offer any comfort. He did not know how much she knew of "the Steel,'' but lies were useless: she would find out soon enough. Its nickname was a corruption of Bastille, and with good reason.

Charlotte remained frozen. At first she felt relief: at least he was not dead. That had been the fear she had not dared to name. Then a kind of darkness closed round her as if it were dusk, not dawn. Arrested! In prison? She had heard more than even Pitt knew of the houses of correction like Coldbath Fields. They were the short-term jails where people were taken before trial, or for brief sentences. No one could survive for more than a year in them; they were crowded, brutal and filthy. It had been one of Aunt Vespasia's passions to get rid of at least the worst of the epidemic jail fever.

But surely Pitt would only be there for a few hours—a day at most—until they realized their mistake.

"Ma'am?'' the constable interrupted anxiously, his blue eyes puckered and very earnest. "Mebbe you should sit down, ma'am, take a cup o' tea.''

Charlotte looked back at him in surprise. She had forgotten he was still there. "No.'' Her voice seemed to come from far away. "No, I—I don't need to sit down. Where did you say he was—did you say Coldbath Fields?''

"Yes, ma'am.'' He wanted to say something else but the words eluded him. He was used to horror and misery, but he had never had to tell a colleague's wife that he was charged with murder—of a prostitute! His face was blurred with pity for her.

"Then I'll have to take his things.'' She was reaching for a solid idea, something practical she could latch on to, something she could do to help him. "Shirts. Clean linen. Will they feed him?''

"Yes, ma'am. But I'm sure a little extra won't come amiss, if it's plain like. But 'ave yer got a brother, or someone as could go for yer? It in't a very nice place fer a lady.''

"No, I haven't. I'll go myself. I'll just make sure the maid is up to care for the children. Thank you, Constable."

"Yer sure, ma'am? In't nuffin' I can do?"

"Yes, I'm sure." Leaving him on the step, she closed the door gently and walked back towards the kitchen on wobbling legs. She bumped into the door lintel on the way in, but her mind was so dazed it was moments before the pain of it registered. In time there would be a purple bruise, but all she could think of now was Pitt, cold, hungry, and at the mercy of the warders of the Steel.

Very carefully she cut the fresh loaf, buttered the slices, and then carved the cold meat that was to have done them all for the next two days. She wrapped the sandwiches and put them in a basket. Next she went upstairs and took out his newly laundered underlinen and a good shirt, then realized that was foolish and chose the oldest ones instead. She was still at the press on the landing when Gracie came down from her attic bedroom and stopped on the last stair.

"You lost summink, ma'am?"

Charlotte closed the cupboard doors and turned round slowly.

"No, thank you, Gracie, I have it. I must go out. I don't know when I shall be back; it may be late. I took the meat for Mr. Pitt. You'll have to find something else for us."

Gracie blinked, hugging her shawl closer round her.

"Ma'am, you look terrible white. 'As summink 'appened?" Her little face was pinched with dismay.

There was no point in lying; Charlotte would have to tell her soon enough.

"Yes. They have arrested Mr. Pitt; they say he killed some woman in Seven Dials. I'm going to take—to take some things for him. I—" Suddenly she was on the edge of tears, she could feel her throat tighten and her voice would not come.

"I always thought some o' them constables was daft!" Gracie said with profound contempt. "Now they really 'as gorn the 'ole way. " 'Ooever made that mistake'll spend the rest of 'is life eatin' worms! An' serve 'im right! Are you goin' ter see the commissioner o' police, ma'am? They can't know 'oo they got! Why, there in't nobody in Lunnon solved more murders than Mr. Pitt. Sometimes I think some o' them couldn't detect an 'ole in the ground if'n they fell in it!''

Charlotte smiled bleakly. She looked into Gracie's plain, indignant little face, and felt reassured.

"Yes I will," she said more firmly. "I'll take these things to Mr. Pitt first, then I'll go and see Mr. Ballarat at Bow Street."

"You do that, ma'am," Gracie agreed. "An' I'll take care o' everythin' 'ere."

"Thank you. Thank you, Gracie," and she turned away quickly and hurried downstairs before emotion could overtake her again. Best not to talk. Action was easier and infinitely more useful.

But when she reached the massive gray tower and gates of Her Majesty's House of Correction and asked to go in, they would not allow her to see Pitt. A red-nosed jailer with a perpetual cold took her basket with the food and the linen, promising lugubriously to see that they reached the prisoner. But she could not come in, it was not visiting hours, and no, he could not make an exception, he would not take a note for her. He was sorry but rules was rules.

There was no argument against such bleak refusal, and when she saw the unreachable uninterest in his watery eyes she turned and left, walking back along the wet footpath, the wind in her face, trying to think of what she would say to Ballarat. Temper passed quickly, fury at the stupidity and the injustice, and she began to think how to be practical. What would be the best way to make Ballarat act immediately? Surely a reasoned and calm explanation of the facts. He could not know what had happened or he would have done something already. He would have contacted the police station which had made such a blunder, and Pitt's release would have been assured as soon as the appropriate message was received.

She took the next public omnibus, which was crowded with women and children. She paid her fare to the "cad," as conductors were known, and squeezed in between a fat woman in black bombazine with a bosom like a bolster and a small boy in a sailor suit. She tried to occupy her mind by staring round her at the other passengers—the old lady with the withered face and out-of-date lace cap, the girl in the striped skirt who kept smiling at the youth with the side whiskers—but sooner or later every thought came back to Pitt and her terrible sense of being shut off from him, the threatening wave of panic at her helplessness.

By the time she got off in the Strand and walked up Bow Street to the Police station Charlotte's heart was knocking in her chest and her legs felt shaky and uncertain. She breathed in and out deeply, but that did not steady her. She went up the steps, tripping on the top one because her feet no longer seemed coordinated. She pushed the door open and went in, suddenly realizing she had never been here before. Pitt came here every day and spoke about it so often she had assumed it would look familiar, but it was much darker and colder than she had expected. She had not imagined the smell of linoleum and polish, the worn brass of the door handles, the shiny patches on the bench where countless people had rubbed against it, waiting.

The duty constable looked up from the ledger where he was writing in studious copperplate. "Yes, ma'am, what can I do for yer?" He sized up her respectability instantly. "Lorst summat, 'ave yer?"

"No." She swallowed hard. "Thank you. I am Inspector Pitt's wife. I should like to see Mr. Ballarat, if you please. It is most urgent."

The man's face colored and he avoided her eyes. "Er—yes, ma'am. If—if yer'll wait a few moments I'll go an' see." He closed the ledger, put it away under the shelf, and disappeared out of the glass-paned door into the passageway. She could hear his muffled voice speaking hurriedly to someone beyond.

She stood on the worn linoleum floor and waited. No one came back, and she knew they were too embarrassed to face her, not knowing what to say. It frightened her. She had expected anger, defensiveness, repeated assurances that it must be a mistake and would be put right immediately. This evasion must mean either that they doubted Pitt themselves or that they dared not express their feelings. Was there no loyalty among them at all, no trust, even after all the years they had known him?

Panic rose inside her, making her sick. Without realizing it she stepped forward, desperate to make a noise, to shout till someone came, even to scream.

The door swung open suddenly and she jumped. The same constable looked at her, this time meeting her eyes.

"If yer'd like ter come this way, ma'am." Still he did not use her name, as if he were ashamed somehow and wanted to pretend she was someone else.

She stared at him coldly. "Mrs. Pitt," she told him.

"Mrs. Pitt, ma'am," he repeated obediently, even the tops of his ears turning pink.

She followed him along the passage, up the stairs, and across into Ballarat's large, warm office. A fire was burning on the grate and Ballarat himself was standing in front of the hearth, feet slightly apart, boots shining.

"Come in, Mrs. Pitt," he said expansively. "Come in and take a seat." He waved his arm at the leather easy chair, but he did not move to allow her the fire.

She sat on the edge, upright. The constable closed the door and fled.

"I'm deeply sorry that I had to send such a message," Ballarat began before she could speak. "It must have been a dreadful shock for you."

"Of course it was," she agreed. "But that is hardly important. What is happening to Thomas? Don't they realize who he is? Have you been to Coldbath Fields and told them? Perhaps they don't believe a letter.''

"Certainly they know who he is, Mrs. Pitt.'' He nodded several times. "Naturally, I made certain of it immediately. But I'm afraid the evidence is quite unarguable. I don't want to distress you by recounting it. I do think, my dear lady, it would be better if you were to go home, perhaps to your own family, and—''

"I have no intention of doing anything so perfectly useless as going home to my family!'' She tried to swallow back her fury but her voice was shaking. "And I'm perfectly capable of hearing the supposed evidence, whatever it is!''

He looked uncomfortable, his rather florid face becoming even more mottled. "Ah.'' He cleared his throat to give himself time to order his thoughts. "If you will allow me to know better, that is because you do not understand what it is. I assure you, it would be far better if you were to leave your interests in my care, and go home—''

"What are you doing to show his innocence?'' she interrupted fiercely. "You know he didn't do it! You must find the evidence.''

"My dear lady''—he held up his hands, plump and well manicured, the firelight catching a gold signet ring—"I must abide by the law, just like everyone else. Of course,'' he said carefully and with a patience so obvious she could taste it in the air, "of course I wish to believe the best of him.'' He nodded again. "Pitt has been a good police officer for years. He has served the community in many ways.''

She opened her mouth to retaliate against such condescension, but he was not to be interrupted.

"But I cannot override the law! If we are to uphold justice, we must abide by due process, like everyone else.'' He was well launched now. "We cannot set ourselves above it.'' He opened his eyes very wide. "Naturally, I do not for a moment believe Pitt would do such a thing. But with all the best will in the world, I cannot and must not say that I know!" He smiled very slightly, showing the superiority of male reason over emotionalism. "We are not infallible, and my judgment of a man is not enough to clear him before the law—nor should it be."

She stood up, facing him with tight, cold rage.

"No one is asking you to be judge, Mr. Ballarat." She glared at him. "What I had expected, before I met you, was that you were loyal enough to fight to defend one of your own men, whom you know perfectly well would not have committed such a crime. Even if you did not know him, I would have assumed you would suppose him innocent and do everything to check the evidence over and over again to find the flaws."

"Really, my dear," he said soothingly, taking a step forward and then meeting her eyes and stopping. "Really, my dear lady, you must accept that you do not understand! This is police business, and we are experts—"

"You are a coward," she said witheringly.

He looked startled, then regained his composure with a smooth, glassy gaze. "Of course you are upset. It is to be expected. But believe me, when you have taken a rest and had a little time to think about it—perhaps it would be wise to leave the matter to your father? Or if you have a brother, or brother-in-law?"

She swallowed hard. "My father is dead, so is my brother-in-law; and I have no brother."

"Oh." He looked confused, an avenue of escape had closed unexpectedly. It was damnable that there was no man to take care of her—for everyone's sake. "Well . . ." he floundered.

"Yes?" she inquired, staring at him furiously.

His eyes wavered and slid away. "I'm sure everything will be done that can be, Mrs. Pitt. But I am also sure you would not wish me to interfere with the law, even if I were able."

He was satisfied with that; his tone grew stronger. "You must compose yourself and trust in us."

"I am perfectly composed," she said chokingly, and left the second half of the reply deliberately unsaid. "Thank you for your time." And without waiting for him to summon any polite parting words, or offering him her hand, she turned on her heel and went to the door. She flung it open and walked out, leaving it swinging.

But anger was a short comfort. It died quickly when she was out in the icy street, brushed by indifferent people, splashed by a passing carriage when she stood too close to the curb. Gradually, as she walked along the Strand towards the omnibus stop, the meaning of it all sank in: Ballarat was not going to do anything. She had expected him to be only a little less outraged than she was—after all, Pitt was one of his own men, and probably the best. He should have been up in arms, doing everything to get this appalling mistake put right. Instead he was backing out, equivocating, finding excuses for doing nothing. Perhaps he was even relieved that Pitt had been silenced. And how more effectively could Pitt be stopped from asking embarrassing questions or unearthing anything that implicated the Yorks, or the Danvers, or Ballarat's superiors at the Home Office and the diplomatic departments that had been penetrated by treason?

She stopped short and a man with a tray of pies bumped into her, swearing in his surprise.

"I'm sorry," she murmured. She stood rooted to the gray footpath as people jostled and grumbled past her. Could that be it? Was it conceivable Ballarat himself—No, surely not. He was only weak, and ambitious. But who had murdered Cerise? What had she known that was still so dangerous, even now, that someone had sought her out in a back room in Seven Dials and broken her neck?

Someone she could still betray—that was obvious. And whoever had done it was afraid Pitt was too close. If it were mere coincidence that she had been murdered just as he reached her, then Ballarat would be doing everything he could to uncover the truth.

She started to walk again, quickly now. She had hold of a definite fact: Ballarat was part of the conspiracy, either because he was implicated or because he was merely weak.

She thought the latter. She and Emily must do something about it, there must be ways—

Then the chill made her gasp. How could she reach Emily? She was a lady's maid at the Yorks'; she might as well be in France! Charlotte could not even be sure a letter would be given to her promptly.

"Extra! Extra!" The newsboy's voice cut into her thoughts as he shouted sharp and high. "Extra! Policeman murders woman in pink! Extra!" He stopped next to her. " 'Ere, lady, yer wan' a paper? Thomas Pitt, a famous rozzer, killed a—" He glanced at her face and amended what he had been going to say. "Killed a woman o' the streets."

Her voice barely came through her lips. "No thank you."

The boy turned away and drew in his breath to shout again. Then she realized it was foolish to run away from it. If she were to be of any use she needed to know. "Yes please! Yes, I will buy one," she called after him, fishing in her reticule for a coin and offering it to him.

"There y'are, lady. Ta." He gave her a penny change and went on his way. "Extra! Rozzer commits 'orrible murder in Seven Dials!"

She pushed it under her arm, out of the way. She would rather look at it alone. The omnibus had nearly arrived, and when it came she climbed on, giving her fare to the "cad," and sat down, this time oblivious of the other passengers.

When she got off it was raining heavily and she was thoroughly soaked by the time she reached her own front door and got inside. She was greeted almost immediately by Gracie, her eyes red-rimmed and her apron filthy. Charlotte took off her sodden coat and hung it up without caring where it dripped.

"What is it, Gracie?" she said impatiently.

"Oh, ma'am—I'm terrible sorry." Gracie was on the edge of tears again, her voice thick with crying.

"What?"

"Mrs. Biggs 'as gorn, ma'am. Never so much as did the floors. Said she wouldn't work for nobody what murdered women. I'm terrible sorry, ma'am—I wouldn't 'a' told yer, but I 'ad to say as why she went, an'—" She gulped deeply, tears running down her cheeks. "An' the butcher wouldn't give no credit. As good as said as 'ow 'e'd sooner we got our meat somewheres else!"

Charlotte was stunned. She had not even thought of that, and here it was, so soon. She felt breathless and a little sick.

"Ma'am?" Gracie sniffed fiercely but it did not stop her crying.

Suddenly Charlotte put her arms round her and they clung to each other, letting the tears come in a storm of misery.

It was several moments before Charlotte was able to pull herself together, blow her nose, and go into the kitchen. She splashed her face with cold water and rubbed it dry so fiercely her red eyes hardly showed. Ordering Gracie about was a kind of relief, chopping vegetables savagely helped to calm her while she tried to think.

She told Daniel and Jemima nothing, doing what she could to behave normally. Daniel was too hungry to be observant, but Jemima noticed and asked what was wrong.

"I have a cold," Charlotte said, forcing herself to smile. "Don't worry about it." She might as well get the initial news over now. She was dreading the lies, but the sooner she started the less horrible it would be. "Papa won't be home for a few days. He's away on a very special job."

"Is that why you're unhappy?" Jemima said slowly, watching her.

The closer she could stay to some kind of truth the better.

"Yes. But don't worry—we'll keep each other company." She tried to smile and knew it was a disaster.

Jemima smiled back, and immediately her lip began to tremble. She had always been quick to grasp Charlotte's mood, whether she understood it or not: she was like a little mirror reflecting gestures, expressions, tones of voice. Now she knew there was something wrong.

"Yes, I will miss him," Charlotte repeated. "And I miss Aunt Emily, too, since she went on holiday. Never mind; I shall have to be busy and then the time will pass. Now eat your supper or it will get cold."

She bent to her own plate, forcing herself to spoon down the stew and mashed potatoes although she was barely aware of their taste. Her throat ached and her stomach felt like stone.

She was barely finished when the doorbell rang. Both she and Gracie stopped, fear returning. Who could it be? For one wild moment Charlotte thought perhaps Pitt had been released and somehow lost his key; then she realized it was far more likely to be some neighbor seeking to confirm the worst, full of curiosity and spurious pity, or worse, another tradesman.

It rang again, more insistently this time.

She looked at Gracie.

"Don't 'ave me answer it, ma'am!" Gracie said urgently. "Y'never know 'oo it is!" She stood up reluctantly. "Less'n I can 'ave yer word ter shut it in their faces if it in't nobody good. I don't say as I can be civil wiv 'em!"

"You have my permission," Charlotte agreed. "Open it on the chain."

"Yes ma'am." And tightening her apron a little and gritting her teeth, Gracie disappeared up the passage. Jemima and Daniel stopped eating, and they all sat, ears straining to hear, as Gracie's heels clicked on the linoleum. There was a moment's silence, the rattle of the chain on the door latch, a murmur of voices too indistinct to identify, then another rattle and returning footsteps.

Charlotte stood up. "Stay here," she ordered.

"Who is it, Mama?" Jemima whispered. Daniel stared at her truculently, frightened and ready to fight.

"I don't know. Stay here." And Charlotte went out into the passage just in time to meet Jack Radley as he came, white-faced, ahead of Gracie. He put out his arms and she walked straight into them. He held her tight, saying nothing at all, and Gracie squeezed past with a little sniff of relief. She thought very highly of Charlotte, but it always needed a man to sort things out properly. Thank heaven one had come.

Charlotte disengaged herself reluctantly. She could not stand here pretending someone else could mend everything.

"Come into the kitchen," she said. There was no fire in the parlor—Gracie had not even thought of it—and the weather was too bitter to take anyone into an unheated room. "Gracie, you'd better take the children up and get them ready for bed."

"I haven't had any pudding!" Daniel said with burning injustice.

It was on the tip of Charlotte's tongue to tell him he would have to do without, until she looked at his face and saw the fear in it, blind, knowing only that she was frightened, too, and his world was threatened. She made an intense effort and controlled her own feelings.

"You're quite right, and I forgot to make any. I'm very sorry. Will you accept a piece of cake instead, if I bring it upstairs for you?"

He regarded her with great dignity. "Yes, I will," he conceded, and climbed down from his chair.

"Thank you."

When they had gone she looked at Jack.

"I read it in the newspaper," he said quietly. "For God's sake, what happened?"

"I don't know. A constable came this morning and told me Thomas had been arrested for killing a prostitute in Seven Dials. It must be Cerise. I bought a newspaper myself, but I haven't had time to look at it yet. I daren't take it out—

248

Jemima can read. I'll look at it this evening, and then put it straight into the stove.''

"I'd put it in the stove now," he said, biting his lip. "There's nothing in it you want to read. He went into Seven Dials to find the woman in cerise. He said he was told where she was by a running patterer—a man who sells news stories—and when he went into the house he was shown upstairs to her room. He says he found her dead, neck broken, and the people in the house say she was all right when they last saw her, and no one else went up except regulars, and they are all accounted for.''

"That can't be true!"

"Of course it can't! They're lying, and I daresay well paid for it. But for the time being, they won't be shaken. It's going to take some work—but we'll do it. Only this time we don't have Pitt to help us.''

She sat down again on one of the kitchen chairs, and he took Gracie's.

"Jack, I don't know where to begin! I went to see Mr. Ballarat. I was sure he would be moving heaven and earth to find the truth, and all he did was talk to me as if I were a child, and tell me to go home and leave everything to him. Only I'd swear he isn't going to do anything at all. Jack—'' She hesitated, wondering if what she was thinking would sound hysterical to him, but what alternative did she have? "Jack, I think he wants Thomas to stay in prison. He's afraid of him!'' She expected disbelief and hurried on to explain herself. "He's afraid of what Thomas will uncover that's embarrassing to people who matter, the Yorks and the Danvers, or the people in the Home Office. Ballarat wants to sweep the whole lot under the carpet. He hopes if he says nothing it will all go away, and he'd rather that, and that someone should get away with treason and murder, than be the one who has to expose what everyone will hate! People can be very unjust, they can hate the person who makes them see what they would prefer not to, who topples idols and shows their clay feet. They blame them for the truth, and the responsibility it leaves us. We don't often forgive those who destroy our illusions. Ballarat doesn't want to be that person, and he will be, by implication, if Thomas discovers what Cerise knew. That's why they killed her—it has to be!''

"Of course it has," he agreed. He reached out across the table and took her hands, quite gently. It was in no way a familiarity, just friendship, and she found herself gripping him back, hard, hanging on. "Do you want me to fetch Emily?" he asked.

"Yes—please do. I don't trust myself to go to the Yorks'.'' She searched for an excuse. "You'll have to tell her it's family illness or something. I don't know how you'll explain knowing her, but you can scrape up a good lie before you get there." The thought of seeing Emily was such a relief, almost like someone lighting a fire in a cold room. Perhaps she would even come and stay with Charlotte. They could work together, as they had done in the past on other cases, ones that mattered infinitely less than this.

"Then what would you like me to do?" he asked. "I've never tried detecting before, and this is a damn sight too important for amateurs, but I'll do whatever I can."

"I don't know where to begin," she said, her misery returning. "Cerise is dead. Apart from the murderer she may be the only one who knew the truth."

"Well, at least we know she wasn't the murderer herself," he pointed out. "Someone killed her, and it would be too much to assume it's coincidence, just as Thomas found her. And we must suppose someone, almost certainly the same person, killed poor Dulcie."

She stared at him. "That means someone in the York house, or one of the Danvers, or Felix or Sonia Asherson."

"That's right."

"But what would any of them be doing in a place like Seven Dials?"

"Murdering Cerise to keep her silent," he answered very

quietly, his face more somber than she had ever seen it. There was an anger in him, a weight she had not found before. "I think that means they knew where she was all the time," he went on. "They could hardly have run into her by chance."

"One of the Yorks, the Danvers, or the Ashersons," she said again. "Emily—" She stopped. Emily was alone in the York house, unable to defend herself except by a disguise of ignorance, and Pitt was imprisoned in Coldbath Fields awaiting trial for murder. Both could end in death.

But Emily was free; at least she could fight for herself!

But surely justice—! The truth? Ballarat would—

She must stop behaving like a child, deceiving herself into comfort, finding excuses to avoid the painful. Ballarat would do nothing.

"I've changed my mind," she said quietly. "Don't ask Emily to come home. The only way she can help Thomas is by staying where she is. Whoever murdered Cerise, and Robert York and Dulcie, is in Hanover Close, and the only way we are going to find that person is by watching them so closely we see what emotions lie behind the facades, who is frightened, who is lying."

He sat still. For a moment she was afraid he was going to argue, point out the dangers to Emily, perhaps even tell her all the accidents that could be made to happen; but he said nothing.

"You and I can keep going as often as possible," she went on. "But we can never see them in their unguarded moments as she can. Have you any idea how much a woman trusts her lady's maid?"

For the first time he smiled. "I imagine about as much as a man trusts his valet," he answered. "Or perhaps a trifle more: women spend more time at home, and on the whole give more attention to appearance."

There was another aspect that needed explaining, Charlotte realized.

"Jack, she probably won't see a newspaper. Maids don't,

especially if there is something sensational in it. The butler will keep it from them." She saw the surprise in his face. "Of course he will! He won't want all his maids swapping horror stories under the stairs, and up half the night with nightmares." It was plain from Jack's face that he had never thought of that, and she realized with a brief shadow of pity that he had very few roots. He was an eternal guest, never a host, too well-bred to be poor, but without the means to keep up with his peers. But there was no time for such issues now. Then she remembered that already one of her own servants had left, and if Pitt was not cleared very soon there would be pressure on Gracie too. Her mother would try to persuade her to find a better place. And come to think of it, Charlotte had no money and she would not be able to keep Gracie anyway, or anyone else. She had enough of her allowance from her own inheritance to eat, at least for a few weeks— The fear loomed up again. She was not only afraid of isolation and insufficient means, but worst of all, life without Pitt. There was not even time to make up for the stupid arguments, to be to him all the things she wanted to be.

She must not think of it, it would destroy her. She took a long breath, her lungs hurting as if the air were sharp. She must fight—anybody and everybody if necessary.

"Please ask Emily to stay there," she repeated.

"I will." Jack hesitated, and for the first time he looked awkward, his eyes avoiding hers, scanning the tabletop, the row of blue-ringed dishes on the dresser beyond. "Charlotte—have you any money?"

She swallowed. "For a while."

"It's going to be hard."

"I know."

He colored faintly. "I can give you a little."

She shook her head. "No. Thank you, Jack."

He searched for words. "Don't—don't let pride—"

"It's not pride," she assured him. "I'm all right for now. And when I'm not . . ." Please God she would have found the murderer by then, and Pitt would be free! "When I'm not, Emily will help."

"I'll go and tell her. I'll say it's a family illness—they'll let me in for that. Even the butler wouldn't be martinet enough to deny anyone the right to that sort of news."

"But how will you explain knowing it? You'll have to explain that, or they'll be suspicious." Always at the front of her mind was the necessity to learn the truth, before everything else. "They won't leave you alone with her, you know. There'll be the housekeeper there, or the other lady's maid, for propriety if nothing else."

He looked taken aback for a moment, then he brightened. "Write a letter. I'll say it's from her family, explaining the situation. She can ask for a day off, to come and visit you on your sickbed."

"Half day," she corrected automatically. "She hasn't been there long enough for one yet, but they might give it to her on grounds of compassion. Please do, Jack—go today. I'll write a letter straightaway, and I'll tell her to burn it as soon as she's read it. There are plenty of fires." She stood up even as she was speaking and went hastily into the parlor, turning up the lights, not noticing how cold it was till her fingers touched the icy surface of the desktop. She took out paper, ink, and pen and began to write.

Dearest Emily,

Something completely appalling has happened—Thomas found Cerise but she was already dead. Someone broke her neck, and they have arrested him for her murder. They have taken him to "the Steel" in Coldbath Fields, to await trial. I went to Mr. Ballarat, but he will do nothing. Either they have told him to leave it alone, or he is simply a coward and is only too glad to be rid of Thomas before he unearths something embarrassing about someone in power.

It is all up to us now, there is no one else. Please stay

where you are and be very, very careful! Remember Dulcie! Half of me wants to beg you to come home with Jack immediately, tonight, so you will be safe; the other half knows you and I are Thomas's only chance. He must have been close on the trail of someone very powerful and very dangerous. Please Emily, be careful. I love you,

Charlotte

She blotted it rather clumsily. It was scribbled, and her fingers were stiff. Then without rereading it she folded it, not very straight, and slipped it into an envelope. She sealed it, put the top back on the ink, and turned the gas down before going back to the kitchen. She gave the letter to Jack.

"I'll be back tomorrow," he promised. "We must plan."

She nodded, overwhelmed with loneliness now that he was going. With him here she did not feel so frightened; even with Gracie's loyalty, and the children, she would be alone when he was gone. Then there would be time to think, and nothing to do all the long, cold night. She dreaded waking in the morning.

"Good night." She forced the moment to come, because waiting for it was worse, and she did not want to weep again. It was pointless, and too hard to stop.

"Good night." Now at the point of going he also seemed reluctant. He was worried for her, and she knew it. Perhaps he really did love Emily. What an unspeakable way to discover it!

Jack hesitated a moment more, then as he could think of nothing further to say, turned and went to the door. She followed to let him out and watched him step into the street, where the wet cobbles shone in the dim gaslight, globes hung like baleful moons in haloes of rain.

He touched her cheek gently, then walked rapidly away towards the main road and the passing hansoms.

* * *

She was so tired she should have slept well, but her dreams were filled with fear, and she woke up many times, fighting for breath, her body aching with tension and her throat sore. The darkness seemed interminable, and when at last the gray dawn came, with rain beating on the window, it was a relief to get up. She was so tired she fumbled with her gown when she went downstairs to draw the pitcher of hot water, then changed her mind and washed in the kitchen anyway; it was warmer. Before dressing she decided to have a cup of tea. The taste of it would wash away some of the gritty feeling and its heat might wash out the tightness in her throat.

She was still sitting at the kitchen table when Gracie came in, also in her dressing gown, her hair down over her shoulders. She looked like a child. Charlotte had never noticed how threadbare her nightclothes were before. She must get her new ones—if she could ever afford it again. She wished she had done it sooner.

Gracie stood still, eyes wide, afraid to speak and uncertain what to say. But her gaze was perfectly steady and hot with loyalty. She longed to ask Charlotte if she was all right but did not dare, in case it seemed impertinent.

"Have a cup of tea before we begin," Charlotte offered. "The kettle's still just about boiling."

"Thank you, ma'am," Gracie accepted with some awe; she had never in her life before sat at the kitchen table taking tea in her nightgown.

But from then on the day got worse. The baker's boy did not call but passed on down the street. The fishmonger's boy, on the contrary, rang loudly, presented the account up to date, and demanded payment in full, with the warning that should madam be buying fish in future—which he appeared to doubt—all transactions would be strictly for payment in cash and on delivery. Gracie told him to be about his business and all but boxed his ears on the doorstep, but she was sniffing fiercely and her eyes were red when she came back to the kitchen.

Charlotte thought of sending her for bread, then realized

how unfair that would be, and perhaps rash; obviously her loyalty was intense and she would retaliate against any jibes, even if only overheard. Charlotte was older and surely could learn to keep the peace. She should not hide behind a girl.

The experience was worse than she expected. She had never been more than civil to most of her neighbors. They knew from her speech, her manner, the quality of her clothes—though cut down from previous years—even the sight of Emily's carriage now and then, that Charlotte was not of their background or stock. On the surface they were civil, even friendly from time to time, but resentment lay close under the surface, fear of the different, envy of privilege; though most of it was long in the past now, it was not forgiven.

She walked down the pavement with the wind pulling at her coat and the rain soaking her skirts. She was glad to reach the corner and the shelter of the grocer's shop. As she went in the door the few women inside stopped talking and stared at her. One of them had a son who was a petty thief, serving six months in the Scrubs. She hated all police, and now was her chance to gain a little revenge with impunity. No one could blame her for it, nor defend the wife of a man who imprisoned other men, and then murdered a prostitute himself. She glared at Charlotte, hitched her basket onto her hip, and walked out of the shop, passing her so roughly that Charlotte was nearly knocked off balance, bruising her and leaving her startled by the suddenness as much as the pain. The other women tittered with amusement.

"Good mornin', Mrs. Pitt, I'm sure!" one of them said loudly. "An' 'ow are we today, then? Not so 'igh an' mighty? Take our turn with the rest, will we?"

"Good morning, Mrs. Robertson," Charlotte replied coldly. "I am quite well, thank you. Is your mother better? I heard she caught a chill in the rain."

"She's poorly," the woman said, taken aback that Charlotte had not retaliated more in kind. "What's it ter you?"

"Nothing at all, Mrs. Robertson, except good manners," Charlotte answered. "Have you finished your purchases?"

"No I 'aven't! You wait yer turn!" And she moved to stand square in front of the counter again, her eyes roving slowly over the shelves, deliberately taking as long as she could. There was nothing for Charlotte to do but contain her temper and wait.

The grocer shifted from one foot to the other, weighing where his profit lay, and chose the obvious. He ignored Charlotte and smiled toothily at Mrs. Robertson.

"I'll 'ave 'alf a pound o' sugar," she said with satisfaction, tasting power like a sweet in her mouth. "Hif you please, Mr. Wilson."

The grocer dipped into his sack and put half a pound little by little into the scales, then emptied it into a blue paper bag and gave it to her.

"I changed me mind." She glanced at Charlotte maliciously, and then back at the grocer. "I'm feelin' rich this mornin; I'll 'ave an 'ole pound."

"Yes, Mrs. Robertson. O' course." The grocer weighed another half pound carefully and gave it to her.

The door opened and the bell rang as another woman entered and took her place behind Charlotte.

"An' I'll 'ave some Pears' soap," Mrs. Robertson added. "Fer me complexion. It's very good, in't it, Mrs. Pitt? Is that wot you use? Not that yer'll be able ter afford it now! Come down in yer ideas a bit, won't yer?"

"Possibly. But it takes more than a bar of soap to make a beauty, Mrs. Robertson," Charlotte said coldly. "Did you ever find your umbrella?"

"No I didn't!" Mrs. Robertson said angrily. "There's a lot o' people round 'ere in't as honest as they makes out. I reckon as somebody stole it!"

Charlotte raised her eyebrows. "Call a policeman," she said with a smile.

The woman glared at her, and this time it was the other woman who sniggered under her breath.

But the verbal victory was brief and gave her no pleasure, and at the baker's it was worse, no jibes, only silence, until she was leaving, when there were whispers behind hands and a nodding of heads. She was asked for cash, and it was counted carefully before being put into the till with a snap. If things became hard, there would be no credit for her, she knew without asking—no allowances, and probably from now on no deliveries. The greengrocer made some excuse about being short of help, even though there was a boy standing idle over the sack of potatoes, obviously waiting for something to do, and Charlotte had to carry her heavy bags home herself. A boy of about nine or ten ran past her yelling, "Ha-ya! Rozzer's in the Steel! They'll 'ang 'im fer sure! Dingle dangle, see 'im dance!" and did a little skip in and out of the gutter.

She tried to ignore him, but the words struck black terror in her, and by the time she got home, soaking wet, her arms aching, shoulders dragging with the weight of her purchases, she was close to despair.

She was barely inside and had just taken off her wet boots and was setting them near the stove in the kitchen when she heard the front doorbell. Gracie looked at her and without being asked went to open it. She came back a moment later, her feet light along the passage, her skirt swishing round the door.

"Ma'am! Ma'am, it's your mama, Mrs. Ellison. Shall I bring 'er through 'ere? It's terrible cold in the parlor. I'll make yer a cup o' tea, then I'll go upstairs an' get on wiv the bedrooms."

Charlotte felt little of Gracie's trust; she was much less certain of what Caroline would have to say. She stood up quickly.

"Yes—yes, you'd better." There was no alternative: she could not ask anyone to sit in the freezing parlor, nor could she bear to herself. Her wet feet were still numb, and the edges of her skirts were steaming as the kitchen's warmth reached them. "I'll make the tea," she added. It would give her something to do. And it would allow her an excuse to turn her back.

"Yes ma'am." Gracie disappeared, her feet tip-tapping lightly on the linoleum.

Caroline came in, having already divested herself of her coat, and since she had naturally come in a carriage, she was not wet except for the soles of her neat high-button boots.

"Oh, my dear!" She held her arms open. Perfunctorily, because there was nothing else to do, Charlotte responded, holding her for only a moment before stepping back. "I'll make us a cup of tea," she said quickly. "I've only just come in myself and I'm perished, and wet."

"Charlotte, my dear, you must come home." Caroline sat down a little gingerly on one of the kitchen chairs.

"No thank you," Charlotte said instantly. She reached for the kettle and filled it, setting it on the hob.

"But you can't stay here!" Caroline argued, her voice ringing with reason. "The newspapers are full of the story! I don't think you realize—"

"I realize perfectly!" Charlotte contradicted her. "If I hadn't before I went to the shops, I certainly do now. And I am not running away."

"Darling, it's not running away!" Caroline stood up and came over as if to touch her again, then sensed her daughter's resentment. "You must face reality, Charlotte. You have made a mistake which has turned out tragically for you. If you come home now, take your maiden name again, I can—"

Charlotte froze. "I will not! How dare you suggest such a thing! You're speaking as if you imagined Thomas were guilty!" She turned round slowly, cups and saucers in her hands. "For the children's sake you can take them, if you will. If you won't, then they'll have to stay here as any ordinary man's would have to. I'm not ashamed of Thomas—I'm ashamed of you for wanting me to run away and deny him instead of fighting! I am going to find out who killed that woman, and prove it, just as I did for Emily when they thought she murdered George—for which she had far more reason!''

Caroline sighed and kept her patience, which made it worse. "My dear, that was quite different," she began.

"Oh? Why? Because she is 'one of us' and Thomas isn't?"

Caroline's face tightened. "If you insist on putting it that way—yes."

"Well, you've been glad enough to have him 'one of us' when you needed him!" Charlotte could feel herself close to losing control, and it made her furious, both with herself and with Caroline.

"You must be realistic," Caroline began again.

"You mean desert him quickly, so people can see I have nothing to do with it?" Charlotte demanded. "How honorable you are, Mama! How brave!"

"Charlotte, I'm only thinking of you!"

"Are you?" Charlotte's disbelief was strident, because she thought what Caroline said was probably honest. It was what other people would think too, and it terrified her. She did not care if she was being unjust, she wanted to hurt. "Are you sure you aren't thinking of the neighbors, and what your friends will say about you?" she went on, mimicking their voices savagely. " 'You know that nice Mrs. Ellison, well you'll never believe it, but her daughter married a policeman—isn't that dreadful—and now he's gone and committed a murder! I always said no good comes of marrying beneath you.' "

"Charlotte! I didn't say that."

"But you thought it!"

"You are being quite unfair! And the kettle is boiling. You are filling the kitchen with steam and it'll boil dry. For goodness' sake make the tea and have a cup. Perhaps you will be able to think a little more clearly. Loyalty to Thomas is all very well, but it is self-indulgent. This has happened, and you must be practical and think of the children.''

She was quite right at least in that the room was filling with steam. Charlotte made the tea, burning her hand on the kettle and refusing to admit it. She set the teapot on the table and fiddled furiously in the cupboard for biscuits. When she found them she spilled them onto a plate and set it down, then poured the tea and passed it. Finally she sat down, hardly more composed.

"I would be very grateful if you took the children," she said carefully. "It would protect them from—from the worst, at least—" She stopped. She had been going to say, "for the time being," and even that thought was a betrayal.

"Of course," Caroline said quickly. "And as soon as you want to come, too, you know there is always a place for you."

"I—am—not—coming," Charlotte said very slowly and deliberately.

"Then go and stay with Emily in the country," Caroline urged her. "Thomas would understand. He wouldn't expect you to stay here. What can you do? Make a show of being brave and letting everyone know you believe he is innocent? My dear, it will only get you hurt, and it will make no difference at all in the end. Leave it to the police."

Charlotte felt the tears running down her face. She fished out a handkerchief and blew her nose, then took a sip of her tea before replying. She could hardly tell her mother that Emily was no more in the country than Pitt was.

"The police are perfectly happy to leave it as it is," she said coldly. "Thomas has discovered something they would prefer not to know. I have no wish to join Emily. I have written to her, of course. But I am a very good detective myself; I shall discover who killed Robert York, and it will be the same person who killed this woman in pink."

"My dear, you cannot know what really happened, or why

Thomas was in Seven Dials with this—this woman in pink.'' Caroline's face was very pale. "We don't know really as much about our husbands as we sometimes imagine.''

Out of her own pain Charlotte was deliberately cruel. ''You mean, as you didn't know about Papa?''

Caroline flinched and the words died before they reached her lips.

Charlotte was sorry, but it was too late. ''But he didn't kill those girls, did he!'' she said, finishing what she had begun.

"No, and I was grateful to the police for proving it,'' Caroline admitted. ''But I could not give back the knowledge of what he had done, nor ever stop wondering at how little I had known him, how much I simply thought I did. Don't press for the truth, Charlotte. You would be much wiser to leave it to the police, and hope they will tell you only what you have to know.''

''If that is the best you can offer, it would be better if we did not discuss it.'' Charlotte stood up, leaving the rest of her tea. ''I'll go and pack some things for the children and you can take them with you now. It will be easier than saying long good-byes. Anyway, there's no point in your going and then having to come back for them. Thank you; I appreciate it,'' and without waiting for Caroline to offer any answer she went straight out of the kitchen and upstairs, leaving her mother at the table with the teapot and the biscuits.

After Caroline was gone, taking Daniel and Jemima with her, holding onto their hands as she had with Charlotte and Emily when they were children, Charlotte felt truly ashamed. She had been unjust. She had expected Caroline to understand things that were completely outside her world. But her mother did not have Charlotte's experience, and it was both unfair and stupid to suppose she could think as Charlotte did. It was not so long ago Pitt had had to be patient with her, excuse her prejudices and assumptions. And what was worse, she had reminded Caroline of pain, disillusionment that still cut deep, tarnishing old memories, which—now that Edward was dead—were all she had. Charlotte had known what she was doing, and done it just the same. When this was all over Charlotte would say something to her; now she was too frightened, too worried to find the words, or to trust herself to deliver them.

She started by being practical. How much money was there, and what had to be done with it? If it came to a choice between food and coal, how should she portion out the resources? The best thing was to check the cellar and see what there was. From now on it would be more potatoes and bread, and less meat. She would have to ask Gracie where the cheapest places were to shop.

Jack came a little before three. It was heavily overcast and the light was already beginning to fade. Gracie let him in and he went straight to the kitchen.

"I saw Emily," he said immediately. "I told the butler a wonderful lie about her sister being ill and that I knew it through Lady Ashworth, for whom Emily—sorry. For whom Amelia had worked before. They swallowed it all." He swung his coattails aside elegantly out of habit and sat down at the table. He looked at Charlotte very soberly. "She agreed to stay there; in fact, she insisted. I hope to God she'll be all right. I've racked my brain for some way to protect her, but I can't think of anything. She's got a half day off on Saturday, and she said she'll meet you in Hyde Park on the first seat as you go in nearest Hanover Close, at two in the afternoon, regardless of the weather. Until then, what can I do?"

"I don't know," Charlotte admitted. "I went to the prison yesterday, but they wouldn't let me see Thomas. I only know what I read in the newspapers."

"I went out and got them all." He could not keep the anxiety from his face. "They say he asked people all over the city where he could find Cerise. Several street sellers will swear to that. It seems the running patterer who actually took him to Seven Dials only watched Pitt go in; he didn't go in himself. It was a brothel, of sorts, and the landlord says Pitt asked him to describe the woman very closely and only wanted to see her if she was the right one. The landlord took him up. No one else passed, and when the man went up a few minutes later he found Pitt bending over with his hands around her neck." He was very pale. "I'm sorry."

She searched his face, but his gaze did not waver.

"Then there's no point in going to Seven Dials," she said as calmly as she could. "Not that I ever thought there would be. The answer is in Hanover Close. I must go and see Veronica York again. Will you take me?"

"Of course. And I'll take you to Coldbath Fields as well. You shouldn't go alone."

"Thank you." She tried to think of something else to say, and failed.

This time she was allowed into the prison, a great cold place whose massive walls were like misery set in stone, condensation making even the inner corridors feel cold and sour. Everywhere was the smell of human sweat and stale air. The warden did not look at her as he spoke, and she was led into a small room with a scarred wooden table and two upright chairs. This privilege was granted only because Pitt was still technically an innocent man.

It took all the strength she possessed not to weep when she saw him. His clothes were dirty, the clean shirt she had brought him was already torn, and there were bruises on his face. She dared not imagine what there might be on his body that she could not see. Neither wardens nor prisoners had any love for a policeman turned murderer. The warden commanded Charlotte and Pitt to sit at opposite sides of the table while he stood upright in the corner like a sentry and watched them.

For several moments she just sat and stared. It would be ridiculous to ask him how he was. He knew she cared; that was all that was necessary, and there was nothing she could do to alter any of it.

Then the emotion became too strong and she spoke simply to break the tension.

"Mama has taken the children. It will be easier for them, and for me. Gracie is wonderful. I sent a letter to Emily. Jack Radley took it to her. I asked her to stay where she is—don't argue with me. It is the only way we shall learn anything."

"Charlotte, you must be careful!" He leaned forward, then as the jailer stepped towards them, realized the uselessness of it. "You must get Emily out of there—it's too dangerous!" he said urgently. "Someone has already killed three times to keep the silence over what happened that night in Hanover Close. You mustn't go again. Send a letter to say you are sick, or that you're going back to the country. That would be better. Promise me! Leave it to Ballarat, he'll handle it now. They haven't told me who he's put on the case, but whoever it is will come and see me, and I'll tell him all I know. We must be getting close for them to have killed Cerise. Promise me, Charlotte!"

Her hesitation was only momentary. She would defend him in whatever manner necessary, and by whatever means she could find. She did not stop to think, or weigh judgment, any more than she would have done had Daniel or Jemima been in the street in front of a runaway horse. It was as instinctive as gasping for breath when the water closes over your head.

"Yes, Thomas, of course," she lied without a flicker. "Emily will stay with me for a while, or I'll stay with her. Don't worry about any of us, we'll be perfectly all right. Anyway, I'm sure Mr. Ballarat won't take long to discover the truth. He must know perfectly well that you couldn't have killed Cerise. Whyever should you?"

Some of the fear eased out of his face and he tried to smile. "Good," he said quietly. "At least I know you're all right. Thank you for your promise."

There was no time for guilt; the hangman waited. She smiled back. "Of course," she said with a gulp. "Don't worry about us."

10

Emily watched the ashes of Charlotte's letter crumbling in the morning room fire and felt a numbness, a sense of disbelief invade her mind. It was impossible. Thomas arrested for murder and imprisoned—it was absurd! Any moment now reality would reassert itself. She should not have burned the letter; she must have misread it. She looked at the red hollow in the coals where the paper had collapsed. There were only little incandescent folds left, and even as she watched, the draft caught them and they shivered to pieces and were consumed.

The door opened behind her and the butler came in.

"Are you all right, Amelia?" he said gently. There was concern in his voice, even something close to a personal tenderness. Dear God! She could not be coping with that now!

"Yes thank you, Mr. Redditch," she said gravely. "My sister has been taken ill."

"Yes, so Mr. Radley said. It was very good of him to come. Lady Ashworth must think most highly of you. What is it your sister suffers from?"

267

She had not even thought of that. "I don't know," she answered helplessly. "The—the doctors don't know—that's what is so worrying. Thank you for letting me have Saturday afternoon. It's very good of you."

"Not at all, my dear girl. Edith can cover for you; goodness knows you've covered for her often enough! Now you go into the kitchen and sit down. Take a cup of tea and recover yourself." He touched her arm gently, and his hands were warm.

"Thank you, Mr. Redditch," she said quickly. "Sir."

He stepped back reluctantly. "If there is anything I can do, please feel you may ask," he added.

She wanted to thank him, to smile and meet his eyes, let him know his kindness was not unnoticed, but she dared not. It might only cause more hurt in the end.

"I will, sir," she said, looking down at her apron. "And I'll go and get a cup of tea, as you said. Thank you." And she hurried past him out into the hall, through the baize door and into the kitchen.

She sat in the kitchen with the large round teacup in her hands, her mind whirling as she tried to think what to do. Her first instinct was to rush to Charlotte to be with her, to protect her from the jeers, the doubts, and to be with her in the long evenings when there was nothing else to interrupt the fear.

But Charlotte was right; pain was incidental, it must be overcome alone if need be, because there was no time for comfort. They could not afford to huddle together for today's hurt at the cost of tragedy which would darken all tomorrows. The answer was in the truth, and that lay here in Hanover Close. As Amelia, Emily was the only one with any chance of finding it.

She could no longer allow things to progress at their present pace. Obviously it all had to do with the woman in cerise, and whatever had happened here in this house three years ago. Perhaps it had been between her and Robert York;

maybe there had been a third person. But Emily believed one of the women who was here now either knew or suspected the truth, and she was determined to wring it from her somehow.

What made people crack? Shock, panic, overconfidence? Pressure gradually increased until it was unbearable—that was it. There was no time to wait for mistakes to happen. Three years had accomplished nothing, and Loretta certainly was not one to give way to carelessness; her guard was impenetrable. One had only to look at her bedroom with its tidy drawers, everything in its place, all her gowns with their matching boots and gloves, to know that. Her underwear was extremely expensive, but it was all coordinated, nothing odd or impulsive. Her dinner gowns were individual, highly feminine, but there were no experiments, none of the errors of judgment Emily had in her own wardrobe, attempts to imitate someone else's panache that had not quite worked, shades that had not flattered after all. There was nothing in the entire house that did not suit Loretta, either among her personal belongings or in the general furniture. Loretta did not make mistakes.

Veronica was different, a generation younger, and far more beautiful by nature. She had more flair, more courage; sometimes she ordered things on impulse and they were marvelous—that black gown with the jet-encrusted bodice was superb, better than anything Loretta could ever wear—but the gray silk was a disaster. Loretta would have known that and never run the risk. Sometimes Veronica was uncertain, full of self-doubt, and that made her rash; she tried too hard. Emily had been amazed at first to see her change her mind as to what she would wear, or how she would dress her hair. Yes, Veronica might well break under pressure, if it was severe enough, sustained enough.

It was a cruel thought, and an hour ago Emily would not have entertained it—but an hour ago she did not know

269

Thomas was in prison awaiting trial for his life. She regretted her decision, but she did not consider any other.

She finished her tea, thanked the cook for it with a meek smile, and set out to go upstairs and begin. The first thing she did was to find a pair of Veronica's boots which needed resoling to give her an excuse to go out. A breath of fresh air and a walk would be a kind of freedom, and she was longing just to be alone, to move swiftly without being closed in by walls. She had never realized before how little time a maid ever had unwatched or supervised by someone; and even in weather like this she missed the opportunity to be outside, to see the sky other than in tiny pieces blocked off by the frame of a window. The claustrophobia of being available all the time, of having her solitude or her company ordered for her, was increasingly difficult to bear, even though there was a certain pleasure in sharing the evenings, the simple humor, and at times a little fun. But the main purpose was to be able to account for her news when she returned.

Today no one questioned her as she left with the boots under her arm.

At five o'clock Emily was back and in Veronica's room, laying out clean linen, when Veronica came in. "I'm so sorry about your sister, Amelia," she said immediately. "You're very welcome to take Saturday afternoon off to go and visit her; if she should get any worse, please tell me."

"Yes ma'am," Emily said solemnly. "Thank you very much. I'm hoping she'll get better, and there are people with worse troubles. I just took your black boots to the cobbler's and I heard them say down there that that policeman who came here about the stolen silver and things has been charged with murdering a woman in a magenta pink dress, to do with some investigation he was on—" She stopped, staring at Veronica's face, which was suddenly bleached of every vestige of color. It was exactly what she had hoped for, and although she was perfectly capable of pity, it did not make the slightest difference to her continuing.

"That must be the same man that upset you so much, ma'am. No wonder! I suppose we should all be grateful he didn't lose control of himself with you, or heaven knows, you might be like that poor woman. Except of course I can't imagine you wearing such an unflattering color. From the description it was wicked."

"Stop it!" Veronica's voice rose close to a scream. "Stop it! What does it matter what color she wore?" Her face was white as a sheet, her eyes glittering. "You are talking about a human being who's been murdered! Life just—snatched . . ."

Emily's hands flew to her face. "Oh, ma'am! Oh, ma'am, I'm terribly sorry! I clean forgot about Mr. York! Oh, I am so terribly sorry—please forgive me. I'll do anything . . ." She stopped, as though she were too upset to speak, and simply gazed at Veronica through her spread fingers. Did her dreadful pallor reflect the memory of Robert's death, or was it a sign of guilt? Surely there was panic in her expression; had Veronica known Cerise, and did she know now who had killed her?

For several seconds they stood staring at each other, Veronica in shocked silence, Emily studying her through wide eyes, affecting abject contrition. At last it was Veronica who spoke. She sat down on the side of the bed and Emily automatically began to undo her boots for her.

"I—I didn't know anything about it," Veronica said very quietly. "I don't see the newspapers, and Papa-in-law didn't mention it. Did they describe her, this woman"—she swallowed—"in pink?"

"Oh yes, ma'am." Emily recalled everything she could of the descriptions of Cerise. "She was tall, rather on the thin side, not at all full-figured, especially for a—a woman of pleasure, but she had a very beautiful face." She looked up from the boots, buttonhook in hand, and saw Veronica's horrified eyes. Her protruding leg was rigid, and her knuckles on the side of the bed were white.

"And of course she was wearing that peculiar color of very violent magenta pink," Emily finished. "I think 'cerise' is the right name for it."

Veronica made a little sound as if she were about to cry out, but tension strangled the word in her throat.

"You look terrible shocked, ma'am," Emily said ruthlessly. "They say she was a woman of the streets, so perhaps she's no worse off. Quicker than disease."

"Amelia! You sound as if—"

"Oh no, ma'am!" Emily protested. "Nobody deserves to die like that. I only meant her life was pretty wretched anyway. I know girls who have lost their places, been dismissed without a character, and had to go on the streets like that. They usually die young, either of working twenty hours a day or the pox, or someone kills them." She kept on watching Veronica's face and knew she had touched a deep pain, a wound that was still bleeding. She turned the probe. "That policeman said he was questioning her about a crime he was investigating. Perhaps she knew who broke in here and killed poor Mr. York."

"No." It was a whisper, little more than a sigh of breath forced between the lips.

Emily waited.

"No." Veronica seemed to collect her strength. "Policemen must have more than one case at a time. What on earth would a woman like that know of this—of this house?"

"Maybe she knew the thief, ma'am," Emily suggested. "Perhaps he was her lover."

For some unfathomable reason Veronica smiled. It was ghastly, like a rictus, but there was the shadow of bitter humor in her eyes. "Perhaps," she said softly.

Emily knew by some change in the air, a difference in the tensions of the body, that the immediate weakness was past. She would get no more from Veronica now. She finished with the boots, took them off, and stood up.

"Would you like me to draw you a bath before dinner,

272

ma'am, or would you prefer to lie down, perhaps with a hot tisane?''

"I don't want a bath." Veronica stood up and went to the window. She spoke with growing decision. "Go and make me a tisane, and fetch a slice of bread and butter from the kitchen. In fact, two slices."

Emily had a strong idea it was not so much the bread Veronica wanted as an excuse to be rid of her, but she had no choice but to obey.

She fairly ran along the passage and down the stairs, earning a sharp word of reproof from the housekeeper for her unseemly behavior.

"Yes, Mrs. Crawford. Sorry, Mrs. Crawford." She slowed down to a more dignified walk until she was out of sight through the green baize door, then quickened into a scamper again. She asked Cook's permission as a matter of policy, then put on a kettle and sliced the bread and butter so rapidly she made a mess of the first piece; it was too thin and fell to bits.

" 'Ere!" Mary said helpfully. "You got 'ands like a navvy today! Let me do it for yer!" And she cut two wafer-thin slices, buttering each on the loaf first, a trick which Emily had not learned.

"Thank you; bless you!" Emily said with real gratitude, then hopped from one foot to the other waiting for the kettle to boil. But she had learned her lesson and she did not spill it.

"S'right," Mary said approvingly. "More 'aste, less speed."

Emily flashed her a smile, picked up the tray, and went back upstairs with it as quickly as her long skirts would allow, unable as she was with her hands full to hold them up. She stopped outside the bedroom door, hearing a murmur of voices, but even standing motionless, her cheek to the panel, she could hear no distinct words. To disturb whoever was within might cut short the very conversation she must over-hear!

The dressing room!

She put the tray down and very softly tried the handle of the dressing room door, making sure the latch did not click. She swung it open, picked up the tray, and put it inside on the chest of drawers, closing the door soundlessly. The door to the bedroom was closed, she had done it herself out of habit. Now she needed to open it so fractionally the movement would not catch the eye of anyone in the bedroom, even if they were facing it. Of course, if they saw the handle move it would all be over: she would be caught eavesdropping without a shadow of an excuse.

She bent to the keyhole and put her eye to it, but she could see only the corner of the bed and a small edge of blue skirt over the chair. It was only the dress laid out for the evening. But she could hear the voices much more clearly. The answer was obvious: she must kneel with her ear to the keyhole. Carefully she took a pin out of her hair and put it on the floor as an excuse if she were caught; then she knelt to listen.

"But who was it?" Veronica's voice was desperate, thick with something very close to panic.

Loretta's answer came back, reassuringly gentle. "My dear, I cannot even guess! But it has nothing whatever to do with us. How could it?"

"But the dress!" Veronica cried. "That color!" The words seemed to cause her physical pain. "The dress was magenta!"

"Pull yourself together!" Loretta snarled. "You are behaving like a fool!"

For a moment there was silence and Emily wondered if Loretta had slapped her, as one does with hysterics; but there was no gasp, no indrawn breath, no sharp sound of flesh on flesh.

Veronica's voice shuddered and the next words were forced through sobs. "Who . . . was . . . she?"

"A harlot," Loretta replied with ice-cold contempt. "Exactly what she seemed to be, I should imagine. Although God knows why that idiot policeman should have broken her neck!"

Veronica's question was so soft Emily strained to hear it, her shoulders hunched to keep her ear to the lock.

"Did he, Mother-in-law? Was it he?"

Emily did not even notice the cramp in her knees or the aching muscles in her neck. Nothing was further from her mind than the tea getting cold on the chest of drawers. She could hear no sound in the room, not even a rustle of silk.

"Well, I assume so!" Loretta answered after what must have been only seconds, but seemed an age. "Apparently he was found with his hands virtually round her neck, so one would presume so. There seems no other easy explanation."

"But why?"

"My dear, how should I know? Perhaps he was so obsessed with getting his information he tried to throttle it out of her, and when she couldn't tell him he lost his temper. It hardly matters to us."

"But she's dead!" Veronica's distress was thick in her voice, even violent.

Loretta was becoming annoyed. "Which is nothing whatsoever to us!" she retorted. "What is one street woman more or less? She had a pink dress—I daresay many women do, especially of that occupation." Then she spoke more urgently and with a peculiar rasping tone. "Get ahold of yourself, Veronica! You have much to gain, and everything to lose—everything! Remember that. Robert is dead. Let the past stay in the grave where it belongs, and make yourself a decent future with Julian Danver. I've done everything I can to help you, God knows, but if you give way to fits of the vapors and maudlin thoughts every time there is a tragedy somewhere, then even I cannot carry you through. Do you understand me?"

There was silence. Emily strained till she could hear her

own heart thumping, but there was not even a movement beyond the keyhole.

"Do you understand me?" Loretta's voice was low and grating, without patience, devoid of pity. Had Emily not heard the words quite plainly, it would have sounded like a threat. Loretta had comforted and supported Veronica for a long time now, and her strength, let alone her patience, seemed to be wearing thin. She too had suffered a loss; Veronica was on the brink of finding another husband, but Loretta would not find another son. Little wonder she thought it was time Veronica behaved less self-indulgently.

"Yes." Veronica's voice sounded defiant, yet there was no conviction in it. "Yes, I understand." And she began to weep.

"Good." Loretta was satisfied. There was a crackle of taffeta as she sat back. Apparently she was not interested in Veronica's tears. Perhaps she had seen too many of them.

There was a brisk knock on the door and Emily shot halfway to her feet, tripped on her skirt and fell flat. This time her hair really did come undone; the pin she had removed must have been vital. Frantically she hitched up her skirts and stood up properly; then she let them fall and smoothed her apron to make sure she was decent. She grabbed for the tray, then realized the knock had been on the outer door to the bedroom, not on the dressing room door.

The relief was overwhelming, so physically sharp her legs were shaking. She had time to put the tray down again, pin her hair rather better, take the tray and go out onto the landing and knock at the bedroom door herself.

When she went in Veronica was sitting on the big bed looking exhausted, bright smudges of color in her cheeks; Loretta was perfectly composed, at least on the surface. Piers York stood there looking slightly puzzled, a frown of incomprehension on his usually benign face. It might have been the angle of the light, but for the first time Emily also saw the deep sadness, in an expression in his eyes that stripped quite naked a patience and a disillusionment. Then he spoke and it vanished.

"What have you got?" He regarded Emily curiously. "Tea and bread and butter? Put it on the dressing table."

"Yes, sir," Emily moved to obey, putting aside the silver-backed brushes and hand mirror. She did not offer to pour; if they left it awhile they might attribute the tea's coldness to their own delay.

"Amelia!" Loretta said sharply.

"Yes, ma'am?" Emily tried to look demure as an insecure pin slid out of her hair and fell on the dressing table with a tinkle, and a coil of hair unwound down her cheek.

"For heaven's sake, girl!" Loretta's rage exploded. "You look like a—a dollymop!"

Emily knew what a dollymop was: the cheapest of pros-titutes, who could be tossed down anywhere for a few pence. The hot blood in her cheeks betrayed her, but she could not give the insolently innocent answer that leapt to her tongue. Nor could she afford to retaliate on equal terms, or she would lose her job—and Pitt's life might depend on it. Choking with the injustice, she lowered her eyes so Loretta could not see the hatred in them. "I'm sorry, ma'am," she whispered, forcing the words between her clenched teeth. "I stood out of the way and brushed against the curtain. I must have pulled out one of my pins."

"Indeed." Loretta made no attempt to hide her total skep-ticism. "It doesn't say much for your ability to dress hair! Well, when I write your references I shall say nothing about the matter, although your manner has not always been what I would wish. But your mentioning this vulgar crime in Seven Dials to Miss Veronica is inexcusable. We do not have ser-vants in this house who know about such things, let alone discuss them. Next thing you know we shall have all the maids in hysterics and the whole household at a standstill. I am sorry you have proved unsuitable, but no doubt you will find another position. You may work out the week, till we find someone to replace you. Edith cannot possibly do the work of two, and I need her for other things. Now you may get on about your business. Leave the tray there.''

Veronica shot up like a jack-in-the-box. ''She is my maid!'' she said rather loudly, staring at Loretta. ''And I am perfectly satisfied with her—in fact I like her! And I shall keep her—forever, if I choose! And she heard about the murder doing an errand for me; she told me because she knew I was upset when that policeman called here before. Now he won't be back, and I for one am delighted.''

Piers shook his head. ''Pity,'' he said with regret. ''Can't imagine what can have made him do it. Seemed such a civilized chap to me. Must be some explanation, I suppose.''

''Rubbish!'' Loretta said swiftly. ''Really Piers, sometimes I wonder how on earth you succeed as well as you do. Your judgment of people is—infantile!''

The change in his face was so subtle it was not a movement of any one feature, but Emily knew instantly that Loretta had trespassed too far, although she herself did not seem to realize it.

''I think the word you were looking for was 'charitable,' '' he said very quietly.

''Do you also take a 'charitable' view of the maid coming in here looking as if she'd just got out of bed?'' Loretta demanded with icy disgust.

Piers turned and regarded Emily curiously. There was the faintest glint of humor in his eyes. ''Have you been scuffling with one of the menservants, Amelia?''

She looked back at him perfectly steadily.

''No, sir, I have not; not now, nor at any time.''

''Thank you,'' he said gravely. ''The matter is settled. I think it is time we all changed for dinner.'' He put his hands in his pockets and walked casually to the door.

''I am keeping my maid.'' Veronica stared at Loretta. ''If she goes, it will be because I don't want her, not because you don't!''

278

"Drink your tea," Loretta replied without expression, but Emily knew from her face, the calm power in the set of her mouth, that her defeat was only temporary. Time was short.

But then time was short for Pitt anyway.

Loretta went out and closed the door with a firm click. Veronica ignored the tea and ate the bread and butter. "I've changed my mind," she said, staring into the mirror. "I'll wear the crimson dress."

The following days passed grimly. Emily tried hard to be the perfect lady's maid so that not even Edith could find fault with her. She ironed many articles three and four times, redampening them and smoothing them again and again with the flatiron till they were flawless. Her back and arms ached, but she would not be beaten by a crease in a piece of cotton. There was no time to sit down and swap gossip, as she would have liked to, since there was also the possibility that someone else on the staff might have known something.

There was always the chance that Veronica's resolve would weaken or her courage fail, and Emily would find herself given notice again. She bit back any smart replies, forcing herself to act meekly, to walk with her head less high and without the slight whisk of skirts that was natural to her.

On the other hand she went out of her way to flatter Mrs. Melrose, the cook, who became a first-class ally, since she disliked Mrs. Crawford already. Emily worked on the principle "My enemy's enemy is my friend." She did rather well with the butler also. Normally it was a tactic she would have despised, but she must survive here if she were to be any use to Charlotte or Thomas, and there was no time for fine moral niceties.

The tweeny and the scullery maid were the lowest forms of life in the household, but the tweeny in particular was an observant child and not unintelligent, and Emily was able, through a little kindness, to draw quite a lot of information from her. Of course, the girl knew nothing about Robert

York, and very little about the family at all; but she had very definite opinions about the rest of the servants. There was no room to be subtle.

On Saturday Emily took her afternoon off and met Charlotte in the park in a fine, driving rain. It was bitterly cold and they huddled together, pulling collars higher and burying their hands in muffs, but at least it was highly unlikely that they would be observed. Who but the illicit or those bound in the utmost haste from one place to another would be out on such a day? Even the homeless chose the comparative shelter of the streets rather than the open wastes of the park, where the wind could sheer unchecked across the flat gray-green winter grass; and forbidden lovers had no eyes for anyone but each other.

They exchanged news, which gave them both some new insights, but no conclusions beyond what they already knew: the murderer was in Hanover Close, and either Veronica or Loretta knew, if not who it was, then at least why the crime had been committed. But how to break their silence was still a mystery.

Charlotte was frightened. She hovered on the edge of begging Emily to leave the York house. Three times she started to, and then the almost paralyzing fear for Pitt drowned out everything else and her words died in her throat. Not that it would have made any difference; Emily had no intention of retiring from the fight and sitting by while they tried Pitt and hanged him.

Which did not mean Emily was not also frightened. After hugging Charlotte good-bye, she sniffed back the tears and turned from the park gates to run along the wet pavements in the rain, past the carriages in the streets, along the wrought iron railings and down the area steps into the kitchen. She was so cold she was shaking inside. She piled her sodden coat and boots into the laundry room to dry, ate a silent supper at the kitchen table, and went up to her room. She lay

280

in bed still shivering and thought how she might trap the man or woman who had murdered three times already and had hidden the crimes so well that the only person suspected was Pitt.

She woke in the dark with a scream in her throat and her body clenched with terror as a footfall made the merest tap in the bare passage outside her door. Soundlessly she slid out of bed, the cold air on her skin cutting through her thin nightgown like a blow. By the dim light of the badly curtained window, she grasped the one wooden chair and wedged it under the door handle. Then she scrambled back into bed again, pulled her knees up to her stomach, and tried to get warm enough to go back to sleep, so that she would not be useless in the morning, either to work or to match wits with a murderer, trap them, and survive to show the proof.

She got up in the chilly gray dawn in time to remove the chair, so that when Fanny, the tweeny, called to waken her she knew nothing of it. The day was full of tedious, time-consuming chores and Emily learned nothing that seemed to be of value.

This was pointless! It could go on for months! She must force the issue.

Late in the evening she crept into the pantry, pocketed half a dozen biscuits dipped in chocolate, and made two cups of cocoa. She carried them upstairs, where she knocked on the tweeny's door and, when it was opened, whispered her invitation.

Five minutes later they were curled up, feet under them, on Emily's bed, sharing the biscuits and sipping hot cocoa. Emily began to gossip.

It took ten minutes before she could bring up the subject of Dulcie's death.

"Whatever was she doing leaning out of the window?" she said, eating the last biscuit. "Do you suppose she was calling to someone?"

"Nah!" Fanny said scornfully. "If'n there'd bin anybody

there, they'd 'a said, wouldn't they? I mean, nobody saw 'er fall! Anyway, she weren't like that.''

"What do you mean?" Emily affected innocence.

"Well . . ." Fanny hunched her shoulders in a shrug. "She weren't a flirt. She were sort o'—proper. Quiet like.''

"And nobody saw her at all?" Emily said incredulously.

"It were dark! She fell out some time in the evening. We was all inside.''

Emily gazed at her. "How do you know? Do you know where everyone was?''

Fanny screwed up her face. "Well, we would be, wouldn't we? Where else would anyone be on a wet night in the middle o' winter?''

"Oh.'' Emily sat back against the thin pillow. "I thought maybe you actually knew where everyone was: at supper in the kitchen, or in the servants hall.''

"No one knows when she fell out," Fanny explained patiently. "Any'ow, she were there at supper wiv us 'erself.''

"You mean—'' Emily opened her eyes wider. "You mean she fell during the night? What was the last time anyone saw her?''

"Edith said good night to 'er 'baht 'alf nine," Fanny replied, thinking hard. "Me an' Prim was playin' cards. Dulcie weren't feelin' that special, so it must 'a bin after that, mustn't it?''

"But that doesn't make sense!" Emily persisted. "Why should she be leaning out of a window during the night? You don't think—'' She took a deep breath and waited. "You don't think she had someone climbing in?''

"Oh no!'' Fanny's shock was genuine and profound. "Not Dulcie! You mean a—a follower? Never! Not 'er, she weren't . . .'' Her little face set in practical lines. "Any'ow, if'n yer was going to 'ave a follower in the 'ouse, yer wouldn't 'ave the poor soul climb up no drainpipe to an attic winder; yer'd creep down an' let 'im in the scullery door, wouldn't yer? She weren't daft! But she weren't loose neither.'' She finished the last of the cocoa and looked at Emily over the rim of her cup, then automatically pushed her hair out of her eyes. "Know what I reckon, Amelia?"

Emily was agog, leaning forward to urge her on. "What?"

Fanny's voice dropped to a hoarse whisper. "I reckon as she saw summink the night Mr. Robert were murdered, and someone came back an' murdered 'er, in case she told that rozzer as was 'ere askin'!"

Emily breathed out in a careful sigh of amazement. "Oh Fanny! You could be right! You think there was a break-in?"

Fanny shook her head vigorously. "No, there weren't—we'd 'a known. Mr. Redditch is most partic'lar, 'specially after there were that terrible robbery when Mr. Robert were murdered. All the doors and winders is looked ter special every night afore 'e goes ter bed 'isself. 'Im or Albert goes over every one."

"Well, could anyone have got in before that?" Emily asked eagerly.

"Nah!" Fanny smiled at her innocence. " 'Ow? There's only the front door, an' yer can't come in that 'less someone opens it for yer; and the back door'd mean 'e 'ad ter come through the kitchen, and there's always people there, Cook or Mary at least, an' on a night wiv guests, near all of us."

"Who were the guests that night? Do you know?"

"The two Danver gentlemen and the ladies, Miss 'arriet and the old Miss Danver, an' Mr. and Mrs. Asherson. 'E's ever so 'andsome, Mr. Asherson, in a sort o' broodin' way. I know Nora's always on about 'im. I reckon as she's got a fancy for 'im rotten!" She sniffed, unconsciously imitating the housekeeper's tone. "Silly little article! What'd she get out of it, 'ceptin' misery?"

"Then it must have been someone already in the house," Emily whispered back, entirely forgetting her accent, but Fanny appeared not to notice. "Or someone in the house let in another person?"

"Like 'oo?" Fanny was indignant. "In't none of us servants 'd do that! Anyway, we weren't none of us 'ere when Mr. Robert were killed, 'ceptin' Mary an' Dulcie 'erself. An' Mary's in the kitchen and nobody came through that way or we'd all 'a seen 'em. Come ter that, Albert was on in the 'all.''

"So it was someone here," Emily agreed. "The only other possibility is that Dulcie crept down during the night and let someone in herself—or Mary did, I suppose." She added that only in the interests of strict logic; she did not believe for a moment that either girl had done such a thing. She had the information she wanted: it had happened after dinner and could have been before the guests left, but there had definitely been no break-in. "Fanny, I think you're right!" She leaned forward, gripping Fanny's thin arm. "You'd better say nothing to anyone at all—in case you fall out of a window as well! Promise me.''

Fanny shook her head, eyes grave. "I won't! Oh, believe me, I won't. I don't want ter end up squashed on the pavement like 'er, poor thing. An' you better keep a still tongue too.''

"I swear!" Emily said with conviction. "And I'll put a chair against my door.''

"You better 'ad," Fanny agreed. "Me too!" She uncurled her legs and slid to the floor, hugging her nightgown round her, shivering now the cocoa was finished. "G'night, 'melia.''

But even with the chair wedged under the handle Emily did not sleep easily. Several times she woke with a start, uncertain if she had heard footsteps in the passage outside, and whether they had stopped outside her door. Could someone have tried the handle? The wind rattled the loose sash frame, and she froze in terror, waiting till the sound came again and she could be certain what it was. Suspicions churned in her mind, slipping in and out of dreams.

With daylight courage returned, but she was still nervous; it took all her concentration not to make any mistakes. As she went from one pedestrian duty to the next, she was always aware of other people, of movement, shadows. By evening she was so tired she could have wept with exhaustion. She felt imprisoned in the house, hurried from one place to another with never any time to be alone, yet carrying her loneliness like a weight inside. And always time was the enemy. In a way it was a blessing to have work to occupy her.

Charlotte could only imagine what might be happening to Emily after they parted in the rain at the park gates. It was useless to think about it; she could do nothing. And she must keep lying to Pitt or he would know she was working to find the truth—and then he was certain to realize that she was doing so because Ballarat was doing nothing—no one would do anything. The loneliness of having to lie to him was one of the worse pains she had ever known. The luxury of hiding nothing, carrying no knowledge alone, was something she was so used to she had forgotten its value. Now it would only be selfishness, and she did not even consider it. Nevertheless, the hurt caught her by surprise.

But there were small kindnesses, friendships where she had not thought to find them. A strange little man in a coster's coat and cap brought her a bag of herrings and refused to be paid, hurrying away into the rain without looking back, as though embarrassed to be thanked. One morning she found a bundle of kindling sticks on the back step, and two days later there was another bundle. She never saw who left them. The greengrocer became curt to the point of outright rudeness, but the coal merchant continued to deliver, and she thought his sacks were if anything a little fuller.

Caroline did not come back, but she wrote every day saying that Daniel and Jemima were well and offering to do anything she could to help.

The letter that touched her most came from Great-aunt Vespasia, who was ill with bronchitis and confined to her bed. She had no doubt whatsoever that Pitt was innocent, and as soon as the time was appropriate, if it should come to such a ridiculous pass, she would instruct her lawyer to act on his behalf. She also enclosed ten guineas, for which she hoped Charlotte would not be silly enough to take offense. One could not fight on an empty stomach—and quite obviously a fight was on hand.

The writing was shaky and a little crooked on the page, and Charlotte was struck with cold shock as she realized that Aunt Vespasia was old and frailty was catching up with her.

She stood in the kitchen in the early morning holding the blue deckled paper in her hand. It seemed as if all the good and certain things in the world were fading fast; there was a chill so close to the skin no fires could dispel it.

She went to visit Pitt again, waiting in the shivering rain with other quiet, sad-faced women whose fathers, husbands, or sons rotted away in the Steel. Some were violent, some greedy, brutal by nature of circumstance, many merely inadequate to cope with life in the struggling, overcrowded streets where only the strongest endure.

Charlotte had time for pity, time to wonder and think about these other women—it was easier to ache for another's pain than work through the realities of her own. That made it easier to face Pitt and lie, smiling as if she had confidence and smothering her fear if she occupied the storm of emotion inside herself with something else.

When at last she was permitted in she was not allowed to touch him, only to sit across the table and stare into his face, seeing the dirt and the bruises, the hollows round his eyes where shock could not be hidden by his forced smile. Never in her life had she had to live so difficult or so complete a lie. He knew her so well, she had never succeeded in deceiving him before. Now she met his eyes and lied as easily as if he had been a child instead of a man, someone to be protected and comforted with stories while she bore the truth.

"Yes, we are all perfectly well," she said quickly. "Although of course we miss you terribly! But we have enough of everything, so I haven't had to ask Mama or Emily for any help, although I'm sure they'll give it if it should be necessary. No, I haven't been back to the Yorks'. I'm leaving it to Mr. Ballarat, as you said. . . . Well, if he hasn't sent anyone to see you yet it must be because he doesn't need to.'' She kept mastery of the conversation, permitting no time for interruptions, questions she could not answer.

"Where's Emily? At home. They wouldn't let her in here, she isn't family—at least, not close enough. Sisters-in-law don't count. Yes, Jack Radley is being very helpful. . . .''

Emily was in the laundry room doing the job she disliked most intensely: ironing the starched frills of cotton aprons, half a dozen of them. Somehow Edith had taken advantage of some absence of mind to maneuver Emily into doing her share as well. She looked up in surprise when Mary came to the door, glanced all round her, then slipped in and closed it, fingers to her lips.

"What is it?'' Emily whispered.

"A man!'' Mary said urgently, her voice so low her words were almost swallowed. "You got a follower!''

"I haven't!'' Emily denied fiercely. She certainly did not need that kind of trouble. And it was totally unjust; she had encouraged no one. In fact, she had given the butcher's boy a flea in his ear when he had smiled at her, impudent creature.

"Yes you 'ave!'' Mary insisted. "Scruffy, 'e is, an' looks like 'e just bin up a chimney! But spoke awful nice an' polite, an' if'n 'e were washed 'e could be real nice, I reckon.''

"Well, I don't know him!'' Emily said fiercely. "Tell him to go away!''

"Won't you even come and see—''

"No! Do you want me to lose my character?''

" 'E's awful keen.''

"I'll be thrown out!'' Emily exploded.

287

"But 'e says 'e knows you!" Mary tried once more. "C'mon, Amelia; 'e could be—Well, d'you want to stay a lady's maid all your life?"

"It's a lot better than being out on the street without a character!" Emily hissed back.

"Well, if you're really sure. 'Is name is Jack suffink."

Emily froze. "What?"

" 'Is name is Jack suffink," Mary repeated.

Emily dropped the iron. "I'll come! Where is he? Has anyone else seen him?"

"You changed yer mind pretty quick!" Mary said with profound satisfaction. "But yer'd better be sharp! If Cook catches yer, yer'll be in dead trouble. 'E's at the scullery door. On wiv yer! 'Urry!"

Emily ran from the laundry room along the corridor, through the kitchen and scullery to the back door, with Mary close behind her, keeping watch for cook's return.

Emily could hardly believe what she saw. The man standing in the rain on the back steps beside the coke scuttles and rubbish cans was dressed in a dark, ragged coat that came past his knees, and his face was all but hidden by a broad-brimmed hat and a lock of sooty hair that fell over his brow. His skin seemed grimy, as if he had indeed come down a chimney.

"Jack?" Emily said incredulously.

He grinned, showing startlingly white teeth in his filthy face. She was so glad to see him she wanted to laugh, but realized immediately her laughter would turn to tears. It all rushed through her in a torrent so fierce she said nothing at all.

"Are you all right?" he demanded. "You look dreadful!"

Then she did start to laugh, a little hysterically, but stopped herself when she realized Mary could hear her. She controlled her voice with an effort. "Yes, I'm fine. I put a chair under my door at night. But I need to talk to you. How is Charlotte?"

"It's very hard on her, and we're not getting anywhere."

There was a shout inside the scullery and Emily knew someone was back who would betray her, if not Cook then Nora.

"Go!" she said quickly. "I'll go to the cobbler's in half an hour or so—wait for me round the corner. Please!"

He nodded, and by the time Nora's curious face came round the outer door he had slipped up the area steps and disappeared.

"What are you doing out 'ere?" Nora said sharply. "I thought I 'eard you talking to someone!"

"Well, you know what 'thought' did!" Emily snapped back, then regretted it; not that she had any compunction about Nora, it was just unwise to antagonize her. But it was too late to retreat now, or it would only make her suspicious. "For that matter, what are you doing out here?"

"Er . . ." Nora had obviously come to catch Emily out, and now she was confused. She lifted her chin a little higher. "I thought if there was someone 'ere 'e might be bothering you! I came to 'elp!"

"How kind of you," Emily replied sarcastically. "As you see, there is no one. I came to see how cold it is. I'm going on an errand; I shall need a greatcoat."

"Of course you will!" Nora said waspishly. "What else do you expect in January?"

"Rain," Emily replied with growing confidence.

"It is raining! Couldn't you see that through the window?"

"Not much. I was in the laundry." She stared at Nora's handsome bold eyes, daring her to make an open accusation.

"Very well then." Nora shrugged elaborately; she had elegant shoulders and she knew it. "Then you'd better be on your way, and don't take 'alf the afternoon about it!"

Emily went back to the laundry room to finish the last apron. She folded it and put away the flatiron, then collected her hat and coat, and after telling Mary where she was going, she set out up the area steps and along Hanover Close towards the main thoroughfare, waiting with every footstep to see Jack, or hear him behind her.

She nearly bumped into him round the first corner. He still looked a sight, and he did not touch her but walked respectfully beside her as if they were both exactly what they appeared: a lady's maid on an errand and a sweep's man taking a short time off.

As they walked she told him about the extraordinary conversation she had overheard between Veronica and Loretta, and the only conclusion possible from her discussion with the tweeny.

He in turn told her what little news he had of Charlotte.

By the time that was completed she had Veronica's boots and was on the way back to Hanover Close. It was raining harder, her feet and her skirts were wet, and the soot was beginning to run in black trickles down his face.

"You look fearful!" she said with a rather painful smile. She was walking less and less quickly. She was dreading going back into the house, not only because this was a moment's freedom from duty and fear, but, surprisingly sharply, because she would miss Jack. "Your own mother wouldn't know you!" she added.

He started to laugh, at first very quietly, then more heartily as he gazed at her straight, mud brown coat, her plain hat and sodden boots.

She began to giggle as well, and they stood in the street together streaming wet, laughing on the edge of tears. He put out both his hands and took hers, holding her gently.

For an instant she thought it was on the edge of his tongue to ask her to marry him, but whatever words he had were quickly swallowed back. She had all the Ashworth money, the houses, the position; he had nothing. Love was not enough to offer.

"Jack," she said without giving herself time to weigh or judge. "Jack—would you consider marrying me?"

The rain was washing the soot off his face in black drops.

"Yes please, Emily. I would like to marry you—very much."

"Then you may kiss me," she said with a shy smile.

Slowly, carefully, and very gently he did; and standing there, filthy and cold in the rain, it was exquisitely sweet.

11

P*RISON LIFE* was unlike anything Pitt had imagined.
At first the sheer shock of his arrest, of being suddenly
and violently thrust from one side of the law to the other,
had numbed his feelings, robbing him of all but the most
superficial reactions. Even when he was taken from the local
cells to the great prison at Coldbath Fields, the reality of it
was purely sensory. He saw the massive walls and heard the
door shut, metal clanging on stone, and the strange sour
smell assaulted him, catching in his throat. He could taste it
on his tongue, but still it did not touch his emotions.

When he woke the following morning, stiff, muscles tight
with cold, memory flooded back, and it all seemed preposterous. Any minute someone would come, full of apologies,
and he would be taken out and given a good breakfast, hot,
probably porridge and bacon, and lots of steaming tea.

But when someone did come it was only the regular jailer
with a tin dish of gruel, ordering Pitt to get to his feet and
get ready for the day. Pitt protested without thinking, and
was told curtly to obey orders or he would find himself at the
crank.

The other prisoners regarded him with curiosity and hatred. He was the enemy. Were it not for the police, none of them would be here in this prolonged torture, cramped in the narrow, airless cells of the treadmill, endlessly stepping on slats that gave way under them as they struggled to keep abreast in the slow-turning wheel. Fifteen minutes in one of its cooplike stalls with the hot air suffocating the lungs was all any man could bear; then he had to be taken out before he collapsed.

If one were not eager enough at this, there was punishment ever available. For outright rebellion a man could be birched or flogged; for lesser offenses such as insolence or refusal to obey orders a man could be required to do shot drill. It was the third day before Pitt found himself ordered to this, for answering back, laziness, and causing a brawl.

The men were lined up in a hollow square outside in the bitterly cold exercise yard. Each man stood three yards from his neighbor and was given a twenty-five-pound iron cannonball to place at his feet. At the command he must pick it up and carry it to his neighbor's spot, put it on the ground, and return to his own spot, where he would find a new ball put there by the man on his other side. This senseless passing round and round of shot could be kept up for seventy-five minutes, till shoulders stabbed with pain, and muscles were torn and backs too sore to straighten.

Pitt's offense had been a stupid quarrel picked by another prisoner, who felt compelled to swagger in front of his companions. Had Pitt been paying more attention to his surroundings he would have noticed the man's brittle temper, the slight bounce to his walk, his curled fingers. Pitt would have understood the glitter as the man's eyes moved from side to side to see who was watching him, and whether admiration was there, the peculiar mixture of fear and respect that the weak have for violence. He would have recognized the man's sharp grin as that of the bully on parade.

But his mind was on the brothel and Cerise's dead body

thrown carelessly on the gaudy bed, as he tried to recall the few moments when he had seen her face. Had she really once been so beautiful, or possessed of such charm and wit, that Robert York had been bewitched by her into betraying his country? He would have been risking not merely the love of his wife, which he might or might not value, but his position in the Foreign Office and in Society, the things which governed the whole style of his life. If he had been caught, the best he could have hoped for would have been a cover-up, for his family's sake, and to prevent a scandal, which the government would not want; at worst he would have been brought here, where Pitt was, Coldbath Fields, or somewhere like it, to await trial, and very probably the hangman's noose.

That reminder was enough to overwhelm him with such anger and fear Pitt was careless of the immediate danger. He did not see the momentary swagger, the quick glitter in the man's eyes, nor recognize the challenge. The man was marking his territory. When the man spoke, Pitt replied tartly with the first answer that came to his tongue, and before he realized it he had placed the bully in a position of having to defend himself to keep from losing face. It was stupid, an idiotic scuffle that ended with both of them on shot drill and Pitt bending, straightening, carrying the shot, replacing it, walking back, until he thought his back was broken and the sweat drenched his clothes. When it finally stopped, they stuck to him in clammy cold and the ache of tortured muscles was so sharp that for four days he could not move even in his sleep without pain.

Days went by, and Pitt became accustomed to the routine, the wretched food, always being cold except when labor made him sweat and then the worse chill afterwards. He hated always being dirty, he loathed the lack of any privacy even for essential functions. He was lonelier than he had ever been in his life; and yet never alone. Actual physical solitude would have been a blessing, a chance to relax the tension, the awareness of enmity, and to explore the thoughts crowding inside himself without prying, cruel eyes watching, probing for weakness, prurient to invade.

The first time Charlotte came was the worst experience of all. To see her, talk and yet always be overheard, without being able to touch her, to have to struggle to put into words communication that was too intimate, too formless for such a quantifiable and public medium. His own thoughts were chaotic. What could he possibly say to her? That he was innocent, of anything except perhaps gullibility somewhere, but he was not even sure where? Perhaps it was only stupidity. He still had no idea who was the spy, or who had killed Robert York. Certainly he was guilty of failure! He had failed both Charlotte and the children. What would happen to them? What was happening now? She must be suffering all the fear, the shame of being thought a murderer's wife. And in time the poverty would come as well, unless her family helped. But the misery and the humiliation of lifelong dependency was hardly an answer.

How could he even say he loved her in such circumstances, with a dispirited and contemptuous jailer listening? And he wanted to, to put away forever the brief anger he had allowed to mar the last few days before he'd been taken away.

She had looked pale. She had tried hard, but she could not keep the shock from her face. He could not remember afterwards what they had said—something and nothing, just noises. The silence between the words had been more important, and the shining tenderness in her eyes.

The second time had been better. At least she seemed unaware of the reality of the prison, and she was confident Ballarat was doing everything to get him released—more confident than Pitt was. Ballarat had not come anywhere near Coldbath Fields, nor had he sent anyone, except a constable, who was embarrassed and had asked only the most obvious and meaningless questions.

"What was yer doin' in Seven Dials, Mr. Pitt?" The

"Mr." was so habitual he could not drop it, even here. He fiddled with his pencil and avoided Pitt's eyes.

"I went there with a running patterer because he told me the woman I wanted to question was there," Pitt had replied irritably. "I already told them that!"

"So you went lookin' for 'er?"

"I told them that, too!"

"What for, Mr. Pitt?"

"Because she was a witness in the murder of Robert York."

"Would that be Mr. York of 'anover Close, as was killed by a burglar three years ago?"

"Yes, of course it would!"

"An' 'ow do yer know that, Mr. Pitt?"

"She was seen in the house."

"Oh yes? 'Oo saw 'er?"

"Dulcie Mabbutt, the lady's maid."

" 'Ow do yer spell that, sir?"

"Don't bother; she's dead. She fell out of a window."

The constable's eyes had opened wider and for the first time he looked directly at Pitt. " 'Ow did that 'appen, sir?"

Was it worth telling him? What if he were the only one who ever came, just as a formality, so all the right papers could be filled in? Now might be the only chance. He must try.

"I think someone overheard her tell me about the woman in cerise." He watched the constable's face. "The library door was open."

"You mean she were pushed?" the constable said carefully.

"Yes."

The constable concentrated hard. "But this woman in pink was an 'ore, Mr. Pitt. Why should anyone care that much about 'er? Gentlemen 'as their pleasures, we all knows that. If 'e were careless, it's a domestic matter, in't it?"

"She wasn't just a whore," Pitt had said gravely, keeping

his temper because he had to. What could he do to persuade this round-faced constable that there was conspiracy and treason in this ordinary, rather sordid tragedy?

"No, sir?" the constable inquired, his eyes narrowing a little.

"There are secret papers missing from the Foreign Office, from the department where Robert York worked before he was murdered."

The constable blinked. "You sayin' as 'e took 'em, Mr. Pitt?"

"I don't know. Felix Asherson and Garrard Danver also work there, and of course many others. I do know the silver vase and the first-edition book that were reported stolen the night he was killed never turned up at any fence's or pawnshop in London, and no regular villain anywhere in the city knows anything about them, or about the murder."

"Are you sure o' that, sir?" The constable looked dubious.

"Yes I am! What the hell do you think I've been doing these past weeks?"

"I see." The constable licked his pencil but could think of nothing to write.

"No, you don't see!" Pitt said angrily. "Neither do I. Except Robert York was murdered, Dulcie fell out of a window, and the woman in cerise, who was seen in Hanover Close, had her neck broken in a bawdy house in Seven Dials—just before I got to her."

"An' yer still say it weren't you as done it?" There was no skepticism in his face now; rather he seemed to be looking for confirmation.

"Yes."

The constable had not pressed the matter any further and had taken his leave with a look of deep concentration on his blunt face.

The days blurred into a long, dark procession. It never seemed light in the Steel. Even the exercise yard was narrow and walled so steeply the frail winter daylight was lost in it, and bent over the back-breaking shot, or huddled with other miserable, sour-smelling prisoners, Pitt felt the darkness creep into his mind like mold. The outside world became remote, a story in a children's book.

Then gradually, in spite of himself, he was drawn into noticing his fellows: Iremonger, who was middle-aged and pasty-faced, accused of practicing abortion. He proclaimed his innocence with stoic resignation, not expecting to be believed. He obviously knew some medicine and exercised a certain compassion. He knew how to treat the small wounds gained at the crank, the worst punishment of all, where a man turned a spindle connected to a drum full of sand; the weight of the spoon-shaped cups lifting against the dead inertia tore the muscles even more than the shot. Iremonger also doled out advice and peculiarly intimate sympathy for those who suffered from the treadmill harness.

There was Haskins, the bully who had fought with Pitt, a sad, shallow man who had won the few victories in his life through violence; he was respected to his face but mocked behind his back. There was Ross, a handsome, genial man who lived off the earnings of prostitutes and was in for some stupid theft. Ross saw nothing wrong in either occupation: one fulfilled a need, the other was merely making the best of an opportunity. When he was released he would do precisely the same again. The concept of right and wrong in anything except personal loyalties was unknown to him. In spite of himself, Pitt could not dislike him.

Pitt also noticed Goodman, who was small, overwhelmingly greedy, but an excellent raconteur, even if it was probably all lies. He was in for embezzlement from his father-in-law, and like most of the others, proclaimed his innocence, if not of the fact then of any moral fault in the matter. His weasellike face was full of indignation. On the other hand, his fertile imagination, and some education, made his company, on the few occasions they were permitted to speak, a relief from the corroding boredom.

And there was Wilson, a man so savage in his rage he lashed out at everyone; Wood, ignorant and angry with a world which had no use and no place for him; fat Molloy, who had spent most of his life in prison and feared the outside world in spite of his repeated longing for it; and poor little Raeburn with drooping eyes and mouth, who stole simply because he was hungry and incapable of earning his way.

At first Pitt hated them all because they were part of the Steel, and everything that trapped and held him, all the ugliness and the perpetuity of the place.

Then through small acts, glimpses of pain, he was reached. At first these incidents seemed trivial; a brushing of the surface of his mind, more an irritation because he had no emotion to spare than any real empathy.

Then a stupid and pointless tragedy involving Raeburn jerked Pitt violently out of his self-pity. Raeburn was a purposeless, simpleminded little man who seemed inadequate to face the world. He had only one thing of which he was proud: though he was promiscuous and he stole, he did not tell lies, not even to escape punishment. Now and again he boasted of it and no one minded; it was boring and they took for granted that he was harmless, and he challenged no one's territory. There was a tacit understanding that one did not victimize Raeburn. He filled the role of a house pet.

On this occasion, when Pitt was sunk deep in his own misery, the permanent cold, the hunger, and the emotional loneliness and fears he was being forced with every succeeding day to face more openly, a jailer's watch was mislaid, and by some mischance Raeburn was accused of having taken it. He swore he had not, but the jailer, who did not know him, did not accept the denial. Raeburn was removed to solitary confinement. He was terrified of being alone, he had no thoughts to fill the silence and it threatened to obliterate him. When they came for him he lashed out, and for that he was undeniably guilty. They dismissed the charge of thieving as no longer important; now he had assaulted a warden. He was put in a cell in isolation, uncomprehending, still swearing he had not taken the watch.

At night in his bunk, shivering in the dark, Pitt could hear Raeburn crying out, sometimes loudly, "I didn't do it! Tell 'em I didn't do it!" Other times it was only a confused babbling that sank away into silence.

He was a weak little man, and the one thing he valued had been removed. His only worth was that everyone knew he did not tell lies, but now someone had not believed him. His solitude was vast, like annihilation itself, and he had nothing to cling to. He either would not or could not eat.

A week later they took him away to the Bedlam asylum for the insane, and within a short time he was dead.

The effect on the other prisoners was surprisingly deep. While he had been alive Raeburn was tolerated with a mild contempt, but there had been a tacit comprehension that his honesty had been one small light in the darkness of his loneliness and stupidity; it was his mark of identity in a nameless sea. He had no other strength, nor was he aware of any other virtue. His weaknesses had let him down so often they were intimately known.

When he was taken away there rippled through the others a kind of anger that for once had nothing to do with selfishness. Raeburn's fate brought them as close to pity as they could come.

The incident marked Pitt deeply. He willed himself to forget it, but Raeburn's cries repeated themselves in his head and his imagination filled in the picture of the man's shallow, droop-eyed face, witless with fear, stained with weeping.

His own self-pity dissolved into anger. From hating the other men, he surprised himself by managing to forget, sometimes for hours on end, all the world of difference between himself and them, and felt only the pain they had in common.

At night, lying in the cold, he turned over every possibility in his mind. He could speak to no one about his own case, but they could not stop him from thinking.

Surely the key to it lay in the treason. Who was the spy? At first he thought it had been Robert York, seduced by Cerise, perhaps with some spy master behind her. Then since Dulcie's death, which he was certain had also been murder, the suspects had been narrowed to either someone in the York house or one of their visitors that night, the Danvers and the Ashersons, who also had access to the Foreign Office.

Now Cerise herself had been murdered—by whom? The unknown spy master who was afraid Pitt would find her and that she might knowingly or unknowingly betray him?

He was growing confused. It made no sense. If there was such a figure, shadowy, unknown, then that person had no part in the murder of Dulcie. It had to be someone Pitt knew, someone he had already seen and talked to. Dulcie had been killed because she had seen Cerise, there could be no other reason. That was borne out by the fact that Cerise herself had been murdered when it became inevitable that Pitt would find her.

But why had Robert York been killed? Was there something he knew, something he had seen or heard? Was it what he had done, and thus could reveal?

Perhaps there had been a real thief, someone Robert York would have recognized when he interrupted and caught him. Perhaps Cerise had not succeeded in her attempts to seduce him, and had sent a thief instead. Then who was the thief? Someone known to Robert York, strong enough and skilled enough—and cold-blooded enough—to kill him with a single blow, even when he was prepared and presumably on his guard. After all, if you disturb a burglar in your house in the middle of the night, and you recognize him and know his intent, then surely you would understand he could not leave you to reveal him, as you would be bound to?

Julian Danver, Garrard Danver, possibly, although he was twice York's age—or Felix Asherson? Pitt did not even consider Piers York; he would hardly have needed to offer any explanation for being in the library of his own house, whatever the time of night.

But the Danvers and Asherson all worked at the Foreign Office themselves. It did not make sense that they should steal secrets from Robert York.

Pitt lay awake in the bitter night, hearing the now familiar sounds of uneasy movement, the echo of coughs, groans, someone swearing, and further away a man weeping with hollow, racking sounds of despair.

He was no further forward. The pieces did not fit. Who was Cerise? he wondered, hovering on the borders of sleep, his mind snatching at shadows. It all hinged on her.

In the morning the gray immediacy of the day returned, crowding his senses. He could close his eyes to some of it, even turn his mind from the sounds, becoming numb to the creeping cold, but he could never completely shut out the sour smell. It was there with every breath, the taste of it at the back of his throat, making his stomach querulous.

There was no stillness to think.

With darkness came the illusion of solitude again, and his mind returned to gnaw the question. He turned it over and over and no answer seemed to satisfy him. It still seemed most likely that Robert York had interrupted someone, and he was killed because of his knowledge, as was Dulcie, and, of course, Cerise. But knowledge of what?

The constable returned, graver this time, and he did not mention Ballarat at all.

"So it was the maid, Dulcie, as first told you about this woman in pink, Mr. Pitt?" He frowned, looking at his notebook and then up again. " 'Ow did you find 'er in Seven Dials?"

"With a lot of work," Pitt replied flatly. "I walked the

streets asking costers, flower girls, sandwich sellers, theater doormen, prostitutes."

The constable shook his head slowly. "Must 'a taken a fair while, sir. Weren't there no better way, nobody as knew nuffink?"

"Nobody who would speak, except Miss Adeline Danver, and she only saw the woman for a moment on the landing in the gaslight."

"That'd be Mr. Julian Danver's aunt?"

"Yes. But naturally Miss Danver didn't know where to find her."

The constable screwed up his face. "I could check that with 'er, Mr. Pitt."

"Well, if you do, for God's sake be careful! The last person to speak to the police about seeing Cerise fell out of a window to her death immediately after."

The constable sat silently for several moments, then slowly began chewing his pencil. "Who do you reckon she was, this woman you calls Cerise, Mr. Pitt?"

Pitt leaned a little more heavily on his wooden chair.

"I don't know. But she was beautiful; everyone who saw her said she had style, glamor, a face that one remembered. Felix Asherson admitted there was information missing from his department of the Foreign Office, which is also where Robert York worked."

The constable took the end of his pencil out of his mouth. There were teeth marks where he had bitten into it.

"Mr. Ballarat didn't believe that, Mr. Pitt. 'E made some inquiries, very discreet like, in several places, and there's been no use made of anything that could 'a come from there. And 'e asked them as would know."

"They don't have to use it straightaway!" But Pitt felt he was fighting on sinking ground. Ballarat did not want to believe there was treason; he was afraid of facing his superiors and telling them something they would be so loath to believe, something that was frightening and innately a criticism of not only their competence but their honor. He was frightened of their anger, of having to muster arguments to persuade them of such a thing, showing them that the blame would be laid at their door. He wanted to be approved of; he had social ambitions that were far deeper than his professional or financial dreams. He liked good living; he liked petty authority, but he had not the courage for real power: the hazards, the envy, and the unpleasantness that it carried were prices he had no stomach to pay. He had been entrusted to prove there was no treason, or if there had been, that it had been safely covered up, and to discover it now would signal the utmost failure.

The constable was staring at him, chewing his pencil again viciously.

"I dunno much about that, sir. But it all seems a bit unlikely to me. I 'spect what men likes in a lady is as different as what they likes fer their dinner, but she didn't seem anythink but ordinary ter me: dark 'air, darkish sort o' skin, bit sallow like—prefer a bit o' color meself. Not a bad face, but nothin' special, an' not much shape to 'er. Not what you'd call 'andsome at all."

"She had grace," Pitt said, trying to find words to explain the subtlety Cerise had had in life to this simple, straightforward man. "Spirit. Probably wit."

"Beggin' yer pardon, Mr. Pitt, but she looked more like a maid who'd lorst 'er character and taken to the streets to me."

"She was a courtesan." He looked at the constable's earnest, confused face. "A very high-class prostitute, one who selected her own customers—just a few—for a very high price."

The constable shrugged. "If you say so, Mr. Pitt. But I'll tell yer this: she'd scrubbed a few floors in 'er time. A look at 'er 'ands and 'er knees'd tell yer that. I seen too many women with them callouses not ter know. They didn't come from prayin', that's for certain."

Pitt stared at him. "You must be wrong!"

"No, Mr. Pitt. I looked at 'er proper, very careful, poor soul. It's me job, an' I knows 'ow ter do it. See, we 'ad no name for 'er"—a flash of pity crossed his face—"we still 'aven't, come ter that."

A staggering and dreadful new thought was beginning to take shape in Pitt's mind: what if it were not the real Cerise he had found, but someone else, a helpless victim left there to fool him? Suppose the whole thing had been contrived to get rid of him, to land him precisely where he was now, in the Steel, helpless, entombed alive. Someone had murdered that wretched woman in order to cripple Pitt. Someone had been watching him, planning for him to arrive and be caught exactly where he was—while the real Cerise was still alive! Did Ballarat know that? Was he deliberately protecting her by turning away from the case, pretending he believed the obvious, and that Pitt was guilty?

Then how high did it go, this corruption, this treason?

No, he could not believe Ballarat had done it knowingly. He was too smug, too small in imagination. He had not the courage to play such a high game. He was complacent, insensitive, lacking imagination, a moral coward, a social climber, but he was English to the bone. In his own stubborn way he would have died before committing treason. If there were no England, what would be left for him to enjoy? What else was there to aspire to? No, Ballarat was being used.

But by whom?

"Are you all right, Mr. Pitt?" the constable said anxiously. "You look awful—taken back."

"You're sure about the calluses?" Pitt said slowly, trying to keep the despair out of his voice. "What about her face? Was it beautiful? At least, could you imagine she might have had grace, a kind of loveliness?"

The constable shook his head slowly. " 'Ard ter say, Mr. Pitt."

"The bones!" Pitt leaned forward impatiently. "I know

about the swelling, the discoloration. But her bones. I can't remember.'' He waited, eyes fixed on the constable's face.

"I'm sure about the calluses," he said carefully. "And as well as I can reckon, sir, she were more or less ordinary, quite good, not plain, as yer might say, but nothin' special neither. Why, Mr. Pitt? What is it you're thinking?"

"That it wasn't Cerise, Constable, it was some poor creature dressed in her clothes and murdered to implicate me. Cerise is still alive."

"Gor' blimey!" The constable breathed out slowly. There was only the faintest skepticism in his voice, a mere shadow of doubt in his plain, round face. "What do yer want me ter do, Mr. Pitt?"

"I don't know, Constable, God help us. At the moment I have no idea."

12

CHARLOTTE'S THOUGHTS were running parallel to Pitt's, although at this point, of course, she did not know it. She began by assuming that Pitt was telling the absolute truth. He had looked for Cerise quite openly, and after dogged police work had been approached by someone who had led him to the house in Seven Dials, where he had arrived at precisely the right time to find her with her neck broken, and thus be caught in the appearance of having killed her himself.

Was that a coincidence, or had the killer organized her death to fall just that way, in one act silencing Cerise and disposing of Pitt? A stroke of superb fortune, or genius?

What had Cerise known that was worth the extraordinary risk of killing Dulcie to keep Pitt from her? Surely that had been a far more impulsive and dangerous murder. It must be something damning: the truth about Robert York's death, or the identity of the spy—which were probably the same thing.

It still seemed most likely that Robert York had been Cerise's lover, and she had tricked or seduced him into giving her secrets, which she had taken back to her master. Then she and Robert had quarreled, and he had threatened to tell

307

the truth. Either Cerise or her master had murdered Robert to protect themselves.

Then why had Cerise been killed? Had she regretted Robert's death? Perhaps she had not bargained for murder. Or had she cared for him in her own way? By all accounts he was handsome, elegant, and witty, and apparently had a reserved character that might make him unusually attractive to women. Or had Cerise simply lost her nerve and become a risk to her master, a liability? Had this master figure in the background learned that Pitt knew of Cerise through Dulcie, and attempted to get rid of all those close to him?

Her heart sank with a misery that was becoming familiar. The murderer could be anybody! There was no clue whatsoever as to who had broken the library window and murdered Robert York. Anyone could have gone to the house in Seven Dials if they knew Cerise was there.

But only members of the three families in Hanover Close could have pushed Dulcie out of the window! Charlotte had met them all, had sat and talked with them politely, and one of them was continuing the slow, deliberate, judicial murder of Pitt.

She got up abruptly from her seat by the kitchen stove. It was dark now. Gracie had long ago gone upstairs to bed. There was nothing more she could do tonight; she had twisted her mind round every fact or supposition she knew and the realization was undeniable: she would not solve it by thinking.

They would not let her see Pitt again for another four days. It was useless to ask Ballarat to help, but she might find the person who was actually working on the case, the constable who had questioned the brothel owner, who had seen Cerise's body. And she must go back to Hanover Close, because that was where the answer was, if only she could find the first thread that would begin the unraveling.

Even though she was weary with anxiety and exhausted from doing all the heavy housework herself, still she slept badly and was awake long before the cold dawn. By seven she was in the kitchen, riddling out the fire herself and building it up. When Gracie came down at quarter past she found it done and the kettle boiling. She opened her mouth to object, then saw Charlotte's pale face and thought better of it.

By late morning Charlotte was walking briskly in the icy sunlight under the bare trees on the edge of Green Park looking for Constable Maybery. The duty officer at Bow Street had informed her, unhappily, that Maybery was investigating the death of the woman in pink. He had been loath to tell her, but he was even more unwilling to face the prospect of dealing with a hysterical woman in the police station. He hated scenes, and from the look of her flushed face and brilliant eyes, this one might very soon fall into that category.

Charlotte saw the blue figure in his tall hat and cape just as he emerged from Half Moon Street into Piccadilly. She dashed across the road, heedless of oncoming carriages, infuriating the drivers, and caught up with him in a most unseemly run.

"Constable!"

He stopped. "Yes, ma'am? You all right, ma'am?"

"Yes. Are you Constable Maybery?"

He looked puzzled, his round face wrinkled in apprehension.

"Yes, ma'am."

"I'm Mrs. Pitt, Mrs. Thomas Pitt."

"Oh." Conflicting emotions crossed his face: embarrassment followed by sympathy, then an eagerness to speak. "I went an' saw Mr. Pitt yesterday, ma'am. 'E didn't look too badly, considerin'." His eyes flickered doubtfully for a moment. There was no guilt in his expression, however.

Charlotte's courage returned. It was just possible he did not believe Pitt was guilty. Perhaps that relief in his face was a sign that they were on the same side.

"Constable—you are investigating the death of the woman

309

in pink? What do you know about her? What was her name? Where was she before she came to Seven Dials?''

He shook his head very slightly, but his eyes remained perfectly steady. ''We don't know nothin' at all about 'er, ma'am. She got to the 'ouse in Seven Dials only three days before she was killed, an' she gave the name o' Mary Smith, an' nobody ever 'eard of 'er before. She said nothin', and they didn't ask. O' course, in that kind o' business people don't. But one thing, ma'am, Mr. Pitt seemed very certain as she was—'e said a 'courtesan,' very expensive an' pickin' 'er own custom. But I saw the body, beggin' yer pardon for discussin' it, ma'am, but the body as I saw in Seven Dials 'ad calluses on 'er 'ands, an' on 'er knees. Not 'eavy, like, but I seen 'em enough to know 'em. She weren't livin' like no expensive kept woman. I reckon as 'e must be wrong about that.''

''But she was!'' Charlotte was nonplussed. Whatever she had expected, it was not this! ''She was a great beauty! Oh, not traditional, certainly, we knew that. But she was extraordinary; people noticed her. She was very graceful, she had style, panache. She could never have scrubbed floors!''

He stood firm. ''You're wrong, ma'am. She may 'ave 'ad character; since I never saw 'er alive I couldn't tell. But she were quite ordinary to look at. 'Er skin weren't particular. Bit sallow. She 'ad good 'air, if yer like it black, an' she was definitely on the thin side. In fact, I'd say skinny. No ma'am beggin' yer pardon again, but I seen 'er, and she were ordinary.''

Charlotte stood still on the pavement. A carriage went by at a spanking pace, its brief wind tilting her hat. Then the woman was not Cerise—she must be someone else. Someone else had been killed to put Pitt, and all of them, off her trail. Perhaps it was only a fortunate accident that Pitt had found her at just that moment and had been arrested for her murder—or was that, too, part of the plan? She must be even more important than they had thought.

Then a startling idea came into Charlotte's mind. It was horrifying, perhaps mad, certainly dangerous—but there seemed to be nothing else left.

"Thank you, Constable Maybery," she said aloud. "Thank you very much. Please give my love to Thomas, if—if you're allowed to. And please, don't mention this conversation. It will only worry him."

"All right, ma'am, if that's what you want."

"Yes, most definitely, please. Thank you." And she turned round and hurried away towards the nearest omnibus stop. The new idea spun crazily in her mind. There must be something better, something saner and more intelligent—but what? There was no time to wait. There was no one left to question, no physical evidence to produce like a rabbit out of a hat, to force a confession. The only thing was to startle someone violently, forcing a betrayal—and she could think of no other way than the wild idea forming in her mind now.

She did not go home but to Jack Radley's rooms in St. James's. She had never been there before, but knew the address from writing to him. Normally he spent as little time there as possible, preferring to be someone's guest in one of the fine town houses. It was both more pleasant and easier on his frugal finances. But he had promised he would be available as long as this crisis lasted, and she did not hesitate to call upon him.

The building was a good second best, and not an address one would be embarrassed to mention. She asked the porter in the hall and was told courteously, with only the slightest frown, that Mr. Radley's rooms were on the third floor, and the stairs were to her left.

Her legs were tired when she got there, and there was no view to reward her effort, since his rooms were at the back. She knocked sharply on the door. If he was not there she would have to leave a note. She shifted from one foot to the other impatiently in the few minutes till the door opened—in fact she had been on the point of rattling the handle.

311

"Charlotte!" Jack looked startled, caught out; then self-concern vanished and he welcomed her in. "What is it? Has something happened?"

She had little time to look round. A few weeks ago she would have been consumed with curiosity—a person's home said much about them—but now she had neither the time nor the need. Doubts of Jack had died without her noticing. She observed only that the rooms were elegantly furnished but small, and she had economized enough herself to recognize it in others.

"Well?" he demanded.

"I have just met the constable who is investigating Cerise's death."

His face darkened. "What do you mean, 'just met'?"

"I found him." She brushed the means and the circumstances aside. "Coming out of Half Moon Street. But the important thing is, he described the body. Jack, I'm sure it isn't her. It was made to look like her, but it was just some poor woman in a pink dress—"

"Just a minute! Why?"

"Because of her hands, but even more her knees."

His face was incredulous; he looked almost as if he might burst out laughing.

"Calluses," she exclaimed peremptorily. "From scrubbing floors. But Jack, what it means is that the real Cerise is still alive! And I have an idea. I know it is extreme, even idiotic—but I've racked my brains and I can't think of anything else at all. I need your help. We must go again to the Yorks', and the Danvers must be there, too, and as soon as possible. Time is getting terribly short."

Every vestige of humor left Jack's face. No trial date had been set yet, but it would not be long and he had never pretended to her that it might. Now he listened with total gravity. "What else?" he asked.

"I must know at least two days in advance, so I can make arrangements."

"What arrangements?"

She hesitated, uncertain whether to tell him. He was likely to disapprove.

"Don't be stupid!" he said abruptly. "How can I help you if I don't know what you're doing? You aren't the only one with brains, nor the only one who cares."

She felt for an instant as if he had slapped her. She was about to retort, when the truth of it overwhelmed her. It was surprisingly painless, in fact. All at once she felt less alone than she had since Pitt's arrest.

"The Danvers come to dinner regularly—next time I'm going to dress up as Cerise and make an assignation with each of the men it might have been," she said frankly. "Only Piers York, the Danvers, and Felix Asherson were there the night Dulcie was killed. I'll start with the Danvers, because Aunt Adeline saw Cerise at their house."

Jack was startled. He hesitated for a long, tense moment, struggling for a better idea himself. When nothing came, he conceded doubtfully. "You don't look much like her—that is, like the descriptions of her," he said at last.

"I'll meet them in the conservatory," she reasoned. "The light's very poor in there, and I'll have the right color dress, and a black wig. If I can pass for long enough to get a reaction it might be enough." The plan sounded desperate as she described it, a very slim chance, and she felt her hopes, thin as wraiths, drain from her grasp. "If he even knows me, it will prove something!"

He felt her panic and put his hand on her arm gently. "It might be dangerous," he warned.

Danger would be marvelous; it had the kick and the fire of hot wine, and seemed very close to outright victory. No one would turn up unless he knew Cerise, and if anyone threatened her with violence it could only be because she was too close to the truth.

"I know," she said with a surge of excitement. "But you'll be there, and Emily. I need Emily's help. I've worked it all

313

out: I'll take the dress and wig in a bag and give them to Emily, beforehand; then when we are there after dinner I shall pretend to be faint and excuse myself. Emily will 'look after' me, so I can slip up to her room and change. Then she'll watch and tell me when to go down to the conservatory, she said the Yorks have a large one, to keep my trysts.''

"You're leaving a lot to chance," he said anxiously.

"Can you think of anything better?"

He hesitated for a moment. "No," he admitted. "I'll do everything I can to keep all the others occupied in the withdrawing room. I'll make some riveting conversation." He smiled bleakly. "For heaven's sake, promise me if there is the slightest danger you'll scream. I mean it, Charlotte."

"I promise." She giggled a little wildly. "Although it would be awfully difficult to explain, wouldn't it? What on earth should I say I was doing in their conservatory dressed in a hideous gown and a black wig, screaming my head off, when I was supposed to be upstairs with the vapors?"

"I should have to say you'd taken leave of your wits," he agreed with a very twisted grin. "But better that than dead— and whoever it is has already killed three times."

Her laughter suddenly stopped, becoming tight in her throat. Bitter tears sprang to her eyes.

"It will be four, with Thomas," she said.

She made her assignations by letter, using as few words as possible, and leaving them unsigned. She had no idea what Cerise's handwriting looked like, nor what her real name was. She used expensive notepaper, wrote only the time and place, and instead of sealing the letters in an envelope, she tied each one with a broad piece of ribbon in a vivid, almost painful magenta. It was the best she could do.

Emily had written to her banker and provided money so Charlotte could purchase the dress and the wig, and Jack had taken them to Hanover Close, posing as a coalman this time and carrying coke inside to the kitchen for them. How he arranged it Charlotte never knew, and she was too preoccupied with her own preparations to ask.

That evening she dressed in a very simple smoke gray and white gown of Emily's, judiciously let out by Emily's maid. It was not nearly as flattering on Charlotte with her darker complexion and mahogany hair as it had been on Emily's apple-blossom fairness, but it had the one merit Charlotte was looking for now: it was very easy to get in and out of. She dressed her hair with the minimum of fuss, so it could be squashed flat under a wig without removing a hundred pins first. The result did not make her look her most attractive, but it could not be helped. Jack was tactful enough to refrain from commenting, although his face registered slight surprise, quickly replaced by a smile and a wink.

They arrived at Hanover Close a few minutes late, as was the acceptable thing to do, and were handed down from the carriage onto the icy pavement. Charlotte took Jack's arm up the steps and into the lighted hall. As the door was closed behind them she felt a moment's panic, then forced herself to think of Pitt, and said rather too effusively, "Good evening, Mrs. York, how kind of you to invite us."

"Good evening, Miss Barnaby," Loretta replied with far less enthusiasm. "I hope you are well? Our city winter is not disagreeing with you?"

Only just in time Charlotte remembered that she was going to be taken ill after dinner. She chose her words carefully. "I do find it—a trifle different. There is a very little pleasure walking in the streets here, and the snow seems to get dirty so quickly."

Loretta's eyebrows rose in faint surprise. "Indeed? I have never considered walking."

"It is very good for the health." Charlotte managed to sound agreeable without actually smiling.

In the withdrawing room Veronica was standing by the hearth in a very fine gown of black and white, looking considerably more composed than the last time they had met.

She welcomed Charlotte with what seemed like genuine pleasure, especially when she saw her very indifferent gray gown.

The usual greetings followed and Charlotte was relieved
to see that everyone the plan required was present: Harriet
looking pale; Aunt Adeline in an unfortunate dress of vivid
brown, which made her eyes the more startling; Loretta in
salmon pink, her bodice stitched with pearls at once individual and utterly feminine. But far more important, the men
were there: Julian Danver, smiling with candid directness;
Garrard Danver, elegant, more elusive than his son, quick of
wit, and she thought perhaps more original. Piers York was
there as well, welcoming her with the sincerity that is a mixture of long practice and genuine awareness of privilege and
its responsibilities. Good manners were as natural to him as
rising early, or eating all the food on his plate. He had been
taught them in the nursery and now they were ineradicable.

With Jack's help, Charlotte devoted her mind to the usual
trivial conversation that preceded dinner. Dinner itself was
quite ordinary; the talk meandered from one unimportant
topic to another. It was an uneven party in that there were
four unmarried women present and only three unmarried
men, one of them being Garrard Danver, who could have no
possible romantic interest in his daughter or his sister, and
presumably not in Veronica, who was shortly to become his
daughter-in-law. Since he was twenty-five years Charlotte's
senior, she would have been most unlikely to have been
paired with him in anyone's mind, even supposing he had
any desire to remarry. And of course Jack was assumed to
be her first cousin and therefore unsuitable.

Nevertheless Loretta was a skilled hostess. Tonight she
seemed to be using all her very considerable charm and poise
to strike a perfect balance between dominating the company
and making everyone else feel at their best. If she tried a
little harder than usual, or if her hand gripped the stem of
her wineglass so her knuckles were momentarily bloodless,
perhaps it was her daughter-in-law who had given her very

real cause for anxiety. She could not be blamed if she was nervous in case, even at this point, Veronica should show some trace of the hysteria, the willfulness, or the latent jealousy so ugly to any man, and which had come through her fragile exterior so very lately in the imagined privacy of her bedroom.

Since it was such a small company and the hour was a little later than usual for the end of dinner, Jack rather boldly suggested that they not separate but all retire to the withdrawing room together. He did not even glance at Charlotte: he was playing his part to perfection.

It was time Charlotte took her cue. Everyone was rising to leave, the table was littered with half empty dishes and crumpled napkins. The gas in the chandeliers was hissing gently and the flowers underneath them looked waxy white, artificial; they must have come from the conservatory.

Charlotte felt ridiculous now that the time had come. There had to be a better way. It would never work—they would see right through her, and there would be nothing for Jack to do except say she was mad. Nursing the sick aunt had turned her wits!

"Miss Barnaby, are you all right?" It was Julian Danver's voice coming to her out of a mist.

"I—I beg your pardon?" she stammered.

"Elisabeth, are you ill?" Veronica came back to her, her face full of concern.

Charlotte wanted to laugh—she had created the desired effect without even trying. She heard her own voice answering automatically. "I do feel a little faint. If I might go upstairs for half an hour, I'm sure I shall recover. I just need to rest for a short while. It's really nothing."

"Are you sure? Shall I come with you?" Veronica offered.

"No, please—I should feel most guilty dragging you from your party. Perhaps your maid . . ." Was she being too obvious? They were all staring at her—perhaps the whole charade was perfectly transparent. Did anybody really behave like this?

"Of course," Veronica agreed and the words were such a relief Charlotte could feel the blood rush back into her face and she felt like laughing. They would put her down as a hysteric! For goodness sake, she must get out of the room and upstairs.

"I'll call Amelia," Veronica said quickly, going to the bell. "If you are quite sure?"

"Oh yes!" Charlotte said too loudly. "Quite!"

Five minutes later Charlotte was upstairs in Emily's small, cold attic bedroom. She looked at Emily, and pulling a face, she slipped out of the gray and white dress. Emily presented her with the glowing dress of almost violent cerise.

"Oh Lord!" Charlotte closed her eyes.

"Come on," Emily urged. "Get into it. You've already made up your mind; don't waver now."

Charlotte stepped into it and pulled it up. "Cerise must be a remarkable woman to look ravishing in this! Fasten me up. Come on, I've only ten minutes to get to the conservatory. Where's the wig?"

Emily finished the fastening and passed her the black wig. It took them several minutes to get it right and to apply the rouge Charlotte had brought. Emily stood back and looked at her critically.

"You know that's not bad," she said with considerable surprise. "In fact, you look quite dashing, in a garish sort of way."

"Thank you," Charlotte said sarcastically, but her hands were shaking and her voice was not quite level.

Emily was watching her closely. She did not ask if Charlotte still wanted to go on with it.

"Right," Charlotte said more firmly. "See if the passage is clear. I'd hate to meet the parlormaid on the stairs."

Emily opened the door and looked out, took half a dozen steps—Charlotte could hear her feet on the boards—then

318

came back again. "Come on! Quick. You can get down these stairs, and if there's anyone coming we'll duck into Veronica's room."

They scuttled along the corridor, down the stairs, and onto the main landing; then Emily stopped sharply and held up her finger in warning. Charlotte froze.

"Amelia?" It was a man's voice. "Amelia? I thought you were looking after Miss Barnaby?"

Emily started down again. "Yes I am. I've come to get her a tisane."

" 'Aven't you got any upstairs?"

"Not peppermint. Would you get me some? I'll stay here in case she calls—I don't think she's well at all. Please, Albert."

Standing above her, at the head of the stairs, Charlotte could hear the smile in her voice and picture the soft look. She was not in the least surprised when Albert agreed without a murmur, and the next moment Emily was back at the bannister again, whispering fiercely to her to hurry.

Charlotte came down so rapidly she almost fell on the last step. She catapulted across the open hallway and through the conservatory door into the blessed dimness of the sparse, yellow night-lights. Her heart was beating like a trip-hammer, she felt as if her whole body must be shaking, and no effort could fill her lungs with enough air.

She stood under the ornamental palm at the far end of the pathway, so she could see the door to the hall. If anyone came she could step forward and the light would catch primarily her shoulder and skirt, showing that burning color; her face would remain in the shadow of the overhanging frond.

But would anyone come? Perhaps Cerise never made assignations by letter. Or maybe her writing or the words she used were utterly different from what Charlotte had written, and the recipients would recognize that instantly. She had given Julian Danver the earliest time. If he were going to come he should be here any moment. In fact, he was late. How long had she been here?

She could hear the faintest sound of footsteps somewhere in the house—probably Albert in the hall. They were not coming this way. Closer to her there was a steady dripping of moisture from one leaf to another, and finally onto the damp earth beneath. The smell of vegetation was overpowering.

She tried to occupy her mind and failed utterly. Every train of thought dissolved into chaos, driven out by the tension that was tightening like the slow turning of a ratchet. Her hands were sticky and felt like pins and needles. Was she going to stand here in the dark under a potted palm half the night?

The whisper startled her so violently it could have been at her shoulder—she did not even know what the words had been.

He was standing just inside the doorway, eyes wide, the yellow light making his cheeks look unnaturally haggard and chiseling his nose more finely.

Charlotte stepped forward just enough to present a clear silhouette against the green, and for the light to catch the searing pink dress.

He was surprised when he saw the color, the smoothness of her bare shoulder and the slender curve of her neck, the black wig. For an instant the pain in him was totally naked. It was too late to call it back—Garrard Danver had loved Cerise. The storm of it had left the wrack in his face. In spite of himself, he came towards her.

She had no idea what to do—conspiracy, infatuation she had been half prepared for, but not such pain.

Unconsciously she backed towards the palm, and the light above her fell on her bosom.

Garrard stopped. His eyes were hollow, he was like a caricature, ugly and beautiful; even in his despair there was self-knowledge, a shaft of irony.

Then she understood. Of course: everyone had said Cerise

320

was thin, nearly flat-chested, and Charlotte was rather well endowed. Even with a tight dress and unflattering camisole she still could not pass for the elegant leanness Cerise was said to have.

"Who are you?" he said very quietly.

"Who did you think I was, when you came?" She had thought of that question long before.

His smile was ghastly. "I had no idea. I never imagined you were whom you pretend to be."

"Then why did you come?" It was a challenge.

"To see why you wanted me, of course! If you've black-mail in mind, you're a fool! You're risking your life for a few pounds."

"I don't want money!" she said sharply. "I want—" She stopped. He was close to her now, so close she could have lifted her hand and touched his cheek. But she was still in so deep a shadow that he had not recognized her. There was someone else in the doorway, someone motionless with horror, and yet with such a passion of jealousy in her face she might truly have seen hell in the quietly dripping leaves and the two figures standing almost touching each other, and that harsh, incandescent, outrageous dress.

Loretta York. Garrard turned very slowly and saw her. He did not look embarrassed, as Charlotte had expected, nor ashamed. The wretchedness in his face was fear—and worse than that, a kind of revulsion.

Water slid off the leaves and landed on the lily petals with a faint *plink*. All three of them stood motionless.

At last Loretta gave a little shudder and turned on her heel and went out.

Garrard looked at Charlotte, or rather at the gloom where she stood. His voice was hoarse, he had to make two attempts at speaking.

"Wha—what do you want?"

"Nothing. Leave. Go back to the party," she hissed.

321

He hesitated, peering at her, unsure whether to believe her or not, and she retreated, almost backing into the palm.

"Go back to the party!" she whispered fiercely. "Go back!"

His relief was flickering, but he did not wait: all he wanted was to escape. A moment later she stood alone in the conservatory. She tiptoed to the door and looked out. There was no one in the hall, not even Emily. Should she risk running upstairs now, or wait until Emily gave her the signal? Perhaps this emptiness was the signal? If Albert came back it would be too late.

She was at the foot of the stairs without having made a conscious decision. It was too late to go back. She picked up the magenta taffeta of her skirt and ran up as fast as she could. Please heaven there would be no one on the landing, nor anyone on the stairs leading to the servants quarters.

She got to the top, breathless, her heart pounding. The narrow passage was deserted, nothing but doors on either side. Which one was Emily's? Hellfire! She had completely forgotten! Panic rose inside her. If anyone came she would have to dive for the nearest room and hope it was empty.

There were footsteps on the stairs now! She scuttled to the door, turned the handle, and pushed it. She was only just inside when the footsteps reached the top. She waited. If they came in here there was nothing at all she could do. Frantically she looked around for something to hit them with. She could not be hauled downstairs like a common housebreaker!

"Charlotte! Charlotte, where are you?"

Relief nearly made her sick. She felt heat and icy cold rush over her, prickling on her skin. She pulled the door open with shaking hands.

"I'm here!"

Ten minutes later she was downstairs in the withdrawing room again, her hair a trifle disheveled; that was easily explained by saying that she had been lying down, and yes thank you, she was quite recovered now. She remained fairly quiet, not wanting to risk the amazing luck she had had so far. Her hands still trembled a little and her mind was crowded with anything but stupid conversation.

The party broke up early, as though by common consent. By quarter to eleven Charlotte was sitting beside Jack in the carriage, telling him about Garrard and Loretta in the conservatory, and the expressions she had seen in their faces.

Then she told him what she proposed to do next.

Ballarat agreed to see her with reluctance.

"My dear Mrs. Pitt, I am sorry you have been caused such distress, believe me," he protested. "But there is really nothing I can do for you." He rocked backwards and forwards on the soles of his feet and stood again in front of the fire. "I wish you wouldn't harrow yourself in this way! Why don't you go and stay with your family until, er . . ." He stopped, realizing he had painted himself into a corner.

"Until they hang my husband," she finished for him flatly.

He was acutely uncomfortable. "My dear lady, that is quite—"

She stared at him, and he had the grace to blush. But she had not come to antagonize him, and giving free rein to her feelings was self-indulgent and stupid. "I'm sorry," she apologized with difficulty, swallowing her loathing of him because his fear was so much greater than his loyalty. "I came to tell you I have discovered something which I felt I must tell you immediately." She ignored his exasperated expression and went on. "The woman in pink who was killed in Seven Dials was not the same woman in cerise whom Dulcie saw in the York house and Miss Adeline Danver saw on the landing in the Danver house. That woman is still alive, and is the witness that Thomas was looking for."

A twinge of pity touched his face and vanished again. "Witness to what, Mrs. Pitt?" he asked with an effort at patience. "And even if we could find this mysterious woman—if she exists—it would hardly help Pitt. The evidence is still there that he killed the woman in Seven Dials, whoever she was.'' He sounded eminently reasonable, certain of his rightness.

''Yes it is!'' Charlotte's voice was rising and there was a sharp note of panic in it in spite of herself. ''Someone dressed that woman in a pink dress and killed her to protect the real Cerise, and to get rid of Thomas at the same time. Don't you see?'' she asked, her tone scathing with sarcasm. ''Or do you imagine Thomas pushed the maid out of the window as well? And presumably killed Robert York too—God knows why.''

Ballarat put his hands up ineffectually, as if he would pat her, then saw the passion in her eyes and backed away instead. ''My dear lady, you are overwrought. It's very understandable, in your circumstances, and believe me, I have the deepest pity.'' He drew breath again and steadied himself. Reason must be paramount. ''Robert York was killed by a burglar, and the maid fell quite accidentally.'' He nodded. ''It does happen sometimes, unfortunately. Extremely sad, but not in the least criminal. And really, my dear lady, Miss Adeline Danver is quite elderly, and I believe not the most reliable witness.''

Charlotte stared at him in disbelief at first, and then with sickening comprehension. Either he was frightened of all the unpleasantness, the anger, the blame if it were true and there really was treason in the Foreign Office—or else he was part of it! She looked at his rounded jowls, his blustery complexion, his lidless brown eyes, round as buttons. She could not believe he was a brilliant enough actor to seem so much the ambitious man tricked and caught out of his depth. For a second that passed like a ripple of wind over the surface of a pond, she was sorry for him; then she remembered Pitt's bruised face and the fear she had seen in his eyes.

''You are going to feel very foolish when this is all over,'' she said icily. ''I had thought you had more love for your country than to allow treason to flourish merely because uprooting it might prove distasteful, and embarrass certain people whose favor you would like to keep.''

Ballarat's face mottled purple as a turkey cock, and he took a step forward. "You insult me, madam!" he said furiously.

"I'm glad!" She glared at him with scorching contempt, cutting off his words. "I had feared I merely spoke the truth; prove me wrong and no one will be happier than I. In the meantime I believe what I see. Good day, Mr. Ballarat." She walked out without looking back, leaving the door open behind her. Let him come after her and close it himself.

She knew what she must do. Ballarat had left her no choice. Had he promised to investigate she would have left it, but now there was nothing else she could think of. There was a ruthlessness in it of which she would not have thought herself capable, but it was shocking to her how easily it came, because she was fighting to protect those she loved more than herself, whose pain she could not bear as she might have her own. Her response was primal and nothing to do with the mind.

Charlotte had understood that look in Loretta's face in the doorway of the conservatory. She was in love with Garrard Danver—totally, obsessively in love, which was not hard to believe. He had a grace, an individuality that was unusual. And he would be a challenge to most women; there was something elusive in him, the suggestion of great passion beneath his rather brittle shell and self-protective humor, if only one could find the secret of touching the heart or the soul inside. To lovely Loretta, bored with the charming but controlled Piers, the hint of something much wilder might be irresistible.

And obviously Garrard had loved only Cerise. All that hunger and flood of emotion, all Loretta dreamt of awakening herself, had been plain in his face when for a moment the sight of Charlotte outlined in the half light, and the flame of the dress, had stirred an anguished memory.

She must get them all together and press and press until someone broke. Garrard was the weakest link. He was afraid—she had seen that in his face too—and repelled by Loretta's hunger for him. Charlotte could remember when a man had once felt such a lust for her and Caroline had blindly thought him suitable as a husband. Charlotte had been nearly hysterical when left alone with him briefly. It had seemed ridiculous later; Caroline had been angry, not understanding. It was years ago now and the incident had vanished from her mind, until she saw Garrard's face in the lamplight and the peculiar mixture of horror, embarrassment, and revulsion brought it back with such precision that it made her skin crawl.

Garrard was the one she must press with all the force she had.

But there was no way within her power to make the Yorks invite the Danvers, the Ashersons, and herself, and no one else. They might not ever do it—certainly not within the few remaining days before Pitt would be arraigned and brought to trial. To have such a gathering in Emily's house would be inexplicable, and Jack had no facilities either, although Emily would willingly have financed the event. No, the answer lay with Aunt Vespasia, and surely she would be willing.

Accordingly Charlotte abandoned the public omnibus and recklessly took a hansom cab to Aunt Vespasia's house. Having paid the cabbie and released him, she climbed the shallow steps up to the front door and rang the bell. She had been here many times before and the maid showed not the slightest surprise at seeing her.

Vespasia received her in the boudoir, which was full of light and space, sparsely furnished in cream and gold with touches of deep green. A great green fern in a jardiniere stood against one wall. Only the steeply banked fire saved it from chill.

326

Vespasia herself looked more fragile but she still had the perfect bones of the amazing beauty she had been forty, even thirty years ago. She had aquiline features, heavy-lidded eyes under arched brows, and coiled hair like old silver. She was dressed in dark lavender, with a high fichu of Brussels lace at her throat.

"How are you?" Charlotte asked immediately, and it was not merely good manners, or the need for help. There was no one outside her family, and few within it, she cared for as much as she did for Aunt Vespasia.

Vespasia smiled. "Quite recovered—and probably far better than you, my dear," she said frankly. "You look pale, and considerably fatigued. Sit down and tell me how you are progressing. What may I do to help?" She looked beyond Charlotte to the maid, who hovered in the doorway. "Tea please, Jennet, and cucumber sandwiches and some cakes—something with whipped cream and sugar icing, if you please."

"Yes m'lady." And Jennet disappeared, closing the door softly.

"Well?" Vespasia demanded.

When Charlotte left, her plans were perfected down to the finest detail. She felt immensely better for the food, and realized she had not been eating as she should—either she'd forgotten or she had no heart for it. Aunt Vespasia's determination eased a great deal of the despair tightening inside her. She had very gently encouraged Charlotte to let go of the self-control which had kept her dry-eyed and rigid for so many days. Charlotte wept fiercely, with abandon. Naming all her fears, rather than forcing them down inside her like black devils, had robbed them of some of their horror; now that she had spoken them aloud and shared them, they no longer seemed unconquerable.

When Aunt Vespasia sent a handwritten letter two days later to say that the dinner was arranged and the invitations accepted, it was time to prepare Jack for the last and best gamble of all. Emily knew of it also, in as much detail as Charlotte dared tell her in a rather oddly coded letter, delivered by Gracie by omnibus.

Jack was far more nervous than Charlotte had expected when he collected her at quarter to seven on the evening of the dinner. But as soon as she was settled in the carriage and had a chance to weigh her thoughts, she realized that this was her own blindness. Just because he had done all he could right from the beginning, never questioning Pitt's innocence or Emily's harebrained plan to go to the Yorks', did not mean he had no emotion under his rather casual exterior. After all, he was born and bred in a society where manner was all; one very quickly became out of fashion if one either loved or offended, and real emotions were apt to embarrass, which was even worse. They could disturb the peace of mind, unsettle, spoil the pleasure, and that was inexcusable. If Jack were worth anything, then of course he was nervous. He probably had a sick fluttering in his stomach just as she did, and a racing heart, and hands that were clammy no matter how often he wiped them.

They did not speak on the journey. They had made all the plans they could, and there was no time for trivia. It was bitterly cold, a rare winter night when the ice was crackling hard on the road and in the frozen gutters. The keen wind off the sea had blown the fog clear, and even over the city the smoke did not obscure the stars, which seemed to hang low as if someone had exploded a chandelier across the sky.

Vespasia had chosen Charlotte's gown for the evening, and had obtained it for her, disregarding her protests. It was of deep ivory cream satin, touched here and there with gold, the bodice scattered with pearls. It was quite the most flattering garment she had ever worn, low-cut and with a beautiful bustle. Even Jack, who had wined and dined with the great beauties of the age, was startled and impressed.

They were shown into Vespasia's withdrawing room and

found her seated by the fire on a high-backed chair as if she were a queen receiving court. She wore gun-metal gray with a choker of diamonds and pearls, and her hair above her arched brows was coiled like a wrought silver crown.

Jack bowed and Charlotte, without thinking, dropped a curtsy.

Aunt Vespasia smiled; there was deep conspiracy in it. The situation was desperate, but there was also exhilaration going into battle.

"England expects that every man will do his duty," Aunt Vespasia whispered. "I believe our guests are about to arrive."

The first to come were Felix and Sonia Asherson, looking agreeably surprised to be there. Vespasia Cumming-Gould was something of a legend, even to their generation, and they knew of no reason why they should be among the very few invited to her house. What had seemed in Sonia to be an unbearably placid complacency, in this light appeared merely the rather regular cast of her features and an expression of politeness.

Felix appeared frankly interested. He could be extraordinarily charming when he wished; he knew how to flatter without words, and his infrequent smile was devastating.

Aunt Vespasia was nearly eighty. As a child she had seen the celebrations after the victory of Waterloo; she remembered the Hundred Days and the fall of Napoleon. She had danced with the Duke of Wellington when he was prime minister. She had known the heroes, the victims, and the fools of the Crimea, the empire builders, statesmen, charlatans, artists, and wits of the greatest century in the history of England. She was happy to play with Felix Asherson and kept the smile on her own lips flawlessly unreadable.

The Danvers were shown in ten minutes later. Julian seemed perfectly at ease; he felt no compulsion to show off or to push himself into the conversation. Charlotte decided Veronica might well be fortunate.

Garrard, on the contrary, was quick to speak, his face drawn, his hands moving nervously as though stillness were an unbearable strain. Charlotte instinctively scented the kill, and hating herself for it made no difference at all to her intentions. The choice lay between Garrard Danver and Pitt. It was no choice at all.

Harriet Danver was also far from comfortable. She looked more fragile than she had on previous occasions, although it was possible that was due to her wearing a shade of smoky lavender which echoed the shadows in her pale skin and made her eyes look even larger. Either she was very much in love and finding the pain unendurable, or there was some other knowledge or fear preying on her mind.

Aunt Adeline was dressed in topaz and gold, which suited her very well. There was a slight flush on her cheeks, which robbed them of their usual sallowness. It was several minutes before Charlotte realized Adeline felt vastly complimented to be invited to Aunt Vespasia's home, and the occasion had excited her greatly. Charlotte felt a sharp spear-thrust of conscience. She would dearly like to have abandoned this, but it was not possible.

Last to come were the Yorks, Veronica ethereal and magnificent in black and silver, sweeping in with her head high and color in her cheeks. She checked herself almost before she was through the door at the sight of Charlotte standing close to Julian Danver. His admiration for her was extremely obvious; and it was equally obvious, just for an instant, that Veronica had never before appreciated what a potential rival Charlotte might be. Little Miss Barnaby from the country was a considerable beauty, when she chose! Veronica's greeting had lost several degrees of warmth by the time they met in the center of the floor.

For once Loretta also looked less sure of herself; her aplomb was a shadow of her old certainty. As always, she was meticulously groomed, exquisitely feminine in golden peach, but the fluidity had gone, the wound Charlotte had

330

seen in the conservatory was still raw. She did not look at Garrard Danver. Piers York was grave, as if aware of tragedy without knowing its nature or direction; either that, or he chose to ignore it. His face lit when he saw Vespasia, and Charlotte realized with surprise that they had known each other for years.

All the customary greetings were made, petty courtesies exchanged, but already the undercurrents had begun to pull, to tear and distort.

For half an hour they talked of the weather, the theater, figures of fashion and politics. They all seemed to be enjoying themselves except Garrard and Loretta. If Piers had any reservations he was too practiced to reveal them.

Charlotte found her attention wandering. She must not begin yet; she would wait until dinner. Begin too early and she could dissipate the very tension she was seeking to build. They must all be seated, facing each other, with no escape except the violent act of physically leaving a hostess's presence. Only illness could excuse that.

The moments dragged by, the inane conversation fell word by word as she watched their faces and planned. Felix was enjoying himself, even with Harriet, and gradually she lost her pallor and joined in. Sonia was swapping gossip with Loretta. Veronica was flirting with Julian, looking in his eyes, ignoring Charlotte. Vespasia smiled and spoke to each of them in turn, drawing out small, self-revealing comments, and now and again her eye caught Charlotte's with the faintest nod.

At last dinner was announced and they went in, two by two, taking the places Vespasia had set for them with meticulous forethought: Harriet next to Felix Asherson and opposite Jack, so he could see any expression in their faces; Julian next to Charlotte; and most important, Loretta and Garrard next to each other, under the chandelier, so no flicker of muscle, no shadow in their eyes could escape Charlotte directly opposite.

Soup was served, lobster bisque, and conversation flagged. Next came the fish, deviled whitebait, then the entrée of quenelle of rabbit. When they were just beginning the removes of quarter of lamb, Aunt Vespasia regarded Julian Danver with an agreeable smile. "I understand you are quite a rising star in the Foreign Office, Mr. Danver," she said. "A most responsible situation, not without its dangers."

He looked surprised. "Danger, Lady Cumming-Gould? I assure you, I seldom leave the extremely comfortable and eminently safe rooms of the Foreign Office itself." He smiled at Veronica quickly, then back again at Vespasia. "And even if I were posted abroad to some embassy, I would insist on it being in Europe."

"Indeed?" Her silver eyebrows rose. "In what country's affairs do you specialize?"

"In the affairs of Germany, and its interests in Africa."

"In Africa?" she asked. "I believe the kaiser has some imperial designs there, which may inevitably conflict with ours. You must be involved in delicate negotiations."

His smile remained. All the other conversation had stopped and faces were turned towards him.

"Of course," he agreed.

The corners of Vespasia's mouth curled upwards very slightly. "And do you never fear betrayal, or even some slight, quite honest mistake that could hand the advantage to your opponents—your nation's opponents?"

He opened his mouth to reply, dismissing her fears; suddenly the words died and a shadow touched his face. Then he banished it.

"One has to be careful, of course, but one doesn't speak of state matters outside the Foreign Office itself."

"And of course you know exactly whom to trust." Charlotte made it more of a statement than a question. "I imagine treason begins little by little. First a small confidence elicited, perhaps by someone in love." She glanced at Harriet and then back at Felix. "Personal loyalties can make such a mess of morality," she said quietly, aware of what she herself was doing even at this moment, aware of friendship, the unwritten laws of hospitality—and of love that overrode them all. It was not that she thought she was right, or that love excused it, simply that it was elemental, as an animal protects its own.

There were spots of color in Felix's pale cheeks. Sonia had stopped eating, and she clutched her fork in a white hand whose knuckles shone. Perhaps she was not as complacent as she seemed after all.

"I think you are—romanticizing, Miss Barnaby," Felix said awkwardly.

Charlotte looked at him innocently. "Do you not believe in the strength of love to overcome judgment, Mr. Asherson, even for a moment?"

"I . . ." He was caught. He smiled to cover his dilemma. "You press me to be ungallant, Miss Barnaby. Shall I say I know no woman, however charming, who would ask me questions I was not free to answer?"

For a moment Charlotte was beaten. But then if it were so easy, it would not have eluded her thus far.

"You don't know the mysterious woman in cerise?" The words were out before she had time to judge them. She saw Jack's eyes widen and Aunt Vespasia let her fork fall onto her place with a little click. Veronica held her breath, staring at Charlotte as if she had cast aside a mask to reveal a reptile's form. Garrard's face was bloodless, his skin yellow-gray.

It was Loretta who broke the silence, her voice grating in the stillness. "Really, Miss Barnaby, you have a taste for the melodramatic which is unfortunate at best. I think you would be well advised to reconsider your reading matter." There was only the slightest quiver in her words, barely a tremble. Of course she did not know Charlotte had seen her face in the conservatory doorway. "You should not read novels of the trashier sort," she continued. "They coarsen the taste."

"I think she has been reading the newspapers," Jack said hastily.

"Certainly not!" Charlotte lied with a touch of irony. "I heard it from a running patterer! It was quite unavoidable; he was crying it out all over the street. Apparently this marvelously beautiful woman led some poor diplomat into revealing secrets, and then betrayed him. She was a spy."

"Rubbish!" Felix said loudly. He stared straight at Charlotte, avoiding even the slightest glance at Harriet or her father. He might have wavered had he looked at Garrard—his face was so ghastly he seemed to be suffering some physical pain. "Rubbish!" Felix said again. "My dear Miss Barnaby, running patterers make their living by entertaining the masses. They invent half of it, you know."

For a moment the tension eased. Charlotte could feel it slipping away. She must not lose it: the murderer was here at this shining dinner table with its silver and crystal and white flowers.

"But not out of nothing!" she argued. "People do fall passionately in love—so deeply they would forfeit everything, betray all the old loyalties." She looked round at their faces as if she were appealing to them. Veronica was numb, her dark eyes enormous, absorbed with some inner horror—or was it fear at last? Was she after all the real Cerise, and was that why Garrard had known Charlotte was an imposter? He had just left Veronica in the withdrawing room. He said he came only because he feared blackmail, but if that were so, why did he not marry her himself? Or had she tired of him and chosen his son instead? Perhaps Julian was her mistake, her weakness—she had loved in return. Or was Julian simply a way into a more powerful position? He was destined for higher things than his father, perhaps even a cabinet position.

Did Loretta know that, or had she guessed? Her face was ashen, but it was Garrard she stared at, not Veronica. Piers was confused; he did not understand the meaning of what had been said, but he knew the fear and the passion that was in the air. He looked like a soldier readying himself to face enemy fire.

Harriet looked wretched, embarrassed, and Sonia was pale with defeat.

Aunt Adeline spoke. "Miss Barnaby," she said quietly. "I am sure such things do happen, from time to time. If we are capable of great feeling of any sort, there is always the chance it may lead to tragedy. But does it serve any good end that we should delve into it? Have we a right to know other people's griefs?"

Charlotte felt the blood hot in her cheeks. She liked Adeline and she doubted she would ever be forgiven this total hypocrisy and deceit. "Not tragedy," she agreed a little less steadily. "Not if it concerns no one else. But treason concerns us all. It is our country, our people, who are betrayed."

Harriet put her hands up to her face, white with horror.

"There was no treason!" Felix shouted. "Good God, any man can fall in love unwisely!"

Harriet drew her breath in a gasp of anguish so sharp it was audible to all of them.

Felix swung round. "Harriet—that's all! I swear, I never betrayed anything!"

Garrard looked as if he had been struck. Veronica gaped at Felix, her mouth open, her eyes like sockets in her head.

"Felix, you—and Cerise?" Loretta started to laugh, at first a gurgle in her throat, then it rose higher till it was out of control, on the brink of hysteria. "You—and Cerise! Do you hear that, Garrard? Do you?"

Garrard shot to his feet, upsetting wine and water over the cloth.

"No!" he cried desperately. "It's not true! For God's sake, stop. Stop!"

Felix looked at him, appalled. "I'm sorry," he whispered, staring past his wife to Harriet. "I'm sorry, Harriet. God knows I tried!"

"What?" Julian demanded. "What the hell are you all talking about? Felix! Did you have an affair with this woman—this Cerise?"

Felix tried to laugh and it died in his throat. "No! No I didn't—of course I didn't." There was such bitter humor in his voice that he could only be speaking the truth. "No. I was trying to protect Garrard, for Harriet's sake. Isn't that obvious? Sonia—I'm sorry."

No one bothered to ask why. The answer was only too obvious in Harriet's face, and indeed in his own. That domestic tragedy was laid bare; there was no mystery left to uncover.

"Father?" Julian turned to Garrard. Now realization was coming to him, and a dawning of pain. "If you did have an affair with this woman, what does it matter? Unless . . . you killed her."

"No!" The cry came from Garrard like the howl of a mortally wounded animal. "I loved"—his voice dropped— "Cerise." He glanced at Loretta with a hatred stripped of all its veneer of irony, weariness, disillusion. "God—damn— you!" The words were choked from him. There were no tears on his face, he was past weeping, but his pain pulsated through the brilliant lights and the glittering reflections.

There was thick silence. For a long, hot moment no one understood. Then at last Julian grasped the sword. "You betrayed the department," he said very slowly. "You told Cerise about the Anglo-German partition of Africa. That's what Felix was covering up for you! Because of Harriet!"

Garrard sat down very slowly, suddenly stiff. "No." His voice had lost its fire of hate, everything had gone out of him. "Felix didn't know I took the papers, only that I loved Cerise. But the secrets had nothing to do with Cerise." He looked up again at Loretta, and all the passion of hate flooded back. "I took them for her!" he cried, his voice shaking. "She blackmailed me into it!"

"That's ridiculous," Piers said quietly. "For pity's sake,

336

man, don't make it worse than it has to be. What on earth would Loretta want with secrets like that? Anyway, as I understand it, the negotiations are going very well. Aren't they?''

"Yes." Julian's brow furrowed. "Yes they are. No one has used your wretched information!''

"Well then." Piers sat back, his eyes touched with sadness. Perhaps his dreams of Loretta had died a long time ago. "Your charge doesn't make sense.''

Charlotte remembered Loretta's face in the conservatory doorway and knew that in her was the consuming passion of desire and rejection that governed this tragic, violent story. "Yes it does," she said aloud. "The information wasn't taken to be used in negotiations—''

"Ha!" Julian exploded derisively. He had seen hope and he clung to it.

"Something much more powerful." Charlotte cut across him. "Once you have paid blackmail, you have to go on paying; you have put yourself in your blackmailer's power. That was what she wanted—power. To exercise whenever she wanted, power to destroy whomever she chose. Wasn't that it, Mrs. York? He loved Cerise, not you. He didn't love you, didn't want you. You revolted him—and you never forgave him for that." She met Loretta's eyes and saw that she had drawn the ultimate pain, and a hate so terrible that Loretta would have murdered Charlotte if she could. In an instant, as their glances locked, they both knew it.

"Did you think that wretched woman in Seven Dials was Cerise?" Charlotte continued pitilessly. "Is that why you broke her neck? You wasted your effort. She wasn't Cerise, she was just some poor maid who'd lost her character and fallen on hard times!''

"You murdered her!" Garrard accused Loretta, his voice high and harsh. "You thought it was Cerise so you broke her neck!''

"Be quiet!" Loretta was cornered, trapped, and she knew

337

it. Her soul had been stripped naked in front of all the people round the table; her rejection had been exposed for them all to see and taste. And Garrard was lost forever, even the power to hurt him was gone. She did not know how to fight anymore.

Garrard had burned under her threat all these years, dreading the meetings with her, always afraid one day she would betray his weakness, ruin his reputation and strip him of his position, his career. Now it was gone anyway, and he took his revenge.

"You murdered her," he repeated steadily. "You dressed that poor damn woman in that dress so you could blame that wretched policeman! How did you find the woman? Who was she? Some maid you'd dismissed, and still knew where to find?"

Loretta stared at him dumbly. It was the truth and it was painted on her face too clearly to be worth denying.

"And Dulcie?" he went on. "You pushed her out of the window. Why? What did she know—or see?"

"Don't you know?" She started to laugh hysterically. "Oh dear, Garrard—don't you know?" Tears streamed down her face, her voice getting wilder and higher every moment.

Jack stood up and moved towards her. "Asherson!" he said sharply.

In a daze Felix rose and came to help. Between them they half lifted her from her chair and took her from the room.

Vespasia stood also, stiffly, her face pale. "I am going to telephone the police. Superintendent Ballarat, I believe it is. And the home secretary." She looked round the table at them. "I apologize for such an—an unfortunate dinner party, but you see, Thomas Pitt is a friend of mine. I cannot sit by and see him hanged for a murder he did not commit. Please excuse me." Head high, back like a ramrod, she swept out of the room to exert all her influence, to call on old friendships and have Pitt released, now, tonight.

In the silence behind her no one moved.

But it was not over. There was still Cerise, the real Cerise. And who had murdered Robert York, and why? Had that also been Loretta? Charlotte believed not.

On shaking legs she rose too. "Ladies, I think we should retire. I cannot imagine anyone feels like eating anymore. I certainly don't."

Obediently they pushed back their chairs and straggled through to the withdrawing room. Adeline and Harriet went together, leaning a little on each other, as though physical proximity could give them strength. Sonia Asherson hugged her hurt to herself, tight-lipped.

Lastly Charlotte followed at Veronica's elbow. In the hallway she drew her aside into the library. Veronica looked round, startled, as though the book-lined shelves unnerved her.

Charlotte stood against the door, blocking it.

"There's still Cerise," she said quietly. "The real Cerise. The woman Garrard loved. That's you, isn't it!"

"Me?" Veronica's eyes widened. "Me! Oh God! How wrong you are! But why? Why do you care? Why have you done all this? Who are you?"

"Charlotte Pitt."

"Charlotte—Pitt? You mean—you mean that policeman is your—"

"My husband. And I'm not going to let him hang for murdering that woman."

"He won't," Veronica said harshly. "Loretta did it. We all heard her say so. You don't have to worry."

"It isn't finished." Charlotte turned the key in the lock. "There's still the real Cerise, and whoever murdered your husband. I don't think that was Loretta. I think it was you—and Loretta knew it. She protected you because of her own blackmailing of Garrard, even though you killed her son. That's why you hated each other, and yet neither of you could afford to betray the other!"

339

"How—I . . ." Veronica shook her head slowly, incredulous.

"There's no purpose in denying it." Charlotte could not afford pity now. This was Cerise; she might not be a spy after all, but she was a ruthless, passionate woman, and a murderess. "Was it to marry Julian? Did you get tired of Robert and murder him, so you could marry Julian?"

"No!" Veronica was so ashen Charlotte was half afraid she was going to faint. And yet she was Cerise—Cerise with the flair, the panache, the courage.

"I'm sorry, but I cannot believe you."

"I am not Cerise!" Veronica put her hands over her face and turned away, crumpling in a heap onto the sofa. "Oh God! I suppose I'd better tell you the truth. It isn't what you think at all!"

Charlotte sat carefully on the edge of a chair, waiting.

"I loved Robert. You'll never believe how much, not now. But when we were married, I thought I had everything a woman could want. He was—he was so handsome, so charming and sensitive. He seemed to understand me. He was a companion, more than any other man I'd ever known. I—I loved him so much." She closed her eyes, but the tears seeped through, and she gulped.

In spite of herself Charlotte was filled with pity. She knew what it was to love so much your whole world was filled with it. She, too, had suffered loneliness.

"Go on," she said softly. "What about Cerise?"

Veronica made an intense effort, her body shaking, her voice husky as if the words cut her.

"Robert grew—cool towards me. I—" She swallowed and her voice sank to a whisper. "He became—uninterested in the—the marriage bed. At first I thought it was me, that I didn't please him. I did everything I could, but nothing . . ." She took a moment to control herself, then struggled on. "It was then I began to think there might be someone else." She stopped, the pain of memory too strong for her.

Charlotte waited. Instinct made her want to rush forward, put her arms round Veronica and hold her, enfold the pain and ease it, touch her so she was not alone. But she knew she must not, not yet.

At last Veronica mastered herself. "I thought there must be another woman. I found a kerchief in the library. It was a bright cerise color, vivid, vibrant. I knew it wasn't mine, or Loretta's. Then a week later I found a ribbon, then a silk rose—all that dreadful color. Robert spent a lot of time away from home; I thought it had to do with his career. I could accept that; we all have to. Women, I mean."

"You found her?" Charlotte said very quietly.

Veronica drew a deep breath and let it out with a shuddering sigh.

"Yes, I—I saw her, very briefly—right here in my own home. Just the back of her as she left through the front door. She was so—so graceful! I saw her a second time, at a theater I shouldn't have been at. I only saw her at a distance across the balcony. When I got there she was gone." She stopped again.

Charlotte believed the story in spite of herself; the wound was too real to be painted. The memory still hurt Veronica with a raw and twisting pain.

"Go on," Charlotte prompted, this time more gently. "Did you find her?"

"I found one of her stockings." Veronica's voice was thick with the agony of reliving it. "In Robert's bedroom. It was so . . . I wept all that night. I thought I should never feel worse in my life." She gave a little choking sound, half laugh, half sob. "That's what I thought then! Until the night I knew Cerise was in the house. Something woke me. It was after midnight and I heard a footstep on the landing. I got up and saw her come out of Robert's bedroom and go downstairs. I followed her. She must have heard me and slipped into the library. I—" She stopped again; her voice died away, thick with tears.

341

"I went in too. I faced her," she managed after a time. "She was—beautiful. I swear she was." She turned and looked up at Charlotte, her face smudged, blurred with misery and defeat. "She was so . . . elegant. I faced her, accused her of having an affair with Robert. She started to laugh. She stood there in the library in the middle of the night and laughed at me as if she would never stop. I was so furious I picked up the bronze horse from the desk and threw it at her. It hit her on the side of the head and she fell. I stood still for a moment, then I went over to her, but she didn't move. I waited a moment and still she lay there. I felt for her pulse, listened for her breath—nothing! She was dead. Then I looked at her . . . more closely." Her face was ashen; Charlotte had never seen anyone look so exhausted. Her voice was so low it was barely audible. "I touched her hair—and it came away in my hand. It was a wig. It wasn't till that moment that I realized who it was. It was Robert himself— dressed as a woman! Robert was Cerise!" She closed her eyes and pressed her hands to them. "That was why Loretta blackmailed Garrard. He was in love with Robert, and he knew all the time who he was. That's why she protected me. She hated me for it, but she couldn't bear to have the world know her beloved son was a transvestite.

"After I knew he was dead I went upstairs. I think I was too shocked then even to weep; that came later. I went to Loretta and told her, and she came down with me. I didn't even think of lying then. We stood there in the study, she and I, and stared at Robert lying on the floor in that terrible dress, and the wig beside him. There was rouge on his face, and powder. He was beautiful, that was the most obscene thing about it!" Weeping overtook her, and without thinking this time Charlotte knelt beside her and put her arms round the thin, aching shoulders.

"And you and Loretta changed his clothes, dressed him in his own nightshirt and robe and destroyed the cerise dress and wig, and then broke the library window?" she concluded; she knew this was what must have taken place. "Where are the things that were supposed to be stolen?"

But Veronica was sobbing too deeply to tell her. Three years of fear and pain had broken at last, and she needed to weep till she had no strength left, no emotion.

Charlotte held her and waited. It hardly mattered where those few objects were. Probably in the attics. They had not been sold, that much Pitt had made sure of.

The rest of the house must be busy with private tragedies: Piers with Loretta and the police, poor man; whatever disillusion he had suffered in the years since the first bloom of his marriage, no loneliness of closed doors of the heart could have prepared him for this. Felix would be smarting from the newly opened wound of his love for Harriet. It was quite hopeless; divorce would ruin all of them and no happiness could lie that way; and now Sonia had been forced to see it, understand it, and know that others saw it also. She could no longer hide her pain behind pretended blindness. Or perhaps it had been real—maybe she had known nothing. And Aunt Adeline would grieve for them all.

Julian would be far too busy with his own family's despair to disturb Charlotte and Veronica now. He would be only too grateful to leave 'Miss Barnaby' to comfort his fiancée in what he supposed was no more than shock.

Minutes went by, stretching in the silent room. Charlotte had no idea how long it was until Veronica finally exhausted herself and sat up, her face a travesty of its former loveliness.

Charlotte had only a meager handkerchief to offer.

"I suppose they will hang me," Veronica said very quietly, her voice quite steady now. "I hope it is quick."

To her amazement Charlotte answered immediately and without a quiver. "I don't see why they should. I can't think of any reason why they need to know about it. You only meant to hurt him; it was a hideous mischance that the blow hit his temple and killed him."

Veronica stared. "Won't you tell them?"

343

"No—no, I don't think there's any point. I used to think I was a very civilized person, but since Thomas has been in prison, and might have been hanged, I discover that I have a savagery in me that doesn't think first when I must fight for those I love—love more than I can understand, or control. I don't know if it's right, but I think I know how you might have felt."

"What about Julian? Won't he—won't he hate me anyway, because he thinks I'm Cerise, and that I drove Garrard to . . ."

"Then tell him the truth."

Veronica looked down. She was too exhausted to weep anymore. "He'll leave me anyway. I killed Robert, and lied for three years to hide it. I didn't know about Loretta and Garrard, but I don't suppose he would believe all of that."

Charlotte took her hands. "If he leaves you then he doesn't love you as you want to be loved, and you must learn to live without him. Perhaps in time there will be someone else. Losing Robert was not any fault of yours. Nothing was lacking in your love; no woman could have held him. But Julian is different. If he really loves you, then he will still love you even when he knows. Believe me, we all have something to be forgiven. Love that expects perfection—no past with mistakes, pain, learning—is only hunger. No one grows to maturity without acts to be ashamed of; in accepting that, we love not only the strengths but also the weaknesses, and real bonds grow between us. Tell him. If he's worth it, he'll accept your past—if not immediately, then in a little while."

For the first time Veronica lifted her chin. Her eyes widened, and there was a stillness in her; the violence inside calmed and her fear slipped away. "I will," she said very softly. "I will tell him."

There was a knock on the door—gentle, requesting permission.

Charlotte stood up and went to turn the key. "Come in."

The door swung wide and Aunt Vespasia stood there with

a tiny smile on her face. She stood aside. Behind her stood
Emily, still in her maid's dress but without the apron, and
Jack with his arms round her. Beside them was Pitt, filthy,
his face hollow, shadowed round the eyes and marked with
bruises. But it was radiant with a smile of joy so intense he
looked positively beautiful.

For more high-stakes murder and mystery
in Victorian England, read on to sample

Treason at Lisson Grove

the latest Charlotte and Thomas Pitt novel
from Anne Perry

CHAPTER

1

"THAT'S HIM!" GOWER YELLED above the sound of the
traffic. Pitt turned on his heel just in time to see a figure dart between the rear end of a hansom and the oncoming horses of a
brewer's dray. Gower disappeared after him, missing a trampling by
no more than inches.

Pitt plunged into the street, swerving to avoid a brougham and
stopping abruptly to let another hansom pass. By the time he
reached the far pavement Gower was twenty yards ahead and Pitt
could make out only his flying hair. The man he was pursuing was
out of sight. Weaving between clerks in pinstripes, leisurely
strollers, and the occasional early woman shopper with her long
skirts getting in the way, Pitt closed the gap until he was less than
a dozen yards behind Gower. He caught a glimpse of the man
ahead: bright ginger hair and a green jacket. Then he was gone,
and Gower turned, his right hand raised for a moment in signal, before disappearing into an alley.

Pitt followed after him into the shadows, his eyes taking a moment or two to adjust. The alley was long and narrow, bending in a dogleg a hundred yards beyond. The gloom was caused by the overhanging eaves and the water-soaked darkness of the brick, long streams of grime running down from the broken guttering. People were huddled in doorways; others made their way slowly, limping, or staggering beneath heavy bolts of cloth, barrels, and bulging sacks.

Gower was still ahead, seeming to find his way with ease. Pitt veered around a fat woman with a tray of matches to sell, and tried to catch up. Gower was at least ten years younger, even if his legs were not quite so long, and he was more used to this kind of thing. But it was Pitt's experience in the Metropolitan Police before he joined Special Branch that had led them to finding West, the man they were now chasing.

Pitt bumped into an old woman and apologized before regaining his stride. They were around the dogleg now, and he could see West's ginger head making for the opening into the wide thoroughfare forty yards away. Pitt knew that they must catch him before he was swallowed up in the crowds.

Gower was almost there. He reached out an arm to grab at West, but just then West ducked sideways and Gower tripped, hurtling into the wall and momentarily winding himself. He bent over double, gasping to catch his breath.

Pitt lengthened his stride and reached West just as he dived out into the High Street, barged his way through a knot of people, and disappeared.

Pitt went after him and a moment later saw the light on his bright hair almost at the next crossroads. He increased his pace, bumping and banging people. He had to catch him. West had information that could be vital. After all, the tide of unrest was rising fast all over Europe, and becoming more violent. Many people, in the name of reform, were actually trying to overthrow government altogether and create an anarchy in which they imagined there would be some kind of equality of justice. Some were content with blood-soaked oratory; others preferred dynamite, or even bullets.

Special Branch knew of a current plot, but not yet the leaders behind it, or—more urgently—the target of their violence. West was to provide that, at risk of his own life—if his betrayal were known.

Where the devil was Gower? Pitt swiveled around once to see if he could spot him. He was nowhere visible in the sea of bobbing heads, bowler hats, caps, and bonnets. There was no time to look longer. Surely he wasn't still in the alley? What was wrong with the man? He was not much more than thirty. Had he been more than just knocked off balance? Was he injured?

West was up ahead, seizing a break in the traffic to cross back to the other side again. Three hansoms came past almost nose-to-tail. A cart and four clattered in the opposite direction. Pitt fumed on the edge of the curb. To go out into the roadway now would only get him killed.

A horse-drawn omnibus passed, then two heavily loaded wagons. More carts and a dray went in the other direction. Pitt had lost sight of West, and Gower had vanished into the air.

There was a brief holdup in traffic and Pitt raced across the road. Weaving in and out of the way of frustrated drivers, he only just missed being caught by a long, curling carriage whip. Someone yelled at him and he took no notice. He reached the opposite side and caught sight of West for an instant as he swung around a corner and made for another alley.

Pitt raced after him, but when he got there West had disappeared.

"Did you see a man with ginger hair?" Pitt demanded of a peddler with a tray of sandwiches. "Where did he go?"

"Want a sandwich?" the man asked with eyes wide. "Very good. Made this morning. Only tuppence."

Pitt fished frantically in his pocket; found string, sealing wax, a pocketknife, a handkerchief, and several coins. He gave the man a threepenny bit and took a sandwich. It felt soft and fresh, although right now he didn't care. "Which way?" he said harshly.

"That way." The man pointed into the deeper shadows of the alley.

Pitt began to run again, weaving a path through the piles of rubbish. A rat skittered from under his feet, and he all but fell over a drunken figure lying half out of a doorway. Somebody swung a punch at him; he lurched to one side, losing his balance for a moment, glimpsing West still ahead of him.

Now West disappeared again and Pitt had no idea which way he had gone. He tried one blind courtyard and alley after another. It seemed like endless, wasted moments before Gower joined him from one of the side alleyways.

"Pitt!" Gower clutched at his arm. "This way! Quickly." His fingers dug deep into Pitt's flesh, making him gasp with the sudden pain.

Together they ran forward, Pitt along the broken pavement beside the dark walls, Gower in the gutter, his boots sending up a spray of filthy water. Pace for pace, they went around the corner into the open entrance to a brickyard and saw a man crouching over something on the ground.

Gower let out a cry of fury and darted forward, half crossing in front of Pitt and tripping him up in his eagerness. They both fell heavily. Pitt was on his feet in time to see the crouched figure swing around for an instant, then scramble up and run as if for his life.

"Oh God!" Gower said, aghast, now also on his feet. "After him! I know who it is!"

Pitt stared at the heap on the ground: West's green jacket and bright hair. Blood streamed from his throat, staining his chest and already pooling dark on the stones underneath him. There was no way he could possibly be alive.

Gower was already pursuing the assassin. Pitt raced after him and this time his long strides caught up before they reached the road. "Who is it?" he demanded, almost choking on his own breath.

"Wrexham!" Gower hissed back. "We've been watching him for weeks."

Pitt knew the man, but only by name. There was a momentary break in the stream of vehicles. They darted across the road to go after Wrexham, who thank heaven was an easy figure to see. He was taller than average, and—despite the good weather—he was wearing a long, pale-colored scarf that swung in the air as he twisted and turned. It flashed through Pitt's mind that it might be a weapon; it would not be hard to strangle a man with it.

They were on a crowded footpath now, and Wrexham dropped his pace. He almost sauntered, walking easily, swiftly, with loping strides, but perfectly casual. Could he be arrogant enough to imagine he had lost them so quickly? He certainly knew they had seen him, because he had swiveled around at Gower's cry, and then run as if for his life.

They were now walking at a steady pace, eastward toward Stepney and Limehouse. Soon the crowds would thin as they left the broader streets behind.

"If he goes into an alley, be careful," Pitt warned, now beside Gower, as if they were two tradesmen bound on a common errand. "He has a knife. He's too comfortable. He must know we're behind him."

Gower glanced at him sideways, his eyes wide for an instant. "You think he'll try and pick us off?"

"We practically saw him cut West's throat," Pitt replied, matching Gower stride for stride. "If we get him he'll hang. He must know that."

"I reckon he'll duck and hide suddenly, when he thinks we're taking it easy," Gower answered. "We'd better stay fairly close to him. Lose sight of him for a moment and he'll be gone for good."

Pitt agreed with a nod, and they closed the distance to Wrexham, who was still strolling ahead of them. Never once did he turn or look back.

Pitt found it chilling that a man could slit another's throat and see him bleed to death, then a few moments after walk through a crowd with outward unconcern, as if he were just one more pedestrian about some trivial daily business. What passion or inhumanity drove him? In the way he moved, the fluidity—almost grace—of his stride, Pitt could not detect even fear, let alone the conscience of a brutal murderer.

Wrexham wove in and out of the thinning crowd. Twice they lost sight of him.

"That way!" Gower gasped, waving his right hand. "I'll go left." He swerved around a window cleaner with a bucket of water, almost knocking the man over.

Pitt went the other way, into the north end of an alley. The sudden shadows momentarily made him blink, half blind. He saw movement and charged forward, but it was only a beggar shuffling out of a doorway. He swore under his breath and sprinted back to the street just in time to see Gower swiveling around frantically, searching for him.

"That way!" Gower called urgently and set off, leaving Pitt behind.

The second time it was Pitt who saw him first, and Gower who had to catch up. Wrexham had crossed the road just in front of a brewer's dray and was out of sight by the time Pitt and Gower were able to follow. It took them more than ten minutes to close on him without drawing attention. There were fewer people about, and two men running would have been highly noticeable. With fifty yards' distance between them, Wrexham could have outrun them too easily.

They were in Commercial Road East, now, in Stepney. If Wrexham did not turn they would be in Limehouse, perhaps the West India Dock Road. If they went that far they could lose him among the tangle of wharves with cranes, bales of goods, warehouses, and dock laborers. If he went down to one of the ferries he could be out of sight between the ships at anchor before they could find another ferry to follow him.

Ahead of them, as if he had seen them, Wrexham increased his pace, his long legs striding out, his jacket scarf flying.

Pitt felt a flicker of nervousness. His muscles were aching, his feet sore despite his excellent boots—his one concession to sartorial taste. Even well-cut jackets never looked right on him because he weighted the pockets with too many pieces of rubbish he thought he might need. His ties never managed to stay straight; perhaps he knotted them too tightly, or too loosely. But his boots were beautiful and immaculately cared for. Even though most of his work was of the mind, out-thinking, out-guessing, remembering, and seeing significance where others didn't, he still knew the importance of a policeman's feet. Some habits do not die. Before he had been forced out of the Metropolitan Police and Victor Narraway had taken him into Special Branch, he had walked enough miles to know the price of inattention to physical stamina, and to boots.

Suddenly Wrexham ran across the narrow road and disappeared down Gun Lane.

"He's going for the Limehouse Station!" Gower shouted, leaping out of the way of a cart full of timber as he dashed after him.

Pitt was on his heels. The Limehouse Station was on the Blackwall Railway, less than a hundred yards away. Wrexham could go in at least three possible directions from there and end up anywhere in the city.

But Wrexham kept moving, rapidly, right, past the way back up to the station. Instead, he turned left onto Three Colts Street, then swerved right onto Ropemaker's Field, still loping in an easy run.

Pitt was too breathless to shout, and anyway Wrexham was no more than fifteen yards ahead. The few men and one old washerwoman on the path scattered as the three running men passed them. Wrexham was going to the river, as Pitt had feared.

At the end of Ropemaker's Field they turned right again into Narrow Street, still running. They were only yards from the river's edge. The breeze was stiff off the water, smelling of salt and mud where the tide was low. Half a dozen gulls soared lazily in circles above a string of barges.

Wrexham was still ahead of them, moving less easily now, tiring. He passed the entrance to Limehouse Cut. Pitt figured that he must be making for Kidney Stairs, the stone steps down to the river, where, if they were lucky, he would find a ferry waiting. There were two more sets of stairs before the road curved twenty yards inland to Broad Street. At the Shadwell Docks there were more stairs again. He could lose his pursuers on any of them.

Gower gestured toward the river. "Steps!" he shouted, bending a moment and gasping to catch his breath. He gestured with a wild swing of his arm. Then he straightened up and began running again, a couple of strides ahead of Pitt.

Pitt could see a ferry coming toward the shore, the boatman pulling easily at the oars. He would get to the steps a moment or two after Wrexham—in fact Pitt and Gower would corner him nicely. Perhaps they could get the ferry to take them up to the Pool of London. He ached to sit down even for that short while.

Wrexham reached the steps and ran down them, disappearing as if he had slipped into a hole. Pitt felt an upsurge of victory. The ferry was still twenty yards from the spot where the steps would meet the water.

Gower let out a yell of triumph, waving his hand high.

They reached the top of the steps just as the ferry pulled away, Wrexham sitting in the stern. They were close enough to see the smile on his face as he half swiveled on the seat to gaze at them.

Then he faced forward, speaking to the ferryman and pointing to the farther shore.

Pitt raced down the steps. His feet slithered on the wet stones. He waved his arms at the other ferry, the one they had seen. "Here! Hurry!" he shouted.

Gower shouted also, his voice high and desperate.

The ferryman increased his speed, throwing his full weight behind his oars, and in a matter of seconds had swung around next to the pier.

"Get in, gents," he said cheerfully. "Where to?"

"After that boat there," Gower gasped, choking on his own breath and pointing to the other ferry. "An extra half crown in it for you if you catch up with him before he gets up Horseferry Stairs."

Pitt landed in the boat behind him and immediately sat down so they could get under way. "He's not going to Horseferry," he pointed out. "He's going straight across. Look!"

"Lavender Dock?" Gower scowled, sitting in the seat beside Pitt. "What the hell for?"

"Shortest way across," Pitt replied. "Get up to Rotherhithe Street and away."

"Where to?"

"Nearest train station, probably. Or he might double back. Best place to get lost is among other people."

They were pulling well away from the dock now and slowly catching up with the other ferry.

There were fewer ships moored here, and they could make their way almost straight across. A string of barges was still fifty yards downstream, moving slowly against the tide. The wind off the water was colder. Without thinking what he was doing, Pitt hunched up and pulled his collar higher around his neck. It seemed like hours since he and Gower had burst into the brickyard and seen Wrexham crouched over West's blood-soaked body, but it was probably little more than ninety minutes. Their source of information about whatever plot West had known of was gone with his death.

He thought back to his last interview with Narraway, sitting in the office with the hot sunlight streaming through the window onto the piles of books and papers on the desk. Narraway's face had been intensely serious under its graying mane of hair, his eyes almost black. He had spoken of the gravity of the situation, the rise of the passion to reform Europe's old imperialism, violently if necessary. It was no longer a matter of a few sticks of dynamite, an assassination here and there. Rather, there were whispers of full governments overthrown by force.

"Some things need changing," Narraway had said with a wry bitterness. "No one but a fool would deny that there is injustice. But this would result in anarchy. God alone knows how wide this spreads, at least as far as France, Germany, and Italy, and by the sounds of it here in England as well."

Pitt had stared at him, seeing a sadness in the man he had never before imagined.

"This is a different breed, Pitt, and the tide of victory is with them now. But the violence . . ." Narraway had shaken his head, as if awakening himself. "We don't change that way in Britain, we evolve slowly. We'll get there, but not with murder, and not by force."

The wind was fading, the water smoother.

They were nearly at the south bank of the river. It was time to make a decision. Gower was looking at him, waiting.

Wrexham's ferry was almost at the Lavender Dock.

"He's going somewhere," Gower said urgently. "Do we want to get him now, sir—or see where he leads us? If we take him we won't know who's behind this. He won't talk, he's no reason to. We practically saw him kill West. He'll hang for sure." He waited, frowning.

"Do you think we can keep him in sight?" Pitt asked.

"Yes, sir." Gower did not hesitate.

"Right." The decision was clear in Pitt's mind. "Stay back then. We'll split up if we have to."

The ferry hung back until Wrexham had climbed up the narrow steps and all but disappeared. Then, scrambling to keep up, Pitt and Gower went after him.

They were careful to follow from more of a distance, sometimes together but more often with a sufficient space between them.

Yet Wrexham now seemed to be so absorbed in his own concerns that he never looked behind. He must have assumed he had lost them when he crossed the river. Indeed, they were very lucky that he had not. With the amount of waterborne traffic, he must have failed to realize that one ferry was dogging his path.

At the railway station there were at least a couple of dozen other people at the ticket counter.

"Better get tickets all the way, sir," Gower urged. "We don't want to draw attention to ourselves from not paying the fare."

Pitt gave him a sharp look, but stopped himself from making the remark on the edge of his tongue.

"Sorry," Gower murmured with a slight smile.

Once on the platform they remained close to a knot of other people waiting. Neither of them spoke, as if they were strangers to each other. The precaution seemed unnecessary. Wrexham barely glanced at either of them, nor at anyone else.

The first train was going north. It drew in and stopped. Most of the waiting passengers got on. Pitt wished he had a newspaper to hide his face and appear to take his attention. He should have thought of it before.

"I think I can hear the train . . . ," Gower said almost under his breath. "It should be to Southampton—eventually. We might have to change . . ." The rest of what he said was cut off by the noise of the engine as the train pulled in, belching steam. The doors flew open and passengers poured out.

Pitt struggled to keep Wrexham in sight. He waited until the last moment in case he should get out again and lose them, and, when he didn't, he and Gower boarded a carriage behind him.

"He could be going anywhere," Gower said grimly. His fair face was set in hard lines, his hair poking up where he had run his fingers through it. "One of us better get out at every station to see that he doesn't get off at the last moment."

"Of course," Pitt agreed.

"Do you think West really had something for us?" Gower went on. "He could have been killed for some other reason. A quarrel? Those revolutionaries are pretty volatile. Could have been a betrayal within the group? Even a rivalry for leadership?" He was watching Pitt intently, as if trying to read his mind.

"I know that," Pitt said quietly. He was by far the senior, and it was his decision to make. Gower would never question him on that. It was little comfort now, in fact rather a lonely thought.

He remembered Narraway's certainty that there was something planned that would make the recent random bombings seem trivial. In February of last year, 1894, a French anarchist had tried to destroy the Royal Observatory at Greenwich with a bomb. Thank heaven he had failed. In June, President Carnot of France had been assassinated. In August, a man named Caserio had been executed for the crime. Everywhere there was anger and uncertainty in the air.

It was a risk to follow Wrexham, but to seize on an empty certainty was a kind of surrender. "We'll follow him," Pitt replied. "Do you have enough money for another fare, if we have to separate?"

Gower fished in his pocket, counted what he had. "As long as it isn't all the way to Scotland, yes, sir. Please God it isn't Scotland." He smiled with a twisted kind of misery. "You know in February they had the coldest temperature ever recorded in Britain? Nearly fifty degrees of frost! If the poor bastard let off a bomb to start a fire you could hardly blame him!"

"That was February, this is April already," Pitt reminded him. "Here, we're pulling into a station. I'll watch for Wrexham this time. You take the next."

"Yes, sir."

Pitt opened the door and was only just on the ground when he saw Wrexham getting out and hurrying across the platform to change trains for Southampton. Pitt turned to signal Gower and found him already out and at his elbow. Together they followed, trying not to be conspicuous by hurrying. They found seats, but separately for a while, to make sure Wrexham didn't double back and elude them, disappearing into London again.

But Wrexham seemed to be oblivious, as if he no longer even considered the possibility of being followed. He appeared completely carefree, and Pitt had to remind himself that Wrexham had followed a man in the East End only hours ago, then quite deliberately cut his throat and watched him bleed to death on the stones of a deserted brickyard.

"God, he's a cold-blooded bastard!" he said with sudden fury.

A man in pin-striped trousers on the seat opposite put down his newspaper and stared at Pitt with distaste, then rattled his paper loudly and resumed reading.

Gower smiled. "Quite," he said quietly. "We had best be extremely careful."

One or the other of them got out briefly at every stop, just to make certain Wrexham did not leave this train, but he stayed until they finally pulled in at Southampton.

Gower looked at Pitt, puzzled. "What can he do in Southampton?" he said. They hurried along the platform to keep pace with Wrexham, then past the ticket collector and out into the street.

The answer was not long in coming. Wrexham took an omnibus directly toward the docks, and Pitt and Gower had to race to jump onto the step just as it pulled away. Pitt almost bumped into Wrexham, who was still standing. Deliberately he looked away from Gower. They must be more careful. Neither of them was particularly noticeable alone. Gower was fairly tall, lean, his hair long and fair, but his features were a trifle bony, stronger than average. An observant person would remember him. Pitt was taller, perhaps less than graceful, and yet he moved easily, comfortable with himself. His hair was dark and permanently untidy. One front tooth was a little chipped, but visible only when he smiled. It was his steady, very clear gray eyes that people did not forget.

Wrexham would have to be extraordinarily preoccupied not to be aware of seeing them in London, and now again here in Southampton, especially if they were together. Accordingly, Pitt moved on down the inside of the bus to stand well away from Gower, and pretended to be watching the streets as they passed, as if he were taking careful note of his surroundings.

As he had at least half expected, Wrexham went all the way to the dockside. Without speaking to Gower, Pitt followed well behind their quarry. He trusted that Gower was off to the side, as far out of view as possible.

Wrexham bought a ticket on a ferry to St. Malo, across the channel on the coast of France. Pitt bought one as well. He hoped fervently that Gower had sufficient money to get one too, but the only thing worse than ending up alone in France, trying to follow Wrexham without help, would be to lose the man altogether.

He boarded the ferry, a smallish steamship called the *Laura*, and remained within sight of the gangplank. He needed to see if Gower came aboard, but more important to make sure that Wrexham did not get off again. If Wrexham were aware of Pitt and Gower it would be a simple thing to go ashore and hop the next train back to London.

Pitt was leaning on the railing with the sharp salt wind in his face when he heard footsteps behind him. He swung around, then was annoyed with himself for betraying such obvious alarm.

Gower was a yard away, smiling. "Did you think I was going to push you over?" he said amusedly.

Pitt swallowed back his temper. "Not this close to the shore," he replied. "I'll watch you more closely out in mid-channel!"

Gower laughed. "Looks like a good decision, sir. Following him this far could get us a real idea of who his contacts are in Europe. We might even find a clue as to what they're planning."

Pitt doubted it, but it was all they had left now. "Perhaps. But we mustn't be seen together. We're lucky he hasn't recognized us so far. He would have if he weren't so abominably arrogant."

Gower was suddenly very serious, his fair face grim. "I think whatever he has planned is so important his mind is completely absorbed in it. He thought he lost us in Ropemaker's Field. Don't forget we were in a totally separate carriage on the train."

"I know. But he must have seen us when we were chasing him. He ran," Pitt pointed out. "I wish at least one of us had a jacket to change. But in April, at sea, without them we'd be even more conspicuous." He looked at Gower's coat. They were not markedly different in size. Even if they did no more than exchange coats, it would alter both their appearances slightly.

As if reading this thought, Gower began to slip off his coat. He passed it over, and took Pitt's from his outstretched hand.

Pitt put on Gower's jacket. It was a little tight across the chest.

With a rueful smile Gower emptied the pockets of Pitt's jacket, which now sat a little loosely on his shoulders. He passed over the notebook, handkerchief, pencil, loose change, half a dozen other bits and pieces, then the wallet with Pitt's papers of identity and money.

Pitt similarly passed over all Gower's belongings.

Gower gave a little salute. "See you in St. Malo," he said, turning on his heel and walking away without looking back, a slight swagger in his step. Then he stopped and turned half toward Pitt, smiling. "I'd keep away from the railing if I were you, sir."

Pitt raised his hand in a salute, and resumed watching the gangway.

PHOTO: © DIANE HINDS

ANNE PERRY is the bestselling author of two acclaimed series set in Victorian England: the William Monk novels, including *Blood on the Water*, *Blind Justice*, and *A Sunless Sea*, and the Charlotte and Thomas Pitt novels, including *Death on Blackheath*, *Midnight at Marble Arch*, and *Dorchester Terrace*. She is also the author of a series of five World War I novels, as well as thirteen Christmas novels, most recently *A Christmas Escape*, and the bestselling stand-alone historical novel *The Sheen on the Silk*.

WWW.ANNEPERRY.CO.UK

To inquire about booking Anne Perry for a speaking engagement, please contact the Penguin Random House Speakers Bureau at speakers@penguinrandomhouse.com.